CINDERVEILED MAGIC

WHITE HAVEN WITCHES
BOOK FOURTEEN

TJ GREEN

Cinderveiled Magic

Mountolive Publishing

PO Box 28, Vila do Bispo CTT

8651-909 Portugal

Copyright © 2025 by TJ Green

ISBN Paperback 978-1-991313-41-6

ISBN Hardback 978-1-991313-42-3

www.happenstancebookshop.com

www.tjgreenauthor.com

Contents

One

There was a chill breeze blowing in from the sea, but Helena ignored it, too entranced with the mid-week Beltane procession that wound down to the harbour and the beach beyond.

White Haven, as usual at these seasonal celebrations, was packed with visitors who had come to enjoy the spectacle and immerse themselves in the magic of the celebrations, and it was certainly magical. There was a sense of anticipation, as if something unusual might happen. Helena sincerely hoped nothing would. These processions had a way of gathering all of the magic in White Haven and amplifying it.

The participants of the parade were a mix of ages, and all wore fancy dress with painted faces or masks depicting dryads, nature spirits, and animals. At the head of the parade were the May Queen and her consort, the Green Man, regal and imposing as they led the procession of jugglers and drummers to the bonfire on the beach.

It reminded Helena of when they had dressed up at Yule. She had loved every second of it, apart from the murderous Winter Queen and Jack Frost, of course. But participating in the parade had been wonderful, the energy infectious. It had empowered her, reinforcing her need to be in White Haven more often. Avery, who was watching with her, thought she understood, but she didn't. Not really. *How could she?* She was of this time, with mobile phones, computers, trains, planes, and electricity, but this was Helena's second lease on life, five centuries after the first one, and she wanted it all.

"I never tire of seeing this," Helena said to Avery, in her guise as Clea, Avery's gran. "It was a shame we couldn't do such a thing in my lifetime."

"At least you get to see it now. Although, as I do recall, you led the All Hallows' parade well enough as a ghost," she said, casting Helena a sideways glance.

"Ah, yes. That." She smirked at the memory. Even as a spirit, it was invigorating to lead the procession. "It was lots of fun. All those shocked faces! As *I* recall, it was very helpful to you!"

"Your participation raised lots of questions."

It was the start of the real awakening of White Haven's magic, Helena realised. Finding the grimoires and releasing their trapped ancestral magic had been one thing, but the events that followed had exacerbated everything. As a spirit lurking on the sidelines, she had seen it unfold. A period of almost two years in which Avery's life had changed completely.

"I'm cold," Avery said, shivering as the last of the procession passed and the crowd straggled behind them. "I'm heading back home to look at those spells again. There's still time before I need to meet Alex in the pub."

"You want to cast one tonight, don't you?" Helena asked, eyes fixed on Avery, who shuffled as if evading the question.

"I just need to see them again."

"You're obsessed. It isn't healthy."

"I'm interested in our family spells. There's nothing unhealthy about that," Avery said, temper clearly rising.

Helena knew that Alex was as perplexed as she was about Avery's obsessive interest in the dragon spells in the early part of her family grimoire. Perhaps she would be, too, if she had seen the dragon and the dragon eggs.

Avery stepped closer to Helena, raising her voice to be heard above the crowd of revellers, and repeated her earlier argument. "The spell we cast to release Morwenna from her curse was incredible. Spells using dragon-based ingredients are ripe with potential. I can't believe you're not more interested, or in fact, haven't researched them before."

"I was busy surviving—and failing—in what was an increasingly fraught time. And I had children." *Children she never saw reach adulthood. Children she was never able to teach magic.* Her tone was harsher than she'd intended, and guilt flashed behind Avery's eyes.

"Sorry," Avery said. "That was thoughtless. But things are different now, and I'm fascinated. Especially at this time! This is a fire festival, and Beltane's energy is all around us. This is the perfect time to cast at least one of those spells. I honestly thought you would have insights. Aren't you even the tiniest bit interested?"

"Of course I am, but this is the Beltane parade! I can't believe Alex is in the bloody pub! At least the rest of the coven is around here somewhere." Briar was watching with her grandmother, Tamsyn, her cousin, Rosa, and the two children. Reu and El were already down on the beach with Stan.

"To be honest," Avery said, pulling her coat around her, "he has seen so many parades that we really don't feel we need to see them all anymore. Plus, the pub will be busy, so it makes sense that he's there." Of course, they had also honoured the event with the Cornwall Coven at Rasmus's house, so the rest of the coven considered the parade in White Haven a bonus. "I'll head down to the beach later, though. A few libations won't go amiss," she said, laughing.

Helena sighed, resigned. She didn't want to continue on her own, and Clea's old friends were avoiding the crowds. *Her friends*, she reminded herself. "All right. Let's head home and get out of this chill. I can see you won't drop this, and I want to make sure you don't do something stupid."

Avery bristled at the insult. "I'm not a child, and just to remind you, I have researched endlessly!"

"I know. We are swimming in dragon books." So much so that Helena had been dreaming of dragons, wyverns, draca, and wyrms, all looking like the gilded illustrations in one of the books.

"And I am virtually the same age as you, so don't give me that grandma tone."

"I am your grandmother," Helena pointed out, "plus several 'greats' too, so I can't help it." Although, she certainly didn't feel it.

Avery poked her tongue out in a childish gesture that made Helena giggle, and led the way through the square that was dominated by the enormous, beribboned maypole, and up the hill to their flat. Helena was glad to get out of the wind that was distinctly chillier the higher up they went. *So much for May heralding warmer weather.*

White Haven had been dressed for Beltane, and the streets were lined with pots of spring flowers and hanging baskets, courtesy of Greenlane Nursery, and the shop fronts were decorated equally as energetically. It was comforting to know their traditions continued, and it fed the town's magic, too.

Fortunately, the house was warm, and Circe and Medea wound around her ankles. Helena petted them absently as Avery headed to the attic, and Helena to the kitchen for wine. Avery was intent on casting a spell that night, and Helena had every intention of finding out why. Something significant was motivating her, but she had no idea what. Neither did Alex, she'd discovered after a furtive conversation. When she reached the attic a few minutes later, she found Avery already settled at the table, attention turned to the open grimoire, candles and the fire alight, and the glint of a stored-up argument in her eyes.

Helena prepared herself. "Avery, I'm not sure we should be casting any of these yet. I feel there are hidden meanings in them that we don't understand."

"I know, but they have so much untapped potential," Avery said, lips twisting with frustration. "I hate being defeated."

"Consider it the thrill of the chase."

"We've chased enough. This is the time for action."

"Action for what purpose? These are transformational spells. What are we transforming?"

Avery shuffled in her seat and averted her eyes, fiddling with the grimoire instead. "I just find them interesting."

"Interesting my arse! Of course they're bloody interesting, but that's no reason to go charging in. I smell bullshit." Helena leaned her elbows on the table and steepled her fingers under her chin, fixing Avery with her most grandmotherly stare. "Something is bothering you. You've had my grimoire for almost two years, and have used it and cast spells from it, but always with good cause.

Now that you have discovered these dragon-based spells, it's like you've gone off tangent!"

Avery protested. "Not off tangent. I'm investigating and researching. It's what I do. I'm book obsessed. Something you are, too. And I'm talking to Clea, who's lurking back there. Maybe you, too, Helena. Plus, you are a witch, and like me, enjoy expanding your magic and spell repertoire. This is all this is."

Helena adjusted her approach and softened her tone. Avery was hiding something, and she needed to know what. "I feel I know you well now. You have a firecracker temper, but you are not stupidly impulsive. I have Clea's memories, too, remember. You are thoughtful, clever, inventive, and deeply intuitive. Clea loves all of those qualities, you know."

"Does she? I didn't know." Her combative tone vanished. "I think I have some of those qualities from her. She was always so calm and thoughtful, and her spellwork was precise. She taught me so much, more than my mother ever did," she said regretfully, eyes dropping to the grimoire again.

"She misses the conversations you used to have. With her daughter, Diana, and your sister, too. She regrets the important conversations she can't have anymore. Her thoughts aren't rational, you understand," Helena hurriedly added. "I don't want you to think they are. They're muddled. I sense them faintly in the background, but I push them aside. I try not to access her memories, either. It would be rude. But there's always a rush of love every time she sees you. You remind her of your mother, too."

"Do I?" Avery looked genuinely surprised. "But we're nothing alike."

"Maybe nothing you see, but Clea does."

Avery sipped her wine, as if steadying herself. "I still don't understand how you can function so well in her body."

"Her brain is quite capable of running her body. It's just her memories. My own memories, plus my magic, override that. She doesn't struggle. I don't think she's aware, most of the time."

"But I found you suffocating."

"Because you were younger and certainly more aware than your grandmother. You can't compare the two. She has consented," she reminded Avery.

Helena now felt guilty for trying to steal Avery's body when they were under All Souls' Church. Giddy with being seen, she was desperate for more, but she should never have tried that. Not with her own descendant. Helena had been jealous of Avery, an ugly admission, but true. Inhabiting Clea's body was better, even though she was old. But she wanted more, if she could only work out a way to do it.

"I know." Avery sighed as if the weight of the world was on her shoulders. "I still feel guilty about it, even though I love seeing her here, and you. It's...odd. But you have her memories, even though you respect her privacy. Does she know why my mother really left? Or Bryony?"

Helena frowned as she reached for her own drink. "I thought you knew, although, you never really talk about it." Actually, she never discussed it at all. "Or your father."

"Oh, *him*!" Avery huffed. "When he discovered my mother was a witch, he left and we never saw him again. I was a baby, and Bryony a toddler. What a bastard."

"I guessed he'd left, but I didn't know you were so young. Have you seen him since?"

"No, and my mother never mentioned him, except when I asked. And then she left, too. We discovered when we started looking for our missing grimoires that many of our ancestors didn't stay in White Haven. Reu's did, obviously, but the others left. You never mention them," Avery said, a bite of criticism to her tone. "You know—Thadeus, and Imogen, Alex's ancestor. Plus the other three. I forget their names."

"I know who Imogen was, Avery. She was my best friend. As for Thadeus, he was a lying creep who I loved. That was a severe lack of judgment on my behalf, and youth was no excuse. The others were all wonderful people. None of us—myself included—deserved what happened to us. You have no idea of the fear we lived with."

Helena could feel it now. Beltane magic was swirling. Beltane wasn't just about passion; it was a time when the veils were thinning again. *Were the ancestors stepping closer?* And then she thought she might have an inkling about Avery's research. El had been dealing with her own issues about her estranged parents. *Had this brought something up with Avery?* She knew she'd been supporting El.

"Avery, have you found a spell to transform feelings? Emotions? Desires, even? Is this need to cast a dragon-based spell about your mother? Your family?"

Unexpectedly, tears welled in Avery's eyes. "It might be."

Helena reached forward and clasped her hand, Clea's concerns mixing with her own. "I'm sorry. I had no idea you had been mulling on this. Just be honest and tell me what you want."

"They both left when I was sixteen. Sixteen! Said they couldn't bear to be in White Haven anymore. My sister left only months after my mother. What is *that* about? Was it White Haven, or was it me?" Avery was flustered now, her colour rising.

"Of course it wasn't you! Why would it be?"

"Because I don't hear from them at all! Leaving White Haven is one thing, but why aren't they in touch? They don't even see Clea!" A gust of wind swept through the attic, rattling pages and guttering candle flames. Avery's agitation always stirred up elemental air, her closest element. "The more I think about it, the angrier I am! How dare they!"

The fire roared in the fireplace as smoke eddied across the room, and Helena knew that she had reached the root of the issue.

"Avery! Stop it. I understand that you are upset, but this is not the time to wreck the attic and suffocate us." She squeezed her hand. "Please, take a breath, and calm down. I will help you."

"You didn't sound like you would."

"Because I needed to understand your motivations. Now I do. Is this to do with El and her shadow work?"

The wind dropped and Avery sighed. "Yes. The fact that her parents didn't go to the wedding upset her, and I wondered why I wasn't upset more, and then the more I thought about it, the more I realised I *am* upset. I have a great life here, but it's been tricky at times."

"Very tricky," Helena said, considering that a gross understatement.

Avery shrugged. "So why aren't they here helping?"

"I would assume they have no idea of what has happened here. Where are they?"

"Not together, as far as I know." Avery's eyes hardened. "I decided they should come here and see exactly what they're missing."

"A command?"

"A coax."

"You can't mess with people's free will, Avery. You know that."

"Just a nudge, then. I wanted them to suddenly desire to come here, just for a few days."

"Ah! I see. You're transforming their feelings. What if they hate it here, and you hate them for their attitude? Or they love it and decide to stay and ruin the life you have here? Have you considered that?"

"But if they liked it and just wanted to visit more often, that would be nice."

"I don't think you can presume anything so specific. If you miss them, why don't you just phone them?"

"Why don't *they* phone *me*?"

Helena was used to Avery's headstrong moods, as was Clea. Helena recognised them because they were like her own, too. "Fair point, but if you reach out, you might be surprised."

"I haven't been before. That's why I stopped calling."

Helena sighed, frustrated for Avery, and appalled at her family's behaviour. She had died to protect her children. "Show me the spell."

"It's just a little one," she said, pulling the grimoire towards her.

"It's dragon magic. It's never little. We saw that at Crag End!"

"Well, that's true," she reluctantly admitted. She smoothed out the page and showed it to Helena. "It's an ember spell. Quite intriguing, actually. The spell includes the ash of dragon bones, and we have plenty of that thanks to the baby dragon's sacrifice. Plus, I kept some ash from the Beltane fire we had at Rasmus's a few days ago."

"So you've been thinking about this for a while."

"Yes, and seeing as dragons are creatures of fire, it makes sense to cast it now."

The spell was written in tiny, crabbed handwriting, and illustrations lined the edges. Helena had seen it years ago in her own lifetime, but hadn't studied it properly. There were so many spells with scribbled annotations, pen and ink drawings, and colourful illustrations, that it became overwhelming. It was only when she needed to find a spell that she really studied them. Recent weeks had revealed a surprisingly large collection of dragon-based spells that even in her own time weren't used anymore. Dragons were a figment of myth.

This particular spell was worked around the embers of a fire, and a variety of roots and herbs were mixed with dragon bone ash. It was indeed a transformation spell. One that changed feelings and beckoned the recipients home.

"A hearth spell, too," Helena said thoughtfully. "Clever. Bringing someone back to hearth and home."

Avery smiled. "A lovely name, I've always thought."

"It's an old-fashioned term. I like it, though. The connotations of warmth at the heart of the house. It says here that you need something of the person you're beckoning, too."

"I know, but I don't have anything. I thought maybe using old photos might help."

"Perhaps. You know," Helena said, easing back in her chair, "they could be furious with you for this. Will you think on it first?"

"I have been thinking on it."

"Think some more! Beltane energy isn't going anywhere yet. You have time. You should talk to Alex about it."

"He'll think I'm needy."

"Don't be ridiculous."

"Aren't you interested in meeting them?" Avery asked, a challenge in her eyes.

"I must admit I am, but I'm not sure like this."

"But you said Clea misses them. You'd be doing her a favour."

"Avery Hamilton, you're being very sneaky!"

"Come on, Helena! I know you're interested. Let's cast it together."

"Why do you need me? Surely you can cast it on your own?"

"I think that two people casting the calling will have more power. Plus, you carry ancestral magic, and have Clea's magic to boot."

"I have ancestral magic?"

"Of course you do. You're my ancestor."

Helena considered her request, and couldn't deny she was interested. Seeing as she was essentially a spirit who spent a great deal of her time in the spirit world, she did carry a different kind of magic.

"Plus," Avery continued, excited now, "it will be like we are casting as the Triple Goddess. I am the Maiden, you're a Mother, Clea is the Crone."

Helena snorted. "You're hardly a maiden!"

"You know what I mean."

Helena drummed her fingers on the table, unable to deny that the more they discussed it, the more intrigued she was. *What was*

Avery's mother like? Was her sister as headstrong? And were they still practicing witches?

Finally, she relented. "All right. There's time before we go to the beach. Talk me through it."

Two

B riar pressed a glass of mulled cider that she had bought from one of the beachside traders into Tamsyn's hands. "Here you go. This will keep you warm."

"Thanks, my lovely. I'm really enjoying all this. Are you sure I'm not keeping you from your friends?"

"I'll be with them soon enough. Besides, they're your friends, too. Look." She pointed across the crowded beach to where El and Reuben stood with Stan, who was waiting to perform the libations around the enormous fire. Cassie, Ben, and Dylan, the three members of Ghost OPS were close by, still filming the events for their website. Briar also knew that they were looking for therians. "I bet Newton's around here somewhere with his sergeants and the community officers."

Tamsyn nodded, her sharp eyes missing nothing. "I saw that nice Hamid and Kevin earlier this evening, patrolling. They *know* about this place and you, don't they?" She emphasised the word "know" intentionally.

"Of course. Newton told them at Samhain last year, and it's a relief, actually. With the amount of weird happenings that occur here, it would be hard to keep them out of it. At least now they know what to worry about and what not to."

"Like therians?"

"Exactly." Briar studied the crowds—a mix of the costumed performers, townsfolk, and visitors as she sipped her own mulled cider, wondering if some of Lord Wentworth's extensive family might be there trying to glean where the dragon eggs were hidden. "I don't think they'll give up searching for *you know what*."

"No, nor do I. I still want to meet a dryad, by the way," she said nudging Briar. "I don't know how long I have left, so to meet a creature of the Otherworld would be a dream. The horrible sprites at Christmas don't count."

Briar was aghast, and she focussed fully on her tiny grandmother. "Don't say that! You're stronger than most. I can't bear the thought of you dying."

"It's the one great certainty of life, and I'm old." Tamsyn didn't sound upset or resigned, just accepting. "At least I've met you. And those lovely Nephilim, of course." Her eyes flashed with humour. "I'm leaving you the house, you know. Well, you and Rosa. You'll share it. I rather hope you don't sell it, but of course, it will be up to you."

The drumming, laughter, and the flashing light from the fire-jugglers faded to insignificance as Briar focussed fully on her grandmother. "I hate that you're talking about this, but no, I didn't know. Thank you." She pulled Tamsyn into a hug. "I love that house, and I have no intention of selling it. I hope Rosa doesn't, either."

"Not as far as I know. Now that most of it is repaired and clean, she loves it as much as I do. And much of that is down to both of you." Tamsyn squeezed her hand. "You've worked so hard up there. Especially in the garden. It looks beautiful."

Tending Stormcrossed Manor was one of Briar's absolute pleasures. She had kept her allotment, despite Tamsyn inviting her to use the garden to grow her huge selection of herbs in. She had resisted initially, as she hadn't known how long that arrangement might last, but now she could perhaps move all her plants there. Something to discuss with Rosa.

"You could even move in. Now, if you wanted," Tamsyn added. It was a regular invite that Briar always refused. "You have a bedroom already."

"I love my cottage, and it's convenient for my shop, but thank you. Maybe I'll stay the occasional weekend sometimes. Is Rosa driving you mad?" She often thought Tamsyn was glad of company other than the highly-strung Rosa who found magic hard to accept.

Tamsyn laughed. "No more than usual. Beth and Max make up for her oddities."

"Why are you bringing this up now? Is something wrong?"

"No." Tamsyn's attention was on the revellers again, but her gaze suggested she saw something else. "I'm dreaming of the white stag again. I wonder if it's calling me."

"Dreaming, not seeing?"

"Just dreaming. But dreams carry signs, don't they?"

Suddenly frightened, Briar stepped in front of Tamsyn and gripped her shoulders, forcing her to look at her. "Are you ill? Tired? I can make you a strengthening herbal potion."

Her beetle-black eyes settled calmly on Briar's. "I feel the same as always. My bones creak, and I can't do as much as I used to, but nothing worse than normal."

"Then perhaps you're seeing portents. We've wondered that before."

They had discussed it months ago, but had decided nothing definite. And then the white stag vanished. Tamsyn, however, was a Seer, although her powers had waned long ago when she had been forced to withdraw to Stormcrossed Manor and manage the banshee. Since the White Haven Coven had successfully banished it, though, Tamsyn's natural powers had resurfaced. They weren't as strong as Beth's, but Briar was thankful for that. Beth still struggled with them, although Alex had helped her manage them considerably.

Tamsyn patted Briar's cheek. "I don't want you to worry, but I needed you to know. Perhaps the stag portended the therians and the dragon eggs. And Nelaira's plans. They are considered Otherworldly messengers. Maybe it's signalling that new Otherworldly events are imminent."

"If they ever stopped," Briar said, considering what it might portend now. *Please not Tamsyn's death.*

"Anyway," Tamsyn said, brightly. "I can see Rosa and the children, and from the tired look on Beth's face, it's time to go home. Go and join your friends and enjoy the rest of the night."

"I'll come and say goodbye, but promise me," Briar said, holding her grandmother's attention, "that you will tell me when you see it again."

"Of course."

Unfortunately, the night that had been so full of fun was now edged with darkness. Potentially the white stag had heralded several big events in White Haven. Wyrd's magic and the arrival of Jack Frost and the Winter Queen. *Was this a sign something else was about to happen, or was it just a continuation of the dryads and the dragon eggs and* therians?

Briar knew she couldn't ignore it, so she had to tell the rest of the coven soon. And Newton, of course. *What the hell was she going to do about him?*

Newton might be strolling through White Haven's crowded beach, but he had other things on his mind, like dragon-obsessed therians.

He considered them an immediate threat to the paranormal world and Cornwall's peace, so he had assembled a comprehensive list of Lord Wentworth's family and distributed it to Moore and Kendall, as well as Kev and Hamid, White Haven's community police officers. They had the most consistent and recognisable presence in White Haven, even more than Kendall who lived above The Wayward Son, so they were on the constant lookout for them. Obviously, the witches knew too, but they were busy with their shops, and it was unlikely the therians would go near them. Hamid and Kev, however, patrolled the streets regularly, and had added Ravens' Wood to their route.

Despite their supposed truce, Newton didn't trust Wentworth at all. He'd even investigated his associates. Maggie Milne was keeping a close eye on Julian, his nephew who lived in London, and had compiled a list of his friends, too. Between them they had uncovered what they had called a large conspiracy of therians. It seemed the best collective noun to describe them, barring any other name. Of course, there were plenty of therians everywhere, but Lord Wentworth's conspiracy seemed particularly large, well-funded, and highly educated. Newton didn't like it one bit.

In an effort to share the management of Cornwall's widening paranormal issues, he had given Moore and Kendall more responsibilities. He had placed Kendall in charge of overseeing the therians. The young detective sergeant was eager to help and very competent, and kept in regular contact with Jasper, the head of the Penzance Coven. Moore, of course, kept an eye on Ravens' Wood. His beloved bloody liminal zone. He also now liaised with the other Cornwall Coven head witches. It wasn't Avery's job to report back to Newton, and he wanted to keep the policing part of it out of her hands. Both his sergeants were currently strolling through the crowds together, ensuring there were no disasters. All in all, he was very pleased with how things were working out.

Not that Newton could relax, though. With eight major celebrations over the course of the year, they acted as trigger points for magical happenings. And he was slap-bang in the middle of one of the most powerful. *Beltane.* Paired with Samhain, they were the biggest fire festivals over the year and shared the same thinning of the veils between worlds. A time when the ancestors stepped closer, and the wild spirits of the Otherworld would gather. Energy was rising, along with the flames of the bonfire. The drumming was heady and intoxicating, drinks were flowing, revellers were dancing, and fires flared all along the beach. God knows what kind of hedonistic behaviour was happening within the dunes. As long as no one was hurt, he didn't care.

He was in the mood for some hedonism himself. He blamed Beltane passion for that, not Briar, who looked particularly pretty in the firelight, with bare feet and a long, peasant-style dress swirling around her ankles. *Behave,* he instructed his loins. *Now is not the time. It will never be the time to be with Briar.*

A shrill whistle summoned his attention, and he turned to where Stan stood on a raised stage equidistant between the road and the bonfire. A local band, The Devil's Brew, were about to start playing their own brand of folk and rock, which sounded a bizarre mix to him, but first Stan would give his offering to the gods. He wore a suitably Druid-like robe in deep purple with silver trimming, and he raised his hands as he summoned the crowd's attention. El and Reuben, the happy newlyweds, were next to him, looking bemused and excited.

When Stan had everyone's attention, he started his speech. He welcomed the visitors, thanked the townsfolk for their efforts in decorating the town, heaped praise on the parade, flattered the May Queen and her consort, and then thanked Reuben and El for their monetary support and the flowers from Greenlane Nursery that allowed White Haven and the parade to be so impressive. "So now," Stan declared, throwing his hand wide, "it is time to give our offerings to the gods and ask for their blessings."

El handed him a grandiose silver chalice, and Reuben poured red wine into it with a flourish. A drink that Newton knew also had herbs and a spell cast on it. The witches had decided if they were getting involved, they may as well do it properly. Stan then marched down to the edge of the fire and sprinkled the drink into the flames as he intoned something portentous that Newton couldn't quite hear. The drumming intensified in accompaniment, resounding through him, and the eerie notes of a tin whistle, low and melodic, drifted on the air and sent chills up Newton's spine. He half-expected to see a fey creature perched on the rocks, but instead it was one of the band's musicians, a young woman who looked almost as ethereal.

As Stan completed the offering, the crowd roared with approval. However, it was as he returned to the stage that something odd happened. The flames roared and cinders exploded outwards in a shower like fireworks, sending a plume of twisting smoke that created unearthly shapes over the crowd before finally breaking up. The crowd screamed and pulled back, and then, as everything settled, cheered again. Stan covered his shock well, and waving at the crowd, urged them to have a good night.

But Newton knew that wasn't planned, and from Reu and El's expressions could see they weren't responsible. It was as if the music, the energy, and the libation had conjured something.

Something unbidden.

Alex poured himself half a pint of Doom and headed to the corner of the bar where Zee was enjoying a moment of peace with a half pint of Skullduggery Ale.

The Wayward Son had been busy earlier that evening, but now that the procession was underway, many customers were outside and would no doubt be heading to the beach for the fire.

He took advantage of the lull and raised his glass to Zee. "Let's hope it stays this quiet until closing."

Zee laughed. "Isn't being busy good for business?"

"It was, and now peace is good for my head." He drank thirstily, wishing it was a full pint, and then called over to Marie who was cleaning the tables. "Take a break. It can wait."

She waved him off. "No, I'd rather do it now, just in case. That way you might let me go early." She wiggled her hips. "I'm going dancing on the beach!"

He laughed. She was always cheeky. "Give it half an hour, and if we're still quiet, you can go."

"Cheers, boss."

"Are you heading to the beach later?" Alex asked Zee, pulling over a stool to sit down next to him.

"Sure. I'm not one for early nights, and the street noise would just keep me awake anyway. It's a shame my brothers and Shadow aren't here—other than Eli, of course. They'd love it. I think he's out there with one of his harem."

"How are things with Nelaira?" Alex knew that the dryad had bewitched Eli in some way, and that they'd had a night of passion to seal the deal with hiding the dragon eggs. "Briar said he seemed distant for days, although I gather he's okay now."

"There's no doubt that it shook him up at the time. He thought he'd be trapped in the wood, forever beholden to Nelaira, which is admittedly a terrifying idea. However, he seems back to his usual self, but Eli never says much. Keeps it all locked in." Zee patted his chest. "Except with Briar. I think he shares with her."

"Yes, they do seem close." Alex had often wondered about Briar's relationship with Eli in recent weeks, but like Eli, she didn't really share her thoughts on her relationships. Not with him, anyway. If she had confided in Avery, she certainly hadn't told him anything. As for what might happen with Newton, Alex had no idea. He had decided long ago to keep out of it. "Where are your brothers and Shadow, then?"

Zee grinned. "France. Niel is with Mouse, and they needed help with a job. They left a few days ago."

"Something illegal?"

"Perhaps. I said the less I knew, the better."

"Intriguing." Alex had visions of them breaking into old vaults or temples to steal treasure. "Dangerous, I presume?"

"Probably. I think they are meeting up with Lucien."

He was referring to the enhanced human who Barak and Estelle had rescued from Black Cronos's clutches. He sounded like some kind of universal soldier to Alex. "A reunion, then. And JD?"

"Causing trouble in London, of course. When he's not ensconced in his Emerald Cave."

"And I thought life was interesting here. Now I feel spectacularly boring." But the second Alex finished his sentence, he felt a ripple of something Otherworldly, and he gripped the bar top as if he might be shaken off his stool. "Shit! Did you feel that?"

"I felt something, but clearly not as much as you."

Alex studied the room, but the few customers present continued to laugh and chat over drinks while Marie ferried plates and glasses to the kitchen.

Zee's dark, expressive eyes became pensive. "What was it? I felt a sort of shiver in the air, as if another type of energy had arrived."

Alex didn't answer, instead walking to the front door of the pub and exiting to stand on the narrow street. Zee followed him. The night was cool, but the brisk wind of earlier had dropped. Laughter and music carried from the beach, along with the hum of conversation from a few passersby. Alex wasn't sure what he expected, but everything looked normal enough.

"Alex," Zee said, breaking his silent contemplation. "What do think it was?"

"I'm not entirely sure, but it felt like a presence. Something old. Maybe Otherworldly. Fuck it. Has Beltane summoned something?"

"Like what? A ghost? A god or goddess?"

Alex shook his head. "I don't know."

"It might be something good," Zee suggested. He didn't look convinced, though.

"I doubt that. The sooner I can talk to the coven, the better."

Three

Reuben walked to the top of the dunes, El matching his long strides, both eager to see the broad expanse of the beach after the explosion of cinders only moments earlier.

"I sincerely hope this has nothing to do with damn dragons," he said, heart already pounding with anticipation.

"With luck, Ghost OPS have caught something on their cameras." El pointed down to where the group clustered together with Newton. "Maybe it was just some damp wood."

"Damp wood? That's utter bollocks, and you know it. I felt it. Almost like a physical presence. That fire has given birth to something." He scanned the beach, both hoping and dreading to see something unnatural that could explain what he'd experienced, but all he saw were endless crowds and sporadic beach fires. Behind him, within the sheltered warmth of the dunes, he heard giggles, a result of Beltane passion, no doubt.

"Everything looks perfectly normal now," El said, but she looked uneasy. "However, I can't deny that I also felt something unusual. Something my own magic responded to, if I'm honest."

"Really?" He spun to look at her, worried for her safety. "Like what?"

"I presume it's because something happened in the fire, and that's my element. Sorry, I know that's vague." She squeezed his arm and gave him a reassuring smile. "I'm fine, though, so don't worry. I'd love to cast a spell to try to unveil if anything odd is amongst us, but that would be far too risky."

He searched her face, hoping she wasn't hiding anything from him. "If you're sure, but tell me if that changes. As far as an unveiling spell goes, that could be a bloody disaster if there *is* something down there. We'd have hordes of screaming people stampeding across the beach."

"Might be better than people dying. Or being possessed."

"Please stop talking. I was hoping for a quiet Beltane, with nothing but us having loads of sex."

"We have been having loads of sex."

"I meant more of it."

El giggled. "You are incorrigible."

"I am filled with passion for my beautiful wife." He loved that word. It made him feel even more connected to El than before. He teased her. "As your husband, I am taking full advantage of my conjugal rights."

"I've noticed. You're like a horny rabbit."

"No. Horns on rabbits do not work."

"Silly bugger. But seriously," she said, staring at the large bonfire, "what *was* that? And what do you mean, 'the fire has given birth?' I've never heard anything more horrific. It sounds primordial."

"What if it's a phoenix? That's not horrific."

"A phoenix rises from its own ashes, not a Beltane fire, and I'm pretty sure we didn't sacrifice one tonight."

Reuben saw Ghost OPS and Newton approaching. Newton's jaw was clenched, but the Ghost OPS team looked excited. Reuben prepared himself. "You know," he said to El before they arrived, "I can ask Silver later. If I can journey with him, I might see an unusual aura or something. He might have felt the disturbance in the force." He smirked at her, wondering if she'd get the film reference.

"It's not bloody *Star Wars*!"

"You see? This is why I married you."

"You're such a tit. I hoped White Haven was settling into some kind of normalcy after our honeymoon, even though we know we have therians living on St Michael's Mount. I mean, it's a long way from here, and they haven't caused trouble here before."

"But the dragon eggs they covet so badly are hidden in Ravens' Wood. Plus, there are shit-stirring dryads, and our adventure-loving Nephilim friends. White Haven will never be normal, and thank the gods for that."

"For a man who used to deny his own magic, you've come a long way."

"Thanks to you."

Before she could respond, Dylan bounded to the top of the dune, waving his camera at them. "We need your help. I filmed some of that weird smoke, but we can't make it out. Can you help?"

Dylan was the IT and camera-obsessed member of the paranormal hunting trio, who also had a degree in some branch of folklore that Reuben could never remember.

"So you saw it, too?" El asked, edging behind Dylan to see the screen. "We wondered if we'd imagined it, but I can't deny what I felt."

"Which was?" Newton asked.

"Something that struck a chord with my own magic. It gave me the tingles."

"No tingles for me," Reuben said. "It felt stronger than that. More defined. I couldn't say what it was, though."

El glared at him. "He said it felt like the fire had given birth to something."

"Really?" Cassie's eyebrows shot up. "Wow. That's intriguing. Like a mythological creature?"

"For fuck's sake," Newton muttered. "Not something else."

Reuben concentrated on the video of the swirling smoke. "I can't make out much at all, Dylan. Although, that might be a face." He squinted at the camera. "Can you clean it up?"

"Of course, but not until I get back to the office."

"Why were you recording it, anyway?"

"We always film the celebrations here." He grinned. "I was immortalising Stan's libations for our website. These videos always pull in traffic."

Ben had been surveying the crowd, no doubt looking for clues, but now he said, "We won't be going back to the office for a while. Plenty more research to do here first. Fortunately, I brought the EMF meter with me."

"As if you're not attached at the hip," Cassie pointed out.

"Let's split up, then," Reuben suggested. "Briar is here somewhere, and Alex and Avery will be along soon. Maybe Zee, too. Perhaps it left a trace we can follow."

"And Helena is here," El reminded him. "She could help, too. But what are we looking for? What we felt could have just been a release of Beltane energy that has now vanished. It is a fire festival, after all."

Reuben shook his head. "That's just wishful thinking. That fire has conjured something, and although I'm sure it isn't on the beach anymore, we still have to look. It will have an energy signature of sorts, surely."

Resigned, Newton pulled his phone out of his pocket. "Time to organise the team, then."

Avery knew she was being headstrong and unreasonable, but also felt that it was justified.

Her mother and sister *should* visit White Haven. Years of little to no contact was unacceptable, and although she thought she'd made her peace with it, talking to El had made her realise that it wasn't okay at all. She had a good life in White Haven, and she wanted to share it with them. Surely they would want to share theirs. Although perhaps they already did with each other. Just not her.

Plus, a little niggling part of her was worried that maybe they were in trouble.

"I could have nieces or nephews!" she said to Helena. "Or stepbrothers or sisters."

"Or neither." Helena settled on a large floor cushion in front of the fire, the gathered tools and ingredients close to hand, the embers hot and glowing. "But there's only one way to find out. Are you sure you want to do this?"

"Yes." Avery picked up the grimoire and sat next to Helena, placing the satisfyingly weighty book in her lap.

They sat in candlelight only, and the room was pleasantly dark. Already Avery felt her magic gathering in anticipation of the rite. In the flickering firelight, the words of the spell danced on the page, almost as if responding to the flames themselves, and the tiny illustrations seemed to shift like settling embers. As usual, Avery had tweaked the spell to suit her needs, and had written it in special ink in her own grimoire. Here, in her family home, seated before a family hearth, the spell would be potent. Especially with three generations of witches casting it. *Was she prepared for what it might do?* She wasn't entirely sure, but if she didn't cast it now, she wouldn't have the courage again, and she would forever wonder.

Helena had changed into a long, flowing gown and had encouraged Avery to do the same, and Avery adjusted her skirt as she mentally prepared herself. "I think you're right about changing, Helena. We don't normally adopt ritual clothing, but it does give the whole thing a bit more *oomph*."

"It's about your state of mind. Your magic is great with or without ritual clothes, but if you're dressed for it, then you're more focussed. Well, I am, anyway. We always used to dress appropriately. The old coven, that is, and I've been feeling its lack recently. Now I feel better. It doesn't have to be dramatic robes, just something you keep special. Or what you decide is special for a given spell." Helena smoothed down her dark green silk dress that she had bought and then embroidered with delicate flowers and leaves to make it her own.

"I still can't get over how clever you are at sewing."

"No TV back then," Helena explained. "I spent hours doing embroidery. Are we ready?"

"Yes."

"No second thoughts?" Helena stared at her intently, as if trying to read her mind.

"No. I am very sure. Let's begin."

The spell invoked elemental fire, and Avery added her own element, air, to it as well. While Avery spoke the words, Helena added the herbal spell ingredients, weaving intent with strength as she repeated the lines. As Helena added the small chippings of the nine sacred Beltane woods, the embers glowed with fierce intensity, the heat burning Avery's cheeks. Ash, Alder, Birch, Hawthorn, Hazel, Holly, Oak, Rowan, and Willow. Then Helena added the ash from the Cornwall Coven's celebrations, withholding that of the dragon bones until the end.

Avery used the traditional words for the sacred woods with a twist, all the while focussing on transformation. "Nine woods in the embers glow, burn them quick a' burn them slow. Heart of hearth must bring to me, close bloodline of family. By these images find them soon, call them back on witch's broom, let Beltane flames transform their will tonight, heedless of whim, desperate my plight. Home is beckoning, White Haven implores, for when three witches summon, you must answer our call."

Helena added the old photos of Avery's mother and sister to the flames and then stirred the dragon bone ashes in too, and the embers burned fierce and hot.

Avery finished the spell, reaching for Helena's hand as she did. "Ember's hearth, fire's breath, transform your heart to needs unmet. A turn of fancy, a call on the wind, a visit home will see you set. By the Goddess—Mother, Maiden, Crone—as we say it, so shall it be."

The flames in the fireplace leapt higher, curling into the chimney, a spiral of smoke and powerful intent that Avery felt in the depths of her core. They both withdrew as sparks flew, and Avery felt the shift. The call had gone out.

And then she felt something else. A deep pulse of energy that blew through the room, lifting Helena and Avery's hair and making the flames flicker wildly.

"Was that you?" Helena asked as it settled.

Avery shook her head. "No. And I don't think it was the spell, either."

Ben walked across the sand, tracking from the bonfire and through the knots of people, not bothering to hide his EMF meter as he searched for strong signals.

He knew that probably no one would care, but also that everyone was having far too good a time to bother with what he was doing. He had decided that starting at the main bonfire would be the best option, and to work outwards from there. Dylan had fixed his tripod on a dark section of beach well away from the main fire, and Cassie had the other EMF meter and was searching in the other direction with Reuben.

He hadn't progressed very far when Kendall, the DS, caught up with him. "Anything useful?" she asked, looking hopeful. She was dressed informally that night, in dark jeans and a jumper, along with a lightweight jacket, but she still managed to give off that professional police air that was instilled into them in training.

"I'm picking up low levels of electromagnetic energy, but nothing conclusive."

"If you do find something, can you tell us what it is?"

He shook his head. "Unlikely. This is just the early stages of our investigation. Of course, if Dylan can see a shape once he refines the video, that could help a lot." His EMF meter whined, and he whirled around, trying to target where it was coming from. "Fuck it. Therians."

"Are you sure?" Kendall asked, instantly on high alert.

He pointed towards two young men and a woman gathered around a small fire, watching them with arrogant smiles. Ben waved cheekily. "I think we should say hello."

"I agree." Kendall strode towards them, and Ben glanced around as he hurried after her, hoping they wouldn't need back-up. Reaching the group, Kendall went straight to the point. "Lord Wentworth's family or friends, I presume?"

"What's it to you?" a young, dark-haired man asked with a sneer.

"I'm DS Kendall. We've been expecting you here. Let me see," she said, narrowing her eyes and pointing at them one by one. "Ah, yes. Peter and Veronica Mills, and Enzo Rinaldi."

All three had been lounging on a rug on the damp sand, but now they rose to their feet with the uncanny fluidity of rising cobras. Ben stepped closer to Kendall in solidarity, impressed she had known them all.

"How the hell do you know our names?" Enzo asked. Olive-skinned with honey blond hair, he looked like he spent his winters skiing and his summers on a yacht.

"We've made it our business to know all of Wentworth's asso-ciates."

"That's *Lord* Wentworth to you," Veronica said, arrogance oozing from her every pore.

"He's whatever I want to call him," Kendall said easily. "Thief, trickster, kidnapper... *Therian*. Just like you three. You should be careful of what you get up to for him. Why are you here?"

Ben wondered if their arrogance would vanish, but it didn't.

Peter drew himself upright. "It's a festival. We're here to celebrate, just like everyone else."

"And," Enzo added, "we aren't causing any trouble. Unlike you." His gaze slid to Ben. "You killed our friends."

So they knew who he was. Unnerving, but inevitable. It seemed everyone was keeping tabs on each other. Ben shrugged, mentally trying to work out how quickly he could access the spell jars in his pack, just in case he needed them. "Your friends were trying to kill us. It left us with little choice."

Kendall interceded as Enzo stepped towards Ben. "Back off and calm down. As long as you're not causing trouble, you're welcome here. Just don't start searching for anything that doesn't belong to you."

Enzo glanced at Ben's EMF meter, a gleam in his eyes. "Are *you* searching for something?"

"I'm always searching for something. It's my job. And I found you. Lucky me."

"You're searching with the police?" Veronica asked, her tone disdainful.

"It's my job, too," Kendall assured her. "Enjoy the rest of your night."

They walked away, Ben resisting the urge to look over his shoulder, even though he could feel them watching. "They know something is here."

"Not necessarily," Kendall reasoned, keeping her stride unhurried. "They looked relaxed around that fire."

"Maybe they are responsible for whatever happened, and they're watching the consequences play out."

"It's possible, but let's not jump to conclusions, or give them reason to suspect anything is wrong. Let's find the others before their suspicions grow. The last thing we want is them adding to the issue."

"I am determined to finish my search," Ben said, aggrieved. "I'll just have to do it later."

Unfortunately, the trail might have gone cold by then.

El joined Briar, who was still talking to Stan, while the others spread along the beach, trying to detect the strange energy that had emerged from the fire.

"Are you two okay?" she asked them. "I presume you had that weird experience too, Briar?"

Briar nodded, obviously perturbed. "Yes, and now I'm wondering if that's what my gran's white stag meant."

"She's seeing it again?" El and the rest of the coven knew all about the white stag.

"In dreams this time. I'm so worried. I keep thinking that it's foretelling her death."

"Briar!" Stan said, aghast. "Of course it doesn't mean that."

"You don't know that. Neither does she. But you're probably right and I'm being too negative. I'm just aware that she's old, and I've only just found her."

El, all too aware of the importance of family recently, hugged her. "She may be old, but she's strong. Plus, she saw it months ago, and she's fine. Maybe it's a warning about tonight."

Stan was wringing his hands with worry, eyes darting over the crowds. He'd been so excited earlier because the parade had been a huge success, and now he looked haunted when he turned back to El. "You're talking about that explosion of sparks, aren't you?"

"I'm afraid so. We don't want to jump to conclusions, but we're sure that something came out of that fire. That's why we're searching the beach now. Not," she added hurriedly, "that we're expecting to find it immediately, of course. Just a clue as to what it might be."

Stan's lips tightened. "Do we need to evacuate the beach?"

El exchanged a worried glance with Briar. "No, I'm sure not. It vanished so quickly. Whatever it is could be harmless, anyway. I mean, it might just have been Beltane energy releasing itself," she said, repeating her earlier argument. It sounded lame, though, and she knew she was downplaying what she'd felt, as if by telling herself that she'd imagined it, it would just go away.

"Or you're just mistaken?" he added hopefully, eyes widening in a plea. "Maybe it's the old Ravens' Wood branches that carry a little more punch."

"We better not have sacrificed a dryad," Briar said, voice squeaking with horror.

"Of course not! It was all dead wood."

El hadn't even considered that, but she was sure that wasn't what had happened. *If they had, did that mean the dryads would attack White Haven? Would the trees march on the town?* She shook her head to dispel such a dramatic idea. "Stan, you stay here, and just relax," she said, summoning positivity she didn't feel. "Briar and I will continue the search. I'm sure no one is at risk, or they would have been attacked already."

Unfortunately, before they had walked more than a few paces, Moore caught up with them. "Kendall has phoned. Three therians are on the beach, further along, and they know we're searching for something, which means we have to stop."

"What?" El frowned, confused. "That's nuts."

"No, he's right," Briar said. "We have no idea what it is, which means we don't want them benefitting from it. There's too much we don't know." She turned to look along the beach. "Avery and Helena have just arrived with Alex and Zee. We should just hang around the fire as if nothing has happened."

El fretted, at war with herself. She wanted to downplay the burst of sparks, and yet the faint recognition of something fire-elemental was growing stronger with every passing minute, as if it had kindled a spark within her own magic. "But we'll lose whatever it is!" El said, an air of certainty and inevitability finally exerting itself.

"Better than alerting the therians even more," Moore said regretfully. "We can regroup and decide what to do next."

And in the meantime, El thought uncharitably, *the creature that had been born in flames was free to go wherever it wanted. Perhaps that was the therians' plan all along.*

$\mathcal{F}our$

Avery woke up groggily on Thursday after a very late night at the beach, feeling worried and sidetracked.

They had lingered by the fire until most revellers had gone home, even waiting for the three therians to leave before they did. They had eventually exited over the dunes, and Zee had followed them, watching as they reached a car parked on the road and then exited the town. *That was a relief, at least.* The witches and everyone else then searched the area, but found nothing at all, leaving them all to wonder if they had imagined seeing something in the fire—except, they knew they hadn't.

Alex was sprawled next to Avery, lying on his stomach, hair spread over the pillow, the gentle rise and fall of his chest telling her that he was still sleeping. She slipped out of bed and into the spell room to stare at the remnants of the fire that she and Helena had stoked the night before, wondering if her mother and sister might already be making their way to White Haven. Or perhaps they would be casting counterspells to stop it. She raked through the cold ashes, ensuring all was a fine powder, and then gathered them up into a small jar that she sealed with a cork and wax before placing it on her shelf. *Best to keep it.* She might need it later.

But when she turned back to the room, she found Alex in the bedroom doorway zipping up his jeans, his chest bare, staring at her. He was obviously confused. "What are you doing?"

"Just keeping the ashes," she said vaguely.

"Please don't tell me you cast one of those dragon spells last night." And then his eyes widened. "Are you responsible for that odd thing we all felt?"

"No! That was something very different!"

He crossed his arms over his chest and leaned on the door-frame. "What did you do?"

She shrugged, suddenly sheepish. "I cast a little spell."

"To do what?"

"I thought it would be good to see my mother and sister. That's all."

"That's *all*? Holy shit, Avery. That's huge!" He walked to the table where the old grimoire lay, still open to the page, with her own spell next to it. "I knew you were interested in these old spells, but not enough to cast one." He brushed his hair back from his face, eyes full of worry. "Why didn't you tell me?"

"Because you'd have thought I was nuts."

"I always think that."

"Alex!"

He laughed. "I'm kidding. Don't you trust me?"

"Of course I do. But I didn't want you to talk me out of it. Helena tried to."

"So Helena knows?"

"She wheedled it out of me."

"Yes, she's been as worried as me. We've talked about your obsession."

Avery felt stung by that knowledge. "Really?"

"We were just worried," he repeated, trying to calm her down. "I defended you, saying that researching is your thing. I actually thought, however, that you would talk to me about whatever was bothering you. What does Helena think?"

She shuffled, feeling guilty at her subterfuge. "She thought it was a bit reckless, but eventually helped me."

"Were you planning on ever telling me? Because it looks like you're trying to hide it."

"Of course. I would have last night, but then everything else happened." She sat on the chair, legs like lead.

He sat opposite her, voice heavy with sarcasm. "Great. So you summoned your mother and sister. They are going to be thrilled! Everyone just loves to be coerced into doing things against their will."

"I already feel guilty, so don't make it worse."

"So why do it if you feel guilty?"

"Because at the time I was really cross with them. Not one word in years, except a bloody Christmas card."

Alex leaned forward and squeezed her hand. "I get it. I'm just not sure that this is the answer. However, it's done now. Where exactly are they going to stay? We're not swimming in space here."

"The spell might not work. If it does, they might not arrive for weeks, or even come together."

He cocked his head. "I know your magic. And Helena's. I'm sure it will work."

"To be honest, it felt right, as soon as we cast it. A potent heart of the house, heart of the family hearth spell." Even now she felt the energy of the magic they'd released.

Fortunately, Alex's good sense of humour returned and he sniggered. "What the hell will they make of Helena?"

Avery laughed, too. "What have I done?"

"Fuck. I'll be in a house full of women, and two of them might be really pissed at being here. I should move in with Reuben."

"Perhaps we both could. They could stay here alone."

"You've invited them! You can't just abandon them."

"You can't abandon me to them!"

"I bloody well can." He shook his head. "No, of course I won't, especially after last night." Avery knew he had felt the strange presence, too. "We need to decide what we're doing today. If your family show up in the middle of all this, they might well turn around and leave again. They might do that anyway."

"I just want to see them. Even an hour will suffice."

"What worries me is that I felt that weird whatever it was in the town, not on the beach, so it moved quickly."

"We felt it here, too, which means it could be anywhere by now. Maybe it's not our concern anymore."

"Except it is, and you know it. And I'm sorry that you miss your mother so much. I didn't realise."

Avery shrugged. "Neither did I. Most of the time I don't even think about it. It will pass. Seeing what El is working through has stirred it all up. Anyway," she rubbed her eyes, feeling the sleep in them. "Coffee time before I open up for the day." It would be busy at work with so many visitors. It had been all week.

However, before she could walk downstairs, Alex's phone started to ring, and he ran to the bedroom to pick it up. She knew even before he answered it that something was wrong. She could feel it. She studied his expression as he turned towards her, and watched resignation sweeping over his features as he ended the call.

"Well?" she asked.

"It's Newton. There are two dead bodies on the beach. Consumed by fire, by the look of it. We're too late. Whatever this is, it has already started."

"What could have done this?" Newton asked, trying to contain his anger. "They're burnt to a crisp!"

Arthur Davison, the Forensic Pathologist and recipient of his anger, rolled his eyes. "You're the expert here, Newton, not me."

"But you deal with the paranormal!"

"I ascertain the manner of death, not who caused it. If there was a weapon, I might have more luck. I shall know more after the post-mortem, of course."

"I need them to be identified quickly."

"I know. I'll do what I can."

"Poor buggers. They were having fun, by the look of it, and this is how it ended."

Their bodies lay entwined together in the dunes, in a hollow out of the wind. Only husks remained, and the bare remnants of clothing. The rest of the forensic team were spread out, combing the area for any clues. Kendall had been the first on scene after an early morning walker had spotted their bodies, and Zee had gone to the beach with her. He stood on the top of the closest dune, keeping a look out for the witches.

"Can I take the bodies?" Arthur asked. He'd arrived much quicker than usual.

"Give me just five minutes. I'm waiting for my other team."

Arthur nodded, knowing full well what Newton meant. "All right. I'll walk down to the sea to give them some space. Just make sure they don't touch them."

Newton joined Zee on the dune. The sea was grey, matching the leaden skies overhead. Rain was coming. "Thanks for coming with Kendall. I worry about her being alone at times like this. Just in case the perpetrator is loitering."

Zee shrugged. "Happy to help. I didn't want her to be alone, either."

"I take it you didn't hear anything?" The beach was a short distance from the town.

"No, or see anything. Have any of them?" Zee gestured to the row of houses on the road opposite the beach.

"We're about to start the door-to-door enquiries. I would have thought they would see flames at night, but if everyone had a late night and a skinful, maybe not." The familiar list of things he needed to do was drowning out all other plans he'd had for the day.

Zee pointed to the witches a short distance away. "Here they come." Zee waved to attract their attention, and within minutes, they had joined them.

"No Helena?" Newton asked Avery.

"She's averse to burnt remains, not surprisingly," Avery said. "And she's waiting at the house for a visitor."

Newton felt callous for even asking. "Ah, of course. Sorry. Anyway, thanks for coming." Newton handed out paper shoes and gloves before leading them down to the victims, leaving Zee on lookout duty. "Sorry to call you out, but I'd like your advice before the bodies are removed. I'm paranoid that this is dragon-related. Please tell me I'm wrong."

Briar blanched at the sight of the bodies. "Those poor people."

"This can't be caused by dragons," Reuben said, crouching to examine them. "The one we had is dead, and the two eggs are safely housed elsewhere."

"But they were killed by fire, and so far there is no sign of any accelerants," Newton told them.

Alex, El, and Avery crouched down too, all running their hands inches above the remains to feel for energy signatures, while Briar investigated the ground around them. Newton felt guilty for asking her here. She was always more affected by death than the others, but he didn't want to exclude her, either.

He crossed to her side, ever a moth to a flame. "Sorry. I know you hate this."

She looked up at him, smiling in resignation, strands of her dark hair whipping across her face in the wind. "So do you. I bet you're already thinking about breaking the news to their family."

He swallowed at her accurate assessment of him. She knew him so well. "Yes, one of my least favourite jobs, but that doesn't just apply to me. It's every policeman's dreaded duty."

"It's still horrible. I'd rather help to track down whatever—*whoever*—did this, so don't worry about me."

"I always worry. That's my job, too." *Especially about you.* "Plus, you need to open up soon."

"If we're a few minutes late, so be it. Eli can open the shop anyway, so I might go to Ravens' Wood first."

"To collect herbs?"

"That, and to ensure that the energy up there isn't changing. It's Beltane, and last year it was really odd there. The Otherworld was so close. Now, with dragon eggs somewhere in its interior, I just wanted to check. I should have done it earlier, but I ran out of time."

Briar had been there with Hunter last year, and Newton felt his old jealousy rising. It was unreasonable and he knew it, and he wanted to make amends. "Should I go with you?"

"No. You'll be busy enough. Plus, I'm collecting herbs, and that will take a while."

Then he had a better idea. "Would you mind taking Moore? He's my Ravens' Wood liaison now. You know how he loves that place. I'd like him to assess it too, and I know that with you he'd learn so much more."

"Of course! Moore is such a lovely man. Your liaison? Interesting!" she teased him. "You're delegating now."

"I have to. This bloody place keeps me busy."

"You used to hate all this paranormal stuff, but..." she studied his face, and he held his breath, "you don't anymore. You've grown into it. Accepted it. even. You've found a way to make it work."

Was there a hint of regret in her eyes for how things had ended between them?

"I accept a lot of things now, including witchcraft." *Including you. But what the hell was he doing when there were two dead bodies virtually at his feet?* "Anyway, does your magic feel anything unusual?"

"It's not earth magic, that's for sure. It must be elemental fire, but as to what wields it..." She turned to her coven who had been talking quietly over the bodies. "What do you guys think?"

El was the first to look up, her blue eyes stormy. "It's very strong elemental fire. As you know, fire is my element, and this feels pure to me. It's a feeling that's been growing all night long."

She stood in one smooth fluid movement, and the other witches stood up, too. "I think there's only one thing it can be. A fire spirit. Pure, elemental fire."

"Which makes sense," Reuben added. "It was born in the Beltane flames."

"Plus," Alex added, "I felt a presence at the pub."

Avery nodded too, all in agreement. "I felt it in our house. Only something purely elemental could travel that fast—or perhaps displace enough energy to create such a wave."

"Which means *what*?" Newton asked, feeling out of his depth.

"We're not sure," El admitted. "I need to do a little research. For example, if we're right—and I don't want to presume too much yet—we don't know how it was born in the flames. These things don't happen spontaneously, surely? So, it comes down to the wood in the fire, or the libation that Stan used, or something else entirely. The herbs we put in the wine shouldn't have caused this. We'll sift through the fire's ashes and see what we can find."

Zee had strolled down to listen, and he frowned. "But what form does a fire elemental take? Is it just energy?"

"Or is it," Briar suggested, "a salamander?"

"A lizard?" Newton asked, thinking he was hearing things.

The witches looked at each other as if in silent communication, but it was Avery who answered. "Essentially yes, but made of pure fire in form. They move through it as easily as we move through air. They are creatures of energy, though, not actually physical lizards." She shrugged. "That's the best way to explain it for now. I'll obviously look into it, as well as explore other options."

"Oh, just great. A giant bloody lizard."

"Well, actually, it might be quite small," Reuben said sheepishly.

"Forget the fucking size! Why is it killing people?"

Alex shrugged. "We don't know. Maybe it's weak and needs food, and that was the way it consumed them. Although, pure energy shouldn't need food, in theory. They have been linked to djinn, however."

Panic kicked in at the thought of another Otherworld entity loose in White Haven, but he lowered his voice, trying not to overreact. "Djinn? You must be fucking kidding me."

"We're just telling you the lore, Newton," Alex said, calmly, "and frankly this is just speculation. Let's hope Dylan has found something helpful in the footage."

Newton could feel a pounding headache starting, so he reminded himself of Briar's words. He was accepting all of this now. It was who he was. The new Newton. He shook himself mentally and cut to the crux of the matter. "How do we catch whatever this is?"

"At this stage, we have no idea."

"But," Reuben added, "we should consider that this thing will be as attractive to therians as dragons. Just so you know."

Newton's mind was filled with images of giant lizards striding across White Haven, or djinn swirling in sand along the beaches, and therians gaining unassailable powers. "In that case I shall update my team, and you lot need to gather as much information for me as possible. This will hit the news, and that means widespread panic. So do it quickly!"

Five

Dylan's eyes ached from staring at his computer screen for so long, but he finally sighed and leaned back, satisfied with his work.

"Okay, I have something, but I'm not sure I believe what I'm seeing."

Ben and Cassie had been at their own desks in their office in Falmouth, but they quickly coasted to Dylan's side on their desk chairs.

"Why?" Ben asked, before he'd even looked. "Is it a mess?"

"Holy shit!" Cassie said, leaning into the screen to see the frozen frame. "Is that a lizard with legs?"

"Thank the gods," Dylan said, sighing dramatically. "I thought I was hallucinating."

"Lizards always have legs," Ben corrected her. "Snakes do not. But I see what you mean."

Twisting within the flames was a lizard that was as tall as Dylan, but slender and made entirely of flames. It had two long legs like a human, shorter arms—or perhaps front legs—like an amphibian, a long tail, and scaly skin. Except it wasn't really skin. It was also flame, barely discernible from the fire around it, and it was visible for seconds only.

"Can you enhance it?" Ben asked, transfixed.

"No. This is as good as it gets, and it took me a while just to get this. I've had to play around with the colour saturation. It's pure flame. If I run the video, you'll see. Pay attention."

He scrolled back and then hit play. He had been filming Stan's libation from a side angle, and once Stan had thrown in the wine, he had panned back and turned to film the flames leaping up, sparks exploding, a sizzle of smoke, and the spectators' faces beyond that looked demonic in the light. A nice touch, he'd thought at the time.

"Look right into the centre, within the sparks. It lasts bare seconds and then it vanishes."

Cassie leaned in further so that she was inches from the screen. "I don't know how you even spotted that. It's so quick! And thin. It's like it turned and vanished. But where to?"

"I don't know. I've played you all of it. I'll slow it down so you can see it frame by frame." Dylan adjusted the settings. "See? It just springs up in the middle like a damn jack in the box."

"And the sparks came with it," Ben observed, already making notes in his ever-present notebook. *He'd have made a good detective in another life*, Dylan realised. *Methodical. Analytical.* Now he was recording the time stamps. "Stop. Replay. And again," he directed. Finally, he sagged back, hands gripping the desk. "It has eyes. It's like it assessed where it was, and vanished into thin air."

"But if it's flame," Dylan said, trying to articulate his thoughts coherently, "where does it go so that we can't see it?"

"Ooh, there!" Cassie jiggled in her seat like a child and jabbed at the screen. "Rewind and play it again."

"It's not a tape," Dylan corrected her.

"You know what I mean! You're so pedantic."

"Says the woman who corrects me over every psychological term."

She flipped him the bird, eyes on the screen. "Look at the top of the flames, just on the left, above the crowd. There! A golden ball."

"It's a spark," Ben complained. "There are loads of them."

"No. This is different. It's bigger, like an actual orb, and it floats away. It doesn't wink out like the sparks."

Dylan enhanced the image. "Shit. You're right. It's like it has its own little aircraft."

Ben looked at him incredulously. "An aircraft?"

"What would you call it?"

"Not that!"

"I kind of like it."

"Let's think of something more appropriate, shall we?"

Cassie interrupted their squabble. "You're associating the orb with the giant lizard?"

"Aren't you?" he asked, confused.

"Well, not necessarily, no. What if they're unrelated?"

"You're suggesting there are *two things* in that fire?" Ben said, voice laced with intrigue as he scribbled notes again.

She shrugged. "Just saying that it's possible. Did you film further out, Dylan?"

"No. Not then, anyway. I have later footage of when we searched. Why?"

"Say it is just one thing, if it likes flames, it must have searched for more. There were plenty of fires on the beach. Perhaps it found another place to shelter."

"But they were smaller fires."

"It can obviously change its shape."

"Or they can," Ben pointed out. "There could be several of them."

"You know what the lizard is, right?" Cassie asked.

"I suspect it's a salamander," Dylan said, considering what he knew of them. "The idea of them began in ancient Greece, and then Paracelsus classified them as one of four elemental beings. There are all sorts of myths associated with them."

Ben nodded. "St Elmo's Fire."

"Exactly."

"I've heard of that," Cassie said, "and I don't mean the film. What is it?"

"It's a spectral fire that appears in a ship's rigging. In the Medieval period it was associated with fire spirits, or something like that," Dylan said, shrugging. "I'll have to check. Considering White Haven has plenty of fishing boats, that's a bit worrying."

Ben rolled his eyes. "Please. It's bad enough already. If the orb isn't the salamander, what is it? Another fire elemental of some sort?"

"Or a spirit trapped in flames," Cassie suggested, and then shrugged as the two men frowned at her. "I'm keeping an open mind."

Ben huffed. "Yeah, you're right to. I'd better phone Newton and the witches. Now that we have a working theory or two, let's see what else we can find in our footage from last night."

Helena had spent the morning baking. It was one of her great pleasures, especially now that she had a modern kitchen, fresh ingredients, and music to accompany her. Plus, it meant she could consider what to do if Diana and Bryony arrived.

In the moody grey light of the morning, with a thickening mizzle drawing in, it was easy to feel worried about the spell she and Avery had cast. It was as if White Haven knew and was punishing them with miserable weather, which was an extremely paranoid and ridiculous idea, but the mood of the place felt off. After Beltane's antics, that was unusual. Their seasonal celebrations always lifted the town's spirits, but not today. Their spell had drifted up the chimney and across the town, so maybe it had infused the place with a sort of longing.

Perhaps they had released something else, as well. Two poor souls had been consumed by flames overnight, and their early investigations suggested a fire elemental was responsible. Surely it couldn't be a coincidence.

Wiping her hands clean, she headed to the attic and studied the original spell in her grimoire again, comparing it to Avery's. Nothing seemed hidden within the lines. No secret spells within spells. Avery's command was clear and concise. If a fire elemental had arrived in White Haven, she was sure they weren't responsible. But still she lingered over her grimoire. She remembered hiding it so vividly, as if it had happened days ago rather than centuries. She had been so scared. They all had been. Oddly, she had been more scared for her children than herself. The fear rolled in again at the thought, making her short of breath. Then the doorbell rang, and she jumped.

By the gods! Was that Diana or Bryony? What would she say to them?

She hurried down the stairs, trying to compose herself, but stepped back in shock when she saw Caspian on the doorstep, looking as well-groomed as always. "It's you! Come in." She put her hand over her heart, realising she wasn't ready to face either woman yet. "What a relief."

"Who were you expecting?" he asked curiously as he followed her up the stairs to the open-plan living area.

She laughed, wondering how much to say, and then decided to tell him everything. Everyone would know soon enough, and he was Team White Haven, as the coven called it, despite being a Faversham. "Avery and I used a spell to summon her mother and sister to White Haven last night. I thought they might have arrived."

Caspian's eyes widened with surprise. "Well, that's unexpected."

"I know. I'm sure you don't want to hear all about that, though."

"Actually, I would. Consider me intrigued!"

"Coffee first?"

"Please. If you have time." He lifted his head and inhaled. "Smells wonderful in here."

"I've been baking for their potential arrival. It was just to distract me, really, and hopefully appease them for casting such a naughty spell."

"Avery's idea or yours?"

"Avery's."

He laughed. "I thought as much."

She prepared the coffee and took a handful of shortbread biscuits off the cooling tray. "The only thing I'm wondering," she confessed, "is whether we inadvertently did something else. Is that why you're here? Did you hear the news?"

He shook his head, eyes fixed on her intently, and he reminded her so vividly of Thadeus, the long dead father of Ava, her oldest child, that she swayed, suddenly dizzy, and gripped the counter.

"Helena? Are you all right?"

She took a breath. "I'm fine." *How much to say?* She and Caspian had reached an accord, but she had murdered his father, and Thadeus, his ancestor had fathered her child. *How tangled it was...*

He cocked his head, suddenly serious. "Are you ill? Is Clea ill? Is that the news?"

"No. Nothing like that. I think I'm having one of those mornings, and I'm wondering if the hearth spell has stirred up other things. Let's take the coffee upstairs and you can look at this spell with me. Then we can talk properly."

"I take it Avery and Alex are working?" he said, taking the tray from her as he followed her to the attic. "I didn't go into the book shop. I presumed it would be busy in there."

"It's heaving, but I don't think Avery is there yet. She and Alex are helping Newton. Long story, which I'll get to."

"That sounds ominous, but it's you I was after, really."

Intrigued, Helena sat at the table, grounding herself in the here and now, the family magic thick and reassuring in this space, as was Alex's now. The descendant of her wonderful friend, Imogen. It still thrilled her to think that their descendants were now together, just like El and Reuben. A full circle.

Caspian took over and poured the coffee, placing it in front of her. "You look horribly pale. You're worrying me. What's going on?"

"You came here for a reason. Not to hear an old lady babbling on."

"My news can wait."

"You are so like him," she said, studying his face and his hands. "Taller, but commanding just like he was. The depths of his passions were so extreme that it took me by surprise."

"You've never talked about Thadeus before, and I didn't want to ask. He betrayed you. I'm sorry." He looked scared, as if she would throw him out.

"It's not your fault. I killed your father. I have far more to apologise for."

"You did me a favour, although I didn't see it immediately. Well," he paused looking into his cup, "perhaps I did, but didn't want to acknowledge it."

"We'll forgive each other, then. I reacted like any mother would when she sees her children threatened. That's what Avery feels like to me, although that's complicated, too. At the time my spirit was released, I envied her youth. I attacked her. Did she tell you?"

"*Attacked* her? No!"

"It was momentary, when she was spirit-walking and I was a ghost. I tried to possess her body forever. Such a terrible thing to do." She sipped her hot coffee, desperate to clear her head. "This hearth spell is stirring up memories. It must be that. And Beltane, of course."

"The veils are thinning." Caspian nodded. "It can be an uneasy time. So, is *this* the news?"

"No. Two bodies were found on the beach this morning." She summarised it all for him, telling him what they suspected. "I'm surprised you didn't see the police on your way here."

"I used witch-flight. A fire elemental?"

"Perhaps. Now you know why I'm worried about the hearth spell, although Avery swears it wasn't responsible, and from what I experienced, I agree. Just weird timing." She took a bite of buttery biscuit, hoping the sugar would help clear her thoughts. "So, how can we help you? Is it Morwenna?"

A slight flush spread across his cheeks. "Sort of. She—we—need a strategy to proceed with her ex. I thought you could help."

"You haven't done that yet?" Helena missed things when she wasn't in Clea's body.

"No. Obviously we broke the curse, and her ex, Jed, knows that, as does Kitty and her old friend, John, who cursed her. Morwenna recovered for a few days before calling Jed. She spoke to Ysella, her daughter, just to ensure she was safe, and then confronted him. Essentially, he is still holding out on any custody arrangement."

"Is he refusing to let her see her daughter?" Helena asked, outrage building.

"Yes. I think now he's scared that if she visits Morwenna, she will kidnap her. Ridiculous, of course. So now they are circling each other."

"Remind me. Is he a witch?"

"No. Just John and Kitty. Her ex-friends are lying low now, but are no doubt keeping an eye on things. Jed, by the way, denies being involved at all. Bullshit, of course."

"Tricky," Helena said thoughtfully.

"Estelle wants to raze him to the ground. Morwenna won't hear of it. He's still the father, is her argument."

"Maybe Estelle should take her anger out on Kitty."

"She might yet." Caspian smiled tightly. "She carries vengeance around like most women carry a handbag."

"Sometimes, it's the only thing that sustains us." Helena drummed her fingers on the table. She used to be diplomatic. Perhaps she still had some skills. "Will your coven be involved?"

"Yes, and Mevagissey's. Oswald, bless him, is circumspect. Cautious. Ulyssess, on the other hand, is keen to rip Jed's head off, and so am I. Every option so far ends with violence. I need a middle ground. Plus, there is weight in numbers."

Helena desperately wanted to know if Caspian and Morwenna were romantically involved yet, but that felt a little forward. And then she cast that thought aside. *Life is too short.* "Does she know how you feel about her?"

He almost inhaled his biscuit, and crumbs shot everywhere. "What do you mean?"

"You know exactly what I mean. If you like her, make it happen. I know!" She waved his objections off. "She's recovering from the curse, complicated ex, teenage daughter, blah, blah, blah. But it's Beltane. When you next see her, just kiss her!"

He laughed. "It's tempting. Reu has said much the same. It seems everyone knows I like her, but I'm trying to be considerate."

"She's probably wishing you'd just get on with it. She doesn't strike me as the forward type to do it herself, plus she's been hurt badly so she probably fears rejection. Promise me you will." She leaned forward to emphasise it, because suddenly it felt absolutely essential that he did. "Caspian, I mean it! Go and see her today. Be like Darcy on the field at dawn."

"Darcy?"

"*Pride and Prejudice.* Keep up!"

"All right." He straightened with resolve. "I will. I'll do it. Today! So, let me see this hearth spell."

"Okay. And I," she countered, "will consider some options for the ex."

Six

Alex was sitting with Zee and his coven around a table under the window in a beachside café called Tide and Thyme, drinking coffee and eating breakfast while discussing their latest dilemma. Although, perhaps *dilemma* was an understatement.

Everyone was despondent, and the weather didn't help. The mizzle was thickening, the grey skies matching their collective mood, and the horizon had vanished.

"At least," Alex said, trying to put a positive spin on things, "Ghost OPS has confirmed our suspicions. It's still a terrible scenario, but at least we know what we're up against. We just have to work out how to find it."

"Or *them*," Zee reminded him. "The mysterious orb might not be connected to the giant salamander."

"Let's just focus on the big fire elemental first," Alex said, trying not to feel overwhelmed.

"What do we do with it?" Reuben asked. "Banish it? Send it back to where it came from—which is where?"

Avery pushed her empty plate away. "I honestly don't know. Pure elemental spirits are strong, but in theory it surely wants to return to its own natural state."

"Isn't it in its natural state?" Zee asked. "It's fire!"

"Yes, but it shouldn't exist like this on our plane," Avery insisted.

"Maybe they do," Zee suggested. "We just haven't met one until now."

Alex shook his head. "No, they do not naturally exist in this world. Not unless called upon. That's what I've read in my grimoire, anyway."

"Exactly," Avery said, agreeing with him. "I've been doing lots of reading around dragons, and fire elementals popped up. I'll have to check the details, but I think in the Medieval period they were summoned to aid with spells. Plus, salamanders have been equated with newts in old-fashioned spells."

Briar nodded. "'Eye of newt' and all that. Although, that's mustard seed."

Alex studied El, who was looking out of the window, brow furrowed, lost in thought. "You're a fire witch, El. You wield it far more effectively than me. Have you got any insights?"

She turned to him, as if summoning herself back to the present with difficulty. "I felt a certain resonance with it last night, but I can't describe it more than that. It's like a part of me—my elemental magic, I suspect—recognised it. However, I can't name it, or say exactly how I feel. It's just as if some part of me knows part of it."

"What about your grimoire?" he persisted. "Any salamander summoning spells?"

"I remember seeing some in the very early section of my grimoire, but I never paid full attention to them. They seemed too unreachable...as if they were a bit of a joke. That sounds terrible."

Avery shrugged. "Old spells are hard to decipher, and some use language and concepts so different to our own that they feel unrelatable. I think, though, that fire elementals were summoned because of their transformative abilities. They are just like dragons in that respect. Fire transforms, consumes, and regenerates. And of course, actual fire salamanders were used in spell work according to historical sources."

Briar shuddered. "Gross."

"We used a dragon," Reuben reminded her. "We aren't exactly a shining example of not utilising dead animals in spells. I still feel like shit about that."

"It's pointless debating it," El said. "We did it for a very good reason, and it worked."

Alex turned to Avery. "You said salamanders were used practically in spell work, which sounds nuts to me, but that doesn't make it impossible. I think we've all seen enough to know that it's very possible. We've just lost the method, but we still have instructions. Zee, did you ever see anything like that back in your original time?"

"No, but I saw plenty of other interesting things, and I am descended from an angel, so you won't find me discounting anything. Something about alchemy and salamanders rings a bell, so maybe JD has more information." He frowned. "I hesitate to bring him in on this yet, though. It's complicated enough."

"I agree. Let's see how we get on first."

"Maybe," El suggested tentatively, "this is a consequence of the dragon spell. It could have had unforeseen ripples."

"But it was weeks ago," Zee pointed out.

"Spells take time to manifest."

Avery was keeping quiet and looked uncomfortable, and Alex knew exactly what she was thinking. She needed to admit to the spell that she'd cast the night before, and she didn't want to. He

was both annoyed and bemused by the whole thing, but ultimately saddened. He'd had no idea that she'd been mulling over
her missing mother and sister, and he felt terrible. Even worse,
she'd gone to Helena for help. He was trying not to feel put out
about it, but he was, even though her explanation was logical.
Pushing his wounded ego aside, he looked at Avery meaningfully,
and she nodded, resigned.

"I have a confession to make, actually," she started. "Although,
I don't think I'm responsible for this at all, everyone should at
least know all the facts."

While she explained everything, Alex looked out at the crowds
that were already filling the area around the harbour, despite the
weather. Energy remained high after the parade the day before,
and the performers would remain in the town, adding to the
week's festivities. Cafés and pubs would be full all day, his own
included, and bad news would travel fast. The police presence
down by the beach was certainly hard to ignore. And then he saw
a familiar face. Sarah Rutherford, the news reporter, had arrived
with her small team and was striding purposefully towards the
beach. She had been filming the parade yesterday and interview-
ing the locals and tourists. *Maybe that explained why she had
arrived so swiftly.* Alex's thoughts drifted, and he wondered if
Stan had heard about the deaths yet. They would have to catch up
with him. With luck the mist would hamper the fire elemental.

His thoughts spiralling, he turned back to the table, hearing
Avery say, "So, anyway, it might have been a bit reckless, but it's
done now."

"Unfortunately, we have no room to put our potential visitors
up," Alex added, giving Reuben a hopeful, pleading smile. "If
they arrive, any chance of a room at your place?"

Reuben smirked. "For you or them?"

"I'd like to say me, but I mean them."

Avery threw a balled-up napkin at him. "You're so mean."

"I'm kidding."

"Actually," El said, laughing, "one of them can use my flat. I can stay with Reuben for a few days. I'm there more often now. Or Helena could have my place, and one of them could have her room? If they arrive, that is. I will be thrilled to meet them, Avery, and I can completely understand your motivation, although frankly, I don't care if I never see my parents again. I am set on that."

"I should admit," Alex said, staring at Avery, "that I might not be that polite, all things considered. They've upset you, and that pisses me off. It all depends on how they behave when they arrive."

"I might not be that polite, either," Avery confessed. "I could just throw them out and send them away within hours of their arrival."

"We'll work it out," Reuben said sagely. Following his marriage, he had been relentlessly positive. It was exhausting. "I'm happy to give them rooms."

"Cheers, Reu," Alex said, slapping him on the shoulder. "Now that's sorted, I should tell you that Sarah Rutherford, the news reporter, is heading to the beach with her camera guy."

"Already?" Reuben asked, turning to look out the window. "Bollocks."

"Newton will keep it under wraps as much as he can for now," El said. "No one will know it's a paranormal crime. But I guess we need a strategy. I presume we all need to head to work soon?"

There was a flurry of nods around the table. The Beltane parade was normally on a Saturday, but Stan and the council had opted for a midweek event for a change. The witches had joined the Cornwall Coven for their big celebrations on Sunday evening, the night of Beltane proper.

"Although," Briar said, fingers twisting a curl of her hair, "I'm heading to Ravens' Wood first, and I'm taking Moore with me. I need herbs, and he needs to meet Nelaira. Newton's request."

"*What?*" Zee clenched his mug so hard that Alex thought he might break it. "You're introducing him to that sneaky bitch! Is that wise?"

"It's just an introduction. I'll warn him, of course."

"Warn him never to meet her alone. You have seen the effect she has on Eli."

Reuben looked between them. "But Eli is okay, right?"

"He's fine," Briar reassured him, but she looked guarded. "Plus, Nelaira will have no interest in Moore. He can't give her anything, and well, as lovely as he is, he's not Eli."

"I still wouldn't trust her," Zee said darkly. "I know what you're saying. Eli has power, but so has Moore, and she might see him as being vulnerable. Which he totally is."

Briar nodded and checked her watch. "I have time to make him an amulet first. Dryad magic is strong, but it will help. While I'm there, I'll ask about salamanders. Anyway, why did you ask, El? About opening, I mean?"

"Because we need to start searching for this thing. We need a strategy. As Reuben said, when the therians get wind of this, they will want it."

"Helena can help us," Avery said. "We should consider the white stag, too," she added, turning to Briar. "If Tamsyn is seeing it again, it's important."

Alex considered their options. "A fire elemental must want a fire, so maybe we should light one to lure it in. In the flat perhaps, Zee? In our place too, Avery."

"Sure," Zee said with a sigh. "I'd love a salamander in my fire."

"And I'll light my forge," El said. "But if it arrives, what then?"

"We were talking about djinn earlier. Maybe we bottle it. What?" Reuben said to the muttered responses of his coven. "It's a legit suggestion."

And so it starts, Alex thought, as the debate erupted and he called for the bill.

The hunt was on.

Briar thought that Ravens' Wood was at its most Otherworldly when she arrived at close to eleven that morning with Moore.

The wood was positioned on the hillside above the town, butting up against White Haven Castle, and the mizzle was thicker here. Once they were under the trees, the whole place took on a spectral appearance, and Briar was glad she wasn't alone as they followed the winding paths deeper into the interior, ravens squawking loudly at their passing.

"Are you sure you want to meet Nelaira?" Briar asked Moore, his eyes darting everywhere.

"Of course." His hand settled on the amulet tucked under his shirt, moisture beading on his red hair and skin. "It's good of you to make this for me. Do you really think I'll need it?"

"Nelaira has grand ambitions for Ravens' Wood, and although she and Shadow seemed to have come to an agreement—with Eli's help, of course—we must be circumspect." She didn't want to say too much beneath the trees where anything could be listening, but he was aware of the circumstances.

"I'm always wary," Moore said, reassuring her. "I've been policing for years. Not much gets past me. I love this place, but I'm no fool."

"I know." She was very fond of Moore. "What exactly is your role supposed to be here?"

"I won't be having weekly meetings with the dryads, that's for sure. I'll just be keeping an eye on things. Newton is pretty ambivalent about this place, but I love it. If you think anything is amiss—any of you—talk to me first."

"We will. I'm probably here more often than any of the coven. I come here for the herbs and plants. They have an unusual potency—not surprisingly. I'll show you some of the paths I use the most. In the daylight, I consider this place to be safe, but I'd be wary of trying to reach the heart of the wood. I don't think you can, anyway," she said, recalling Eli's words. "It's a whole other place."

"Through the veil," he said, as if it was totally normal.

"I guess so."

"How's its energy now, after Beltane?"

"Edgy. It feels wilder."

"I agree. It's..." Moore paused, lifting his head as if listening. "Unsettled. As if something has unnerved it." He looked shocked at his own statement. "Sorry. That just struck me."

"Don't apologise. That's wonderful. It's your intuition talking. Never ignore it." She smiled. "You *are* attuned to this place. Perhaps you should try this." Briar slipped her boots and socks off and wriggled her toes into the earth, then placed her hands on the closest tree. The cool, damp loam felt deliciously wonderful around her toes, and the hum that she always sensed from the earth intensified. Her awareness expanded as she absorbed the myriad sounds and scents around her, and the scattered energy of the wood became more palpable. There was something that she couldn't quite place. A tone that was so deep it was almost out of reach. Like a tolling bell beneath the waves. She shook her head as if to dispel it. *Odd.* "You don't need to be a witch to feel this, Moore. You just need to be quiet and pay attention."

After a moment's hesitation, he took his shoes off too, and followed her example, and for a few moments they stood silently. Moore smiled. "I used to do this as a kid. I loved this place. It made me love the supernatural. I always knew there was something different about it."

Briar had completely forgotten that Moore had received implanted memories of the wood. The strange and complex magic that the Raven King and the Green Man had woven when they created it so that everyone believed it had been there forever, except the people who had actually been present at its inception. *If she told him the truth now, would that change things for him? Had someone already said, perhaps, and he had forgotten?*

Moore continued, "It feels bigger than it is. The wood, I mean. As if I'm grounding in something enormous."

She decided not to say anything. He could feel the wood's past size, and that was important. "That's because you are. The ancestral roots of this place are beneath our feet and spread far wider. I'm sure you've spoken to Ben and Stan. They saw it in its prime at Samhain last year when they went back in time. But you're right about it being unsettled. I can feel something really odd. Let's try and find a dryad, but we'll keep to the outer paths for now."

A distant dog bark and shout reassured them both that they weren't alone and they pushed on, continuing to talk quietly, with Briar stopping every now and then to collect herbs and roots.

"They'll come soon," she reassured Moore, partially distracted by the unusual feeling she'd had. "They are drawn to my magic, although they are in general curious about humans."

Finally, when other sounds had quieted and they had reached a shallow hollow between trees, Briar felt the dryads' presence, so she stopped and called out, "I feel you watching. We have questions, if you wouldn't mind answering. I also need to introduce you to a friend."

A young, male dryad stepped out from behind a tree, as ethereal as a dandelion seed. "We knew you'd come," he said without preamble. "We need your help."

"Why? What has happened?" Moore asked quickly.

He levelled his liquid brown eyes at him. "I have seen you before. You are not a witch."

"He's a policeman," Briar said, then realising that term would make no sense to a dryad, added, "he enforces order. Keeps things safe."

He didn't take his eyes off Moore. "I remember you from when the hunters came here. When they imprisoned some of us. You helped."

Moore smiled. "I did. I helped open the doorway to release them. What's wrong?"

"Beltane brought the Goddess here. The elementals followed to pay their regards, as is common at this time. One, however, has escaped and must be found. It has wreaked…" his voice caught, as if choking back a sob. "Devastation."

Several things he said were warring for Briar's attention, but one in particular took precedence. "Escaped? You mean the fire elemental?"

His eyes widened. "You have seen it?"

"It has killed two people," Moore said, "and has since disappeared."

"What do you mean by escaped?" Briar repeated, confused. "Was it a prisoner?"

"No. He is a prince amongst the fire elementals. He escaped from the retinue that paid respects to the Goddess."

"A prince!" Alarmed, she looked at Moore, who was as dumbfounded as she was.

A salamander prince? Was that a thing? No wonder the wood felt unsettled. *A retinue of them!* And then the word *devastation* struck her. The word she should have paid attention to first had she not been so consumed with their own concerns.

"What did it do? What devastation did it cause?" Briar looked around, realising there were many dryads gathering in the mists. They seemed sombre. Frightened. "Where is Nelaira? I would have thought she'd be here to greet us."

"Nelaira is dead. The elemental killed her."

$\mathcal{S}even$

Happenstance Books was reassuringly warm and safe when Avery joined Sally and Dan around midmorning.

The thickening mist was forging up the streets now like a scavenging beast. May had never seemed bleaker, although the bright pots of flowers and hanging baskets were trying their hardest to brighten the place up. It hadn't stopped the tourists, though. The town still heaved with them, and the shop was full. Dan and Sally were with customers, and Avery took over at the till, trying not to think about the elemental. Unfortunately, news of the deaths had spread, and she heard several muttered conversations that she tried to ignore.

Finally, at just after midday, the crowds thinned as they headed for lunch, and the three of them sagged behind the shop's counter. Dan rummaged for biscuits and placed an opened pack of chocolate Hobnobs on the counter after taking a couple for himself.

"Well, that was fun." He crunched into his first biscuit, crumbs exploding outwards. "We haven't been that busy in weeks! I mean, it's great, but knackering."

"So," Sally asked, always direct, "what do you know about the deaths, Avery?"

"Why should I know anything?"

"Oh, please." She rolled her eyes. "Of course you know, even if it has no basis in anything," she lowered her voice, "*magical*. Besides, I heard they were odd deaths. Those poor people."

"How do you know they are odd?"

"Hamid was here earlier, checking in on us. He's very sweet. Looked quite perturbed by the whole thing."

"We are all very perturbed." Avery saw the last customer leave, the bell jangling as the door swung shut, and she slumped on the counter. The outside world was a blur now, the mizzle so very thick. Water streaked down the windowpanes, and she was glad of the twinkling fairy lights that dismissed the gloom. "We think a fire elemental caused it. One arrived in the Beltane fire last night—somehow. Don't ask, because I don't know yet. Hamid helped search, but we didn't actually know what we were searching for at the time. Dylan saw it earlier." She updated them on the phone call she'd received that morning.

"Ah!" Dan said, pulling his phone out of his back pocket. "That's what Dylan has messaged about. He said to call him. I haven't had a chance yet. I suppose he'll want to discuss myths."

"Any suggestions?"

"Plenty, but they are not a typically Cornish phenomenon. Of course, they can appear anywhere, especially when summoned by witchcraft." He cocked an eye at Avery. "Any confessions?"

She flushed, knowing that she had at least one confession to make. "No! Why would I summon one? We just need to find it. But my mother and sister may arrive in the coming hours, days, or weeks, so just be prepared."

"Your mother?" Sally stared in shock. "She left years ago. So did Bryony! Why would they be coming back?"

"I may have cast a small summoning spell. I know I shouldn't," she held a hand up to forestall arguments, "but I did, so it's done, over, finished. Don't lecture me!"

"It is far from done. In fact, it has just begun!" Sally sighed. "I always wondered if this day would come and they would return. I have vague memories of your mum. She was quite stern. She always scared me a little. And your sister just thought I was a pain. She was always so cool."

Dan sniggered. "So, I'll get to meet your mum and sis? Interesting. Avery, that's ballsy."

"Stupid, more like." In the cold light of day, it seemed like insanity. "Besides, the spell might not work. I don't know if I'll be happy or relieved."

"Of course you'll be happy. I hope you're planning to spend time with them," Sally said. "They might have come a long way."

"Are they air witches?" Dan asked.

"No. My sister is a fire witch, and my mother a green witch. Or *were*. Who knows if they still practice now."

"Go on, Sally," Dan prompted her. "Why was her mother stern?"

Sally's expression was distant as she said, "I just always thought she looked cross. I didn't know she was a witch, of course. Or Bryony. She was tall, with thick hair the colour of golden syrup. Bryony was a strawberry blonde. All three were shades of red," she said, smiling at Avery and pulling a strand of her hair affectionately. "All of you had long hair and this *vibe*. I remembered thinking how cool your family was."

Avery gaped at her. "I never knew you thought that!"

"It's not something you admit as a 16-year-old when you're trying desperately to be cool, too. I always thought how lucky I was, though, that you were my friend. I still do." Sally squeezed her hand. "I always knew that there was something different about all of you, even back then. I was shocked when they both left. And then you buried it. You just soldiered on like it never happened, and I never knew what to say. So, I just decided to be there for you, however I could. I've never regretted it, either. Look at us now, all grown up with a beautiful shop and people who love us."

All of a sudden, tears welled, and Avery couldn't find the words to speak.

Dan shot off the stool. "I'll make coffee, and we're closing for lunch. Don't argue." He locked the front door, flipped the sign to *Closed,* and scooted to the backroom, leaving Avery still floundering.

Sally pulled her into a big hug and Avery dissolved into sobs on her shoulder. Sally had seen it all, but from *her* point of view. Not her gran's, who had suffered equally as much but bore it as stoically. Both of them shoring it up. Both of them pretending they were okay with it, to perhaps protect the other.

"You know," Avery said through tears, "me and gran hardly ever talked about it. If she even knew where they had gone, she never said. I asked, of course, but she denied knowing anything, and then we just didn't talk about it all. Clea never encouraged it. And then she was gone, too."

"No wonder you practised magic alone all those years. What do you call it? A solitary witch?"

"Yes, but that's okay. Many are." Avery sat back and snagged a tissue from the box to wipe her tears away.

"Depends on your reasons, doesn't it?" Sally had shed a tear too, but now she sniffed it away, face hardening. "I may not be that welcoming to them when they arrive, but I'll do it for you, if that's what you want."

"You sound like Alex. Well, all of the others, in fact. I don't know what I want. I just cast it—with Helena, after much persuasion—and now I'm wondering what the fuck for. But thank you. I really appreciate everything, Sally."

"That's what friends are for."

"And you're a very good one." Feeling better, Avery took a deep breath. "I'm fine. I'm just having a moment. It's like now that it's surfaced, it won't go."

"Good. Let it out. There is nothing wrong with expressing your emotions, Avery. We women have worked hard to be heard, so let everyone hear it."

Dan called from the rear of the shop. "Coffee is ready, and cake. Home baked! Caspian and Helena are here."

"We're coming," Sally called back. She studied Avery. "Are you okay?"

"Yes. I'm fine. I think just casting it has been cathartic."

"Well, they better bloody come after all this. And remember, any time you want to talk, I'm here."

"I should be more worried about this fire elemental. It's killed two people!"

"We can worry about both. Multi-tasking is what we do best." She grabbed a besom broom that was propped against the wall and winked. "I'm handy with this, remember? I'll hound the elemental out of here if I have to, and maybe knock some sense into your family while I'm at it."

El stoked her forge until it was blazing hot, and once satisfied, turned to examine the objects placed on the many shelves in her small smithy.

Reuben frowned. "I'm not sure this is a good idea."

"What do you suggest, then?" she said, picking up a small clay pot she could seal with a cork and wax, and then placed it down again. She couldn't even remember why she had it.

"I don't think we should try to summon the elemental until we have somewhere to put it. What if it grows so big that we can't get in this room?"

"You're being very dramatic."

"I am examining all options."

"Well, I am considering your suggestion of a vessel to trap it in. Help me look."

"You're taking me seriously?"

"Don't I always?" She turned to look at him, amused.

"You scoffed earlier." Reuben folded his arms over his chest like a petulant child.

"No, *everyone* scoffed, because we're talking about squashing a salamander in a bottle. But it has merit. We need something that can withstand high temperatures. I was thinking brass, but actually, I could make something. In fact, I *should* make something," she said, correcting herself. "I could either enhance what I have, or make something new from scratch." She ran her fingers, covered in ash and smelling of wood smoke from making the fire, across her pursed lips. "I can blend some metals, enhance it with spells, and craft a unique trap. However, that means making a mould."

A hiss of steam filled the room as Reuben dowsed the flames with his magic. "In that case, you do not want that thing coming here until you are ready for it."

"I suppose that's a fair point, but I will need it lit to make the container."

"Well, you need to protect this place first. As for now, this place is out of bounds for fire elementals. I can create wards. You need to be able to work in here unhindered."

El smiled, crossed the room, and kissed him. "You are very sweet, husband."

"I know, wife. It's my job to look after you."

"I haven't become useless all of a sudden, you know."

"I know. I just take my role very seriously, that's all."

"Okay. Then you can start crafting wards, while I get started drafting spells for a container. I need more information first, though. It has to be perfect to work effectively. I doubt we'll get a second chance. Maybe I need Dragonium, which we should have a small supply of, or at least the means to make it." She tried to recall what Shadow has said about the metal and how it could be made from the dragon. "I need a list of potential metals." Excited, she grabbed a pencil and paper from a drawer. "This will be a very interesting challenge."

"Won't a fire elemental just melt a metal container?"

"Not if I do it right. Brass can withstand very high temperatures. Dragonium, as I mentioned, and a blend of others in a unique and special way, along with spells, of course, can keep that from happening. Plus runes and sigils. Damn it. It's a shame

Shadow is away. Fey writing could be useful. Otherworld binding magic is very strong."

"How long will it take?" Reu asked.

"Good question. It depends how big it needs to be."

"In theory, it could be small, if you recall the story of the djinn in the brass lamp, or the genie in the bottle."

"You and your bloody djinn. This is bad enough. Let's see what Dan has to say, and Ghost OPS." Already, time was pressing in. The longer the elemental was out, the more chance it would leave White Haven, or kill more people. Or both, of course. "I need more clay. I'll speak to Dante."

"You're not going to tell him what it's for?"

"No, not specifically."

"Maybe we should ward his place, too. I know he's not in White Haven, but he's close. Plus, his forge is huge." Reuben had been there a couple of times with her, so he knew Dante's forge reasonably well.

It suddenly struck El how attractive his place would be, and how vulnerable Dante was.

"Shit. Let's go right now."

Eight

B riar looked at the burned remains of the once beautiful silver birch and couldn't control her tears.

"I can't believe it. This is murder! Utter desecration."

The tree—Nelaira's tree—had fallen where it had once stood majestically, clearly consumed by flames, bark blackened, leaves curled in on themselves or burnt to cinders. The other trees crowded around in mourning. *No wonder Ravens' Wood felt unsettled.*

A raven called from overhead, and she looked up to find it glaring down at her from a high branch. For a second, she couldn't speak. Words failed her and she fell to her knees, hands on the trunk, the smell of smoke still heavy as if the mist had caught and held it there. Moore crouched opposite her, as filled with grief as she was. Nelaira was tricky, but she didn't deserve this.

When the dryad had broken the news, she had insisted on seeing the evidence for herself before hearing anything else. She had distrusted him, fearing a fey trick. Plus, a part of her wondered if she were really dead, and that maybe she could still heal Nelaira. Save her. Now she felt terrible for doubting him. She also realised that Ravens' Wood was contributing to the mist. It was pouring from it. A mourning veil.

The number of dryads had grown, and they crowded around now, felt more than seen, all shades of grey and green, their mottled skin thick with moss, their voices like keening wind and rushing water. The trees leaned in, their bright green leaves of spring sheltering them from the sky's grey gaze. It seemed impossible that spring was upon them now. It felt more like Samhain.

Moore gathered himself first, directing his question at the young male dryad. "Tell us what happened. Start at Beltane, please."

The dryad sat next to them, eyes on the dead tree. "The Goddess arrived, as is her want at this time of the year, with her consort, the Green Man. The Great Wedding has been long anticipated. It happens not just here, you know?"

Briar shook her head, confused. "No. I don't understand. We were here last time, and I saw her—accidentally, of course. Saw the wedding, somewhere in the depths of this place." She had seen the Green Man, too. Her Green Man who had looked her straight in the eye and told her to run, so she had, with fear driving her all the way. *How she missed him.*

"It was here, and it was not," he said in a singsong voice that lulled like a breeze in the treetops. "This is a place amongst many. Pathways cross. Worlds intersect. It allows all to see the ceremony and offer our respects."

Moore nodded. "I understand. This place is liminal, and worlds collide here. The Goddess marries the Green Man in one place and all places."

"Exactly."

"Which is why," Briar said, thinking of the insanity of their night at Beltane the year before, "we saw satyrs and naiads, and so many other things. And it was four nights ago?"

"Yes. A full night of celebrations. This place is stronger now than last year. More deeply rooted. Plus, we have the dragon eggs and the grove. When the Goddess came, she opened the gateway, and the magic here resonated across worlds, so more than usual crossed, and one did not return."

"The prince of the elementals," Moore whispered, as if caught in a trance.

"Not just any elemental," the dryad corrected as he exchanged worried glances with his kin. "A djinn. One of the highest forms of fire elementals in the Otherworld."

"A what?" Briar said, head whipping up to look at the dryad. That sounded so much more terrifying and powerful. "You didn't say that earlier."

Moore sat back in a pile of leaves, as if his limbs had lost all strength. "Djinn? Actual djinn?"

Flustered, the dryad said, "I'm sorry, but I'm telling you now. And not *the* prince, only *a* prince. One of the many princes amongst djinn. As I said, they do not worship the Goddess, but all offer respects. He stayed, curious as to this place. We allowed it—for a short while. Our celebrations were longer this year, because we have had much to give thanks for." His shy smile was fleeting. "But he had to cross back before the pathway closed. The wedding grove does not stay visible for long. Nelaira told him he must go. He refused. He knew of the dragon eggs."

"How?" Moore asked.

"He is djinn. They know dragons."

"He wanted them?" Briar asked, grief quickly replaced by anger and fear.

"He wanted to see them. Nelaira refused. There was a fight. He was stronger. No one expected this. He just laid his hands upon her, and she was consumed. Her screams..." He shook in grief, and the dryads trembled with him. The trees trembled, too, the earth rumbling beneath them as roots shifted and branches swayed, and more mist rose around them like a shroud.

"This happened when?" Moore asked, all business as he started taking notes.

"Two nights ago, and then he vanished."

Tuesday night, Briar thought, wondering if she'd felt anything untoward.

"He didn't just vanish," a female dryad corrected him. "We rose as one against him, lashed him with our branches. Grabbed him with our roots. We would have ripped him apart if we could have. He could not fight all of us, so he fled in smoke and flame, knowing the full weight of his transgressions. This mist is not just our mourning. It is to counter his fire. All day we searched and mourned and searched again, but he hid so well. Now you say he has left the wood?"

Moore looked at Briar as if to confirm, but nodded anyway. "It seems so. I need to speak to Stan," he said, almost to himself. "Check if they collected any more wood from here yesterday or the day before. Perhaps he hid in a log?"

"Would he need to?" Briar turned back to the dryads. "Can he travel where he wants?"

"Perhaps, but this is not his world," another dryad answered.

Exasperated, Briar asked, "Why kill for dragon eggs? Did he see them?"

"No. The grove is closed, even to him. They are safe. As to why he killed Nelaira?" The young male dryad shrugged. "I don't know. Maybe there is something about the eggs we don't know."

Briar reached out to touch and reassure him, and found his skin cool. "Can you find out more about him? We need details if we are to find him and stop him."

"What details?"

"His strengths and weaknesses. Your lore on how to defeat djinn."

"Especially how," Moore said, "to stop him killing more people and more dryads."

"We will try." The dryad looked lost, confused, as if he had been thrust into this position and was out of his depth. "I will consult the elders."

"Where is Nelaira's body?"

"Gone. Ash." He nodded at the blackened tree on the ground. "When the tree dies, our bodies become earth again. We are one."

She felt silly asking, but she had to know. "Will you have a funeral? Say your goodbyes?"

"We will bury the tree here. It has already begun. The roots will pull her lower over the next few days until she lies beneath our feet in the embrace of earth." His liquid brown eyes filled with tears. "Death does not happen like this. We die of old age, rarely of violence."

"I would like your permission to be here when her body is finally buried. My coven and friends would like to pay our respects. Is that possible?"

"I will ask," he said.

Briar knew it was time to leave them to mourn, but she felt heavy. Desolate. Their grief was filling her up and she had to get out. It was as if Moore had read her mind, and he stood.

"We will leave, but I'll return to find out what you have learned within one full passing of the sun. I promise you that I will find this djinn. Does he have a name?"

"Prince Qabas Nar-Ifrit of the House of the Desert Rose."

Wow. He sounded powerful. "And yours?" Briar asked.

"Alderic."

"Then we will see you soon, Alderic," Briar promised. "In the meantime, stay safe."

Briar realised as they headed home through the mist-shrouded forest, Moore grimly silent, that she needed to tell the coven, and then she would have to tell Eli, and she had no idea how he would take the news.

"You have got to be kidding me," Newton said to Moore, in utter disbelief at what he was hearing. "This isn't the bloody *Arabian Nights*!"

"I wouldn't joke about this," Moore said, gripping his coffee cup in the backroom of The Wayward Son. "That's three dead souls this damn djinn is responsible for. It has scarred Ravens' Wood. Grief is pouring from it. That's where most of this mist is coming from."

Newton exchanged a worried glance with Kendall, who without asking, left the table and headed to the front of the pub as if to confirm his assertion. Newton always ribbed Moore about his love for the wood, but he couldn't joke now. The stakes, which had seemed already so high, had now amplified.

"I'm sorry, Moore. That must have been awful. Poor Nelaira. She was trouble, but she didn't deserve that. It seems that he—this Prince Qabas Nar-Ifrit of the House of the Desert Rose—has crossed Otherworld boundaries, as well as ours. Pun not intended."

Moore shrugged. "I'll know more tomorrow. The dryads were grief-stricken, and if I'm honest, had trouble keeping it together. The young dryad, Alderic, was shaking. Their response was good, though. They scared it, and that means it can be intimidated. He, that is."

"By them, but maybe not by us. Why did it look like a salamander? Is it a shapeshifter?"

"I didn't get that far. Perhaps. I mean, according to fairy-tales, djinn can turn into sand, smoke, and flame. Maybe it's a salamander, too."

"I thought," Newton said, hesitantly, "you'd be excited to see one."

"I would be if I didn't hate him for what he's done."

Kendall arrived back at the table, sitting heavily. "You're right, Moore. What started as sea mist has been added to by the wood. I can't believe we didn't notice. It's rolling down the hill. Well, what I can see of it, which isn't much. The castle has vanished, and most of the wood."

"Sea mist often sweeps up the hills before trickling down," Newton said. "Plus, if it started two days ago, it would have been a slow build. I presume that's when it started, anyway, after Nelaira's death. I can't believe we didn't know sooner."

"Why would we?" Kendall asked. "Dryads are not likely to come into town, and no one has gone there from our group lately.

We've been busy, and they have been too, searching their wood for the djinn."

"Briar considered the same thing," Moore said to him, "but can recall nothing that happened that night that would have made her suspect this."

Newton considered all the many places a djinn could hide, drawing from his memories of fairy tales. "With luck, the dense mist will keep it under control. It's a fire elemental, right? We're saturated in water right now. They supposedly live in deserts, and White Haven is not a desert, but it has dunes and there are plenty of beaches close by. Maybe," he said, brightening, "it has buried itself in the sand dunes. They are always dry, and even in the biggest storms, the sea never reaches them."

"Let's get Ghost OPS to search there, then," Kendall said, reaching for her phone. "We need to update them anyway. They still think we're dealing with a boring old salamander."

"I'd hardly call it boring," Newton said.

Kendall smirked. "Compared to a djinn? A prince amongst djinn, in fact."

"Maybe I should block off the dunes to the public," Newton mused. "The deaths would be a good reason to do that. What if its kin come looking for it?"

"The gateway is closed," Moore reminded him. "It was opened for the Great Wedding only. It's what Briar and the witches saw last year."

The event that scared the crap out of them, Newton remembered. "So much for the Raven King and the Green Man saying Ravens' Wood would never become a portal. They lied. And it's right on our doorstep."

"I don't think even they knew how potent the place would become. Besides, it isn't open to the Otherworld forever. Maybe," Moore said, absently reaching for a cheese and onion crisp from the open bag on the table, "the Winter Queen affected it too, and Wyrd. Perhaps it absorbed some of their magic."

"We can't forget the dragon eggs, either," Kendall added.

"They even alluded to those events changing them," Moore said thoughtfully. "However, the gateway is now closed, and the djinn has no way back."

Newton sighed. "They should have just let him take the eggs. At least then they would be back where they belong."

"We don't know that for sure," Kendall said. "I think they did the right thing."

"Regardless, we have to capture and neutralise him. It's nothing we haven't done before," Newton said more confidently than he felt. "We just need a rock-solid plan."

"Easy," Kendall said with a nonchalant shrug. "Magical traps, flying carpets, spelled chains, a royal palace for his majesty...a grand sandcastle, perhaps!"

Newton ignored her sarcasm. "Right, jobs. You, Kendall, will organise sealing off the dunes. Give Ben full permission to erect as many bloody cameras around the place as they can. Hamid and Kev will need to keep an eye on it all. Liaise with the PCs and see if they have pulled anything from the door-to-door canvassing."

"There's nothing so far," she said. "I already checked. The residents were either on the beach or watching the TV. Those who were looking on from windows said there were so many fires, it was impossible to know if any one of them had relevance."

He huffed. "Bollocks. Moore, you're liaising with Dan. I want as much information about the djinn as possible. You said you'll visit the wood again tomorrow?"

"Yes. I'll go with one of the witches. Or Zee or Eli, perhaps."

"Good. Do *not* go there alone."

"What about you?" Kendall asked, draining her coffee and pulling her jacket on, ready to go out.

"I am going to speak to Jasper and see what Lord Wentworth is up to. In fact, let's see if we can track where those three therians went last night."

Nine

Eli had been having a good morning in the Charming Balms Apothecary on his own. It had been busy, but the customers liked him, and he refused to be rushed, so despite the constant stream of shoppers and the endless requests for teas, lotions, and candles, he handled it with ease.

Music was playing, candles were lit, and it was pleasantly atmospheric. By lunchtime, however, the sales were slowing, and as the final customer arrived at the counter, he was looking forward to food.

His equilibrium had finally returned after being thrown off completely by Nelaira weeks before, but she was firmly relegated as a one-night stand. The weird hold she'd had over him was pushed to the back of his mind, and sex without strings with others had resumed as normal. Plus, it was Beltane. New women with raging hormones had flooded into White Haven, and he was only too happy to oblige. All of his brothers were away, except for Zee who was living above the pub, so Eli was free to indulge his whims. Plus, his new rooms in the outbuilding where Shadow also lived were almost ready. His own place. It had been a long time coming.

However, as soon as Briar entered the shop, he knew something was wrong. She met his eyes with little mirth, scanned the rest of the room, adjusted the Beltane themed window display as if to buy herself time, and then joined him behind the counter, fiddling with the packaging while she waited for him to finish serving.

"Hey Eli, sorry I've been out so long."

"It's okay. It's been breezy here." He smiled at the middle-aged female customer as he handed her the bag of goods. "Here you go. Have a good day and Blessed Beltane."

"And to you." She cast Briar a speculative look, as if wondering if they might be a couple, but Briar was too distracted to notice.

However, Briar followed her to the door, flipped the sign to closed, and locked the door. "I need to chat to you."

"Is it about the deaths on the beach? Do I know them?" he asked, suddenly worried.

"It's not about them. Come to the herb room."

"Briar, you're worrying me. Are my brothers okay? Shadow?"

"They're fine, as far as I know."

Once he was inside the fragrant room, she shut the door behind her and leaned against it, leaving the lights off. It was dark in there, even in the middle of the day, with soft grey light the only illumination from the small-paned window that looked into the tiny, flower-filled courtyard.

"Is it Newton?" he asked, thinking that if something had happened to him, it would be a disaster for Briar, however much she might deny it. He pulled her to a chair. "I'll put the kettle on. I have the perfect tea."

"No." She grabbed his hand. "Sit with me. I have some terrible news, and there's no good way to say this." She took a breath, her dark eyes locking on his. "Nelaira is dead. I'm so sorry. So very sorry. I know you weren't together, but you had a connection of sorts, and now…" She trailed off, eyes still fixed on his.

"What do you mean, dead?" Panic he didn't know he was capable of rocketed through him, swiftly followed by disbelief. "It's not possible. She's a dryad!"

"It's true. She was killed by the same fire elemental that killed the bodies on the beach. He burned her completely." Briar burst into tears. "She's gone. Just ash. And her tree is blackened and dead." She clasped his hands tighter than he thought possible. "I couldn't do anything to save her. It was far too late. I'm so sorry."

Eli thought his brain had turned to treacle. "Dead? But why? I don't understand. What damn elemental?" His voice rose with anger and confusion.

She took a breath, trying to control her emotions, and then launched into a rambling explanation of the Goddess and the Great Wedding, and a djinn that had refused to cross back to the Otherworld who had sensed dragon eggs. *Those damned dragon eggs.*

"Let me get this straight," he said, as his blood pounded and he itched to grab his sword and hack the elemental to pieces. "Nelaira refused to let him see the dragon eggs or have access to their sacred grove, and he killed her for it?"

"Yes." She dashed her tears away, replacing her grief with anger. "He just laid his hands on her and burned her out of fury. I believe she died instantly. Her tree has fallen, and it's blackened and twisted, and the wood is already starting to bury it. They will have a funeral, although I'm sure they don't call it that."

"He killed her out of spite?"

"It seems so. I think he would have attacked the others next, but the wood fought him, and he fled."

"The fucking coward."

"We'll find this djinn, I swear."

Eli felt numb, as if his insides had been scooped out, leaving him a husk. He didn't love Nelaira. It would be a lie to say he had. But they had shared *something*. A connection deeper than he had experienced in a long time, and an attraction that was inexplicable. She was vibrant, seductive, clever, and she had terrified him. And yet now... His hollow interior filled with icy rage, and when he looked at Briar, she flinched. "What's his name?"

"Prince Qabas Nar-Ifrit of the House of the Desert Rose."

Eli saw him in his mind's eye. His brothers had known djinn, fought them on occasions. Dangerous, yes, but not without weaknesses. Most were tall figures swathed in sand and smoke, wearing clothing that was rich and embellished, and they always had secrets. "I will kill him and throw his guts to the fishes."

"You aren't alone. We will all search, but we thought to trap him."

"And send him back? No. Death is the only option. He would not face justice if you sent him back."

Briar stuttered, always wary of violence. "There are other options. Like imprisoning him forever, like in the fairytales."

"No. It is not enough." Eli leaned forward, now gripping Briar's small hands in his. "Perhaps you shouldn't be involved in this."

"What? Do you think I'm weak?"

"I think your heart is too kind for such violence."

"I'll do what I have to, Eli. Please don't doubt me. You should also know that if the therians find out, they might well hunt him, too. If they can't have dragon eggs, a djinn is a good alternative. Maybe better."

"Then the race is on, Briar, because I intend to find him first." Resolve sat side by side with his fiery anger. He hadn't felt so filled with intent for millennia. It was as if he'd been sleeping, and was now finally awake. "I will deliver the justice she deserves. It's a shame I haven't still got Belial's trinkets. That would make short work of him."

"I am very relieved that you haven't. They were toxic. Eli, you're scaring me. You have the look that you had then, and if you remember, you hated the way they made you feel. I had to cleanse that shit out of you."

She didn't normally swear, and it made him aware that he was behaving like a madman. Hating that he was scaring Briar, he released his grip on her hands and sat back. "Sorry. Yes, you're right, but I'm just so angry. It's so unnecessary!"

"As are the two dead people on the beach. They all deserve our compassion. And I have a feeling there will be more dead before this is over."

"I need to see her body."

"She's ash. Only her tree remains."

"Then I'll see that. I have to. Only then will I feel that this is real. I'll go tonight." He felt better for making that decision. Perhaps in the wood he would discover a clue as to how to find this djinn.

"I'll go with you."

"No. They know me. I can easily go alone."

"Then go with Zee if you won't go with me. Ravens' Wood is in mourning. It's unsettled. The land is thick with mist. *Promise me.*" She was almost vibrating with indignation and worry, like an outraged pixie.

He finally smiled. "All right. I promise. But you have to promise me something."

"Not until I've heard what it is!"

"Make things right with Newton."

"Things are fine with Newton."

"Are they? Are they really? You know how he feels about you. Make it happen. If today teaches us anything, it's that life is too short, and you never know what's coming." He put a hand up to forestall her argument. "You know it's true. You can't lie to me, Briar. I see it all. You like him more than you admit—even to yourself."

"But he hasn't said a word about his...*feelings.*"

"Then *you* need to say it. Or are you that old-fashioned?" he challenged, goading her.

"It's not that easy."

"It's exactly that easy." He'd been meaning to say that for weeks. Satisfied, he stood and headed to the kettle, other issues taking precedence. His brain felt like it was on fire, and he needed something mundane to do. *Tea, food, all the normal crap.* "I'll phone Zee to organise tonight. I'm sure he'll be thrilled," he said sarcastically. "Then I want to meet with everyone to decide what we're doing. That's a good reason for you to speak to Newton, right?"

Her eyes flashed with indignation. "I don't need a reason, and I'm not sure I want *that* discussion."

"You do," he said with certainty. "You totally do."

If there was one good thing to come out of this total shitshow, it would be Briar and Newton getting back together, and he totally intended to make it happen.

Once he killed the djinn.

Ten

R euben pulled his car into Dante's courtyard and just
sat for a few moments, listening to the sounds of the
countryside as the engine died.

"Shouldn't he be open by now?" he asked El, noting the
door to the long building was firmly closed. The windows
were as grubby as always, so it was impossible to see inside.

"It's cold today. Although," she looked wary, "he nearly
always has the door open a little. It gets so hot in there. There
are usually a few cars here, too."

"This place is too far out of White Haven for him to be
affected, surely," Reuben reasoned. "There's no way the djinn
could be here. Plus, it's bloody gloomy. No wonder it looks
closed. He's probably sleeping off Beltane. Dante enjoys a
good party, as I recall. Maybe that's why he's not answering
his phone." Dante's forge was in a small hamlet just a couple
of miles out of White Haven, nestled within a fold of hills.
"Besides, how far can a djinn travel? I can't believe I even
asked that question. This is nuts."

"More nuts than a regular old fire elemental?"

"Yes!" Briar had updated them on the latest news as they
were driving, and Reuben was still having problems processing it all. "And it killed Nelaira. I can't believe that, either."

El twisted around to look at him. "This could stir things up badly in Ravens' Wood. Make it more dangerous, perhaps. What if it lashes out on anyone?"

"It's not psychotic."

"It's grieving. People—*beings*—aren't always logical when they're grieving."

Reuben wondered if she was referring to his behaviour after Gil had been killed. He hadn't been logical at all. "No, you're right. I'm still having trouble processing this, though. I mean, both options are nuts, right? A djinn and an elemental," Reuben explained as his mind raced. "One option places me in Medieval Europe with alchemists and witches summoning salamanders to do their bidding, the other in the mystical East."

"And yet, they are potentially the same. Isn't that what we're thinking now?"

"Or the djinn summoned an elemental? Perhaps it doesn't shapeshift at all."

"What a nightmare." El heaved a sigh and looked back at Dante's forge. "We can discuss this later. I'm sure we'll analyse it to death, but let's check this place now that we're here. If he's closed, I can come back tomorrow to discuss moulds. I certainly don't want him opening up to find the damn thing in his fire."

They both exited the car, but Reuben left it unlocked while El progressed to the smithy door and tried the handle. He stood on the carpark, looking around for possible telltale signs; scorched grass, perhaps, a blackened wall, or a trail. His gaze drifted to the roof where he looked for damage to the chimney or roof, but everything was reassuringly normal. Until he saw a curl of smoke.

"El! Wait!"

"What? It's locked."

"Then why is there smoke?" He grabbed El's elbow and pulled her back so they could both see the chimney. "Does he leave his forge lit?"

"I doubt it. Shit. What do we do?"

"We have to check. It might be nothing."

"It might be something." El studied the building as she gathered her magic. "Do we call the others?"

"If it's nothing, we'll feel like idiots. If it is the djinn, then we're prepared. I suspect water magic would be effective against a fire elemental."

"The plan is what, exactly?"

"Let's try talking, and hope Dante isn't dead inside. Let's be cautious, though!"

Now that he'd made his mind up, he crossed the courtyard swiftly, unlocked the door with a spell and eased it open. The darkness was all-encompassing, except for the red glow of firelight, and the scent of ash and smoke was strong. And it was hot. He'd been in the forge once or twice, but it was years earlier; however, he knew the forge was to the right, and after checking to his left to ensure nothing lurked to attack him, he stepped inside and immediately wished he hadn't.

Standing next to Dante's blazing forge was a shadowy figure with its back to them that was well over two metres tall, and which seemed to be cloaked in cinders and smoke. Reuben flung his hand out to El to stop her from entering, but it was too late. She'd already slipped in behind him.

He edged to the side to see it better, and realised that its attention was on the metal that it was forging in the fire, and noted that its hands appeared to be made of flame, too. *What the hell was it making?* As his eyes adjusted to the light, the multitude of objects became clearer. Iron railings, lanterns, statues, wall plaques, scraps of metal, and a variety of tools all in their rightful place, but there was no other creature present.

Deciding to stick with his original plan, Reuben was about to speak, when the creature beat him to it, greeting them in a deep, resonant voice. "Are you going to stand there all day, or do you have something to say?"

Mouth suddenly dry, he croaked out, "Have you hurt Dante?"

"Who is Dante?" He didn't even turn around.

"He owns this place. He's our friend."

"No one was here when I arrived last night. Fortunately." There was an edge of malice to his voice, or maybe it was just impatience and arrogance. There was no discernible accent, either.

Reuben glanced at El, who had stepped to the other side of the long workbench that ran down the centre of the room, magic balling in her hands, and she shook her head as she scanned the floor, and then mouthed, *"He's not here."*

Bolder now, Reuben called, "We just want to talk. What are you doing here?"

"What does it look like, boy? I am making something." The creature turned to the side and dunked metal into a large drum of water. Steam hissed and bloomed, further shrouding the creature.

"I am not a fucking boy. Turn around and look at me!"

"Be on your way. I am busy here." He picked up one of Dante's hammers and started shaping the metal, and that's when Reuben realised there was a whole pile of worked metal on the bench closest to the creature. *A torc, perhaps. An elaborate dagger?*

Reuben wasn't sure what he'd expected, but it wasn't this, and exasperated, he looked at El, mouthing, *"What the fuck?"* He turned back to the creature. "Hey! This isn't your place, and it sure isn't your world, so stop being a dick. We want answers. Are you the djinn that escaped from Ravens' Wood? The elemental?"

"And what is that to you?"

"You killed a dryad."

"And two humans," El added angrily. "That has consequences."

Finally, the creature turned towards them, revealing eyes of blue fire, and fine veins of what looked like molten metals across bronzed skin. Only a portion of his face was visible, and brawny, bronze-coloured forearms. The rest was swathed in the unusual cloak and a head scarf. "Who will mete out those consequences? You?" He smiled, revealing bright white teeth.

"Yes, you arrogant fuck," Reuben replied angrily. "You don't just walk into White Haven, kill people, and get away with it."

"I am Prince Qabas Nar-Ifrit of the House of the Desert Rose. I do whatever I choose without consequence, especially from humans with inadequate magic that is no match for my own." He raised his hands and fire curled around his fingers, and with a shock, Reuben noted his long, talonlike nails. "At least you have magic, unlike most of the mere humans that exist here. That is the only reason you live—for now."

Reuben was so shocked at his appearance that despite his anger, he stepped back almost involuntarily, and so did El. He raised his hands, summoning water so that steam curled around him. "If our world is so inadequate, then leave."

"This shadow world is a pale imitation of my own," Qabas said, looking around distastefully. "However, I have things to do first...unfinished business. Now go, before I turn you both to ash."

Reuben nodded to the metal he'd been forging. "What are you making?"

"As if I would tell you. You wouldn't understand, anyway." He swelled in size, growing so tall that he almost reached the roof, and his eyes blazed with that unnerving bright blue flame. "Now leave while I still allow it!" He threw his hands wide, and fire curled down the aisles towards them.

Reuben retaliated, hurling a blast of water at the creature, but it evaporated before it was even close. El threw a ball of pure magic at it, but the djinn caught it and held it, turning it into molten flame that he proceeded to absorb.

"Go!" he roared, voice shaking the building and chasing Reuben and El out on to the courtyard as if they were autumn leaves caught in a strong wind.

Barely aware of how it had happened, they found themselves on the ground, and the door to the smithy slammed shut. Despite the warning, Reuben tried to pull it open, but it was sealed tight, and all they could hear was the rhythmical pounding of metal on metal as the djinn continued to forge.

El was pale and grubby after rolling across the floor, but she rose to her feet, eyes blazing with fury. "We need to call the others."

Eleven

Helena examined the painting of White Haven's harbour that she had almost completed, while listening to Avery and Caspian talk about Morwenna in the attic room where they had gone after cake and coffee.

Painting was one of her latest hobbies, and she had set her easel up under the window. She needed hobbies in this new world, something to keep her hands busy while her mind worked, and she had discovered that painting had satisfied her creativity on many levels. Plus, Clea liked it. She was painting the harbour from a photo she had taken. Not much had changed from her time, really, except that the boats were modern. The rest was pleasingly familiar. The house that held The Witchcraft Museum was newer, a place that always fascinated her.

"Morwenna is ready to act against her ex?" Avery asked Caspian. "Why now?"

"Because mentally she's ready, and she knows she can't put it off any longer."

"Don't worry," Helena said, hearing the slight panic in Avery's tone. "I'll look into it. You can focus on other things. In fact, I already have a plan."

"You do?" Caspian asked, surprised.

She turned to face them, finding them both watching her. They were a good-looking couple, but there was no doubt for her that Avery had made the right decision in staying with Alex. He suited her so much more. "Yes. You—we—are overthinking this."

"Are we? Her daughter's life is at stake here."

"So is his."

Caspian's eyes narrowed. "I told you she doesn't want Jed's life at risk. He is Ysella's father."

"Ysella." Helena smiled. "Such a lovely name. I didn't say I would kill him or even injure him. I'll just terrify him. There are consequences to being complicit in a curse. I think your sister has the right idea."

"What are you thinking of doing?" Avery asked, lips already pursed in disapproval. She could be so righteous sometimes.

"I'm going to pay him a visit. Just me—the spirit me. I will tell him to start sharing custody or I will haunt him for the rest of his days. I shall appear in smoke and flames, as I consumed your father, Caspian. I gather it's a terrifying look. I think that will impress the seriousness of the situation, don't you?"

Avery gasped. "That sounds like a bad idea."

"Why? I won't be at risk, even if his dodgy little curse-enabling friends are there. I'll make sure Ysella isn't around, of course. Just me and him, nice and cosy." She could already envisage it. "Maybe I can conjure a little ghost of past and future, too. I've found I enjoy Dickens—well, some of his work."

"You could give him a heart attack!"

"Oh please, Avery." She rolled her eyes. "He's not ancient."

Caspian smiled. "Actually, I quite like the idea. As much as I want to meet Kitty again, and John the supposed best friend, that can wait. In fact, waiting will make them nervous. They'll be constantly looking over their shoulders, wondering when we might strike, but dealing with Jed first is the most important. Morwenna needs to see Ysella. Soon.”

“Of course, and Ysella needs to spend significant time with her. Come here, meet everyone. Make it her second home.” She saw Caspian flinch. “What?”

“She wants full custody.”

“Ysella has spent so long with her father, she might not want that. She may want to stay at the same school where all her friends are. That might mean Morwenna has to consider where she lives.”

“But,” Avery leapt in, glancing at Caspian with a worried expression, “Morwenna wants to stay here. She has support here.”

“Exactly, and she probably will. Who knows, Ysella might be sick of living with her father and desperate to move. But first things first, Ysella needs to make that choice, which means I must advise Jed to reconsider his custody arrangement.”

“Once we have dealt with the djinn,” Caspian said. Briar had updated them all via their Witchy WhatsApp group they had recently set up. It saved phone calls and alerted everyone all at once. Once the message had arrived, it had set off a flurry of responses, and a meeting had been planned for after work at Kendall and Zee’s apartment above the pub. “Morwenna will understand. That has to take priority.”

“Trust me, it won’t take long. Get me his address and I can be there quickly using spirit paths. Clea will be waiting here for me when I return.” Helena smirked, very much looking forward to exercising her spirit-self for someone else’s gain. “Perhaps I can find Gil to assist. Two spirits are always better than one.”

“I don’t know if Reuben will agree to that,” Avery said.

"Avery, it's not Reuben's decision. It's Gil's, who is not a child, by the way. And when did you get so sanctimonious, especially after the spell you cast last night? Plus, you were furious when you first heard about the curse. Breaking it almost killed all of us!"

"She has a point, Avery." Caspian's smile broadened, although Avery scowled. "I think it's an excellent idea, but only, Helena, if it will be safe for you. I know you're a ghost, but Kitty and John might well have anticipated that we will strike back. There could be all sorts of traps set up."

"For you, perhaps. Not for me. Although, I will check and proceed carefully, of course, and maybe leave some of my own on my way out. Obviously, nothing to endanger Ysella." The more she considered it, the more she liked it. "Will you find the address?"

"I already have it. We have checked the place out already—I asked Nahum to look into it. He was very happy to help. I considered having him make the threat. He would be terrifyingly effective."

Avery cocked her head at him. "Sneaky, but clever!"

"He found nothing obviously worrying, either, after watching it for a few days. No recent visits from Kitty or John. I can give you the layout of the house, the area, and the garden. It's a regular home, on a regular street."

Helena nodded. "Even better. Good. Yes, I'll go tonight. Let's get it done."

Avery heaved a sigh. "You're right, Helena. I just can't bear the thought of you not being around, if I'm honest. I've got used to it, and I really like it, so please be careful."

"I will, I promise."

Unfortunately, all of their phones started buzzing as another group message arrived, but Avery got to it first. "Shit. The djinn is at Dante's forge. Time to go."

"For the sake of all the gods everywhere," Cassie said, as Ben braked hard, sending the van skidding into the kerb by the forge and Dylan crunching into her side. "I nearly bit my bloody tongue."

The trip from White Haven's beach had been erratic and fast. She grabbed her pack, threw the door open, and staggered onto the lane, closely followed by Dylan. Her attention turned to the smithy, where she saw a thick plume of smoke spiralling out of the chimney, and El and Reuben waiting by the courtyard gate. They arrived at the same time as Briar and Eli, and—*holy shit*—Briar was on the back of Eli's trail bike with a helmet on and wearing his leather jacket. That was a sight she thought she'd never see. Eli kicked the stand down, stepped off in one smooth movement, and pulled his sword from his scabbard. His hair was tousled, his t-shirt revealed his muscled arms, and his jeans moulded to his thighs in all the right places. Cassie thought she might faint from desire. This was Eli as she had never seen him before, and she really liked it.

Eli strode to Reuben's side, eyes on the forge. "Where's the murdering bastard? Inside?"

"Still forging by the sound of it. He's a busy boy."

Now that the van and bike engines had been turned off, the muffled, rhythmical clanging of metal on metal resounded across the carpark.

Eli started to advance on the forge, but Reuben pulled him back. "Just wait. We need a plan, and the others are on their way."

"What's he making?" Ben asked, already setting up his monitoring equipment. "Weapons?"

"Perhaps," Reu said, "but he has powerful magic, and was more than a match for us. He certainly didn't tell us anything."

"He's an arrogant prick," El added viciously. "Said he had unfinished business. At least Dante wasn't there."

"He spoke to you?" Dylan said, shocked. "That's so cool!"

"And supremely unnerving, if I'm honest," Reuben said. "I'm in no rush to encounter him again. No one should be," he added, staring meaningfully at Eli.

"The longer we wait," Eli said, hand flexing around his sword hilt, "the longer he has to get away."

Briar laid a hand on his arm. "The others are coming. I hear them now."

Within seconds, two other cars pulled up, Alex and Zee exiting one, while Avery, Helena, and Caspian exited the other. Zee, like Eli, was armed with a sword. Cassie realised they had all abandoned their businesses to be there. The only people not present were the police, and Reuben stated that was because he didn't want them involved. It wasn't as if they could arrest the djinn. Ghost OPS were there purely to report on any unusual phenomenon that could help them in any way. While they set up their equipment, Reuben briefed them on their conversation. All the while, the constant clanging of metal on metal proved the djinn wasn't going anywhere.

"I guess the plan," Reu said in summary, "is that we kill him or capture him. There are multiple windows, all mainly blocked, one door only, and the chimney, but I doubt djinn need conventional exits. I have no idea how we capture him. El has an idea, but that's nowhere near ready to execute yet. It's sort of why we're here."

"Save your explanations for later," Eli said with growing impatience. "I suggest that Zee and I go in first, engage him in battle, and try to kill him swiftly."

"I think, brother," Zee said, "that will be easier said than done. Djinn are tricky opponents. But obviously, I'm happy to try."

Caspian pointed up to the roof. "Avery and I can cover the chimney exit. Witch-flight will get us up there."

Avery nodded in agreement.

"You three," Eli pointed at Ghost OPS as he took his shirt off and unfurled his magnificent, tawny wings, "stay out here and do what you do best. Witches, you're our backup."

"Wait!" El said. "Balls of pure magical power don't work. He absorbed mine, and Rue's water magic vapourised before it could get close. Then he threw us out. Literally. I presume he knows we're still here."

"We'll use rune magic," Helena suggested immediately. "Or spells that work on his mind, not his body."

Eli shrugged. "You work it out. I'm going in."

Caspian and Avery immediately used witch-flight and appeared in seconds on the roof, while Eli ran to the door with Zee. Cassie stepped away from the witches, leaving them to have a hurried discussion while she focussed on the Nephilim.

Ben's EMF meter whined as he paced closer to the building. "Shit! His energy is off the scale! Even out here."

"Electromagnetics have no boundaries, my friend," Dylan said. He ran after the Nephilim, pressing his face against one of the windows to try to see inside, camera in hand.

Cassie was far too distracted to use her own equipment, watching instead as Eli tested the door, and trying not to stare too obviously at his physique. When he failed to open it, he tried to kick it in. When again it refused to yield, both Nephilim tried to force it open together, their wings expanding as they did so, which temporarily hid part of the building. Firelight bloomed beyond the dirty windows, and a flurry of sparks plumed out of the chimney.

Alex helped the Nephilim, trying a combination of spells to open the door, but it remained stubbornly sealed.

"What the actual fuck?" Eli roared with anger and punched the door. "Come out here and fight, you coward!"

For one heart-stopping moment, the banging of metal ceased, and everyone froze, but then it started again. The inside of the forge now glowed with a fierce light, as if a fire was spreading. *How hot was it in there?*

Ben summoned Cassie's attention. "Cassie! Wipe the drool from your chin and start recording sound. We might pick something up. And have you checked temperatures?"

"Sorry, no. And piss off! I'm not drooling."

Nevertheless, she discreetly ran her fingers over her chin before fumbling to start the audio Electronic Voice Phenomena (EVP) equipment. She presumed it would be useless, so fished her thermometer out at the same time. Ben, meanwhile, was recording his observation notes into his phone. She plugged her earphones in, focussing on higher frequencies, and leaving the others, paced to the end of the building closest to where the forge was. And that's when she heard what sounded like a song. A soft rising and falling of notes that was displayed on the visual part of the recorder in rippling waves. It was hypnotic. Mesmerising, even. She adjusted her audio equipment and drifted forward, feet finding their own way independent of her brain. It must be coming from the djinn. *Was it singing? Did it have an unusual instrument?* She checked that she was recording and moved closer. *Were there words?* Then she knew what it reminded her of. It was like a lullaby. *But for what?*

Then she jumped as another tone entirely sounded. Something as deep and resonant as a bell that she heard very clearly. The musical tone responded. Like a conversation. That's when she realised that there were two creatures in the forge, not one.

She needed a second opinion. "Ben! Come over here and listen!"

Twelve

It was obvious to Alex that the djinn had sealed the doors with magic, and that so far they didn't have the key to breaking through. Even the Nephilim's considerable strength wasn't even close to battering down the door.

Like Dylan, Alex pressed his face to the grubby glass, but could see nothing except an array of metal objects that were impossible to discern clearly. Even twisting as much as possible, he couldn't see to the far side where the forge itself was, and the windows were completed blacked out at that end.

Frustrated, he turned to El. "Is Dante a bloody vampire? It's pitch black in there."

"He says the darkness provides alchemy. He reckons that's why he's so good at metalwork. Fire and darkness. I may also have taught him a thing or two."

"He sounds like the djinn, then. Helena, what did you mean by spells to target his mind?"

"Spells to confuse, like glamour, but I've already tried while you were attempting to get inside. He has an impenetrable protection field. He could give us some tips."

Eli tried to smash the glass windows, which was fairly pointless, because the windows were small and narrow, and no one would have been able to get in, anyway. Not even Briar. Not that she was an option. However, the glass remained impervious to destruction, too.

"So, it's a waiting game," Briar said. "We can't get in. Maybe Cas or Avery could using witch-flight, but that's risky."

"Too risky," Alex said immediately.

"I'm thinking that this is a big fat waste of time," Reuben said, smacking a spell off the closest wall and sending a stone block flying. "He swatted us off like flies. The only way we can take him down is together, and that means having a big spell we can use. Something tailored to him, specifically. Right now, we have diddly squat."

"Guys!" Cassie came running over with Ben. "I've heard something. We think there are two things in there. The djinn and something else. There's a sort of singing that I detected."

El groaned. "Could it be the metal itself? Shadow says that in her world, metal makes a sound. All weapons do, hers included. She said that apparently Excalibur sang sweeter than most."

Alex had several questions about that particular statement, but shelved most for later. "Are you saying he's crafting a weapon? One that answers him? Because that's just bat-shit crazy."

Reuben shook his head. "He was crafting several things. Potentially parts to one weapon, or several."

Cassie's face took on a distant expression as she pressed her headphones to her ears again. "There's a kind of sibilance to it. A hiss. Steam, maybe?"

"Oh crap," Zee said, pressing his ear to the door. "Has he got a pet salamander?"

"Maybe the djinn was the orb, and the salamander was his?" Briar suggested. "Perhaps they were both at the Great Wedding and both are stuck here. The thing is, the dryads did not mention the salamander."

"Perhaps it's his familiar," Helena suggested. "If they have such things."

"Fuckity fuck fuck," Alex said, stepping back as if it might come barrelling out the door. He looked up at the roof and summoned Caspian and Avery down to update them, and they looked just as baffled. "This is just getting weirder. What are we going to do? I can't stay here all afternoon. We've left only two staff in the pub, and it's nuts in there. I have to get back. But equally, I can't go yet!"

Reuben shrugged. "I can stay. I suggest we have a stakeout. Perhaps when it emerges, we can talk. Bargain."

"I'm not bargaining with that monster," Eli said through gritted teeth. "He killed Nelaira and two others."

Alex knew he couldn't leave them, so he phoned the pub, and when Maria reassured him that they could cope for a while longer, he gave himself an hour. While they waited, they paced around the perimeter, discussed spells, watched Ghost OPS, and generally felt increasingly useless and frustrated. The only thing that sustained him was that they had fought Jack Frost and the Winter Queen, both fey creatures, and won. If they could best them, then they could fight a djinn. They just needed to find a weak spot.

It was getting darker as a storm threatened. The drenching mist of earlier that settled on his skin seeped away as the wind picked up, revealing heavy rain clouds gathering overhead. This place was exposed at the end of the small hamlet, and the weather would drive in. He doubted magic would keep them dry easily, but maybe it would give them an advantage over a fire elemental.

Just as Alex decided he couldn't wait any longer, the sound of hammering stopped. Hushed conversations ended, and the slick whisper of metal being withdrawn from scabbards replaced the silence. The door flew open, and Eli and Zee rushed forward, weapons raised.

Then the djinn emerged, and all coherent thought fled Alex's mind.

The djinn was so Otherworldly that he could barely take it in, despite hearing Reuben's description. The cloak of cinders and shadows swirled around it, and only his bright blue flaming eyes remained visible above the dramatic scarf that covered his head and lower face. He raised his hand and sent Eli and Zee spinning backwards like leaves in the wind.

His voice boomed out. "I am Prince Qabas Nar-Ifrit of the House of the Desert Rose. When this is over, you will all kneel before me—even you, Nephilim. The blood of my ancestors is strong, and you are no match for my power." He regarded their stunned faces with amusement, and his voice rang as if with prophecy. *"In this shadow world, my flame burns bright, and all will bask in my fiery light."*

In seconds he dissolved into a maelstrom of sand, coal-black smoke, and sparks, and he spun across the courtyard, the accompanying blast of wind throwing them all off their feet. Then he leapt into the air, caught a current, and vanished.

It was over before it had even begun.

"It was awful," Avery said to Dan and Sally later that afternoon after they locked the shop's door and started tidying up. "There was nothing we could do. He was so powerful, and...magnificent! I feel a total traitor for saying that. I both hate him and admire him."

"Herne's hairy bollocks," Dan said, voice faint and eyes distant. "I think I can imagine him, but I'm probably falling short."

"Trust me. You are." Avery could barely get her head around it. "His eyes will haunt my sleep, I just know it. They were bright blue flames. And his cloak..." she floundered, arms flailing as words failed to explain it, although she had tried several times. "It was smoke and darkness and sand and sparks. You know, like when you're staring into a fire at the end of the night? We hoped the weather would slow him down, but it really didn't."

"Where do you think he's gone?" Sally asked.

"I honestly have no idea. Newton is still sealing off the dunes from the public, but obviously distance doesn't deter it. It might return to Ravens' Wood, but I doubt that from what Briar told us. But what does it want? Apart from our subjugation, of course." *All will bask in my fiery light.*

After their encounter, the group had entered Dante's forge, partly to shelter from the increasingly wild weather, but mainly to look for clues as to what Qabas had been doing. Ghost OPS had set up full spectrum cameras, audio, thermal imaging cameras, and examined everything with black lights. The witches used their magic to investigate. Unfortunately, whatever he had been working on, he had taken with him. Alex hadn't waited, nor Zee, both returning to the pub as soon as they were happy the others were safe. After confirming that their evening meeting was still on, Avery, Helena, and Caspian also left. El and Reuben however were staying to speak to Dante, who was coming to see what the djinn had stolen. As for Eli... Avery had never seen him so angry, even after using Belial's jewellery. Hopefully, Briar would calm him down.

"Well," Dan said, obviously trying to summon a sense of normality, "I've been trying to dredge up my knowledge on djinn, but I'll hit the books later. I've got plenty at home, and Caro can help me. Plus, I'll peruse our shelves before I leave. Dylan will swing by my place tonight. I think El has the right idea, though."

"To trap it in a jar of some kind?" Sally asked.

Dan nodded. "Yes. I'm sure there are other options, but it seems a good one, and potentially easier than fighting it."

Sally adjusted the Beltane window display and straightened the books on the table arrangements while they talked, but she was obviously worried and distracted. She'd straightened the same pile of books twice already. Avery resorted to strengthening her protection spells, taking solace in the shop's magical atmosphere as the rain drummed down with fierce intensity. The mist may have cleared near the forge, but in White Haven it was still drifting down from Ravens' Wood in thick ribbons, nosing through the streets as if it were searching for something. Maybe it was. It seemed none of them were ready to go home, even though the shop was locked.

Avery drifted to the window, squinting to see through the rain driving down the pane. *The djinn was out there somewhere. Would it manifest in the middle of the street? What would she do if it did?*

Avery noticed a car easing down the street as if unsure where to go, the unidentifiable figure at the wheel slowing down to examine the shop before pulling haphazardly onto the pavement. Within seconds, the person flung themselves out of the car, slammed the door, and then pounded on the shop's door so strongly that the bells rattled inside. And they continued to ring, air shifting within the shop as if they had opened a window.

Instantly, Avery summoned her magic for protection as she ran to the door, only to find a familiar face staring back at her through the glass. A face that had more lines around the eyes than when she had last seen it.

"Avery Hamilton!" the woman yelled, nose to the glass as she glared. "You summoned me here against my will in this shit weather!"

It was her mother. Avery froze as they locked eyes, mouth dry, having almost forgotten the spell she had cast the night before.

Sally pushed her out of the way and unlocked the door. "Bloody Hell, Ave, let her in!"

Diana almost bowled Sally over as she thrust her way inside, eyes skimming the room in one swift movement before settling on Avery again. She threw her cowled hood back to reveal a mass of amber-hued hair and sharp hazel eyes that Avery wasn't sure she'd ever see again. Eyes that held no warmth whatsoever. "You did this! You better have a damn good reason!"

Avery's own anger spilled out. "Yes, I have! It's called wanting to see my mother after she abandoned me, virtually disowned me, and hasn't bothered to see me since I was sixteen! I thought it might be nice to see if you were still alive. It seems you are. Feel free to fuck off back to where you came from now. And if you see Bryony, take her with you, too."

Her mother paused, assessing her from her head to her toes. "Are you ill?"

"No. I am exceptionally well and happy, thanks. I thought you should know that, seeing as you *never* ask. Beltane clearly has affected my judgment, though." She flicked at the door that Sally had closed, spelling it wide open again so that a blast of cold air and rain slithered into the shop. "Job done. I'm okay, you're okay. Be on your way." She forced her mother back with another imperious push, using the wind for her own means, and extremely satisfied that her magic was responding strongly. She held it around her, her hair swirling as she faced down her mother who was looking at her in a very peculiar manner. "What are you waiting for? Go on. I'm far too busy for this, and you clearly don't want to be here."

"You summoned us both?"

"Yes! A mistake, *obviously*."

"On your own?"

"Not exactly. But what does it matter?"

"Because that's an extremely powerful spell you cast, young lady."

"I'm an extremely powerful witch, Mother."

Diana's eyes took on a speculative gleam and her shoulders dropped as she studied Avery again. "Interesting. Your magic feels different."

"I'm not sixteen anymore. I have been a practising witch for a long time now."

"There is an ancient quality to your magic."

"Ancestral magic, no doubt. I consult them regularly."

Diana stepped closer, lifting her head as if sniffing out the magic. "Intriguing."

"Not half," a resounding voice called out from the back of the shop, "as intriguing as *you*." Helena strode through the stacks, although of course she was Clea to Diana. She was bristling with anger, and magic shimmered around her. "Always the drama queen, Diana. We have been quite deprived of it, and I'm not sure we've missed it. Either go or shut the door. You are making the shop cold." She nodded to the door behind Diana. "But if you stay, do not be rude. I won't tolerate it."

Diana's mouth fell open in shock. "Mother? You look...different."

"Almost as if I'm a different woman, wouldn't you say?" Helena's mouth twisted into a wicked smile. "Are you going or staying?"

Diana hesitated, looking at Avery as if for encouragement, but Avery remained silent, thinking that she had a busy evening ahead, and her mother was going to make it far more complicated. Plus, she had been so bloody rude, she couldn't bear to encourage her. However, she wanted to know who her mother was now, and perhaps see herself through her mother's eyes. See the woman she had become. Avery felt rather than saw Sally and Dan flank her as if to offer reinforcement, and she could have kissed them for it.

Diana relented. "I think I should stay. It seems things have changed here. I admit, I'm curious."

Curious. As if they were bugs under a microscope. Wind flickered around Avery again, and her mother glanced at her, startled once more.

"You know what they say about curiosity," Helena said with a smirk. She shut the door with a silent spell, and the bells once again jangled longer than they should have, as if warning of danger. "Time to put the kettle on, then. Follow me, Diana. I think you know the way. Or has it been so long you have forgotten?"

Diana's eyes narrowed as she stared at Helena and then at Avery, and then she followed Helena through the shop without saying another word. Avery hesitated before following, needing a moment to gather herself as she watched her mother examining the shelves as she went.

She'd done it. She'd actually summoned her mother, and impressed her with her magic, too. *Was that good or bad, though?*

"Well," Dan said softly under his breath. "Fuck a duck, Ave. That was quite some reunion."

She looked at them, lips pressed into a thin line. "I think I've made a monumental mistake."

Dan winked. "Nothing you can't handle."

Sally hugged her, but when she pulled back, her cheeks were dimpling with suppressed mirth. "Go on. You might need to save her from Helena. We'll finish up here. See you in the morning."

Avery took a breath, squared her shoulders, and headed after them.

Thirteen

"I'm just relieved that Qabas didn't damage anything," El said to Dante, as he examined the interior of the forge carefully and then moved to the huge, locked cabinet that abutted against the end of one long work surface. It wasn't locked anymore, unfortunately.

"He might not have damaged anything, but he's stolen some copper sheets, bronze bars, and brass. A bit of steel too, I think. And he's melted my lock. Bollocks."

El felt terrible. "I'm so sorry."

"It's not your fault." Dante straightened up, brushing his long dreadlocks back from his face. "Not sure I can claim it on the insurance, though. There's no sign of a break-in."

"The padlock is melted right off your cabinet. I think that counts," she pointed out.

"Yeah, but not on the main door. I can try, though." He cocked his head at her, resignation in his eyes. "I suppose that's djinn for you."

"You're taking this remarkably calmly."

"Externally. Internally, I'm freaking out."

"But," El said tentatively, "you know a little bit about me and how I work, and Shadow is different, right?"

"There's different and *different*. Shadow's metalwork was *different*, with properties not known to me before, but I didn't expect this."

"If it's any consolation, neither did we. I'd rather not lie, either." She stepped closer, worried she'd lost his friendship. "I'm still El despite all this. The world just isn't as straightforward as you thought."

"I know. Perhaps I was trying to pretend irrational things were rational, too. I certainly can't do that anymore. Once you know, you *know*, right?"

"Right. I'm still really sorry."

"It's okay, El. We're fine."

"Really? Because I'd hate to lose your friendship."

His steady gaze fixed on her for a few more moments. "No more secrets."

"Are you sure?" she pressed, thinking that he didn't know what he was asking.

"Yes."

"All right. I'm just glad you weren't here. He's killed people."

"Those deaths on the news?"

El nodded. "In the dunes at White Haven."

"Yeah, I saw that Sarah Rutherford interview. Horrible way to die."

El was feeling sick at the thought of Dante being injured. "Maybe you should keep the place closed while he's on the loose."

"I need to work, El. I can't do that. It sounds like he's got what he needed, though." He nodded to where Ghost OPS were still running tests, with Reuben questioning them endlessly. "What are they doing again?"

"Checking for supernatural signatures. They're paranormal investigators. You must have seen them on the news, too."

"They look a bit young."

"Trust me, they're very good." El sighed heavily as she studied the area again. The place still felt charged with magic. Weird, off-kilter djinn magic. "It feels as if a desert wind has swept through here."

"It kind of did. I can see sand on the floor." Dante laughed and shook his head. "What will you do now?"

"Can you work out what he might have made?"

"No way. You might be right with a weapon, but it doesn't sound like he needs one."

"That's true. Maybe it's something to open a portal and return home. Although, that doesn't feel right, either. He said we would become his subjects, in some portentous announcement." She shrugged it off. "We'll work it out. What I actually wanted to discuss with you was about making a mould. I want to craft a jar to trap him in."

"A glorified Aladdin's lamp, eh? Crafted with magic?"

"Yes, and metals he can't break out of. Or should I use another material?"

"Iron, perhaps? Fey don't like it, do they? Does a djinn count as fey?"

El groaned. "Iron! Of course. That's how Gabe trapped Shadow, at first. I'll have to speak to Shadow to check. I have some special fey metal, too. Just a small amount."

He rubbed his cheek, smudging it with metallic dust that gleamed against his dark skin. "What an interesting project. Want some help?"

She grinned. "I thought you'd never ask."

Briar clutched Eli's waist tightly as he rounded the bend and turned into Stormcrossed Manor's driveaway, wondering what on Earth she'd been thinking when she agreed to be a passenger on his bike.

Time was of the essence, he'd said in their shop earlier, and desperate to get to the forge quickly, she had agreed. Plus, she had been intrigued to ride on his bike, seeking something to distract her from thoughts of Newton. It had definitely worked. She had been so terrified and exhilarated that she had barely thought of anything except surviving. Plus, she had wanted to make sure that Eli didn't do anything rash, and with her on the back, she trusted that he wouldn't.

Rather than let him rage around the forge, she had persuaded him to leave and take her to see Tamsyn. With the arrival of the djinn, and Tamsyn's visions of the white stag, she wanted to check on her. Now he eased to a stop on the sweep of drive before the front door, and she stepped off, legs shaking, and drenched from the heavy rain. Because he'd given her his helmet that was far too big—but he argued, better than nothing—his hair was plastered to his head, and his wet clothes moulded to him. She took a breath, reminding herself that a romantic liaison with Eli was not an option, but that looking was just fine.

Stormcrossed Manor brooded in the gloom, as menacing as when she had first seen it all those months ago. Now, however, she knew better than to fear it. The gardens were being tamed, the paintwork had been spruced up, and the house had lost its abandoned and forlorn air. She ran to the front door, pushed it open, and stepped into the hallway lit with lamps that were on far earlier than they would normally be.

"Bloody hell," she said, taking off the helmet and heavy leather jacket. "I wish we'd taken my mini now. I'm soaked."

"But I'm quicker."

"And wetter!"

His eyes travelled down her body, lips curving upwards in a lazy smile. "It's a good job Newton can't see you now. You're not leaving a lot to the imagination, Briar. Or maybe it's a shame he can't see you now. It might spur him into action!"

With a scowl, she cast a spell to take the worst of the water off both of them. "You are incorrigible."

"I'm a fucking delight, as Shadow would say."

Ignoring him, Briar headed along the entrance hall, shouting out, "Hello? It's Briar. I've brought Eli."

Rosa, her cousin, appeared at the top of the stairs, hair bundled up and wearing old clothes, and a paintbrush in hand. "Hi! I thought I heard an engine. The kids and Tamsyn are in her kitchen. I'm painting yet another bedroom. Is everything all right?" She walked partway down the stairs, glancing nervously between both of them. She knew Eli, but not well, because she shopped in Charming Balms occasionally.

"Sort of. Just checking in," Briar said with a shrug. "Has Beth seen anything odd?"

"No, thankfully. Alex seems to have helped her a lot. Is this about those deaths?"

"I'm afraid so," Eli answered, "but there's nothing for you to worry about."

"There's a lot of magic protecting this house, Rosa," Briar told her. "Maybe stay here for a few days, though. I can bring supplies, if necessary."

"So it is bad news."

Eli smiled to reassure her. "We're just being cautious."

"I'm afraid I can't stay here just *because*! I have a part-time job in the library now."

Briar backtracked, eager to calm her down. Besides, she was sure that Prince Qabas had no intention of attacking the public library. "Fair enough. It will be fine."

Nodding, Rosa started back up the stairs. "If you say so. I don't need any more details, thanks. I'll just worry."

When they were alone again, Eli said, "She does like to live in the dark, doesn't she?"

"She's a bag of anxiety," she said, heading to Tamsyn's kitchen in the other wing of the house. "Trust me, it's for the best."

Eli studied the décor, poking his head into rooms as they passed. "It's been a while since I've been here. It looks better."

"They've decorated the areas they use regularly. Lots more to do, though. Wait until you see Tamsyn's kitchen!"

What had been a dank, decaying mess was now full of light and warmth and music, and as usual, Tamsyn was cooking while the kids were painting at the kitchen table. "I thought I'd be seeing you, Briar. You, though," she said smiling at Eli, "I did not. Tea? Or something stronger," she offered, eyes narrowing.

"Coffee, please, if you have it," Eli said, before high-fiving the kids and sitting at the table with them.

Briar greeted Max and Beth, relieved to see Beth looking bright-eyed and happy, before walking to the sink to fill the kettle. "I'll have tea, but I'll make a fresh pot and Eli's coffee." She took a moment to appreciate the kitchen that was now painted a soothing sage green, along with some new wooden cabinets. "It looks good in here."

Tamsyn nodded. "Rosa is handy with a paintbrush, I'll give her that. It keeps her busy and stops her worrying. You two, though, are hiding something. Particularly you, Eli. You're positively vibrating in anger."

He leaned back in his chair to look at her. "You don't miss much."

"I know. Kids, head on upstairs and wash your hands before afternoon tea. And do it properly! I'll inspect your nails when you come back. Bring your mother with you. Remember, no cake for grubby hands. It's chocolate caramel, so you know what you're missing."

They dropped their paintbrushes into a glass of water and raced out of the room without a backward glance.

"Wow," Eli said admiringly. "Talk about well trained."

"You better have clean hands, too," she said.

He wiggled them. "No blood on them today. Unfortunately."

Appalled, Briar threw a tea towel at him. "Eli!"

"There's a killer djinn on our patch, Briar. Trust me, you'll be glad when I find him."

He placed the offending tea towel on the table, unnervingly calm now after his earlier anger, and Briar knew he was storing it up, ready to release it later like a storm. She had seen him after using Belial's jewellery, and couldn't bear to see him behaving like that again. They had to think of a solution, quickly.

Tamsyn considered them both carefully, placed the cake onto a large plate and carried it to the table where she sat next to Eli.

"We have about five minutes before the kids come racing back, so make it quick. Djinn?"

He filled her in on the overnight developments while Briar prepared the drinks. When Eli had finished, Briar said, "Of course, I'm worried about the white stag you dreamt of. Did you see it again last night?"

Tamsyn sagged in her chair. "My beautiful stag was walking through a wood last night, and it was surrounded by what I thought was thick mist, but now believe was smoke. I awoke to the smell of charred wood, and I thought my room was on fire at first, it was that real."

"Could you see flames?" Eli asked, watching her intently.

"No flames, and my stag wasn't scared either, but the path he followed became ever narrower."

"Where did the path go?" Briar asked.

"Just through the trees, but it was pitch black at the end. Again, I thought maybe it was death it was leading me to, but actually, I think it was a different message. I'm not sure what, though. Yet."

Briar placed the pot of tea and cups on the table and handed Eli his coffee as she sat down, pondering Tamsyn's dream. "It could have been mist, because it's pouring out of Ravens' Wood now. It seemed like their version of tears to me. But if you smelled burning wood, I really hope it doesn't mean it was on fire. Was it *our* wood?"

"It was an ancient place, full of wisdom, I could tell that. Timeless," Tamsyn said, her gaze distant, seeing her dream perhaps, not the kitchen. "But I sensed urgency, too. The need to hurry."

And then suddenly Tamsyn's eyes turned white, and Briar tried to smother her gasp as Eli jerked back in shock.

Tamsyn continued, her voice a singsong. "*He's turning towards me, then nodding at the way ahead. His antlers are draped in moss and ivy, and his white flanks are smooth and glossy. 'Quickly, my love,' he beckons. 'Or the wood will burn and the path will close. I will take you. On my back now, quickly. He comes. Do it now before he consumes us all.'*"

Fourteen

Helena studied Diana as she in turn studied the large, open-plan living area of Avery's home, her own impressions mixing with Clea's. Avery arrived after them and also waited, watching silently.

Clea was excited to see her, but angry, too. Like Avery, she was annoyed at her years of absence. Memories of how Diana had looked in her youth enabled Helena to see the current changes. The lines around her eyes and corner of her mouth, shorter hair that was shoulder-length rather than reaching her waist. But still it rippled with amber colours, complimenting her hazel eyes. The family resemblance with Avery was obvious, including their build. Diana was slender still, fifty-something perhaps, but there was something spare about her, as if she was denying herself pleasure. Her lips puckered as she looked around, and Helena realised that she did not like Diana, not one little bit. Diana was hard, whereas Avery was softer, more approachable. But Diana's magic was there at her core, an ember waiting to be coaxed to full flame. That incensed Helena even more. *What a waste.*

Helena had been about to offer her a drink, but now she didn't want to. She felt as if she'd found a poisoned apple in a bowl of fruit. "Something upsetting you? You look like you've eaten something sour."

Diana finished examining the room, taking her time before finally facing Helena, arms crossed over her chest. "Who are you? You are not my mother. She would never talk to me like that."

"It's been a long time, Diana. I've changed. I've learned not to care about those who leave me or those I love. It's a wasted emotion when I have so much else to care about."

Diana twisted to keep Avery in her sight. "I had to get away from this place. So did Bryony. You know that. I was sick of magic and secrets and mysteries and everything that went with it."

"Enough to forsake your daughter and mother? Shame on you. You abandoned your ancestors, too."

Diana's eyes were like ice. "You gave me your blessing."

"I did no such thing. You heard what you wanted to hear." Clea was rousing now; Helena could feel her uncoiling, memories rising unbidden to the surface at the sight of her daughter. "I told you that if that's what you had to do, then so be it. I certainly did not approve. Leaving Avery to cope with no mother or father! Feeling unloved and not worthy! Shameful." She stepped towards Diana, magic rolling around her, glad to see Diana step back. "It's lucky she had me. Her magic has grown stronger than yours ever was. Now yours is a half-dead thing, musty and unused."

However, Diana was no wilting flower, and the accusation made her magic flare, too. "I'll ask again. Who are you? You are not my mother." She glared at Avery. "What have you done to her?"

"Remind me," Avery said, voice laced with sarcasm, "when did you last see Clea?"

"It's been a while, I admit, but don't insult my intelligence." She studied Helena again, eyes narrowed with suspicion. "Your clothes, your expression...everything! You're not her. You called me here so at least be honest with me. I've agreed to stay—as requested," she said pointedly.

Avery turned to Helena. "Go on, then."

Helena smiled. "I am Helena Marchmont, the spirit of your long-dead ancestor who was burned at the stake. Events brought me back, and now Clea's body is my occasional home."

Diana recoiled sharply. "Don't be ridiculous. That's impossible."

"I can assure you, it's not. Don't worry, though. She is unharmed. Clea has dementia now. She lives in a home. Did you even know that? Avery arranged it all." Actually, she knew Diana knew, but she wanted to make her uncomfortable.

"Of course I knew."

"Through a Christmas card!" Avery said viciously. "That you never replied to. I couldn't even call you! The more I think about it, the more I wonder why I summoned you back at all. Just stupid sentimentality."

"I did warn you," Helena said to Avery, but not unkindly. "Never mind. It's done now. We must make the best of it. Perhaps a night would suffice?" She turned back to Diana. "I'm sure you don't need longer than that. I don't think any of us do. Avery just wanted to reassure herself that you were alive. Plus, Clea doesn't really want you hanging around, either. Especially with your aggressive attitude. By the way, she deeply resents you not visiting all these years."

"I had my reasons!" Diana shot back.

"Purely selfish ones," Helena said. "Frankly, I'm appalled with you. I died at the stake to protect my family. You'd have probably sent them there instead."

Helena knew she was being unkind, but she wanted to hurt Diana as much as she'd hurt Avery and Clea. She was comfortable with vengeance, especially with a woman she didn't know. *Although*, she thought, casting Avery a glance, *she was no shrinking violet.*

Diana, momentarily stunned, finally said, "That's a terrible thing to say. I would never have done that. I left, that's all. I knew that you—my mother—would look after Avery." She sagged into a chair, as if all strength had left her. "Avery had the same passion for magic as you. I could tell. I didn't. And this place..." She looked around. "The house. The town. All of it. It suffocated me with expectations. Bryony, too. It was easier to deal with it by pretending it didn't exist."

"By pretending *I* didn't exist!" Avery yelled. "You are an insufferable monster! I am going upstairs to the spell room. I have things to do. If you're staying, you can sleep at Reuben's. I'll call him. You certainly aren't staying here."

Avery marched upstairs without another word, eyes flashing, and Helena decided that was probably for the best. However, perhaps a conciliatory cup of tea might be in order. They had called Diana here, after all.

"Tea?" Helena asked. Diana just nodded. "Take your coat off and sit down, then."

Helena headed to the kitchen, but instead of remaining seated, Diana took her coat off and hung it over the back of the chair and then followed her into the kitchen. "I didn't mean to upset Avery," she said, voice low. Regretful, even.

"Good grief, Di. You must have known what your leaving would do. You're no fool."

Diana didn't answer that, instead saying, "This place has changed a lot. The house, I mean. It's more modern."

"Avery's doing. And Alex's, of course. It's their home together now. Mine only occasionally."

"I have so many questions, I don't know where to start." She looked upwards, to the attic. "I should go and talk to her. Try and explain myself. It's been a terrible start."

"You did shout at her through the door!" At least Diana had the grace to look slightly regretful. "Just wait. She'll calm down—hopefully—soon. Raging at each other won't do any good at all."

"No, it won't. Who's Alex?"

"Alex Bonneville, a descendant of my old friend, Imogen. One of the five families. I presume you know some of your history?"

She nodded in recognition. "They owned the pub."

"He still does."

"They're a couple?"

"And very happy, too."

"And Reuben?"

"One of the Jacksons. The youngest son. The oldest was killed a couple of years ago."

"The Jacksons of Greenlane Manor?" Her eyes widened in surprise.

"Exactly. A lot has happened since you left. White Haven is reclaiming its magic, and so are its witches. They're part of the wider Cornwall Coven now. We all are—I include myself, of course."

Diana looked out of the window, gaze distant, but when she turned back to Helena, she looked as if she'd accepted her fate. "Well, now that I'm here, you better tell me all of it."

"Are you sure? Perhaps it's better not to, considering how you feel. You can leave in blissful ignorance tomorrow."

"No. I should know. It's my responsibility."

"Then let's sit down, because there's a lot to get through. Then you can tell me about what you've been up to. Perhaps we should also discuss where Bryony is."

"So," Ben said to his team once they were settled in the back room of The Wayward Son with drinks and food on the way, "how does the salamander relate to a djinn? As far as I am aware, they are two separate creatures."

"Maybe that just goes to show," Dylan said, helping himself to the communal bag of cheese and onion crisps, "that we know bollocks all about djinn."

"Perhaps it's a pet," Cassie said, eyes dancing with amusement.

Ben frowned. "This isn't funny! That djinn was insanely powerful, and we know what we saw. Our machines don't lie. It was a salamander in the fire, and that was not a salamander we encountered at Dante's. It was a ridiculously powerful djinn prince." He considered what the witches had suggested. "A familiar of some sort was a good suggestion, if the fey even have such a thing. Although, I'm more inclined to think the salamander is a servant."

"Or just something else that arrived with the Great Wedding," Dylan said.

"I wonder," Cassie mused, sipping her coffee, "whether djinn royalty are more powerful than the common herd? Is 'herd' even the collective name for djinn?"

"I think perhaps a flurry. Or maybe a carpet bag of djinn?" Dylan suggested.

"Or a flame of djinn?" Cassie said, eyebrows quirking upwards. "I like that."

Ben sighed and sipped his half a Guinness. *It was going to be one of those conversations.* Not surprising, really. They had all encountered something they had never met before. A slight amount of hysteria was to be expected. "Maybe a sandstorm of djinn," he said, throwing his own suggestion in. "But perhaps discussing how to find it might be of more use? And what relevance the salamander has?"

"Ooh! Sandstorm... Interesting." Dylan nodded, and then seeing Ben's pinched lips, clearly thought better of dwelling on it. "Er, yes. Tracking. Well, we have all agreed that its energy signature is strong, which should make it easy-ish once we're in range, but that still leaves narrowing down its whereabouts. As for the salamander, maybe it shapeshifts, as we discussed. It's a shame Shadow's not about."

"Moore is going back to Ravens' Wood," Cassie reminded them. "He'll learn more there, so it's pointless speculating too much. Let's focus on the dunes. We didn't really detect anything there, did we?"

Ben shook his head. "No. Only around the dead bodies. What does a djinn need to kill people for? The only thing I can think of is for energy. Fuel. It's cold and wet out, so maybe the weather makes it weaker."

Dylan snorted. "Yeah, right. It really didn't look weaker. I reckon El has the right idea. Trap him rather than kill him. Which, admittedly, still poses lots of problems."

They had left El and Reuben at the smithy discussing the finer points of what vessel was the best to trap a djinn in and how to make it.

"Our job," Ben pointed out, "is to help them find it. I get the feeling regular tracking spells won't help. We need to work out where it might hide until it's ready to do whatever it intends."

"Ben! We're forgetting the conversation!" Cassie dug in her pack for the audio recorder. "Plus, I was still recording when it emerged from the forge."

Ben groaned. He knew there was something lurking at the back of his mind. Something he'd forgotten after actually encountering the arresting djinn with eyes of blue fire. "Of course. The whispered conversation."

"It was sort of sing-song," Cassie said, eyes slightly dreamy again. "One low voice, one higher, if 'voice' is even the right word." She played back the recording and passed it over to Ben, but even with the earphones, it was hard to pick up. "We need to analyse this. It's Class C. Impossible to work out properly until we filter it." She was referring to the classification system used for audio recordings.

"I can analyse the djinn, too. I was still filming when it exited the forge," Dylan said. "We analyse the shit out of everything, really. Maybe we'll see the salamander somewhere. If there are two voices, finding out what the other voice belongs to is important, as well as what it said."

"Or," Ben said, recalling what El had mentioned, "the metal itself was talking. The weapon. Although, if I recall correctly when I spoke to Shadow, she said metal sang. That's not the same as a conversation. Dragons were particularly attuned to their call, but fey are, too."

Dylan shrugged. "If there are three distinct sounds or voices, we'll find them back at the lab."

Cassie was searching through the audio, and finally she said, "I've found it! I managed to record the djinn. I'm so relieved." She played it back quietly so as not to disturb anyone else, although as usual, the backroom was mostly empty, spelled for their team to use, along with a small number of locals only. The djinn's voice boomed out his warning. *When this is over, you will all kneel to me, even you, Nephilim. The blood of my ancestors is strong, and you are no match for me.* "Why the hell would he need us to kneel to him? I mean, seriously. Why?"

"Perhaps it's a distraction," Ben suggested. "While we're worrying about that, he's planning something else."

"Which means we shouldn't hang about," Dylan said, draining his pint. "We should skip the meeting later. Or phone in to it instead. We have a mountain of research to investigate and catalogue."

Ben nodded. "I agree. In which case, is there anything else we can do here before we leave?"

"Other than see Dan," Cassie said, "no."

"Let's leave Dan for today," Dylan suggested. "We have enough to be doing. Besides, it's too wet to do anything outside. It's Biblical rain out there! And mist."

Mist caused by grieving trees. Ben loved Ravens' Wood, just like they all did, and had a healthy amount of respect for it of course, but he considered his bond deeper than that of most. He had travelled back in time. Seen it at its most majestic. Met the ancient fey who had once hunted in its sprawling forest. Encountered the deep magic that was soaked in the land, the roots, and the sap. It lingered in his blood and haunted his dreams, even all these months later. To discover that Nelaira was dead was almost a physical blow. He understood Eli's rage. He just expressed it differently.

He rose to his feet, weariness and grief hitting him, as if Ravens' Wood's mourning was soaking into his skin. "Good. Let's hope the djinn is drowning in it. Let's get out of here."

Fifteen

Alex had only just said goodbye to Ghost OPS when Newton entered the pub on his own, looking damp, bedraggled, and cross.

Alex didn't even need to ask what he wanted, and he poured him a lager shandy and placed it on the bar in front of Newton's regular stool. Zee was serving customers at the other end of the bar.

"Bad day?"

"Probably not as bad as yours," Newton answered grumpily as he shook the water off his coat and took a seat. "At least I didn't meet the bastard djinn."

"Yeah, but we avoided the rain. Dunes all sealed off now?"

"Yes, but with this weather, it's hardly likely anyone will go there, anyway."

"It's unlikely to last forever, and it's done now. Has the SOCO team finished?" He pitied them having to work in this weather.

"Yes, hours ago, so at least there's that. Of course, there are footprints everywhere, and we can't discount them. Not in the immediate vicinity, at least. However, I would imagine djinn don't leave footprints. The bodies are at the morgue. I'm waiting on IDs."

"Sorry." Alex had forgotten all about that in the drama of seeing the djinn. "No clues at all?"

"We're hoping a hotel might report someone missing, or a family member saying people didn't come home. Nothing yet. They're probably staying in a cottage or something. It's just shit. I don't know anything! Especially why."

Unfortunately, Alex had no new suggestions. "Did you speak to Jasper?"

"Yes." Newton drained half of his drink and wiped his lips with the back of hand. "There is supposedly a bit more activity noted at the Mount. Jasper knows some of the local fishermen. Apparently, the castle has had a few more visitors than usual. About a dozen arrived just before Beltane. All ferried over on private boats, and all still there. I presume they have some kind of bloody dragon ritual going on." He snorted and drank his shandy again. "We've done a bit more checking on the three on the beach last night."

"Who are they, again?"

"Friends of Wentworth's son. Peter and Veronica Mills, and Enzo Rinaldi."

"Not relatives?"

"No. Posh wankers, though. And shifters, of course. Therians. Ben proved our suspicions."

Alex leaned against the bar. "Other titled families?"

"No, but the Mills come from money, and Rinaldi's daddy is in banking in Milan. Seems there are more moneyed therians than I realised. Unfortunately, we don't know who else arrived, of course. I'm assuming they're all therians, but I can't set up cameras, and I haven't got the manpower to watch them all the time."

"And potentially," Alex said, trying to cheer him up, "it would all be boring bollocks anyway."

"True."

"Although, I would love to see what rituals they do in that temple cave."

"I'm not sure I would. Anyway, the three on the beach last night all went straight back to the Mount. We tracked them using traffic cameras. No loitering at Ravens' Wood."

"That's something, then. This is complicated enough without adding them to it. Where are Kendall and Moore?"

"With Hamid and Kev in the station. They're debriefing and then coming here for the meeting." He looked towards the windows where the rain continued to lash down. "Hopefully it will be better weather tomorrow when Moore goes back to the wood. I might go with him. I feel I should pay my respects."

"You still want the meeting tonight?"

"I think we should pool our knowledge. A lot seems to have happened in twenty-four hours." He stared into his drink, and then asked, "It's hard to know what to do next. I mean, where does a djinn even go?"

"I honestly have no idea. Just one more thing to add to the list."

"How's Briar?" Newton asked, changing the subject.

"Worried about her gran and the vision. She's with her now, with Eli."

"Eli?" Newton's eyes were wary. "Why him?"

"She was on the back of his bike when they arrived at Dante's smithy. They do work together, Newton."

"I know. I've just never known her to go on his bike before."

"Time was of the essence. At least she was there, but here they are now." Alex nodded at the front door as it opened and they ran in, drenched. Briar still wore Eli's leather jacket, and it swamped her small frame. Eli, although wet, didn't look the least bit affected by the weather at all, and amused, Alex noted pretty much everyone watched him stride across the pub to take a seat next to Briar and Newton.

Eli slicked his hair back, revealing his strong cheekbones and seductive eyes. He winked at Newton. "Don't worry, I kept her safe."

Briar glared at him and thrust the wet jacket into his arms. "Large white chardonnay please, Alex. I'm heading to the ladies' to dry off. Hi, Newton. *You*—" she viciously jabbed Eli's bicep with her finger. "Just don't!"

"Just don't what?" Newton asked as Briar walked away. "What's happened?"

Eli smirked. "I don't know. Pint of Skullduggery Ale please, Alex." He nodded to Zee at the end of the bar. "Brother."

Zee held his hand up. "Be over in five."

Newton persisted. "Well, it must mean something."

"She thinks I'm going to spill the beans."

"On what?"

"Her love life."

"She has a love life?"

Alex wasn't sure if he sensed trouble or mischief, but decided not to interfere as he silently poured their drinks.

Eli adjusted his position on the stool to face Newton across Briar's empty stool that was between them. "What would you do if you thought she had a love life?"

He stuttered, face flushing. "Wish her the best, I guess. Has she?"

"I'm working on it."

"For who? Not you!" Newton looked appalled. "She deserves more than being in your bloody harem."

Eli didn't look the slightest bit put out, and his smirk broadened. "Maybe I'm thinking of giving up my harem for love. Briar is funny, clever, thoughtful, and hot! I saw a whole new side to her today when the rain plastered her clothes to her body. Herne's horns." He gave a low whistle. "Wow. I must admit to having thoughts I've never had before. She's very…perky." He sipped his beer, his meaning clear.

Alex knew that Eli was teasing, but where Briar was concerned, Newton, had no sense of humour, and he was steadily looking more crazed, his knuckles white as he gripped his glass. "*Perky*?"

"I think," Alex said, quickly intervening, "that Eli is winding you up. Aren't you?" He shot a warning glance at Eli. At least he hoped he was. *Eli and Briar?* He liked Eli, obviously, but seeing them as a couple… *Really?*

Eli obviously wasn't finished yet, though, and rather than answer, stared at Newton. "Would you fight me for her?"

"Fight for her? With you?"

"I don't mean with your fists, Newton. For fuck's sake, keep up! Would you try to get in there first? Tell her how you feel. Ask her out, properly. Because I'm a contender. I mean, look at me. I'm as hot as they come. I have wings, and muscle definition that *Men's Health Magazine* would do a whole feature on."

Alex now absolutely knew Eli was teasing, and he bit down a grin as he jumped in. "It's pretty obvious to me, Newton," he said tentatively, because let's face it, no man ever wanted to discuss his love life with other men, "that you still like her. Maybe you should try again. I think she'd be interested. Not that we've discussed anything, of course!" He cocked his head at Eli, questioningly.

Eli leaned across to Newton, still provoking him. "How would it make you feel if we were together? Knowing we were having seriously great sex and we were all-in as a couple—bells, whistles, and everything. Would it eat you up inside? Would you forever regret not trying? Again. Because you never really got your head around Hunter."

"Eli," Newton ground out between clenched teeth. "You are treading on thin ice."

"Thank fuck for that. An honest reaction, at last. Then do something about it, Newton. Before I do."

Avery raged around her attic for a good fifteen minutes after she angrily left her mother and Helena in her living room.

She lit the candles with so much intent that they flared a foot in the air before settling down. The smell of scorched wood on the bookshelves had her hurrying over to make sure she hadn't ignited anything else. Then, because it was cold and the rain was battering the attic windows, she lit the fire, incense, and the lamps, slowly moving through all her routines that acted to stabilise her mood and ground her magic.

Mind racing, she adjusted the baskets, tidied books, cleaned her magical equipment, and organised her crystals, although they were fine just as they were. Finally, she sat on the sofa and glared at the offending fire where she had cast the spell, and it was there that her emotions overwhelmed her until the fire was seen only through a veil of tears. She was an idiot. A complete idiot. *Had she really expected a heartfelt reunion full of regret, confessions, and maternal bonding? Of course not. But had she expected to be yelled at on her own doorstep? No.* In fact, although she had the utmost faith in her own magic and her grimoires, she didn't really expect that it would work, especially so quickly. Unfortunately, despite all the reassurances that she'd given Helena, she hadn't considered the consequences at all. And now her mother was downstairs talking to Helena. As Avery should be.

Pull yourself together. Go downstairs and talk like a proper adult.

It was as if with her mother's arrival, she had regressed to her sixteen-year old self, and that was not the attitude she wanted to show at all. She had thrived since her mother and sister had left. *Thrived!* Her magic was strong, she represented her local coven in the larger Cornwall Coven, and she was respected. She had friends, Alex, and a great life. And Helena and Clea had stood up for her. She took a deep breath and released it slowly. She was better than this, and she would prove it. Cool, calm, and collected.

However, just as she was about to head downstairs, movement in the fireplace caught her eye. She had been staring almost vacantly into the flames as she wiped away her tears, but a small golden orb drifted into the fire and settled in the glowing logs at the bottom.

Suddenly alert, she edged forward, eyes on the orb that grew, elongated, and then transformed into a curled lizard made of firelight that nestled into the flames like her cats tucked themselves into corners of the sofa. She glanced over at Circe who was curled next to her. She opened an eye and closed it again, completely uninterested.

Holy shit. The salamander was in her fire. *Did that mean the djinn was, too? Or would it follow?*

She leapt to her feet and raced to the top of the stairs as silently as possible, progressing only a few treads down, so she could still see into the attic. Voices carried to her from below, the conversation sounding calm and measured. Unwilling to go down any further, she called in a low voice, "Helena! Come here!" She lobbed a witch-light down the stairs, sending it bobbing in their general direction. It was dim downstairs, the storm bringing an early darkness. "Helena!"

In moments, Helena and Diana appeared at the bottom of the steps, both staring at her in confusion. She could see traces of her mother in Clea now, but this wasn't the time.

"Helena, come up quickly. The salamander is here! And be quiet." She whirled around and then approached the fireplace carefully. Holding her breath, she was relieved to see it was still curled in the logs, embers shifting around it as what appeared to be little puffs of exhalations made them move. "See it?" she whispered as Helena stood next to her.

Diana started to speak far too loudly. "What is…"

"*Shush!*" they both said furiously.

Avery pointed at the fire and whispered again. "We have a visitor." She put her finger to her lips.

Helena pulled them both backwards to the middle of the room, attention still on the fire. "When did it arrive?"

"Minutes ago. It floated down the fireplace in orb form, and then settled in the flames. What should we do? Can we catch it?"

"What is it?" Diana asked, alarmed. "A lizard?"

"Salamander. A fire elemental." Avery studied her room, filtering through all the various jars, baskets, and boxes she had. *A glass jar would be the obvious answer, but how big should it be? And how to seal it without hurting it?*

Helena's brow wrinkled as she considered their options. "Did you summon it?"

"No. I was just thinking about things, and it appeared."

"Mmm. You released a surge of magic earlier. I felt it. I wonder if that's what called it. And the fire, of course. Are the Beltane woods still in it?"

"Well, most of the ashes from last night are still there. I collected some this morning. There will be traces of the dragon ingredients."

"*Dragon*?" Diana asked, voice rising in surprise.

Avery ignored her. "Do you think it can feel them?"

"I think it's highly possible. It's a creature of the Otherworld, so it's magical by nature, and by all accounts it belongs to their Realm of Fire. It thrives in heat, obviously, so it needs somewhere to rest." Helena edged closer again. "I suspect that it was drawn by your magic *and* the fire—including the magical ingredients."

"But how did it get through my protection spells?"

"Perhaps they weren't specific enough. Or it means no harm."

"Which means that the djinn and the salamander are two separate things, just as we speculated," Avery mused. "And just as Cassie heard."

Helena wiggled her hand in a *possibly* motion. "That's too much to presume. She could have detected the metal singing, as we discussed. Ghost OPS will tell us more later, once they've analysed everything. In the meantime, we should take this opportunity to learn as much as we can. Where is Raven when we need him?"

Avery shrugged. Her familiar did not always stay in the house. Sometimes he vanished for weeks, which was a relief, on occasions. As wonderful as he was, he was also loud and bossy. "Doing Raven things. I could call him, of course, but if we can solve our issues without him, that would save overcomplicating matters." She stared meaningfully at her mother.

"Oh," Diana said loftily. "Am I in the way now? You should have thought that through first. Do you think either of you could spare me the time to tell me exactly what the fuck is going on?"

Helena tutted. "Language."

"I think we are all old enough to cope."

"Well," Avery said, too focussed on the salamander to explain anything to her mother, "one thing is clear. We need to keep the salamander here. If it is a fire elemental that is distinct to the djinn, maybe it can help us. We need to keep it safe and comfortable." Which sounded ridiculous, as if she was adopting it like a pet. "I certainly don't feel anything threatening at the moment. Neither does Circe." The cat was still curled in the corner of the sofa, ears pricked and paws twitching, as if dreaming.

"What if it killed those two people?" Helena asked. "We're risking our lives. Remember, it seemed that the salamander became very large within the flames."

"What reason," Avery persisted, feeling more and more that she was right, "would a salamander have for killing people?"

"Energy to continue to live."

"There were loads of fires on the beach. It didn't need them. Whereas," she added, "the djinn killed Nelaira. We absolutely know that because the dryads saw it happen. Plus, when El and

Reuben confronted him about the human deaths, he didn't deny it. He must have killed them for some warped reason we don't understand right now."

Helena finally nodded. "Fair point. All right, we'll try and keep it here."

"I'll keep the fire going and add magical woods, and," Avery gestured towards the grimoires, mood lifting at the prospect of progress, "keep searching for salamander spells. In fact, Mother dearest, you can help."

"I didn't want to end up in the middle of any magical conundrums. That's why I left!"

"True." Avery turned to face her properly, trying to adopt a conciliatory tone. "I'm sorry. I summoned you selfishly, and have no idea what you might have abandoned, or who, to come here. Call it Beltane madness, or whatever you like. I'll apologise to Bryony if she arrives, too. Feel free to leave at any time. However, my reasons for calling you still stand. I'm curious to know where you went, what you did, and what you do now. You know, life stuff! It would be nice to think you might be slightly curious about us, too. However, please feel free to leave if you hate it."

Her mother exchanged an unreadable glance with Helena. "I have been briefly informed of what's happened here in recent years, and after seeing what's happening now, it seems I'm long overdue a visit. So, I'll stay. But I would prefer a bed elsewhere, if that's possible."

Avery wasn't sure if it was relief she felt, or surprise, but she nodded anyway. "I'll call Reu and El, and message everyone so they're up to date with our latest development."

"I," Helena said, urging Diana to sit at the worn wooden table, "will introduce you to our old family grimoire."

And just like that, after Avery had gently added logs to the fire and watched the salamander basking and stretching in the heat, they sat at the table to consult on spells together—Maiden, Mother, and Crone—as if it was the most natural thing in the world.

$\mathcal{S}ixteen$

Newton had retreated to Kendall and Zee's flat above The Wayward Son to organise his thoughts for the meeting later that evening.

He needed to plan their next moves, collate their known information, discuss strategies with his sergeants, and more than anything else, recover from the shock of his conversation with Eli. *Was he seriously considering pursuing a relationship with Briar? Was she with him?* The notion of some future in which Briar was seeing somebody else had of course hovered on the periphery of his mind ever since she had split up from Hunter, but faced with the very real prospect of her actually hooking up with Eli—who was unbelievably good-looking and no doubt a very skilled lover—horrified him. The thought brought out a cold sweat. He had to admit that he couldn't bear it. *But what else could he do? Leave White Haven? Change his job?* Neither of those options appealed to him at all.

Which left fighting for her, as Eli suggested. *What did that mean? Flowers? Confessing his feelings? Meals? Wooing her?* He stood in the middle of the living room not seeing his surroundings. *Was he that out of touch? Had his job consumed so much of his life that he'd forgotten what to do outside of it?* Suddenly, his future stretched ahead of him. Loveless. Wedded to the job.

Forever lonely. His house empty, dark and grim, as if he lived in a perpetual twilight. While over at Briar's it was all laughter and shagging. He'd enjoyed his brief time with her. Breakfasts on the veranda, cooking over a glass of wine, talking on her sofa into the early hours of the morning. Until his stupid witch aversion got in the way. *What was that even about? Not Briar, that was certain.* With hindsight, it was more to do with the circumstances and the sheer overwhelming evidence of magic that had just unnerved him. Those feelings didn't exist anymore. He was neck-deep in it now, and fully accepted the facts as much as any of his paranormal friends.

Which is when it became very clear to him that he absolutely *did* need to fight for her. If he didn't tell her how he really felt, he would forever regret it. "And if she doesn't feel the same, I'll just have to suck it up," he murmured.

"Suck what up?" Kendall said from the door.

Newton jerked around in shock. "Hernes's hairy bollocks! Are you trying to kill me?"

"I'm entering my flat, you great bloody pillock. Sorry. Guv," she said quickly, to cover for abusing him. "Are you all right? You look miles away."

"I'm thinking." He wiped his brow, hoping she hadn't heard the first part of that sentence.

"In the dark? Mind if I put some lights on?"

How long had he been standing there, lost in his thoughts? The last dregs of evening had been swallowed by the heavy clouds and unceasing rain. Only a pale light was coming through the kitchen windows from the streetlights, and he felt cold. "Yes, of course. I was thinking about our meeting. Where's Moore?"

"Picking up three fish and chips from the chippy on the corner. We're starving and thought you'd be, too."

Kendall moved through the flat, lighting lamps and the fire so that the flames blazed, driving away the sudden chill. The flat looked different to when Alex lived there. For a start, it now contained Avery's sofa, there were a lot more soft furnishings, and artwork graced the walls. The kitchen was cluttered, and both Zee and Kendall's belongings were spread across the room.

"It's hard to believe we were on the beach enjoying Beltane last night," she said. "The weather is bloody awful."

Newton moved to the window. "I see the mist is still thick, too. Still coming from Ravens' Wood?"

"Unfortunately. The whole place feels weird. I've got used to the subtle changes over the past few months."

"Have you?" He leaned against the frame and watched her fill the kettle with water. "How do you mean?"

"You must know. You live here. White Haven has its own distinct energy." Kendall paused to watch him, her short, damp hair sticking up where she'd run her hands through it. "You sort of feel it when you visit, but you can't pinpoint it. The age of it, the feeling that secrets hide around every corner. But when you live here, you start to feel the magic. The little hum that sits under everything. When that changes, I feel it, and right now, its mood is depressed. Squashed."

"That's a very interesting observation," Newton said, as she busied around doing her no doubt usual routine of making tea and pulling plates and cutlery from drawers. "I've lived here my whole life and hadn't considered it."

"Because you've always lived here."

He shrugged, slightly put out. "Perhaps I've taken it for granted." *Like lots of things.*

"You probably sense it and don't always notice, or your mood just changes with it. A sort of symbiosis." Newton wasn't sure he liked the sound of that, but he just nodded as Kendall continued. "I assume today's mood is because Ravens' Wood's mourning is spreading through the town. Plus there have been two very gruesome deaths. That has obviously unsettled everyone. Hamid and Kev have been approached by lots of people seeking reassurance, which of course they have given as much as possible. All day people have been keen to tell them of unusual or suspicious activity, but fortunately haven't mentioned djinns or salamanders. Nothing has leapt out as being worth following up. The vicar at All Souls has added an extra service today and left the doors open all day, too."

"James," Newton said. "Nice bloke. Decent."

"I remember him well from Samhain." Kendall smiled and shrugged. "I've made sure to get to know him, seeing as I'm living here now. I don't want to tread on Hamid and Kev's toes, but I'll try and see him tomorrow, if I have time."

A brisk knock at the door heralded Moore's arrival with the welcoming smell of fish and chips, and it struck Newton how hungry he was. Within minutes of Moore drying himself off with a towel, they were eating around the kitchen table, planning their next moves. Curious about Kendall's comment about White Haven and symbiotic moods, Newton mentioned it to Moore.

He nodded vigorously as he dipped a chip in ketchup. "Well, I don't live here, but I come here often enough. This place has a quality. Some of the other coastal towns do too, but nothing quite like this. We work in the paranormal world, though, so we are sensitive to it. I guarantee lots of people won't notice it, especially if they're just here for a few days."

"But enough do," Kendall pointed out. "That's why the festivals are so popular. I reckon more practitioners come here, too. Maybe that's why those two were targeted on the beach. Maybe they engaged in the magical arts. Not necessarily witches. Might be just regular people, of course."

"Well," Newton said, partly dreading the next day, "I need to go to the post-mortem tomorrow, which means I can't go to Ravens' Wood with you, Moore, like I planned."

Moore looked startled. "I didn't know you were."

"It was an idle thought until Arthur called." He didn't like post-mortems, but who did except Forensic Pathologists? "Who will you go with?"

"I was going to discuss it tonight. What time are they all arriving?"

"Half an hour or so," Newton said, checking his watch. "I think Eli wants to go to Ravens' Wood tonight with Zee. I guess that's your other option, but the weather is crap."

Moore didn't look put off at all. "If they're going anyway, I'll tag along. I can only get so wet."

It struck Newton that perhaps he should discuss his Briar dilemma with Moore, but he quickly rejected it. He didn't need more opinions clouding his judgement or judging his ineptitude. He just needed to get on with it. *Soon.*

Seventeen

Reuben had been shaken up by the events at Dante's smithy. He hadn't anticipated coming face to face with an enormous djinn of indeterminate power. A prince, at that.

However, he had been heartened by Dante's acceptance of their current dilemma and his willingness to help El. He had left them to it for a few hours and gone surfing, despite the rain. Although, *surfing* might have been an exaggeration. It was more like paddleboarding in the shallows that enabled him to regain his equilibrium, as it always did when surrounded by his natural element, and also allowed for a chat with Silver, his water horse familiar, amidst the crashing surf. Unfortunately, Silver had no useful news to impart, but at least no tales of doom, either. He was as intrigued by the whole event as the witches were.

At present, he and the other witches, including Caspian, plus Newton's team and the two Nephilim were gathered in Kendall's flat, and Ghost OPS had phoned in. Normally these meetings were fairly relaxed affairs, as they all knew each other well, but of course Avery's mother, Diana, had never been there before, and she was bristling with a mix of resentment and curiosity from her seat at the dining table, eyes darting everywhere, assessing, listening, and generally being unnerving. Everyone had been welcoming enough, but with a strong dash of wary reserve.

Especially Alex, who regarded her as if a snake had reared in their midst. Reuben was more than happy to have her stay at his house, though. He was planning on asking her just what the hell she had been thinking all those years earlier. However, now they were pooling information, and Reuben was sharing the conversation he'd had with Silver.

"Well," Reuben told everyone, "Silver said much the same thing as he had about dragons. Djinn have strong Otherworldly energy that can cause havoc with our own, but he has no idea what Prince Qabas might want, other than the dragon eggs, seeing as that was what he was arguing with Nelaira about. Ultimately, we really need more information about djinn. Can't we call Shadow?"

"I managed to talk to her earlier," Zee said. He lounged on the rug in front of the fire. "She said the djinn are in general friendly, but aloof. They have their own customs, and have had plenty of issues with dragons in the past. They are skilled metalworkers, and their tears produce diamonds called Tear Diamonds, very imaginatively. They hardly ever cry, apparently, which makes their diamonds incredibly valuable. Shadow also stresses that djinn are not salamanders and do not shapeshift, other than to change into grains of sand or smoke. It means they can travel very quickly, and very likely means he is sheltering in the sand or somewhere underground."

"A bit like vampires, then," Alex suggested. "So it's sort of shapeshifting."

"She also said," Zee added, "they have small horns on their heads and talonlike nails on their feet and hands, but some can manipulate their appearance better than others. Plus, some of them get on better with dragons than the rest of the fey, and some even ride them."

"Ride them?" Moore almost spilled his drink. "I thought they were deadly!"

"They are, but if reared from birth they are more easily tamed, and of course djinn do not fear their fire. Plus, dragons love the song of metals, and djinn weave those well. It helps subdue them. They weave songs into dragon bridles." Zee had clearly been hoarding this information, because he looked very pleased with himself as everyone stared in shock. "Cool, right? It is possible, although she's never heard of him, that this prince is of the type to train dragons. Just a theory. Or he just wants to trade them because of the very pricey gems and metals that dragons can provide. One way or another, he *will* try to steal those eggs."

Newton groaned. "Bollocks! I told you we should never have kept those damn eggs, but you said they would be safe in the bloody wood! Now we have even more problems." He pointed at Eli, who he had seemed at odds with all night. "This is *your* fault. You swore Nelaira would keep them safe. Now she's dead."

Eli regarded Newton icily. "Actually, it was Shadow's idea to hide them in the wood, and just to remind you, Nelaira is dead because she refused to give them up. So far they are still safely in the wood's innermost sanctum where no one can get to them. I have one hundred percent faith that they will remain safe there, but I'll go later to pay my respects and find out exactly what is happening."

"He's right," Zee added, supporting Eli. "If we had stored those eggs at the farmhouse, they might already have been stolen. If necessary, we will camp in Ravens' Wood to protect them, but

I doubt they need our help. The wood already chased off the djinn."

"Exactly," Briar said, intervening swiftly because Newton was still bristling. "The djinn's arrival is completely unexpected, and I honestly had no idea that portals opened during Beltane, or that there would be some kind of mass paying of respects at the Great Wedding."

"None of us did," Reuben said, thinking back to that crazy Beltane night twelve months earlier. "How could we know?"

Newton gave a begrudging grunt and paced to the kitchen counter, no doubt to calm down.

"And the salamander that's currently sleeping in my fireplace?" Avery asked Zee.

"Possibly the djinn's own elemental that he uses to forge weapons, or just an interloper, much like the djinn. Shadow agrees that it was probably some type of weapon that the djinn was making at Dante's."

"Unless someone summoned it, as we discussed earlier," El suggested. "As we've read, some witches used to work with salamanders. They are a powerful tool in witchcraft, if you know how to use them."

"Did you search your grimoire again?" Avery asked.

"I haven't had time, sorry. I've just been too busy, but I remember that some practitioners believe that tiny salamanders exist in every spark and every fire. Unseen, but potent. Elemental beings that are present in our world all the time. I don't believe that, as I've seen no evidence for it. I think it's a Medieval belief that some people like the idea of. However, they clearly exist in some form, because there's one in your fire, and it might help us craft a vessel for the djinn. Big if, of course."

"Can we borrow your grimoire?" Avery asked over the ripple of muted chatter that El's suggestion had caused. "I'm researching them now, but seeing as you have spells, we should check those, too."

"Of course. It's still in my flat, so just fly straight in. My old grimoire, of course."

"Brilliant. Thank you. I'll go as soon as the meeting is done."

Newton frowned. "Do you really think someone summoned it, El?"

"We can't discount it. Dylan saw it in the fire, but someone still could have summoned it, rather than it simply came over from the Otherworld. Maybe a witch did and lost it." She shrugged. "I'm just throwing it out there. If it's been summoned for spell-work, maybe it is used to working with a witch. I don't know, though. It's just a suggestion," she said, trying to alleviate the rising air of worry in the group.

This just added another dimension to the whole issue, and Reuben didn't like it at all, but he trusted they would get to the bottom of it.

"I have an excellent piece of news," Zee said, trying to cheer everyone up. "I spoke to Nahum earlier. You've heard of the Moonfell witches?"

The witches had, but Kendall shook her head. "No. Who are they?"

"A coven of witches who live at Moonfell Manor in London. Edge of Richmond Park, to be exact. The house is amazing, apparently, and the family is steeped in magical ancestors. Even more importantly, they recently found a Wayfinder that allows them to track shifters. Djinn are marked on it, so I asked if we could borrow it. Nahum will call me later once he's spoken to

Birdie. It's Beltane, so they've been having a few issues of their own," Zee said, grinning broadly. "Sounds like a fun place."

A flurry of questions broke out around the group, and several separate conversations started up. Reuben turned to El. "This could be a game changer. If we can track it, and you and Dante can make a suitable vessel to trap it in, that's one big issue dealt with. How we deal with him then is another matter."

"But it could take days to make this container. Dante is still working on it now, and I'm heading back there later. We need to put serious hours into this." El had a smudge of soot on her face, and she smelled of smoke and metal, which to Reuben was very sexy. "In fact, I can see me living at the forge for the next few days. Of course, the salamander may speed things up. Maybe we need to consider how to move it."

"And use it safely," he pointed out. "I'll bring food and drink, but you do need to sleep, and you can't sleep there."

"I know." She squeezed his hand. "I'll stay at yours." She glanced over at Diana, who was tight-lipped as she listened and observed. "I won't leave you alone with her, and Bryony might want my flat—if she arrives. Or maybe Helena will, and Bryony can stay with Avery. I just don't know if I can contain my annoyance with either of them."

"Nor me," Reuben confessed, "but they'll have their reasons, as do your parents, even if we don't agree with them. Is this stirring things up for you again?" El had spent some intense weeks after the wedding dealing with her feelings about her parents' refusal to accept her current lifestyle, and was still working through it. He hated seeing how upset it had made her.

"A little. I can't get rid of years of frustration in a matter of weeks, so I know how Avery feels, and I can't believe how her damn mother can't see the hurt she's caused. Selfish cow." She shot Diana a look of pure annoyance.

"Avery is amazing," Reuben said, looking over at who he considered the de facto leader of their coven, "just like you. You both found your own way. We all have, one way or another. Look at Briar! Anyway," he shrugged, "we have djinn to consider. Just make sure you keep your protection at Dante's strong."

She kissed his cheek. "I will."

They both turned their attention to the rest of the room as Helena asked, "How soon can the Wayfinder be brought here?"

"By tomorrow," Zee said. "Nahum will drive down, with instructions to use it, hopefully."

"So for now, it's a waiting game," Alex said, sagging back into the chair. "If I have time I'll try spirit-walking. The djinn's energy is so distinct from our own, I should be able to see him. His aura will be very obvious. Of course, if he's underground or buried in sand, it won't be so easy. He must be sheltering somewhere."

"If he's plotting something," Reuben pointed out, "he won't be sleeping under the sand, surely. He'll have a base of operation somewhere that's dry and secure."

"Which means we need to narrow places down," Alex said, frowning. "I'll start compiling a list."

"I'll help you," Kendall said. "We need a perimeter of a good few miles all around."

"There are those passages under West Haven," Ben reminded them, his voice emanating from Alex's phone that lay on the coffee table. "Where we found the vampires."

Briar shuddered. "I do not want to go down there ever again!"

Kendall looked equally horrified. "I didn't know you'd encountered vampires!"

"Long story," Caspian informed her. "Not a tale for tonight. But Ben is right. We need to consider it. Those passageways are extensive, and there's probably still access from the beach. Easy for a djinn to find, I would imagine."

Kendall had already started scribbling in her notebook.

"What about the salamander?" Moore asked Avery. "What will you do with it?"

"Keep it safe, and try to discover as much as we can about it. I just hope it's still there now. I put lots of logs on the fire to keep it comfortable, and surrounded it with protection so that the house doesn't burn down. How nuts does that sound? We should probably get back there," Avery said, looking to Helena.

"I can't stay long," Helena said. "Remember, I'm going to see Morwenna's ex tonight." She smiled wickedly at the rest of the group. "In spirit form."

"You're doing what now?" Briar said, looking at her and Caspian in alarm. "I thought we were making a plan?"

"As Helena pointed out," Caspian said, amused, "we were overcomplicating matters. She has a more direct idea that I rather like. So does Morwenna, when I suggested it to her earlier. She wants this to be over now. She's tired of it all."

Reuben laughed at Helena's mischievous expression. "You're the ghost of vengeance present?"

"Something like that." Helena looked smug. "I shall leave Clea comfortable on the sofa while I lay out the new plan for Ysella's wellbeing."

"What if you run into trouble?" Moore asked. "What then?"

"Trust me. I have it all in hand. You do your thing, Moore, and I shall do mine." She looked to Caspian. "I don't need you to be at Avery's, but you can be if you wish."

Caspian nodded and smiled, and it was obvious that he was much happier and more content recently. Reuben was pleased for him. "Yes, please. Morwenna doesn't want to be there, but I'll report back afterwards, if that's okay?"

"Of course. Just be aware that it might take a while, and I'll need an hour or so to prepare."

"Time for a sneaky pint, then. Seems a shame not to while I'm here."

Reuben knew he wouldn't want Helena's spirit descending on him in the middle of the night. She'd be terrifying. But frankly, it was what Morwenna's ex deserved. Everyone was stirring as if getting ready to leave, and so far Diana had barely said a word except in greeting. Reuben figured it must be intimidating to turn up as a newcomer to such a large group who clearly knew each other well. It gave him immense satisfaction that she should see how full Avery's life was. He was looking forward to expanding on it.

"Diana," he called to her, ""I presume you're coming with me?"

"Yes," she said, fixing her direct gaze on him, "I suppose I am. I'd like to follow you there. My car is at Avery's. I think I know where you are, but it's been a while."

"Of course. No problem. El is heading to Dante's now, but will return later." Then he had another thought, thinking that he could do more than just babysit Avery's mother for the night. Briar had looked really concerned earlier after she'd related Tamsyn's strange Seer state of that afternoon. It had worried everyone. "Briar, do you want me to look in on Tamsyn? It's close enough, and I don't mind."

She smiled broadly at him, but darted a nervous look at Diana. "That's very sweet of you, but have you got the time?"

"I've always got time for Tamsyn," he reassured her. "I want to hear more about this stag, too. Plus, I'm sure Diana would love to meet your grandmother."

Startled, Diana just nodded. "Yes, of course."

"We'll get your car first, of course, and drop it off at my place," Reuben said. "Then you can come with me."

"Who's coming with us, then?" Eli asked everyone as he stood and stretched, rolling his shoulders so that his t-shirt rode up to show his abs, and gave Briar a lazy grin. Almost like he was flexing on purpose. Something was going on, but Reuben wasn't sure what. "Just Moore? We should keep the numbers low, in my opinion."

"Agreed," Zee said, standing next to him. "It will be easier for us to stick together."

"Well," Briar started, "I was wondering—"

Alex hurriedly cut in. "I think we witches should focus on spells for djinns and salamanders while we have the time, and get a good night's sleep. Tomorrow could bring more unexpected issues. I have to work for another couple of hours, but then I'm done."

"I second that," Newton said. "Knowledge about controlling djinns is our priority. I'll help Kendall with the list of places, though, before I go home."

Briar looked puzzled, but then nodded. "Yes, fair enough. I'd rather not go back to Ravens' Wood tonight, if I'm honest, but equally, I'm pretty sure nothing will be in my grimoire about djinn."

"Moore," Newton said, "did you catch up with Stan today, about the wood for the town fire?"

"No. It's on my list for tomorrow."

"What about you three?" Alex asked as he picked up his phone and addressed Ghost OPS. "I presume you have plenty to be doing?"

"*Lots* of analysis," Ben said, sounding as if he was moaning, but Reuben knew he loved it. "Good luck, everyone. We'll be in touch tomorrow. Avery, if that salamander is still at yours, we're coming to see it!"

As they all gathered coats and said their goodbyes, Reuben dragged Alex aside while El spoke to Avery, Diana, and Briar. "Alex, is there something I should know? What's happening with Eli and Newton? Things seem frosty."

Alex rolled his eyes as he stepped out onto the landing, pulling Reuben with him. "Eli sort of challenged Newton for Briar."

For a moment, Reuben just gaped at him. "What the actual fuck? Are you serious?"

"Yes. But Eli wasn't. He just wanted to goad Newton into getting things together with Briar. Well, I think so," he qualified, looking not at all sure. "But maybe I'm wrong. It's not like he admitted that to me. However, if Eli wanted to make a move, he'd just do it. Why warn Newton?"

"When did this happen? How?"

"Late afternoon, after they came from Tamsyn's. At the bar. Briar was in the loo. I haven't had a chance to speak to Briar privately, so I know fuck all, really. Frankly, I don't think I want to know. This is on them."

"You must be kidding? This is a small group. It could be disastrous." Reuben liked happy friends, not brooding discontent.

"I know, but I have other things to worry about, like Prince Bloody Qabas. The endless questions of Jago, my chef, who, if you'd forgotten, is now very interested in all things paranormal. He's been pestering me today—again. *And* the unwelcome arrival of my almost mother-in-law. There are a lot of women in my house right now, and another due imminently! I like women, but not intense family bloody reunions!"

"You're getting a bit high-pitched there, mate. I am taking Diana off your hands." And then, thinking it made him sound sexist, said, "Well, Avery's actually."

Alex took a deep breath and rolled his shoulders. "For which we are both very grateful. Thank you."

He lowered his voice. "She really didn't think that spell through."

"Tell me something I don't know!"

Wanting to help his old friend, he said, "We need some quiet time over a whiskey. My snug is always available, as is a bed if you want to get bladdered and sleep it off."

"When this is done, I might well take you up on that. Better get back to the bar now, though. Good luck tonight." After an exchange of manly hugs, Alex headed back downstairs, and Reuben backed into the wall to let his friends leave the flat.

Time to get to know Diana.

Eighteen

Helena was pleased that Diana had left. Her energy was not conducive to haunting Jed, whereas with just her, Caspian, and Avery in the attic room, the mood would hopefully be more grounded.

Avery and Helena had driven to the pub rather than use witch-flight, as they had accompanied Diana, so the first thing either of them did when they arrived home was race up the stairs to the attic to check on the salamander.

"Thank the gods, it's still there," Helena said breathlessly, wishing she'd remember that Clea's body did not like running. The salamander was curled amongst the crumbling logs, sleeping, and she picked up another chunk of wood and placed it carefully in the fire. "It's really very sweet."

Avery giggled. "It's like tucking in a baby."

"A very hot one." Helena straightened up. "Now I'm even more confused as to why it's still here."

"Because it's warm and magical here, must be. I mean, who knows what salamanders do or want? Perhaps, like cats, they sleep for most of the day. Where will you leave Clea?"

"On this sofa, if that's okay. You can keep an eye on things while I'm gone. Well, you and Caspian, when he arrives. I presume you'll be poring through the grimoires for the next few hours?"

"Yes." Avery walked back to the pile of books that were strewn over the wooden table. "I'll re-examine all the spells and stories we found earlier, and try to collate a helpful pile. I'll pick out useful snippets and put them into some kind of logic. There's just so many of them! Which reminds me, I need to fly to El's for her grimoire."

"Just try and keep salamanders distinct from dragons, that will be useful. It seems to me," Helena said, idly turning pages of a book on Medieval spells, "that they are two distinct things. Dragons and dragon-named herbs are spell ingredients. Salamanders are fire elementals that *assist* with spells."

"And it might help El," Avery said, repeating what El had suggested earlier, and both witches twisted to look back at the fire.

"If we can work out how to use it, it will be perfect," Helena said with sure conviction. "What better way to make a prison for a djinn than with the aid of a salamander?"

"*If* they're not already connected."

"They aren't together yet. While I'm in the spirit world, I'll see if I can find anything out."

"How?"

"There are many old spirits where I'm going. I just need to ask around."

"Of course." Avery shrugged. "A chat amongst the inhabitants of the spirit world. Nothing could be simpler."

"Oh! Sarcasm now? Easy for me, a ghost. I spend most of my existence there."

Avery's eyes clouded with worry, as they always did with such a subject. "I don't understand how you can live there. It sounds cold and formless and unpleasant."

"I'm dead there, not living." It was impossible to explain to a warm-blooded creature with a physical body. Only Alex, of all the witches, could understand how different it was, and even he saw it from the perspective of the living, not dead. "Avery, I'm one of them. I've been there for hundreds of years, and I'm powerful in that world, more than I am in this one. Those of us with magic never lose it, even there, and I know my way around. Don't misunderstand me, of course. There are no maps. No fixed places. Time does not exist. In fact, it's weird to return to a body. There I feel no heat, need no light, no gravity. I'm just energy and intention."

Avery nodded and leaned against the table, arms crossed, eyes firmly on Helena. "Let's talk practicalities, then. How do you get to Jed?"

"Distance has no meaning in the spirit world. It's not like actual spirit-walking, either. I am not tethered by Clea. When I leave her, my spirit will be free to go wherever, so I'll travel the highways and byways," she said dreamily. "I'll manifest when he's alone."

"What if there are magical traps?"

"They're not expecting me," she reiterated. "There may well be protection spells because Kitty and John are not stupid, but unless they have been extremely thorough, I'll be okay. It's not like I'll blunder in, either. If the worst happens, then do as you normally do. Bring Clea around gently and take her to the home. But give me a day or two, just in case."

"That long?"

"I suspect that by dawn we'll be done. I'm just being cautious. I can be, you know."

Avery did not look convinced. Her lips were pressed together, and her chin was jutting mutinously. "Could Alex help if you're in trouble?"

"No! Do not send Alex." She stepped forward and squeezed Avery's hands. "I have this in hand. Now, I'll prepare a potion for Clea to relax her. I'm glad Caspian will be here with you. He will stop you worrying, as will Alex, of course, when he gets back later. I'm worried more about your mother than my night's adventures."

Avery groaned and sank into the chair. "My mother. What was I thinking?"

"You wanted to see her. Now you have." Helena couldn't help but smile, though she quickly suppressed it. "It's...interesting. Have you calmed down now?"

"I'm still inwardly seething that she was so rude, but if I put myself in her position, I would shout, too. Then again, I'd never abandon my children in the first place. It must have been weird," she said thoughtfully, "to have received a pull to somewhere that you can't control. It makes me think that it's what it must have been like for Morwenna. That uncontrollable urge that you have no power over. You know, if your plan doesn't work, we can summon Jed here! See how he likes it."

"An interesting suggestion, but let's try my way first. Earlier," Helena said, starting to collect her potion ingredients, "while sitting right here, we chitchatted about polite nothingness with your mother, but you need to talk properly. When you're both calm."

"I know. Did you, while I was up here?"

"So-so. We spent most of that time talking about Clea and me and how it works. She said you looked well, and said she always knew you'd be a powerful witch. We'd have talked more, but our little visitor arrived." Helena collected the final herb and placed it on the table. "At least she'll stay a few more days."

"Does she work? I don't even know that."

Helena smiled. "She's a librarian for a private collection. A love of books is something you have in common. Something we all do."

Avery's eyes widened in surprise. "A librarian? For what private collection?"

"We didn't get into it. Something to ask tomorrow."

"And Bryony?"

"We didn't get around to her, either. If she arrives, it's something we can ask directly."

Helena fell silent as she prepared the potion for Clea, and Avery used witch-flight to go to El's flat. She just hoped Bryony's arrival would be far less dramatic than Diana's.

The rain had eased by the time Eli arrived at Ravens' Wood with Zee and Moore.

All three had travelled together from the pub in Moore's car, the Nephilim reasoning that they could fly home afterwards, and Moore could continue home without having to return to town.

"Are you sure you want to do this?" Eli asked Moore as the DS pulled on his thick waterproof jacket and grabbed a large, heavy torch.

"I'm sure." He patted his chest. "I have my stab-proof vest on under this, just in case. It makes me feel a little better protected. I have no idea what to expect if I encounter a djinn—or even an angry dryad."

Moore's eyes held a gleam of excitement that wasn't tempered by the threat of danger, reinforcing how much he loved Ravens' Wood and the paranormal. A far cry from Newton, who respected it but still distrusted it. Eli still held a trace of doubt about whether he was a good fit for Briar, but then swept it aside. Newton respected the witches' magic and the Nephilim's abilities, and trusted what he knew to be good. That was only sensible. Plus, he loved Briar.

"Just stay close to us," Zee advised Moore as he removed his t-shirt, unfurled his wings, and drew his sword. "It's very different in there at night. I just want to clarify a few things before we head inside. I know we've come to pay our respects, but what do we need to find out?"

"Ways to target the djinn," Moore said. "Weaknesses. How to send him back. And we need to know those eggs are protected."

"And," Eli added, "see if the wood can help us defeat Qabas." His chest tightened, and anger seethed under his calm exterior.

Zee, never one to shirk from a hard question, turned to Eli and looked him square in the eye. "Are you sure you want to do this now? Do you need more time to come to terms with her death?"

"Time will not change my anger, brother."

"We'll achieve more with calm heads than rage."

"I know, but there'll be time for that, too."

He turned to face the wood, aware of Moore and Zee exchanging glances behind him. *Let them. He was fine.*

They had parked below the castle, deciding a brief exploration of the old site would be helpful before heading into the wood. However, the ruins were damp, empty, and devoid of any trace of djinn. Water pooled in hollows and dripped off the remnants of stone walls, and the shells of the remaining rooms were ghostly in the mizzle that was closer to fog on the cliff top.

The air of mourning was stronger here than in White Haven. A palpable sense of loss permeated everything. As Eli plunged beneath the branches and hurried to the tangled interior, he felt as if every living thing had withdrawn from the perimeter to huddle within.

"Was it like this earlier?" Eli asked Moore who walked between him and Zee.

"Similar, but the feeling of loss was less obvious. It has deepened now. Intensified. Briar said she heard a bell toll. Or felt it, perhaps. Deep in the earth."

Eli rested his palm against a tree—not a dryad-filled one—and felt the similar hum that Briar had described. Subdued, like someone curled inward, as if the outside world was too great to bear. Their loss inflamed his anger, and he checked himself. Now was not the time to rage, and he drew a deep, shuddering breath.

"Are you all right?" Zee asked, drawing level with him.

"Her death was so pointless, and this place," his hands swept outwards, "is hurting. I hate it."

"Let's hope White Haven isn't further engulfed in their mourning." He cocked his head. "I can hear something. Singing."

"I hear it, too," Moore said, clutching his torch like a weapon. "Do you think the djinn is here?"

"You're thinking of the song of metals?" Eli asked. "No. This is quite different. It's the dryads. Come on."

He quickened his pace, threading through the tangled paths that seemed even narrower now than they normally were. They really didn't want visitors here. And there were watchers, too. Owls swooped ahead of them, warning of their approach, and mammals skittered underfoot. More than one odd face peered from around a tree trunk, but not dryads; some other fey creature that must inhabit the wild interior.

"They have guards," he pointed out to the others. "I think if we were anyone else, we would have been blocked and turned away by now."

Lights appeared ahead, suspended in branches, golden and twinkling as if a thousand fireflies had appeared, and the route opened up before them. Suddenly, they were there, and the blackened trunk that was Nelaira's remains, thick with the stench of charcoal and smoke, lay on the ground, half consumed by the earth and thousands of unusual mush-rooms. Dryads clustered around it, sitting, standing, and singing. Bells were ringing, but Eli could see no source for them. In fact, he couldn't care less about them, because his attention was fixed on the charred tree.

He fell to his knees, hands on the trunk, not entirely sure what he was feeling. He could see her still, in his mind's eye. Her beauty. Her raw sexuality. Her fire and her bravery. Tears welled. *What a waste of a life.* Memories of their night together flooded his senses. It had been all-consuming. He had never experienced a coupling like that before, and he doubted he would again. He couldn't work out if he regretted it not happening again, or whether he was grateful for his self-restraint, because no doubt he would be feeling a lot worse than he did now.

He struggled to maintain concentration on what was happening around him, and noted the dryads had drawn back to give him space. Zee looked as equally shaken at the surreal situation.

Moore alone seemed to be in control, although he was fighting for composure. "Who made all this?" He gestured at the lights.

"We did," a young dryad said with a note of impatience. "The magic of the inner grove has spread. The elders have allowed it."

"Which means what?" Eli asked, alarmed. "Is the grove open?"

The dryad shook his head. "Of course not. We bring its magic."

"Alderic," Moore said, confirming Eli's suspicions of who the dryad was, "I'm sorry that we're intruding, and are grateful you have allowed us here, but are the eggs safe?"

"Very safe. The elders watch them."

"You're sure the djinn cannot get in?"

"Yes. We are more strongly linked than before. The elders lend us their strength."

"But," Zee said tentatively, "the prince is making a weapon—we think. We heard the metals sing when we found him at a forge earlier. Could a special weapon have an effect here?"

"What type of weapon?" Alderic asked, voice suddenly sharp.

"We don't know, but we are trying to find out. He's hiding somewhere."

Moore asked, "Has he returned here? Even in disguise?"

"No, but this weapon could be a problem. Blades of djinn-fire, crafted with the right magic, could harm our defences."

Eli stood, knowing he needed to focus on this. "How?"

"A blade that can cut through the wood's magical defences would be very dangerous. You know we have our own. We can defend ourselves against all things—even Wyrd's magic and the

Winter Queen could not violate our borders—but with the right weapon…" His voice dropped, and a ripple of unease spread through the dryads.

"Then we need a solution," Moore said decisively. "Did you ask the elders for information on how to fight djinn, as I asked? Their weaknesses? Because we will help you. We are working on a solution now."

Alderic nodded. "I did. Sit, and I will share all, but I must warn you, they are prepared to expand our borders, if necessary, to find him."

"Expand how?" Eli asked, fearing he knew what they meant.

"They will release the old magic, and if needed, we will sweep to the coast and the far hills to catch him. Whatever stands in our way will be destroyed."

Nineteen

Alex had been serving in the pub for less than ten minutes after the meeting when he realised that he could detect the faint but unmistakable energy of a therian.

Caspian was sitting with Newton and Kendall at the end of the bar, helping them compile their list of possible hiding places. Briar had already gone home, citing a long and tiring day. He edged closer to his friends, wiping down the counter and trying to look casual as he scanned the room. "Caspian," he said quietly, "I'm picking up therian vibes. Am I imagining it?" He tried not to disturb Kendall and Newton, who were still focussed on the list.

Caspian moved only his eyes as he glanced at Alex and then to the part of the pub he could see easily without turning. "I hadn't, but let me try now."

The pub was busy, so it was hard to pick anyone suspicious out of the crowd, but Caspian sipped his pint calmly, and Alex continued to scan the room as he collected the dirty glasses that Marie had placed on the bar. No one looked as if they were watching them or listening, and he paid particular attention to those seated nearest to the bar. Most people in here were either in family groups or tables of friends, but there were several couples around. It struck him that the therian—or therians—might be here in animal form. The Wayward Son was an animal-friendly pub, as long as the owners were responsible, so several dogs were curled beneath tables. Or it could be a moth or a fly, or any insect, really. No one looked unduly suspicious.

He edged back to Caspian. "Anything?"

"Yes. Faint. Towards the back of the room. I'd say behind my left shoulder somewhere."

"It might be a dog," Alex said, glancing over Caspian's shoulder but seeing nothing to draw his attention.

Caspian laughed. "Really?"

"Really."

"Doesn't that suggest the owner is a therian?"

"Not necessarily. Should we do something?"

"You think they're spying?"

"Don't you?"

"Hard to stop therians from drinking in a pub, Alex. It could be any old therian. Not Wentworth's lot."

"Is that likely?"

Newton interrupted. "What are you two muttering about? Did you say therian?"

"Yes. We can both feel their magic," Alex said. "As to whether there's one or more, we're not sure. We're just debating whether we should ignore it or not."

"As I've just pointed out," Caspian said calmly, "it could be harmless. Plus, if they're not close to us, what does it matter? Unless they have bionic hearing, of course."

Noting that Marie and their newish barman, a young man called Barnie, were serving customers, Alex grabbed a tray. "I'll collect some glasses. It's unnerving me, so I'd like to know."

He weaved through the tables, heading to the back of the room where several tables had empties to be collected, and started to load the tray. He greeted a few regulars on the way, behaving as casually as possible, but it wasn't until he was making his way back via a different route with a full tray that he felt the strong pulse of therian magic. He paused, trying to cram one more glass on his tray to give him an excuse for delaying, and spotted the source. A couple of women in their late twenties on a small table against the wall with a dog at their feet. He was pretty sure it wasn't the group from the beach.

Rather than pretend he didn't know, he decided to talk to them. It was highly unlikely they'd cause a scene in the crowded pub, surely, and Caspian was right. They could just be there drinking. Beltane had drawn all sorts to White Haven. He walked over to them, smiling as non-threateningly as possible, and rested the tray on their table.

"I'm Alex Bonneville. I own this place. Just wondering if you're friends of the Wentworths. No problem, obviously, if you are," he added hurriedly. "I just like to personally welcome other paranormals to my pub." The dog that had been lounging at their feet suddenly sat upright, eyes fixed on him, and Alex realised it was a dog he'd seen roving through the pub earlier, getting lots of attention as he sought out pats and leftovers. And gossip, no doubt. It was a large, black-haired hound with human intellect behind the eyes. Alex grinned and patted its head. "Nice doggy."

One woman had short blonde hair, and the other had pale brown hair cut into a blunt bob. Both looked suddenly wary, but the woman with the bob spoke first and extended her hand to shake his. "Alex, hi. Yes, we are aware of you. I'm Jak with a 'k,' this is Julie."

"With a 'J?' And who's the doggo? Rover?"

"Mike."

"Nice name for a dog."

Jak affected a withering smile. "No problem being in your pub, I hope?"

"Of course not, but I don't like being spied on."

"We're not spying," Julie said, eyes flashing. "We're drinking."

"Mike has been spying. He's pretty recognisable, and I noticed he's been sniffing around this place. Learn anything interesting, Mike?"

Mike growled in response.

"Look, girls, I have no problem with therians in my pub. I am a witch, after all. But eavesdropping is not cool. Are you friends of Wentworth's? I'm not about to throw you out. I just want to know."

"We're friends of his son, Giles," Jak hedged.

"You're a long way from the Mount."

"We're even further from London. We're visiting."

"Beltane?"

"Amongst other things."

A table vacated nearby, so Alex grabbed a chair, pulled it close, and sat down. "I won't keep you, but what things?"

Julie snorted. "Do you always grill your customers? Or is it because we're women?"

"It's because you're therians, and the last time I met Wentworth's clan they tried to kill us."

"And you," Jak hissed, darting forward, "killed them."

"Not me, actually. My very capable Nephilim friends." All smiles had gone now as animosity flared. "Their fault. They started it. Wentworth kidnapped my friends and was planning on feeding them to fucking dragons, if you hadn't heard."

Jak blinked. "Yes. That was unfortunate."

"That's one word for it. So it's unlikely, isn't it, that you just happen to be in my pub, of all the pubs in White Haven? I'm trying to be courteous here," Alex said, as they looked uneasily at each other. "You weren't part of that group, and I don't want to make enemies." He hesitated, wondering how much to say, but seeing as the news had been reporting on the deaths all day, they had to know. "Especially after what happened overnight."

Jak shrugged. "We're all curious, that's all. Death by all-consuming fire in a sand dune isn't your regular way to die, is it?"

"It wasn't a dragon, in case you're all still fixated on that."

"But you do have our eggs," Julie said pointedly.

"Not *your* eggs," he insisted. "You stole them, and we got rid of them. No one needs a shifter war."

Julie huffed. "You can't just get rid of dragon eggs, and we know you're hiding them, so don't bullshit us."

"I'm not debating it," Alex said with an air of finality.

"But something," Jak said, edging closer, eyes fixed on Alex, "is as powerful as a dragon to kill someone in such a manner."

"Is that so?"

"You know so. You're all very twitchy here." Her gaze slid to the bar, and when Alex turned, it was to find Caspian, Kendall, and Newton watching them. "List making, a meeting upstairs, your investigator friends scanning the beach last night..." She smirked. "Yes, we noticed that. And a weird, unnatural mist that has descended on the town. Something unusual has arrived here, and we want to know what. That's all."

It seemed they hadn't detected the arrival of the salamander in the fire, or surely she would have mentioned that. The therians on the beach last night would have hung around to investigate, too. Or maybe she was just dissembling.

"All you need to know is that we're dealing with it."

"You know what it is, then?" Julie asked.

"We are at the early stages of our inquiry." *By the gods. He sounded like Newton.* "We don't need your help, either, just in case you were going to offer."

Jak, by far the edgier and more threatening of the two—not including the dog that had a low, rumbling growl in the back of its throat ever since Alex sat down—gave him a mirthless smile. "You know exactly what it is. You think you can hide it from us, but you can't. Something has arrived with powerful fire magic, and as far as we're concerned, that's as important to us as dragons."

"Nice that you're so honest about it."

"Which is what you suspect anyway, and why you don't want us involved. Why are we dancing around this, Alex? It's ridiculous. I'll make it clear. If something else can give us an edge over other therians and shifters, we'll take that instead. Happy now?"

"Not really."

She continued, regardless. "All of our cards are on the table. You'll try to stop us again, but this time we'll win. We won't make the same mistakes again. There are more of us here now. Maybe this time we'll get the eggs *and* the new power."

Alex couldn't help himself. He laughed loudly, enjoying the narrow-eyed look of annoyance from the therians. "You are all in way over your heads. You have no idea what's going on, but trust me, you're not winning this one, either. If I'm honest, I'm not even sure we will." He stood, only half-joking, because he genuinely had no idea how they'd fight a prince amongst djinn. "Enjoy your drinks, and keep your mutt under the table, or I'll throw you all out. And if I catch *any* therian trying to eavesdrop in my pub, I will wrap this place up in spells so tight you won't get in again. Or maybe," he grinned maliciously, "you'll get in, but won't get out."

In fact, he thought as he walked away, feeling their belligerent stares between his shoulder blades, *he should probably do that anyway.*

Twenty

Caspian arrived at Avery's just in time to have a last chat with Helena before she returned to her spirit and went hunting.

"Are you sure you want to do this?" he asked her, certain she was, but feeling he should check anyway.

"See this smile?" Helena pointed to her face, her eyes already dancing with excitement. "I am very ready."

"What will you say? Do you want to rehearse?" He was nervous on Morwenna's behalf and his own. He wanted to ask Morwenna out and go to dinner, and all the normal things, but with this hanging over her, he didn't feel he should. Although, to be fair, she'd been giving him lots of encouraging smiles, and they'd shared plenty of coffees.

Helena patted his cheek. "No, I don't need to bloody rehearse. I'll improvise."

Avery met his gaze over her head. "I've argued this myself, but as you know, she's quite headstrong."

"It runs in the family," Helena shot back.

The joke settled his mood, which after the events in The Wayward Son, needed settling. He hadn't told Avery about the therians yet, and certainly not Helena. She could hear it upon her return.

Helena sat comfortably on the sofa with a blanket over her legs, and a bag of knitting on the seat next to her. She drank the potion she'd prepared, and after giving Caspian the empty glass, settled back into the cushions. "This could take a while, so don't stress. You might need to go home and sleep, Cas."

"Oh, no." He shook his head. "I'll wait, unless Avery throws me out."

"Of course I won't," she said, voice rising in shock. "None of us will sleep until this is done."

Helena closed her eyes, and in seconds had slipped from Clea's body. Her ghostly form in her long, black dress with a tight bodice stood before him, and he gasped with surprise. He'd never seen Helena so clearly before as a ghost. The last time was when she had charged at his father, only a whirl of smoke and flames. She was young and pretty, as dark as Avery was a redhead, but he could see the similarities. It was uncanny. The scent of smoke and violets magnified around him, and she gave him a knowing smile.

"By the gods," he murmured.

Then she vanished, and Clea seemed to sink further into the cushions, and even with her eyes closed, the spark that had so animated her faded. Then Clea's eyes opened, revealing a slightly unfocussed gaze, and she smiled at Caspian and patted his knee. "I'll just catch up on my knitting."

Avery crouched down next to her. "Sherry, Gran?"

"Lovely. Did I see Di?"

Avery froze momentarily. "Yes, she's popped out."

"Never mind. We can chat later."

Avery stood and called Caspian back towards the table at the rear of the room. "She'll knit for hours now, with a few sherries.

Then she'll probably nod off." She looked stricken. "She remembered my mother. I feel terrible."

Caspian felt as if he was intruding on a private moment. "She didn't seem upset about it. Look, should I go?"

"No! I'd rather you be here in case something happens. Sounds stupid though, really. What could we do if it went wrong? Grab a seat, and I'll get Gran's sherry. What about you? Wine? Beer? Coffee? Tea?"

"Wine sounds great, red if you have it. I'll help with your research. Mind if I check on the salamander?" He nodded towards the fire, suddenly remembering it was there.

"Course not."

The salamander basked in the flames, looking asleep until it opened one heavily-lidded eye to reveal a pupil of the deepest black. Caspian froze, worried it might attack him or vanish, but then it closed it again, shuffled around, and settled back to sleep. It looked like a lizard made of embers; the bright glow of its reptilian skin had a row of stars running down its spine, and it had a long snout that it tucked under its tail. Its webbed feet twitched as if it were dreaming.

"Cute, isn't it?" Clea said.

"What?" Caspian whirled around at her unexpected comment. "The salamander?"

Clea nodded, but her gaze was distant, as if trying to remember where she was or what she was saying.

She didn't expand on her statement, so Caspian asked, "Have you seen one before? A salamander?"

"Years ago. I accidentally summoned one. Nearly burnt the house down." She giggled. "Didn't do that again."

Caspian sat next to her. He had never summoned an elemental himself, and none of his coven had, either. It was considered risky because they were so volatile. "Can you remember the spell you used?"

"I was a bit tipsy at the time. Just a teenager. Had a lot of trouble sending it back, too."

"Can you remember how you did it?"

"Did what?" she asked, eyes clouding again.

"Sent the salamander back?"

"What salamander?" She picked up her knitting, and the clack of needles filled the silence.

He sighed. She'd gone again.

When Avery returned, and Clea was settled with her sherry, they retreated to the table and Caspian repeated the conversation.

"You're kidding!" Avery said, mid-sip of her red wine. "She summoned a salamander?"

"That's what she said. Why didn't Helena know?"

"She tries not to pry in her memories. She says it's rude."

"She has morals about this?" Caspian asked, amused. Helena could be blunt and unsentimental about most things.

"Quite strict ones!"

"I think that could be one memory well worth investigating." He nodded at the grimoires, papers, and books spread across the table. A year ago, he would have loved to be in this situation with Avery. The intimacy of them around the table. The fire. The wine. The rain drumming on the roof that wrapped them in solitude and privacy. No Alex. But he had moved on. Unwillingly at first of course, but now there was Morwenna. "You've been busy."

"I love research as you know, but I'm swimming in dragons and salamanders. Sorry, terrible metaphor," she said with a wry grin. "Fortunately, I organised lots of dragon spells a few weeks ago. I put the most useful ones in my own grimoire." She tapped the deep red, leather-bound book next to her.

He nodded. "For breaking the curse. Transformational spells."

"Exactly. I've added to them, because I've found more since then, but Helena made a good point. Salamanders help us with spells—traditionally, at least. Dragons are ingredients. Unpleasant, but true."

"I'm intrigued that El wants to use the salamander."

"Me too, but how? Look at it!" She stared at the fire, but it was impossible to see the creature from their position. "How do you direct a salamander?"

He laughed. "I have no idea. Any luck with El's grimoire?" It lay open on the table and gave off a distinctly different energy to Avery and Alex's grimoire. And his own, actually. There was a whiff of metal to it.

"Not yet. I've barely started looking. It's so different to mine," she said voicing his thoughts.

"I'm looking forward to seeing what she has in there. Have you asked the coven?" He meant the Cornwall Coven.

"No, but I probably should. I should probably tell Gen about the djinn, too. I'm amazed she hasn't called."

"Tell her tomorrow. I have news, too. There were therians in the pub tonight. Two girls, and a guy who had shifted to a dog. All roughly late twenties, and not the three from the beach. Alex confronted them. I thought he was mad, but it was the right move. They've admitted they know something is here, and that they want it. They sort of threw down the gauntlet."

"Oh! Shit." Avery sagged back into her chair. "Great. Therians now, too. I'm not surprised, though."

"Of course, they could be lying and already know exactly what killed those people, but they didn't get near to them, unlike you. Unless they shifted to do that."

"Exactly. One of them could have been a gull or something. I'm sure we'd have noticed, though, if one of them was there with us earlier, and all we could detect from the bodies was a trace of magic. We couldn't tell it was a djinn that caused their deaths. How could we? We've never encountered one before. In fact, we thought it was the salamander." She closed her eyes briefly, exasperated. "This is all so confusing. Surely, a djinn hasn't killed two people just because he's arrogant?"

"He didn't admit to doing that," Caspian reminded her, remembering Reuben's account of their first meeting in the forge.

"He didn't deny it, either."

"Maybe he needs human energy to appear more human here. I have no idea why he'd need to, but it's a possibility. It's not like he'll fancy a night down the pub. Or maybe the cold means he needs to fuel himself? It is a creature of the desert, after all, and it's far from warm here, even last night." Caspian rolled his eyes at his own suggestion. It sounded idiotic, but they had to start speculating somewhere.

"He killed Nelaira," Avery pointed out. "That was out of spite."

"No, that's because she refused to grant his wishes. And partly spite, I suppose."

"Wishes." Avery's expression became vague before fixing on him with sudden intensity. "That's what they do, right? Grant wishes?"

"According to myth and folklore, yes."

"Do they have to *want* to grant you a wish, or are they obliged to?"

"I really have no idea. You're thinking of springing a wish on him?"

"Yes, actually. To sod off back to the Otherworld."

He laughed. "If it was only so easy."

"Maybe I should try it, just in case."

"Fighting fire with fire might be exactly what we need here," he said, pulling Avery's more modern family grimoire that was still a couple of centuries old towards him. "Salamander fire."

"Providing they're not working together."

"Clea will most likely have used this book, if she's recalling an actual memory and not a fantasy. I presumed you've checked in here?"

"Diana did. She noted a few spells that mentioned salamanders." She pointed out the stickered pages. "It's the book she's most familiar with. It was all a bit weird. We sat here together earlier before the meeting as if this was something we did together all the time."

He paused. He'd been about to plunge into a search for salamanders and how to use them, but instead said, "Sorry. I should have asked. Are you all right? She didn't seem that thrilled to be in the meeting."

"She was spectacularly angry to be here. Launched at me before she'd even got through the shop door." Her lips twisted in a smile. "I guess I know where I get my temper from."

"Family is never easy. Well, not for some of us, me included. Briar and El, too. And Alex?"

"His dad is fine, but the rest of them not so much, and well, you know about his dead uncle."

"Creepy guy who spelled the script of *Tristan and Isolde*?"

"Exactly."

"Diana could have walked straight out again, but she didn't. That says something."

"I suppose so. Is it horrible to say I'm regretting it?"

"No. What we wish for rarely turns out how we envisage it. I'm sure Reuben will work his charms on her."

Avery laughed. "He's so sweet to do this."

"It seemed to me that she was pretty overwhelmed with your coven and friends earlier. It wouldn't have been like that years ago. For a start, thanks to my father, you were excluded from the Cornwall Coven. She might have kept her magic under wraps. That would have been lonely. Plus, no Briar or El's family. White Haven would have been very different. Your sister clearly didn't feel as strongly connected to her magic, either."

"No. Whereas I always have been."

"At sixteen, it's difficult to reason the motives of others. It's hard enough as an adult. I hope you can come to some kind of peace with it all. Start a relationship again, if only at a distance." Avery nodded, eyes on the grimoires, and Caspian turned his attention to the spellbook again. "Right, salamanders. There must be a common language to use when summoning one. If they are to help us with spellwork, we must communicate."

"Yes." Avery seemed pleased to return to a safer subject. "Maybe there's a spell to talk with them in here somewhere, as well as spells for summoning them. I'll continue to search El's grimoire."

"Maybe a fire witch, such as El, won't need a spell to speak to them. Perhaps it's instinctive."

"I also noticed," Avery said, running through her earlier notes, "that they are transformational creatures, too, just like dragons. Which is logical, right? Fire transforms, rebirth, etcetera. With fire, metals are changed, water turns to steam, ingredients are activated, but fire also gets rid of what no longer serves us."

"Emotions, ways of thinking. Clearing out the old to make way for the new. Fire cleanses. I always use it in rituals." Especially after his father died. He'd wanted to cleanse that toxic part of his life away completely.

Avery nodded. "Salamanders' alchemical abilities are physical and spiritual, but there will be other uses for them."

Caspian checked the time. It was only just past ten o'clock. "Plenty of time for research yet. I'm not tired. You?"

"No, although if I'm honest, today feels like it's packed a week in already."

"I agree. Thank the gods for adrenalin. Or should I say fire energy?"

She laughed. "Bloody Beltane. Dragons, djinn, and salamanders... We need to get as much done tonight as possible," she said, amusement dying. "We can't afford to delay with this. The djinn is already making his preparations for who knows what."

"Better get to it, then."

Unfortunately, they had barely started when someone pounded on the door below as if the hounds of Hell were after them.

"Who is that?" Caspian asked, leaping to his feet.

"Oh, shit. What if it's my sister?"

Avery vanished in a swirl of air, and Caspian followed, both manifesting by the rear door that served as the main entrance to the flat. A figure stood outside, illuminated through the glass panel by the security light. It was impossible to tell if it was male or female, but they were slight of build.

In the seconds since they had arrived, fists hammered on the door again, and with a look of fear and anticipation, Avery shouted, "Hold on! I'm here." She opened the door, as Caspian summoned his magic to attack or defend.

The figure almost fell inside, but caught themselves just in time. It was a woman in her early thirties with reddish-blonde hair that was bedraggled and damp, and behind her were two children, both swathed in waterproofs.

"Avery!" she said, almost breathlessly. "Are you all right? You called me! Are you ill? In trouble?"

Avery faltered. "I, yes... Bryony. I'm fine. Come in! It's so wet."

But Bryony just stared at her and then Caspian. "You're okay?"

"Yes."

"So why did you summon me?"

"To see you!" Avery stepped back to invite her in.

"I've dragged my kids all the way here just for that?"

"Isn't that enough?" Avery yelled, suddenly furious.

Caspian wished he was back in the pub, but decided to intervene in what looked to be another argument, and the weather seemed to agree, because in seconds it intensified again, wind gusting the rain inwards and driving the three people on the doorstep closer.

One of the children plaintively said, "Mum!"

"Perhaps," Caspian said, smiling as casually as he could manage, "we should discuss this inside."

Finally, with a look of sheer annoyance, Bryony crossed the threshold.

Twenty-One

Helena had a secret.

The ways of the spirit world were confusing to the uninitiated, but for Helena, who had existed there for hundreds of years, far longer than she had existed in her living, breathing form, it was home.

In many ways, it was a simpler existence there. There was no need of warmth, food, air or other sustenance. She was pure spirit, where thought mattered more than appearance. However, there were malignant spirits there, as well as weak and needy ones, so in that sense it was much like being human. Epiphany and enlightenment were not achieved at death, unless you actively sought it out. Some did; others did not. It was fair to say that some were old, old souls, who had been around for millennia, while others were brand new.

There were no gods there. No weighing of the good and bad, of justice metered, or rewards. No Hell nor Heaven. Christian concepts she had no patience for. Instead, the afterlife was like a gigantic consciousness that she considered akin to swimming in a vast ocean. Practitioners of the craft who were skilled at walking in the spirit world would venture into the shallows. Helena dived far deeper. However, it was in the shallows where you were closest to the human material world, and could lurk beyond the veil to see the living. At certain times of the year, such as Samhain and Beltane, it was far thinner, and spirits who weren't ready to dive into the depths of the dead would remain there all the time.

Helena considered it unhealthy, which admittedly sounded ridiculous coming from one who now regularly inhabited the body of an old woman, and cared about hair and clothes, but adapting to her surroundings had always been her strength. Except, of course, when history and the Witchfinder had caught up with her. When Avery had first found her grimoire, Helena had been so tied to it that she'd had no choice but to return. Sometimes fate was inescapable. She saw that now. Her entanglement with the Favershams and her sacrifice had been fated. She saw her rebirth in Clea as her reward. As such, helping her descendants was now her priority, closely followed by righting the wrongs subjected to those close to her—especially women. Morwenna fell into that category. When Helena had returned to the spirit world after breaking the curse, she had searched for signs of Kitty. The curse had contained her imprint. Her magic. As it had Morwenna's perfidious friend, John, who had worked with Kitty.

Because what Helena had discovered after many years of her spirit existence, was that witches, because of the nature of their practice, also left their mark in the shallows of the dead, even when they didn't actively venture in. Invocations, spellwork, rituals, their acknowledgement of the world beyond their own, familiars, candle magic, and tarot work meant that even without realising it, they left footprints in the sand. The stronger the magic they worked—and curses were very strong—the deeper were the footprints. Footprints that Helena could follow.

So, because she was close to Morwenna during the curse-breaking, Helena had found Kitty easily. Her footprints were muddy and deep, metaphorically speaking, and she had followed them to John, and then found Jed. She had watched Kitty in the intervening weeks; carefully, because Kitty was a clever witch. Mean and spiteful, yes, but clever nonetheless. She had been furious when she found out they had broken the curse. She had raged with John, her co-conspirator, and had wanted to try to curse Morwenna again. He had refused, saying it was too obvious, and besides, the threat to them was too great. He was right, too. Helena had resisted vengeance because this was Morwenna's business, but had she seen they were trying again, she would have intervened, and it wouldn't have been pretty.

She had also watched Jed. He was a good-looking man, but lacking in character. Seemingly full of confidence, much of it was bluster. Plus, as much as he was wary of witchcraft and Morwenna's magic, he was also quite happy to have it put to use for his own gain. Because as much as he denied it, he absolutely did know about the curse. *How could he not?* Consequently, he was both annoyed it had been broken, and terrified about retribution. Helena had decided not to tell Morwenna or anyone this news, because Morwenna had gone through enough already. That was how she knew that Kitty and John had placed protection on Jed's house, but had not warded against spirits.

Jed's one positive attribute was that he did love his daughter, in a selfish, *you won't see your mother* sort of way. However, if he thought it would stop Ysella's own magic from developing, he was very wrong. Her magic was waxing with her increasing age, and Ysella was also pressing to see her mother more often.

Helena hadn't mentioned this spirit-spying to Avery or anyone else. Endless discussions on the nature of the spirit world did not interest her, although she had talked to Alex on occasions, of course. But not about this. *This was a secret.* A plan, in case all else failed. It was only when Caspian had announced that Morwenna was finally ready to deal with Jed, and she realised how convoluted and ridiculous it would all become, that she had decided to use her connections.

It meant that even though Helena was miles away physically, she was seconds away spiritually, which meant within a very short time of entering the spirit world and leaving Caspian by the fire, his expression full of surprise—and, she noticed, a little admiration—she had found Jed. She now waited beyond the veil, watching him.

The weeks since the curse-breaking had not been kind to him. He'd lost weight and was jumpy. He opened the mail as if every letter contained a bomb, and flinched at every noise. Some were admittedly caused by Helena who rattled windows and slammed doors in an otherwise empty house. Now, Ysella was in bed, and Helena watched him staring into the fire, a book in his lap forgotten, the TV droning in the background.

Perfect.

Helena pushed against the veil by the TV, pleased to see the screen flicker and flash, and then sputter out. Then she broke the light bulb, glass shattering from the overhead light, leaving only a dim light from the lamp on the table. Jed leapt to his feet, book falling on the floor, and she sent a stiff wind to riffle the pages.

"Jed," she called, her voice as cool and incisive as a winter wind, "it is time that we talk, you and I."

He fumbled in a drawer and pulled out a curiously marked knife whose blade burned with witch-fire. He thrust it in front of him, sweeping from left to right as he wheeled around, trying to see her. "Show yourself! Is that you, Morwenna?"

"Morwenna has better things to do than haunt you, you miserable man," Helena said, lowering the temperature with her malevolence.

Keeping a wary eye on the blade that she hadn't seen before, she circled at a distance, choosing to remain unseen for now. It was unlikely that the blade could harm her, but clearly he had taken more precautions than she realised. She studied the room for traps and enchantments that might harm her, but other than the protection sigils and magic she had seen before, there was nothing to hurt a spirit. She had been careful to conceal herself from Kitty and John, even when breaking the curse.

She broke the tense silence. "That's an interesting knife. A present from Kitty and John?"

"What do you know of them?" he asked, still turning in the centre of the room, blade outstretched, hand shaking, and sweat gathering on his brow.

"I know they cursed your wife, Morwenna, with your blessing." She darted in, striking at his hand with icy fingers, and the knife flew from his grip and landed under the TV console.

He shrieked, and then covered his mouth, eyes looking upward. "If you touch, Ysella," he hissed, "I will kill you."

"I'm already dead, Jed, and you've done enough harm to Ysella without my help. Sit." She summoned the armchair so that it flew across the room, rumpling the rug before hitting the back of his knees. He sat with a thump, and she cast a spell to seal the room in silence. Ysella would not interrupt this conversation. "We are going to talk about how you are going to correct that harm and make reparation to your ex-wife." She revealed herself to him, standing between him and the fire, so that the flames could be seen through her, lighting her eyes so that they burned with the fire that had consumed her.

"Shit!" he exclaimed, retreating into his chair as if trying to push it backwards, but Helena's magic had fixed it in place. "Who are you?"

"The Ghost of Vengeance Present." *She rather liked Reuben's name for her.* "I am a busy woman, Jed, so I will make this *very* clear. You will stop hedging and bluffing, and making threats you cannot fulfil, and send Ysella to Morwenna next weekend. Then you shall agree that Ysella can stay for the summer, in Cornwall, should she wish. Of course, you will encourage it."

He spat out the words, "I will not. She shall not learn witchcraft. I do not approve."

"Yet you approved of John and Kitty using witchcraft against Morwenna. I don't see the difference."

"It is to save Ysella."

"Such nonsense. It is about control. You are no different to a million other men. Your methods are coercion, threats, and force." She leaned over him with such swiftness he recoiled in his chair. Helena pushed her face to his, smelling his fear. "Your daughter will see this. She already sees it. She is starting to despise you."

"She is not."

"She most certainly is. Shall I whisper in her ear now?" Helena pressed her cheek against his, icy breath in his ear. "Tell her how cruel you are. How weak. What a spineless excuse of a man you are?" Her hands rested on his shoulders with the strength of steel, but he wasn't struggling. He had frozen in place. "Answer the question, Jed. Shall I? Or will you agree to my demands? Because," she eased back, his cheek almost blue from her icy touch, his eyes wide with fright as she looked into them, "they *are* demands. I am merely trying to sound polite."

"I have rights!"

"So do both of them. I intend to see that they get them. *Do you agree*?" She roared it out so that he jumped in his seat.

Jed was very frightened, but he was also stubborn and vicious. "You have no power over me."

"I could blind you right now. Lay my cold hands upon your eyes and freeze your eyeballs in their sockets," she said, squeezing the end of his nose between her finger and thumb and giving him frostbite. He cried out in pain. "Perhaps I should scar your cheek forever. Maybe a handprint burnt into your skin. I burned in flames for my craft, Jed. Right to my core."

She raised her hand so that flames raced along it, superheating it, and at the same time, revealed the fire's effects. Her burnt skin, ragged hair, smouldering dress, the strong stench of woodsmoke, and the pungent scent of violets that she had conjured the morning of her death to make her think of brighter days. The day her magic was so weak she could not and would not fight, terrified for the safety of her friends and family.

"You are just a ghost," Jed said, trying to convince himself now, but his tentative fingers touched the tip of his nose, and a piece of his blackened skin came away. "I can't feel it! What have you done?"

"Decide quickly, Jed. Do you agree to my demands? To sharing your daughter properly with Morwenna, for this summer and beyond? Because I can set this house on fire right now. Save

Ysella's life and deliver her to her mother, and leave you to burn right here, in a pyre of your own making."

Helena meant it, too. She was furious, and her fury stoked her flames. Still, doubt lurked in his eyes, a feral cunning, and she struck at him, hand slapping his cheek with her burning palm that she left there until his skin withered beneath it and he screamed with pain and horror.

"Let me see," she said, eyes travelling down his body. "What else could I burn?" Her gaze settled on his crotch, and she lifted amused eyes to his. "Shall I?"

"No! All right. I agree."

"To what? State it nice and clearly."

His eyes burned with hatred for her now, and Helena revelled in it. *Let him hate her. It would fuel her even more.*

"I agree that Ysella will visit Morwenna next weekend, and all summer if she wishes."

"And you will..."

"I will encourage her to go."

"And?"

"I agree that she will see her mother more regularly from now on."

"I think it's important to add that you will not take this out on Ysella in any way, because some men think love is proved with violence. Do you agree?"

"I would *never* hurt Ysella. I love my daughter." His voice cracked with fear and pain, and possibly some regret at this turn of events. His cheek was blistering now, and must be very painful. "I never suggested the curse. It was Kitty's idea. She was so insistent. She'd never liked my wife. Or John. He did once, I think. He changed. I just wanted Ysella to be normal."

"It's highly overrated."

She weighed him up. She thought he was sincere. In all the time she had watched him, he had never been violent or threatened his daughter, and as she'd realised early on, he was ultimately weak, but with a streak of cunningness that weak men often had. She nodded. "Good. Because I will be watching, and if you so much as think about hurting Morwenna, physically or magically, I will kill you."

She listened as he ground out his agreement, stuttering now.

Then she stepped back beyond the veil, into the shadows of the living room, allowing the room temperature to return to normal, and his fear to subside marginally. But she planned to watch him all night long, just in case.

Twenty-Two

Reuben pulled onto the sweep of drive in front of Greenlane Manor, Diana's car next to him, and once he'd parked, took Diana's small suitcase out of her boot.

"You're planning on staying a few days, then," he said to her without preamble.

"When summoned, it's best to go prepared. It doesn't mean I was happy about it."

"No, I can see that. How did it feel?"

"Deeply unpleasant. I had a sudden urge to come back here that was irresistible, despite trying my hardest to ignore it. It was a compulsion. Like an addiction."

Much like Morwenna's curse, then, Reuben thought, although he didn't say so. *Had Avery even considered that when she cast the spell?*

Diana's lips were set in a thin line as she surveyed the house. He opened the front door and placed her suitcase at the bottom of the stairs. The lamps were on, casting a welcoming glow, and she took in the broad hall with its tiled floor and the bright, decorative wallpaper.

"This is not what I was expecting," she admitted. "It's far more domesticated, considering you look like a surfer."

"I am a surfer, but I'm also Lord of the Manor now, so I have to keep up appearances," he said, teasing her. "Not that I'm an actual lord, of course," he added quickly. "My dead sister-in-law styled the place. She was a monster, but she knew how to decorate."

"A monster?"

"Long story. I'll show you to your room later, but I want to see Tamsyn first. Ready?" He had no intention of leaving her there on her own. However, she looked tired, so he added, "We won't be long."

"Of course. I seem to have arrived in the middle of a crisis." She tore her gaze away from the house and settled her stare on him. "Or is it always like this in White Haven?"

"We have periods of intense activity," he admitted, preferring not to use the word *crisis,* "and also very settled, boring stuff. Well, regular stuff. White Haven is never boring." He ushered her out of the house and back into his car, apologising for the mess. He was driving his old VW Variant that was always filled with sand and smelled of the sea.

"You live with El?" Diana asked. "She's your girlfriend?"

"Wife now," he said, pride and love swelling at the memory of their wedding. "Most of the time. She still keeps her flat in town. Whatever works for her, I support. It will be great if she moves in fully, but I'm fine if she doesn't want to, either."

"So you're alone in that huge place?"

"I am now." He felt the familiar weight of loss settle in his stomach. "My brother, Gil, died a couple of years ago. There was only the two of us after our parents passed. Gil was eighteen and I was fifteen when that happened. They died abroad. First time they had holidayed without us, and they never came back.

That's why me and Gil were so close." He rarely spoke of his parents' deaths, but all of his coven knew. It wasn't mentioned by common assent. It was sad, but they had died together, and had left him and Gil a legacy of magic to be proud of. "Now there's just me. They must have died after you left."

"I'm sorry. I remember hearing about that happening. It was an enormous shock. It actually happened before I left."

He was so surprised at her admission that he jammed the brake on in the centre of the drive, throwing them both forward, and twisted to look at her. "You remember them from when you lived here?"

"Of course." Her expression was odd. Furtive maybe, or even guilty. Or perhaps it was just the dim light in the car that masked her features. "I might not have embraced my own magic, but I was aware of the other witches who lived here. I chose not to mix with them. My mother always did. Everyone knew her."

His thoughts whirled as he tried to recollect what they had learned when searching for the missing grimoires. "Did you know about the old families and the missing grimoires? Do you know about them now?"

"I know what Helena told me earlier. The ghost who resides in my mother." Her lips tightened and she sat rigidly, shoulders stiff. "Of course the stories of the five old families had been passed down, and we all knew that our ancestor had been burned at the stake, but I *absolutely* did not know about the hidden grimoires. When I lived here, only my family, your family, and Alex's remained."

"Yes," he said, words forming despite his confusion. "There's something about your generation, and earlier ones, I suppose, that meant you didn't stick around. El's family didn't, and Briar's parents didn't, although her grandmother was here all along and she never knew." He should start driving again, but he couldn't. "You weren't friends with my parents?"

"No, not really. I saw them in town. We had a nodding acquaintance. As I said, I kept apart from the other witch families, unlike Avery."

He was sure she must know more about his family, but decided it could wait for another time. He wanted the perspective of another witch, and suspected she was hiding something, but he had no idea what, or why.

"The coven was Alex's doing," Reuben said, driving down the long, winding drive to the lane again. "He united us all. Avery is our unofficial leader, though. She's a natural. I was late to the party. I didn't practice my magic for years. Now I wouldn't be without it. Do you still practice?"

"No. I set it aside when I left. It was a relief, if I'm honest. Not to have to speak of the craft, or practice it or teach it." She sounded bitter, and had looked away, out of the window so that he couldn't see her face, but he caught a glimpse of her reflection in the glass.

He wondered whether to say the next words, and then thought, *fuck it*. "It was a relief to walk away from Avery? Wow. That's cruel."

Her head whipped around, fury sparking in her eyes. "And you're rude. You have no idea…"

"It's *magic*! Of course I have an idea. I'm a bloody witch. It's hardly like finding out you're a member of the mafia!"

"Magic can attract danger."

"I am bloody well aware of that! Were you asleep in that meeting? We met a djinn today, who seems to be a sociopath, but we aren't running away! Avery was sixteen when you left and you haven't been in touch with her since. I don't count Christmas cards as valid conversations."

"I knew this was a mistake." Diana spat the words out. "Take me back. I'll go somewhere else."

"Too late. You're not bloody running out on Avery again. Besides, we're at Stormcrossed Manor now."

The car bounced down the uneven drive, shaking both of them, but Reuben didn't care. His old car had withstood a lot worse. By the time he halted before the front door, he had bounced them into a stony silence, only relieved by the rain pounding on the roof and sheeting down the windows.

"We'll have to make a run for it," he said, nodding towards the front door. "Watch out for puddles."

But she made no move towards the door, instead staring out the window, eyes glittering with the faint light from the lamp by the front door. "I didn't run out on Avery. I left her with Clea, who was far better suited to teaching her magic than me."

"That's bullshit and you know it. Being her mother is not just about magic."

She finally turned to face him. "I am allowed to have a life, you know."

"Of course. But would it have killed you to have kept in touch properly? My wife, El, was deeply hurt by her parents' refusal to accept magic, and then they refused to come to our wedding. That's just selfish and mean. I will never forgive them for hurting her like that. Never. They better never need our help with anything, because they won't fucking get it. At least her aunt, Oli, stepped up to help. She's nuts, but she supports her."

"I presume you all feel this way about me?"

Reuben could feel her magic stirring, despite the fact that she said she never used it. Then again, you could never truly get rid of magic. "Of course we do. Avery is our friend. Alex—her partner—is fucking furious with you. I admit, Avery's actions probably weren't the wisest, but she'll admit that, too." Hoping he wasn't being disloyal, he said, "El's shadow work brought up things for Avery, so you only have yourself to blame for being summoned like this. Do you really have no interest in your own daughter's life?"

"I felt suffocated here. The weight of those years pressed down on me, and Bryony never felt the pull of the craft, either." Diana looked out the window again. "The thought of coming back here was too much, and to speak to Avery was too much, too. I knew Clea would look after her. Better than I did."

"That's no excuse for your behaviour, and you know it. If you think that sorry-for-yourself story will wash with me, you're an idiot." Too annoyed to discuss it further, he slammed out of the car and ran for the front door. Testing the handle, he was relieved to find it locked, and rang the bell. Tamsyn was far too trusting, but Rosa's paranoia meant the place was secure.

Within moments Diana was next to him, and they stood in stony silence until the locks rattled and the door opened to reveal Rosa. She smiled with relief as she stepped back to let him in. "Reuben! I wasn't expecting you." She was wearing paint-stained jeans and a t-shirt, and looked tired.

"I told Briar I'd check on Tamsyn," he said, and they stepped into the hall and shook the rain off. "This is Diana, Avery's mother. Are you still painting?" He barely gave them time to greet each other. "It's late."

"I'm in the mood, and there's so much to do. Plus, I'm keeping out of Tamsyn's way. She's been fine since this afternoon, but preoccupied. I'm giving her space. Come on through." She walked up the hallway, scratching at a dry patch of paint on her cheek. "The children have been a welcome distraction, I think, but they're in bed now."

"Is she still in her kitchen?" Reuben asked, guessing where they were going.

"Of course. I can barely get her to sit in the new living room, even though it's decorated and comfortable." She shrugged. "It's up to her."

Reuben sensed tension again. Rosa and Tamsyn didn't always see eye to eye. "If you're busy," he said, pausing, "carry on painting. I know the way."

"No, I'll come. I'm worried about her. She hasn't had a vision like that in a while." She turned to Diana whose brow was furrowed with confusion. "She's a Seer, but she thought those visions had long gone. It affects my daughter more strongly now. It's something I have had to get used to. We do, don't we, for those we love? Much as it unnerves me," she admitted with a rueful glance at Reuben. "The longer I live in White Haven, the more normal it becomes. I never thought I'd hear myself say that!" She quickened her pace, unaware of how timely her comment had been.

Reuben glanced at Diana, curious to see her response, but she stared everywhere but at him.

The kitchen was glowing in lamplight, the curtains open to the garden that was bathed in inky blackness marred with thick ribbons of mist. Tamsyn sat in her broad-backed armchair by the crackling fire, staring out at the darkness, unmoving and oddly still.

"Gran! Are you all right?" Rosa called out. "It's just Reuben and Avery's mum, Diana. He's popped in to see you."

Reuben circled around the chair to see Tamsyn's face, but her beetle-dark stare was normal as she shifted her focus to him rather than the garden. "I swear he's close tonight, Reuben. Just beyond my ken."

"The stag?"

"Yes. He's a big, bright beast. Always clad in moonlight." She stared out the window again. "I can't believe I had the vision earlier. It was such an old place. So tangled, with such deep, dark, delicious depths. I sound mad, don't I?"

"You never sound mad," he said, pulling a kitchen chair over to sit close to her, while Rosa gestured for Diana to take the opposite armchair. "You're the wisest woman I know. Have you been to Ravens' Wood?"

"Of course. Such a wonderful place. I remember going there as a young woman. It has always had that air of mystery."

Again, he hit that implanted memory that the Green Man and the Raven King had given everyone. "I mean recently."

"Yes, with Briar. And yes," she smiled, "I know of its recent inception, but I still remember it as being there forever."

"So do I," Diana said unexpectedly. "It always unnerved me. I only went once or twice. What do you mean, 'recent inception'? It's Ravens' Wood. It has always been there."

Tamsyn's attention sharpened on her. "The wood is a gift. You're Avery's mother?"

"Yes."

Tamsyn frowned, and her wrinkles deepened and spread like an incoming tide. "Your daughter's magic eclipses yours, and you carry such resentment about it. It's a wonder you aren't crawling under it. It's like a shroud of lead."

Reuben's mouth fell open in shock. "Resentment?" *That might explain a few things.*

Diana ignored him, focussing only on Tamsyn. "What do you mean, resentment? A shroud of lead. You're talking in riddles."

Tamsyn smirked. "You know exactly what I'm talking about. I see her magic on you, still. She called you back."

Reuben glanced at Rosa, glad to see she looked as perplexed as he did. "You see Avery's magic, Tamsyn?"

She didn't take her eyes off Diana, who seemed to wilt beneath her stare. "A summoning, wasn't it? Yes, I see it. A binding cord that has drawn you here. And you can't leave yet, either. Not until it's done."

"You're stuck here?" Reuben seemed to be trapped in a mental loop that he struggled to get out of. "You mean you can't go, even if you wanted to? Which means you're lying! What the fuck is happening?"

Tamsyn clipped him lightly on the leg. "Language."

Reuben dragged his attention from Diana and turned to Tamsyn. "But you're not a witch," he protested. "You're a Seer. How are you seeing magic?"

"You're very handsome, but not always so bright," Tamsyn said, clucking.

"I'm very bright *and* handsome, actually!"

"I'm a Seer, which means I see what might be, but also what is, and it seems my stag is giving my insights a little juice. Tell me I'm wrong, Diana."

Diana sank back into the chair, deflating as if popped. "No, I can't leave. I am bound here, I know it. If I get in my car and try to exit White Haven, I know that I won't be able to. That the magic won't allow it. It's weird. I just know I'm stuck here until something is finished, but I don't know what that is. What am I supposed to do?" Her voice rose with indignation as she stared at Reuben instead.

Suddenly, he knew what must be resolved before she could leave. "Avery used dragon magic to bring you here, and Beltane woods and Beltane energy, but other things arrived that night, and I think that somehow the summoning has been tied to that. The salamander, the djinn, and now you, are all linked."

"And my stag," Tamsyn added. "A foreshadowing he has been trying to show me for months. The stag is tied to the Wild Wood, and there's nothing wilder here than Ravens' Wood. He knew something would come through at Beltane. Something dangerous that could burn the whole place down."

"The djinn," Reuben said, a horrible sinking feeling in the pit of his stomach. "He will burn it down to find the dragon eggs."

"You," Tamsyn said to Diana, "must help us stop him. Only then can you leave."

"And if we fail?" Diana asked, eyes wide and face pale. "What then?"

"We will all be cinders and ash." Tamsyn stood and crossed to the window, hands pressed against the glass, and Reuben followed her. "I think I must visit the wood to find my stag. The only thing is, Reuben," she paused, her voice faltering, "I'm not sure I'll make it back."

Avery watched her sister study her home with as much intensity as her mother had earlier.

Prowling like an inquisitive cat, she touched objects, stared at pictures on the walls, and then paused to look at the mist-shrouded White Haven lights visible through the partly opened blinds.

Wet coats had been flung off and placed on the back of chairs to dry, bags were under the window, the children were on the sofa watching a kid's film Avery had hurriedly found streaming on the TV, and Caspian was in the kitchen making hot chocolate and mulled wine, skills Avery didn't know he had.

Avery had attempted to use magic to dry the coats, but her sister had muttered, "Don't you dare!"

"Like that, is it?" Avery had answered impatiently. "How very sad for you."

"Mulled wine?" Caspian offered, sweeping in with the tray of drinks. He thrust a steaming glass at Bryony, wafting the scent of spices around. "You look like you need it, and it's not like you'll be driving again tonight. And one for you, Avery. I'm Caspian, by the way," he said, a smile forced on his face, "a friend of Avery and Alex."

"Round so late?" Bryony asked archly.

"We have time sensitive unfinished business. Speaking of which," he said, handing the children mugs of hot chocolate with tiny marshmallows on the foamy surface, "I should go and finish things upstairs."

"Thank you," Avery said, thinking Caspian must have used witch-flight to raid the kitchen in the shop for the marshmallows. Dan's stash for when his blood sugars were low—which was always. "Just shout if you need me."

"What's he doing up there?" Bryony asked as he stepped into the attic room and out of view.

"It's our spell room," Avery answered in a low voice, shooting a look of concern at the children, and hating having to hide her magic in her own house. "Can we sit and talk civilly?"

"Do you promise to keep your magic to yourself?"

"*Our* magic, Bryony, let's not lie." Avery sat at the far end of the table, as far from the children as possible, although the TV sound was turned up so it was doubtful they would hear anything. They seemed settled enough, but every now and again they would peer around to look at them, and Avery smiled in an attempt to make everything appear normal. "Besides," she added as Bryony took a large, satisfied sip of mulled wine, "you don't object to *that*."

Her sister's jaw dropped open in horror as she stared at her drink. "You used magic to make this?"

"Caspian did, obviously! You can't brew that in five minutes!" She rolled her eyes. "Just drink the damn stuff. It won't kill you." It was definitely making her feel better. She'd only wished they'd made some earlier.

"It's very good," Bryony admitted, tentatively sipping some more and clearly deciding she no longer gave a crap. "Just what I needed."

"Me, too. Sorry to have dragged you out on such a day. It was much better weather last night. I was feeling a little...headstrong when I cast the spell."

"No surprise there. Some things don't change, unlike this place. It's more modern and relaxed. Very you. Tidier than I expected, though. You were always such a packrat."

"I still am," she admitted with a smile. "But Alex is very tidy. He reigns in my excesses."

"Alex? Do I know him?"

"Bonneville. His family owns The Wayward Son, and now he runs it."

"Oh! That Alex. Nice. He was always hot."

"Still is," she said smugly. Feeling contrite, she said, "I didn't know you had kids, obviously, or I probably wouldn't have cast the spell. How old are they?"

"Juniper is eight and Rafferty is six. Juni and Raff for short. My husband, Lars, is away on business, or I would have left them at home with him."

"Lars?"

"He's Swedish. Well, Swedish dad, English mom. I'm a Lindgren now." She gave a small smile, a slightly sheepish one. Glad to have left her own surname behind perhaps.

"Congratulations." Avery sighed, a mix of emotions racing through her. She had missed so much. *She had been left out of so much.* She bottled it away, reasoning they were talking now, and urged herself to move on.

"I should also add," Avery said, as the wine loosened her lips, "that I didn't know the spell would be as effective. Did you know I summoned Mum, too?"

Bryony blinked in shock. "No!"

"She was furious about it. Do you two keep in touch?"

"She's *here*?" Bryony looked around as if she'd spring from a cupboard.

"No, she's with Reuben. I'm sure you remember the Jacksons." Her sister nodded. "She's staying at Greenlane Manor for the night. There are beds there for you too, although my friend, El, has also volunteered her place. You can stay here tonight, though. It's too late to traipse about with the children. Helena will go to El's place." Although, she had no idea where the children would sleep. Someone would have to be on the sofa.

"I'm totally bewildered. I don't know who everyone is, or why I'm here. Seriously, you just wanted to see me?"

"It's been years, Bryony! Lately, I just wanted to know that you're okay. Christmas cards don't cut it! Weren't you the slightest bit interested in how I was?"

"I knew you'd be fine."

"Bullshit!"

Bryony swelled with belligerence. "I'd have heard if you weren't."

"Now I find out that I have a nephew and a niece, *and* a brother-in-law, and you never told me!" Tears started to well up, mixed with anger again that she smothered. "And you had a wedding that I wasn't invited to. Am I such a monster?"

"Of course not!" Bryony recoiled like she'd been slapped.

"Was Mum invited?"

"Yes, but we hardly ever see her. It's not like we keep in constant touch."

"Why? You have two children. She has grandchildren!"

"It's complicated."

"Why?"

"We have no wish to exacerbate our magic. We keep our distance. I never speak of it, never practice it, and my husband has no idea."

"You live a half-life."

Bryony jutted her chin out. "It's not that way to me. And now I'm back. Surrounded by it. This place crackles with it. As do you. But it feels strangely comfortable, if I'm honest."

Avery took the time to really take in her sister's appearance. She was still as fair-skinned, with reddish streaks in her hair that was longer than Avery's. Her face was still youthful, and she looked happy. Slightly hippy-ish. *Plus*, Avery reminded herself, *she had rushed to White Haven because she was worried about Avery, not furious with the summoning, like her mother.*

"I'm glad you came. It's really nice to see you."

"Your spell was strong, so I didn't really have a choice, but," Bryony pressed on, seeing Avery's expression, "I'm really pleased to see you, too. I can't believe how busy White Haven is! Full of Beltane bustle. Also, if I'm honest, I want my kids to know you, but not the 'W' word, or the 'M' word."

Witch and magic.

"What if it's what they want?"

"I'll cross that bridge when I come to it."

"With a broom?"

"Funny." "

Avery sighed as she looked over at her nephew and niece. "I better tell you what I've been up to, because I'm afraid White Haven is not the safest place to be right now."

"Why?" Her sister was suddenly alert.

"Beltane magic, and some Otherworld weirdness."

Bryony held her empty glass out. "You better top my wine up, then."

Twenty-Three

"That took a lot longer than I expected," Dylan said, pushing the earphones off his aching ears and rubbing his hands through his dreads. "I still can't understand what they're saying, and my eyes feel as if they have been scrubbed with sandpaper."

"You should have gone to bed earlier," Cassie told him. "I did warn you."

He shrugged. "You know how I get."

"Obsessive."

"Yes, that."

While Cassie had sensibly gone home at about ten o'clock the previous night, Dylan had pressed on to the early hours, when even Ben had given up and sloped off for some sleep. Now, at almost eleven on Friday morning, he had finally finished analysing and organising all the audio.

"The good news," Ben said, scribbling notes on the white board in the centre of the long wall in their office, "is that Newton says there were no more deaths overnight in White Haven, or anywhere else, that could be related to the djinn."

"No other smouldering carcasses, then?"

"Dylan!" Cassie lobbed a ball of rubber bands at him. "They were people!"

"I know. I'm tired. But they're still carcasses."

"Spill then," Ben said, ignoring their spat. "What have you found with the audio?"

"I have isolated the music." Dylan turned back to his screen, blinking to clear his vision. "It's high-pitched and very Otherworldly. It gave me goosebumps." He turned up the volume and played the audio he'd isolated from the rest. The sound started softly, a whining whisper that increased in intensity gradually until various chords and notes blended together to create a soaring song that once again caused goosebumps to erupt on his skin. It felt less intense than it had through the earphones, but equally, as the sound filled the office, the air shimmered around them.

"Stop!" Ben yelled.

Dylan hit the pause button. "What?"

"Did you not see the shimmering mass in the room?"

"Yes," he said hesitantly. "Isn't it soundwaves?"

"You can't *see* soundwaves! That could have been a portal."

Dylan rolled his eyes. "It wasn't a bloody portal. It's magic."

"Magic that could open a portal."

"If it was that bloody easy," Dylan pointed out, "I dare say Prince Qabas would have dragged over his family to help him with his Machiavellian schemes."

"Perhaps," Cassie said, voice dripping with sarcasm, "we should measure it like proper investigators!"

"I was planning to." Ben looked affronted. "I just thought we should pause a moment. Besides, that music was spooky."

"But beautiful," she said, grabbing the EMF meter. "Go on, Dylan."

He hit play, and once again, the strange, Otherworldly music filled the air, and the centre of the room shimmered with a translucent beauty, as if all the energy the sound generated gathered there.

Cassie studied the meter. "It's just a weird kind of magic associated with sound. Nothing is changing…" And then Cassie's confident tone faltered. "I see something in there. Someone grab the camera!"

"It's a fucking portal," Ben said, scrambling to grab the video recorder off Dylan's desk. "I told you!"

"Stop harping on! It's just images. Amazing images."

"Like through a portal?" Ben asked belligerently.

"For the sake of all the gods, Ben," Dylan said, leaping to his feet, "give it a rest! I see it, Cassie. I see the desert."

"And a palace," she said, almost breathless. "Towering turrets, all made of red brick."

"Sandstone," Ben corrected, finally calming down enough to enjoy the show. "It's like a mirage."

To be fair, Dylan appreciated his panic. Ben had been swept back in time with Stan months earlier, and only managed to return by a whisker. Of course he wouldn't want to end up doing that again.

The EMF meter whined. "It's okay, just low levels," Cassie reassured them. "There's no swirling, peaking energy that suggests anything is coming through. It's just an image."

All three stood transfixed in the middle of the room, gazing into the misty vision that had coalesced between them. Dylan waved his hand through the edge of it, but felt nothing untoward.

"Amazing," he muttered. "You're recording, Ben?"

"Yes. I think it's the Realm of Fire. Isn't that what Shadow calls it?"

"Yes, four realms, all elemental. She's from the Realm of Earth."

"So," Cassie said, circling it slowly, "the song of the metals has conjured its home?"

Dylan shrugged. "Seems that way. I feel slightly spellbound. I think we're only hearing and seeing this so well because I've enhanced it. Dragons and other creatures apparently find this hypnotic, according to Shadow. Hell, *I* find it hypnotic."

He shook his head as if to banish his brain fog, but the audio track suddenly stopped, and the image vanished, leaving them all blinking in confusion.

"No!" Cassie murmured. "It's gone."

"Maybe," Ben said, ever practical, "we can think of a way to use it to our advantage."

"I need to hook us up to read our brainwaves while it's playing," Cassie suggested eagerly. "That would be fascinating."

"Agreed. What about the djinn's voice, and the other one?"

"I can't hear words," Dylan said, returning to his desk and switching to the next track, "just murmurs, and it's probably fey speech, anyway. It's sing-song, though. Maybe the djinn is singing, too." He nodded to himself. "Yes, I think he's weaving power into the metal. If I put the tracks together, it's like a conversation." He played them together so that everyone could hear. "I wish I knew what they were saying."

"It's sinuous," Cassie said, watching the image manifest in the room again. "Look! There are different colours in the picture now. Flashes of fire, too."

"This is brilliant," Ben said, furiously taking notes. "I agree, Dylan. The djinn is weaving his own magic into metal. The witches might understand this better. Perhaps it's like when they weave spells into things. Incredible. Maybe hearing this would be useful to El and Dante?"

Dylan nodded. "Could be. No harm asking."

"Was there a final voice or track?" Ben asked him.

"It's the weirdest one," he said, changing the tracks so that the final sound they'd recorded filled the room. "It's like whispering embers. It sounds to me like the fire itself."

"Perhaps the salamander," Cassie suggested.

"Possibly, but I think it's just the fire. The djinn is a fire elemental. He had fire on his hands. It looked like it simmered under his skin. It's not beyond the realms of belief that it's fire itself."

Ben shrugged. "We'll assume that's an unknown for now."

Dylan pushed away from his desk, back aching, and headed to the coffee pot in the corner. "I consider that a good few hours' work. At least we've learned a little more. What about you? What have you found?"

"The djinn's energy reading is off the charts," Ben said. "Way different to Shadow's and the witches'. I suppose that's not surprising. It's like he's operating on a higher plane. Or in another plane."

Dylan turned to Cassie, who had opted to look at the film footage while Dylan worked on the audio. "Any good video?"

"And then some. We can see his body under that cloak—sort of. Unless I'm seeing things, he's got no legs at all, and is instead sort of like a column."

"A column?"

"Like a djinn in a cartoon. All smoke at the bottom. Or maybe sand."

"This I have to see!" Dylan scooted next to her, and Ben leaned over her other shoulder.

The footage was taken at the rear of the carpark, from where Dylan had retreated when the djinn emerged from the forge. He'd kept to the side, trying to avoid the witches and Nephilim blocking his view. There was a light shakiness to the image, but Cassie had cleaned it up and enhanced the thermal imaging. The huge cloak that swathed the prince's body was still obvious, but the thermal imaging had revealed what was underneath it. Not only could they see the slender but muscular shape of the djinn's torso, but also the small horns beneath his scarf-wreathed head. He glowed with a vigorous fire that seemed to consume him, but the lower part of his body was amorphous and tapered away to nothing. Like an ice cream cone that hovered a couple of feet off the ground.

Dylan leaned in to try and see the details. "No wonder he looked so tall. He's floating!"

"He looks like he's burning," Ben said. "Look how much heat he's giving off."

Cassie jabbed the screen. "Check out what he's carrying."

Dylan leaned so close that his nose was almost touching the computer screen, unable to see for a moment what Cassie had, and then he realised why. It was as fiery hot as the djinn's body, so it blended in, but he then saw the sickle shape of an enormous sword with a deadly blade that glinted white-hot. In fact, Dylan was sure he saw a lick of fire along it. "Bollocks! A weapon."

"It's what we expected," Ben said, sounding far calmer than Dylan was. "But is it finished? And where is he hiding?" He looked thoughtfully to the middle of the room, as if the mirage they had seen earlier was still there. "We need to calibrate our instruments so we can search for it."

"Isn't Nahum supposed to be bringing that shifter Wayfinder?" Cassie asked.

"So? Two ways to find Qabas are better than one. That's a big, dangerous looking sword. Whatever he's planning will be massive and brutal. The question is, what is he waiting for?"

Alex awoke to murky grey light filtering into the bedroom he shared with Avery, grateful that the house was quiet.

It had not been quiet when he'd arrived home the night before. Avery and her sister, Bryony, were giggly on red wine, two children were sleeping on the sofa, and Caspian was in the attic room, trying to distract himself from Helena's antics by researching djinns and salamanders. Observing that Avery was enjoying her catch-up with her sister, after some polite conversation, Alex left them to it, deciding to talk to Caspian instead, and together they tried to work out what the therians might do next.

Spending time with Caspian wouldn't normally be his first choice, but they were *almost* friends now, and with Caspian's interest now firmly on Morwenna and not Avery, Alex's animosity had faded. Plus, Caspian was a skilled witch who offered useful insights, and whilst drinking several whiskeys, both had relaxed even further. Alex's slight headache now was testament to that. The conversation had moved on from therians and elemental fire spells to difficult parents and siblings, and surprisingly, it was just the few hours Alex had needed in which to wind down, relax, and let off some steam. With Caspian, of all people.

Helena had returned in the early hours of the morning, brimming with mischievous glee that had quickly spread to Alex and Caspian once she'd related her escapades over more whiskey to celebrate. No wonder his mouth felt like sandpaper.

Avery started to move against his side, her pert bottom nestling into him in a way that stirred his desire, despite his headache. She turned over, opened one eye, and groaned. "The light hurts."

"That will be the wine. Whiskey, for me."

"I can smell it." She snuggled tighter against him, arm wrapped over his chest. "I don't care."

He kissed her forehead. "Did you enjoy chatting to your sister?"

"Actually, yes. It was like the last few years melted away. Apart from the wedding, the husband, and the kids, of course."

"Which bothers you."

"I'm trying not to let it, but yes," she mumbled into his neck. "I sort of get why, though. It's the witch effect, isn't it?"

"It seems so. I think we need to make coffee, and then settle your sister at Reuben's. At least he'll have beds for the kids." That had been a shock. He had a niece and nephew. *Sort of.* Juni was sleeping in the bed with Bryony, and Raff was on the sofa. Helena had joyfully headed to El's place, stating she would love her own flat. Alex had a feeling that El had a willing flat sitter forevermore, should she wish it.

Avery rolled over onto her back and stared at the ceiling. "It's made me feel slightly better that Mum and Bryony rarely see each other, either. How weird is that? Why is my mother not interested in her grandchildren?"

"There's clearly more going on than we realise. At least Bryony didn't rage at you."

"She did for a while, which is completely understandable." She turned to face him again, cheek creased from prolonged contact with the pillow. "I did a terrible thing calling them here. It was a summoning they couldn't ignore. If they'd done it to me, I would have been furious."

He had an urge to say, *I told you so*, but didn't. She knew. "You clearly had a need. It's not the best timing, considering what's happening, but who knew we'd have a djinn in White Haven?" He kissed her again, her lips soft beneath his, but if he lingered, he'd want more, and with two kids downstairs that was not going to happen. "Later, Ms Hamilton, when we're alone, I shall take full advantage of you, but until then I'll make coffee and tea and make sure your sister is okay. Then I'll call Reuben."

"I hope my mother behaved."

"As if he would give a crap one way or the other. If she was rude, he'd dish it straight back. I'm hoping he did. I know I want to. It was a bloody good job I wasn't here when she arrived."

Avery smiled. "What would you have done?"

"Yelled back."

"I did that."

He laughed. "I'd have liked to watch, then."

He wanted nothing more than to lie there all morning, doing nothing except read, relax, and have sex with the woman he loved, but instead he hauled himself out of bed, showered, and headed downstairs. The jumble of books and grimoires on the attic table reminded him of all they'd talked about the previous night, but he'd think about that later. Collecting the empty glasses, he walked downstairs, casting a spell to make him silent, and entered the kitchen.

For the next ten minutes he made coffee, cleaned and tidied, and let his thumping head settle. Then the messages started coming in. Reuben, Ben, and Eli, all with updates, all wanting to meet up, and within minutes it was settled. 10:30am at Reuben's, which suited everyone except Briar, who resignedly said she'd be there anyway. She wanted to open her shop, but with Eli also needing to be at the meeting that was impossible. In addition, they wanted Nahum to be there too, and seeing as he was already driving down, he should arrive in time. *With the shifter-seeking Wayfinder, whatever the hell that was.*

"Sorry," Bryony said, startling him out of his thoughts, "I just wanted some tea."

"It's fine, come in." He beckoned her in from where she loitered by the arched entrance to the kitchen, looking as sleepy as he felt. "Just catching up with messages. Kettle has just boiled."

"I didn't hear you in here at all." She had dressed in jeans and a t-shirt, but her face was bare of make-up and her long hair was loose. She looked so like Avery, it was shocking. Her build, her bone structure, even some of her mannerisms.

"I cast a spell so I wouldn't wake anyone. Did you sleep okay?"

"I drank so much wine, I slept like the dead. Plus," she said, adding hot water to the teapot that Alex had already prepared, "I was exhausted after travelling for hours." There was no re-crimination in her voice. Just plain fact.

"Where do you live?"

"The Lincolnshire Wolds."

He frowned, trying to place it, and she smiled. "East of Sheffield. A long drive, especially when you have to find dog sitters, lock up the house, organise children, and all those things. My husband is away on business. He's a Conservation Architect," she added. "It means he travels quite a bit."

"It sounds interesting."

"It is, and he loves it. He's in York at the moment, working on a manor house. I'm sure he'd be very interested in this place." Her gaze swept around the room. "This house *and* White Haven."

"In which case, he'd love Reuben's place."

"The Jacksons. Greenlane Manor?"

"Yes, where your mother is." He wasn't responsible for the summoning spell, but suddenly felt horribly guilty, especially as he'd wanted to shout and rant at Bryony and Diana. But Bryony seemed nice. Normal. Not a monster. "Sorry. It must have been a nightmare yesterday, but Avery…"

She stopped him with a slight shake of the head. "I know. I should have been better at keeping in touch. I left for university and never came back."

Alex frowned. "I didn't know that. I just thought you left without a plan. My memory of that time is quite foggy."

"My mother just up and left. I had a plan, but I'm not sure how much Avery took that in. She was totally absorbed in the craft, angry with Mother, and caught up in her own schoolwork."

"When she was older, she studied in Bristol before coming back here. English Lit."

She smiled. "Always books. For both of us, really. How could it not be when books are the family business? I went to Edinburgh—History and Archaeology with an MA in Heritage Studies. That's how I met my husband, and then we had children. Now I'm a freelance writer for heritage and arts magazines." She shrugged. "Sorry, you probably didn't need to know all that. I feel I need to justify myself, though. As if I ran off with no cause."

"You ran off to pursue the life you wanted. Without witch-craft. I can't blame you for that. Only for not keeping in touch. It hurt her."

"I know. Blimey." She laughed. "This is quite the topic for an early morning. Especially after such a late night. I still haven't seen Gran, either. I seemed to miss her with everything that happened last night."

"Ah, well, Clea had her own things going on last night. In fact," he said sipping his coffee for mental fortitude, "we all have a lot going on right now."

"So I gather. It's far from the sleepy White Haven that I re-member."

"There is nothing remotely sleepy about White Haven, espe-cially right now."

"Avery told me everything. I admit that I'm worried. However, now that I'm here, I don't want to just run off again. I may as well make the most of it. Besides, the strange compulsion the spell gave me is still here. Settled in my stomach. I don't think I could go even if I wanted to."

"No," Alex said, thinking of Reuben's brief message that morning, "your mother can't, either. We're having a meeting today. All of us at Reuben's place, and your mother will be there. You should be part of it. And like I said, Reu's happy to put you up, and there's loads of room. Unlike here."

"I vaguely remember Reuben, but it's not him I'm worried about, just that there's a house full of magic." She glanced back towards the living room, where the noise of the TV was already audible. "I don't want the kids exposed to it."

"This house is full of magic, so it's no different, and I doubt you'll find a place in town at the moment. Everywhere is booked for Beltane. However, Reu's place is warded and protected, so you'll be safe there. Plus, there are huge gardens to play and roam in. The kids will love it." He paused, and then smiled. "You can spend time with your mum, too."

"Yes, that will be interesting." She leaned against the counter sipping her tea as she looked around. "I must admit, it doesn't seem overtly witchy here. Well, apart from the shelves of herbs, but it is a kitchen."

"I take it you haven't seen the attic room yet?"

"You seemed busy up there last night, and we were talking."

"Well, that's where the witchy stuff is. Not sure what your kids will think." However, it was in their blood, whether Bryony wanted to admit it or not.

"Surely quirky Auntie Avery is easily explained away?" Bryony said, hoping for reassurance.

"Not when they see the attic."

Bryony closed her eyes and sighed. "I don't want this, Alex."

"Well, either don't take them up there, which will lead to rampant speculation, or call it book research. Plus, they should totally check out the kid's section in the shop downstairs. I'm sure there's a free book or two down there for them. Sally and Dan are both brilliant with children—they're Avery's friends and colleagues."

"I think I remember Sally." She shook her head, perplexed. "All of these names are suddenly flooding back. I even remember you. You make her happy, that much is obvious. Thank you."

Alex, despite his earlier antagonism, found he actually liked Bryony, and was determined to make the family dynamics work. Avery wanted her family back in her life, and Alex would do what he could to make it happen. *Djinn be damned.*

Twenty-Four

B riar was certain she felt the mournful mood caused by the thick mist that still enveloped White Haven more than the others, maybe because she was an earth witch who was deeply attuned to the land and Ravens' Wood.

It affected her concentration, which was already scattered with thoughts of the djinn, Nelaira's death, and her grandmother's palpable concern about the white stag. Especially after what Reuben had told her of his visit the night before. While she had been mixing potions and searching her own grimoire for information about salamanders and djinn, her sunroom ablaze with candles to drive away the gloom, Tamsyn had been staring into the darkness.

Briar sighed as she stood at one of the windows in Reuben's vast ballroom, looking west across his grounds, with White Haven and the coast, mostly unseen, in the valley below, the dark green rise of Ravens' Wood thick on the opposite hill. It was barely visible in the fog, but every now and again the wind lifted it like a veil, revealing the bones of the castle and the creaking branches of the ancient forest, before it settled again. The chattering clatter of the twigs sounded close to her ears, as if she were amongst the trees in the leafy green twilight, feeling the steady rise of sap mixing with her own blood. She fought to dispel the sudden, disconcerting vision by closing her eyes tightly and then opening them again. In the brief glimpse she'd caught of it, she already thought the treeline looked closer, but perhaps that was just the dryads' threats making her imagine such a thing.

Eli stood next to her, his profile bleak as he too studied the wood. "They weren't joking. I honestly think they could march to the coast. Not sure how, but I wouldn't put it past them."

She tore her eyes away from the view, comforted by Eli's solid presence. "How are you after last night?"

"Pissed off. Angry. And wondering where that fucker is."

"We'll find him. We have a big enough team, and now the mysterious Wayfinder."

She turned to the room behind them and their gathered group of friends, the murmurs of many conversations resonating across the large area. So much had happened in the short space of time since yesterday's meeting, they were all catching up with the latest news.

After the wedding, Reuben had decided the ballroom was too good a space not to use more often, and El had agreed. The long windows and run of doors offered light and spectacular views, the décor was impressive, and the room was perfect for both summer and winter, especially as large fireplaces were placed in the two shorter walls. It was now furnished with large, leafy plants that gave it the air of a conservatory, especially with the dramatic wisteria wallpaper and panels. Lots of comfortable chairs had been placed there—some old, some new—plus several occasional tables, many of which were close to one fireplace. At the other end of the room by the second fireplace was a long, burnished wooden table that seated thirty people. It was no doubt once intended for grand dinner parties, but now allowed for witchy strategy sessions.

El had a hand in it all. Briar could tell, from the placement of lamps, cushions, paintings, and flowers. Briar was pleased that El was finally putting her stamp on the grand house, and although Briar knew she loved her flat, she had a feeling that El might just move in now. It was as if the wedding had granted her the permission she felt she needed to make changes. Reuben's addition was the large TV screen on one of the walls, intended to play Ghost OPS' findings. It was clearly their new centre of the operations.

Stan was overjoyed to be present in the room he had declared his favourite place on Earth. Stan never did things by halves. He had been invited to the meeting, as Reuben felt he should be kept informed of events, and he was warming his hands by the fireplace whilst talking to a tense Diana. Bryony was elsewhere in the house with the kids, exploring, but everyone else was there. Tension rolled around the room, especially from Newton. Briar thought his behaviour as of late was just plain weird. He glowered at Eli, and every now and again, Eli winked at her and acted overly courteous, which alone made her wonder what was going on. But there was no time for idle chitchat. Nahum had just arrived, full of good health and cheer.

He held up a curious metal device for everyone to see. It was the size of a plate, made of various metals inlaid with interesting designs, and looked heavy. "It shouldn't need calibrating, as magic has been built into it by an ancestor of the current Moonfell Witches. It was designed to find shifters, because they were hunters, of sorts. That mark there is for djinn." He held up the device and pointed to a spot on the outer perimeter. "Birdie—their priestess—considers them shifters too, and clearly their ancestors did. They used this very successfully only a few weeks ago to find an ancient group of wolf-shifters. They used some kind of spirit spell, but that's a long story—best saved for whiskey." He waved it off. "Essentially, this should just work, but I told them you'd work it out if it needed adjusting. Birdie says you're welcome to call her, too. I suggest you do. She's amazing. They all are."

El, unsurprisingly, was the first to Nahum's side, and she took the Wayfinder and hefted it. "It's pretty substantial. Ooh!" She took a big breath in. "I can feel the magic, and look at the metal-work!" She walked to the windows to see it better in the natural light, and Briar edged to her side, while Ben turned on his EMF meter to scan it.

"Have you ever seen anything like this before, El?" Briar asked.

"Never. This is incredible." El looked focussed and sharp, despite the many hours she'd spent at the forge the day before, and during the night. "You know, I've always thought I'm a very good metalworker, able to instil my magic into my jewellery well, but this is something else."

"Don't downplay your abilities," Briar said. "I bet you could make something like this, given time."

El barked out a laugh. "Not without serious help. This is way beyond my abilities. I'm just trying to think of how they accomplished it. The spells they must have used, and then the device itself."

El placed it on her palm, her finger nudging the two slender pointers fixed to the centre, one that indicated the moon phases, the other reaching to the outer rim where the miniature shifter figures were etched. It was incredibly beautiful, but so far they weren't moving.

"Will that identify therians?" Alex asked.

Nahum shrugged. "Sure. They're shifters. I think there's a symbol on there for them. Vampires are there, too."

"I can see the djinn's image," Briar said, leaning over the Wayfinder. The body itself was made of brass, but many other metals were inlaid into the surface. Plus, she felt its magic even without touching it. "Like out of a fairytale."

"Not a fairytale," Dylan said, calling from his position by the TV where he was plugging in his equipment. "That's what they look like. Well, that's what ours looks like, under his cloak."

"Ours?" Stan shuddered theatrically. "Don't say that. We don't want to own him, and he bloody well isn't staying."

El called across to Nahum who was leaning against one of the exterior doorframes, chatting with Zee. "Nahum, who made this, again?"

"A guy called Fitz and his friend, Ed. Moonfell had a strange experience over the last few days, and they've learned—and are still learning—lots about them. They were hunters, mainly in India, but across Europe, too. Eighteenth century adventurers."

"That's wicked cool," Reuben said, looking with renewed interest at the Wayfinder. "Awesome. How long can we borrow this for?"

"There's no rush to return it—yet."

"Any idea of how long the range is?" Caspian asked.

"Pretty good," Nahum said. "The witches tracked wolf-shifters across London, but that was with the aid of another spell to guide it. Do not ask me the details, because it's complicated. I don't think you'll need a spell though."

Avery, always eager to expand her knowledge, volunteered. "I'll call if necessary. Perhaps put Birdie on speaker. Cas? Alex?" She looked to both of them for help.

Caspian, however, pointed to El. "El should be in on that conversation. She's the metalwork guru."

Caspian's mood was buoyant that morning, and Briar was glad to see it. They had heard about Helena's encounter with Jed the night before, and Morwenna had already received a phone call arranging a time for Ysella to visit. *One good thing, at least.* Briar hoped Caspian would see more success in his love life than she was having.

As for Helena, although she was quiet, she was full of barely contained delight, so that even her interactions with Diana were good. There were so many different moods in the room, it was hard to keep track of them all. It meant the atmosphere felt strained. Not uncomfortable; just odd. Or maybe that was just her mood.

"You know," Briar said thoughtfully as she considered their other witch friends' abilities, "if you need help with this kind of thing, Nate would be good."

"Eve's friend?" Zee suddenly perked up.

"Yes. He sculpts, right?" she asked her coven for confirmation. Then she turned back to El. "Just in case you want to try and replicate something similar. Not right now, obviously."

El ran a manicured finger over her lower lip—still well-groomed despite metalworking all night long. "I'd start simpler. This would certainly be a challenge. Anyway, I'll learn more as we use it."

"Ed," Nahum explained, "was an engineer, I should point out. Very clever. Member of the Royal Society. If you need someone to help make tools like that, I suggest you involve JD. What he doesn't know isn't worth knowing."

Zee snorted. "Although, you may want to prepare yourselves. He'll annoy the shit out of you."

"The guy who made alchemical weapons?" Reuben asked, eyes widening. They'd all heard about the immortal JD.

"The very same," Caspian said. "Certified genius and borderline insane, but I like him."

"And he adores Maggie Milne," Nahum said to Newton. "Didn't see that coming, I must admit."

Now it was Newton's turn to look surprised. "He does? Maggie? Super sweary Maggie?" He repeated her name as if he'd misheard.

"Yep. They verbally joust with Elizabethan witticisms. It's very funny."

"I really want to meet her," Kendall said to Newton. "For many reasons."

Alex held up his hand. "As delightful as all of this is, can we move on? If El wants JD's help to try and replicate that, great. Same with Nate. But for now, how do we use it? The sooner we start searching the better."

"We should just head out there and start testing it," Nahum said with a shrug. "I can stick around and help. Olivia is busy with work, so I can stay a day or so."

"We're hunting him today?" Briar asked.

"It depends," Alex said, "on how far along El is with making something to put him in."

"Let me just kill him," Eli said, a hard edge to his voice.

"No offence, Eli, but you didn't look close to killing him yesterday."

"You didn't look close to catching him, either."

"This hunt," Briar said, laying a restraining hand on Eli's arm, his muscles cording beneath her touch, "will need strategies. Multiple ones. From what Eli, Zee, and Moore found out last night, Ravens' Wood will take matters into their own hands if we don't sort this out. I'm sure none of us want to see White Haven swamped by an ancient forest. I certainly don't want my grandmother lost in the wood with some mythical white stag, either."

"She saw fire," Reuben said, eyes flicking to Briar and then to the rest of the group. "It scared her, but the stag might offer a solution—if we can work out its message."

Avery stepped forward, her clear voice ringing out around the room, marshalling everyone as she always did, and Briar was grateful for her energy and resilience. "We have various spells that potentially could restrain a djinn or a salamander that you need to see, El. And now we have a Wayfinder. What else have we got?"

Ben waved an arm in Dylan's direction. "We've calibrated our equipment to help hunt. Before we all split up, you need to see and hear what we found. It might especially help you, El."

"Good," she said, "because when I leave here, I'm heading back to Dante. I need extra spells for the vessel we're crafting, and all help is useful. Salamander included."

"Gather around, then," Dylan said, beckoning them.

As they all clustered in front of the TV screen, Diana kept away from the group, but she didn't leave, which Briar found curious. She might profess not to care about White Haven, or confess she couldn't leave, but she could choose not to be involved—and yet here she was, watching Avery through narrowed eyes. Watching all of them as they observed the impressive ten minutes of video footage and listened to strange, Otherworldly music that conjured mirages that left them all talking excitedly at the end of it.

"Brilliant work!" Stan said, clapping Dylan on the shoulder with a resounding smack. "Brilliant. Terrifying, obviously, but wow!"

"Guys!" El held a hand up. "Play the talking bit again. Well, the singing or whatever you call it. I think the pointers moved."

Dylan cued up the track, and El placed the Wayfinder on the table so everyone could see it. "There. A slight flicker in the dial."

"But it isn't pointing anywhere," Helena said.

"Now the weird embers sound," El instructed, not answering her.

Again, the longest pointer twitched.

"I call that a win," Nahum said. "Something about that audio is djinn-adjacent enough to set that thing off. The night the witches used it, it whirled a lot until it settled on the signal, and then it sat true. But they were close when that happened."

El heaved a sigh of relief. "I thought I was imagining it. At least it works."

Stan cleared his throat and wiped his slightly sweaty brow. "I don't know about you, Ben, but that music reminded me a little too well of our own experience. I could feel it in my blood."

Ben nodded, flashing a guilty look at his team. "I've been trying to ignore it, actually, but yes. It felt like a sort of calling."

Cassie looked stricken. "You should have said so!"

"No point. Nothing anyone can do. It's not like I'm be-witched or anything, either. We strayed into the Otherworld in that ancient forest, that's all."

There was nothing 'that's all' about it, Briar thought, watching Ben and Stan. *What a strange experience to have shared.*

"Interesting, though," Cassie said, studying him. "I'm definitely hooking you up later to study your brainwaves."

Briar suppressed a smile. Their group never failed to entertain, no matter how bad things seemed.

Helena had been conferring quietly with Avery, but now addressed them all. "We've faced worse, and at least we know more now. He's crafted a weapon. He wants the eggs, and he'll kill to get them. *Again.* We just have to get to him first. I think for now that just a couple of witches, Ghost OPS, and the Nephilim need to search for him and hopefully find where he's hiding. Then we watch."

"I have to go to the post-mortem," Newton said regretfully. "Just keep me informed."

"We watch from a distance," Alex pointed out. "We don't want to spook him."

El nodded. "I'll complete the vessel to capture him, but I'd like the coven's input later. I'm already weaving some spells into the metal, and we're using iron, which should be effective, but I've also found a really good spell to trap it. The more of us that cast it, the more powerful it will be. I think that by this evening I'll be ready. It's not the most beautiful thing I've ever made, but it should do its job." She turned to Diana. "I don't include you, obviously, although I'm wondering if the Beltane fire spell that seems to have settled in you might help. Your decision, though."

"I haven't used my magic in a long time," Diana admitted, uneasy, "but if you think it can help, I'll be there. I'm sure Bryony will be, as well. However, who will look after the children?"

"I'll ask my cousin, Rosa," Briar said. "She also has two kids, so I'm sure she'll help. So will Tamsyn, my grandmother. Thank you, Diana."

Briar assumed that would have been hard for Diana to agree to help, but also how could a witch really not use her magic? Reuben didn't think he'd used his, and yet he acknowledged he had been for years without realising it.

"We," Avery said, barely looking at her mother and instead focussing on her coven, "will find a way to transport the salamander. Last night we found a spell that should enable you to use it, El, and unsurprisingly it was in your grimoire. It's pure fire energy, so it should enhance your spell's strength."

El shook her head. "Those grimoires never cease to amaze me."

"Your ancestor, Ursula," Helena said to El, "in my generation, did not use a salamander, but fire wasn't her strength. Air was."

"What about mine?" Briar asked, wondering why she'd never asked before. But she knew why. They were always busy with the here and now, and Helena had a wealth of knowledge that couldn't be grasped in a few days every few weeks. Something it was increasingly obvious they needed to address.

Helena smiled. "Agnes was an earth witch and healer. Your roots run deep, my dear."

Agnes. Briar had seen her name in the grimoire, obviously, but hearing Helena mention it again made it all much more real.

El wagged a finger at Helena. "We'll talk about this later. Avery, I'll meet you at yours as soon as we're done here."

"What else can we do?" Briar asked, eager to keep busy. "Obviously not let Ravens' Wood invade the entirety of White Haven. I think I'll take Tamsyn to meet the dryads, as long as Rosa will be okay with the children on her own. If she can meet the stag, even better. I think I should summon Deer to help." She shrugged as she turned to Eli. "Opening the shop seems pointless today. There's too much going on. Plus, what if the djinn returns to the wood today?"

Newton's lips tightened. "Take Moore again."

Moore nodded enthusiastically. "Absolutely. The more often I go, the better my rapport. Plus, safety in numbers."

"You have good instincts there," Briar told him. "Works for me."

"In that case," Eli said, folding his arms across his broad chest, "I'll go, too. I don't want you encountering the djinn without proper backup. Right, Newton?" Eli smirked.

Newton's jaw clenched, and then he just nodded. "Of course."

"And me!" Cassie said. She turned to her team. "One of us should check the wood, and now that our instruments are calibrated, I will."

"Well," Kendall said, "I hate to be a bore, but I'm seeing James, the vicar. I feel he should know what's happening. Plus, I'll liaise with Kev and Hamid."

"I'll join you," Stan said to her, before addressing the wider team. "Say you're successful today, and we find the djinn and catch him, where does Prince Qabas go then?"

"That, Stan," Reuben said, clapping him on the back as he picked up a pastry off the selection on the table, "is the million-dollar question."

Twenty-Five

Newton deeply resented that he had to go to the post-mortem. If he hadn't been required to, he could be spending time in Ravens' Wood with Briar, and now Eli was making his move.

Bollocks.

Although at least Moore and Cassie were there, and Tamsyn, of course. Plus, he was the DI with other responsibilities, and his place was understanding the creature, not swanning around with Briar. He would make it work. It was not too late.

Wanting to see the hunt underway before he left, he parked at the side of the road and studied the long stretch of beach that was inhabited only by a couple of rain-loving walkers, and decided that maybe going to the post-mortem would be better than searching the beach in this weather. He exited the car to speak to Alex and Reuben, who had pulled up in their cars behind his.

"Bloody hell," Alex said with a groan as he surveyed the sea. "I can think of better things to be doing today."

Newton raised his jacket collar, hunching his shoulders. "It's grim weather, that's for sure."

Reuben bounded out of his car eagerly. "It's just rain. You two need to surf."

"Nope, I really don't," Newton said.

The waves pounded into the beach, and everything was grey. The sky, the sea, and his bloody mood. But somewhere out there might be the djinn. It was the logical place to start. Djinn liked sand, and this was where he had arrived, after all. At least Stan had been able to confirm that they had carried extra wood down from Ravens' Wood on the day of the town bonfire. All old wood, all piled at the edge by the carpark ready to be used. One of those old logs must be where the djinn had hidden after fleeing the dryads. *But that didn't make sense.*

"Why," he said, voicing his concerns, "do we think the djinn needed to hide in a log when he seemingly can transport himself anywhere?"

"That's actually a very good question," Alex said, eyes narrowing. "Convenience?

"Maybe he was weakened after killing Nelaira," Reuben suggested. "Or he needed to get his bearings? He is in an unknown world, after all."

Newton grunted. "Maybe. He seemed very powerful yesterday to need to do such a thing."

Reuben shrugged. "Maybe the Beltane fire did that. And killing those people. There are still many unknowns."

"Or maybe," Alex said, "it was just the salamander all alone in there, and the djinn made his own way. I suggest," he added, as Ghost OPS' van pulled up behind them, "that we work logically over the sand."

Newton nodded. "Yes, but I think you should attack it from both ends, and meet in the middle. The less time you need to spend here, the better."

"We only have one Wayfinder," Reuben pointed out.

"But Ghost OPS have calibrated their *whatevers*," he said vaguely. "I trust them. And we have you two." He mustered a cheesy grin.

"Don't force it, mate," Reuben said, frowning. "Your aura is off."

"Aura?" Newton couldn't have been more shocked if Reuben had punched him. "Since when do you talk about auras?"

"I'm more tuned in now that I've been spending time with Silver. What's upsetting you?"

"Djinn," he answered firmly. He didn't want any awkward questions. "I also suggest you focus on the dunes. They're all sealed off, anyway. Let's split the team."

He turned to greet the others before those hideously intuitive witches asked anything else. Zee and Nahum emerged from the back of the Ghost OPS' van, and Dylan and Ben from the front. That should work; one Nephilim, one witch, and one Ghost OPS member to a team.

"Who wants the Wayfinder?" he asked after telling them of his plans.

"Me," Nahum said. "I've received instructions from Birdie. It should be straightforward."

Newton turned to Ben. "You'll lead the other team, then. You happy your EMF meter is sensitive enough?"

"Of course."

"Then I suggest Reuben and Zee are with you, and Alex and Dylan are with Nahum. Everyone okay with that?"

"Works for me," Alex said. "But if we have no success here, we'll have to consider where else we search. Any suggestions?"

Zee shrugged. "Back to Ravens' Wood?"

"Or the next beach," Reuben said. "We'll see what Briar and Eli think. We should keep in touch, too," he said to the other team. "We'll meet in the middle, but of course if you find anything first, Ben, call us. Same goes for us."

"And keep your distance," Newton instructed. "I don't want to scare him off, or risk a confrontation if you find him."

As Ben's team set off to the edge of the dunes, Newton lifted his face, the fine drizzle settling on his skin as the chill wind cut through his coat. He hoped the djinn was finding the weather equally unpleasant. It was hard to see the other end of the beach, the sea mist was so thick, so the gods only knew what it might be covering up. Then he stared up at the cliff top, wondering how Briar was getting on, and hoping that she would be safe.

"Holy shit! El said, crouching down before the fire to watch the salamander. "Look at it! I love it already!"

"But can you use it?" Avery asked, kneeling next to her, the glow from the fire glinting off her red hair.

"I'll find a way." The salamander was curled in its bed of embers, logs smouldering around it, and it looked utterly content, even as it opened both eyes to peer at her, triggering a response deep in her core. "It seriously hasn't moved?"

"Not in twenty-four hours. I've made sure to keep it comfortable." Avery sniggered. "How crazy is this?"

"Only as crazy as all the other crazy things," Helena said, calling from the table at the back of the room.

El laughed. *There was no denying that.* They were in Avery's attic room with Diana and Bryony. Rosa had agreed to look after Bryony's children with Max and Beth, so that Bryony could join the others. The atmosphere felt tense with Avery's family present, and El tried to focus on the issue at hand.

"Maybe it won't want to come with me," El said, doubt creeping in. "Although, with summer coming, you can't keep this fire going forever. What then?"

"It might just disappear anyway, as quickly as it arrived."

The salamander was still staring at El with unblinking eyes, and she smiled at it. "Hello, you gorgeous creature. Would you like to come with me? A new home?"

El conjured a witch-fire to lick around her fingers and reached towards the lizard. It stirred and moved, lifting its head as if deciding whether to move closer, but the heat of the embers made El withdraw her hand. She knew spells to insulate herself against fire, and manipulated the element all the time when she was working on her larger projects, but she had never yet placed her hands in the flames. Partly because she hadn't needed to, and partly out of natural fear. Something perhaps she should address.

"You have a rapport already," Avery observed. "How?"

El shrugged. "I don't know, other than it must recognise my elemental magic. I feel its magic, too. As soon as it looked at me, it was like something responded in here." She tapped her chest. "I almost feel as if I could communicate with it, and yet I don't know how. It's weird, as if I'm blocked. No, *blocked* is the wrong word. Just lacking essential knowledge." El sat back on the rug as the salamander retreated but continued to watch her, and reached for her capacious leather bag, trying to be practical. "I've brought a metal box with me. I figure we can line it with embers and transport it that way."

The metal box was one of many that she'd crafted over the years to contain all sorts of things. She practiced her engraving skills on them, and imbued magic into the metals. They were side projects, and she found she liked storing her candles and other witchcraft paraphernalia in them. Something different to wicker baskets and wood. This particular one was made of brass, an excellent insulating material, and very sturdy, with thick sides and runes etched in, as well as pretty designs, and an ornate latch.

"That's cool," Avery said, taking it off her. "I'd love something like this. I don't know what for, but you know, it's pretty."

"Thank you. I can make you one. I've also brought a thick scarf to wrap around it to insulate the hot metal. With luck, I can transfer it straight to Dante's forge."

Diana cut in, eyebrows raised. "Doesn't your friend, Dante, think this is weird?"

"He's used to my magic. I think he always suspected, and then he met Shadow, our fey friend." El twisted to look at Diana. "He asked some awkward questions after that. She had glamoured herself, but well, we had some odd discussions, then she needed her sword fixed...and well, now he knows."

Bryony was prowling around the attic, examining the herbs, candles, potions, and tinctures lined up on the many shelves. Pausing to investigate Avery's tarot card collection, she picked up a pack and turned to El. "He must be very accepting of you. Not everyone would be comfortable with all this."

"He has a questing mind, but he has never been here, or Briar's herb room, and he certainly doesn't know about Alex's spirit work. This, however," she said, pointing at the salamander, "will obviously prompt more questions. It won't stay with Dante, obviously, but I need Dante's help, so I can't hide it from him. If it doesn't vanish, I'll keep it at my own forge. But again, how, over a long period of time?"

"Your grimoire," Avery suggested, "has spells for summoning them, so maybe they just go somewhere for a while?"

"It's time I checked my grimoire." Leaving the salamander sleeping once more, although part of her was sure it was listening to every word, El headed to the table to where her grimoire was open, the call of the magic within its pages already beckoning her. "You searched this yesterday, then?" she asked Avery as all the witches gathered around her.

"Yes, and that spell," Avery tapped the two pages it was spread across, "looked the most useful."

The spell was in the first third of the grimoire, the pages old and made of vellum. The inked cursive was tightly packed as it coiled across the pages, much like the salamander that was drawn in one corner, curled within embers. Colour had been worked into the text and image, still bright despite the years, preserved by magic. Rich purples, blues, and umber.

"I remember seeing this when I first explored it," El said, fingers stroking the page and tracing the fine lines of the slumbering fire elemental. "I love to illustrate my spells, and when I discovered this, I realised it was a family trait that reached back centuries."

"Ursula loved to draw, it was one of her hobbies," Helena said softly. "I didn't know that about you, El."

"Why would you? I don't think any of us share how we decorate our personal grimoires, and we don't see half enough of you." She met Helena's warm, thoughtful gaze. "When we do, we don't talk about that time. I wasn't sure if it was something we should avoid. If it was too painful."

Helena squeezed her arm gently, as if to reassure her. "It is painful, but also, before the horror, it was a wonderful time. It's actually been healing to talk about it."

Diana cleared her throat. "I would like to hear about that, too."

"So would I," Bryony said.

"You would?" Avery questioned, tone harsh. "I'm surprised."

"I might not wish to use my magic," Diana said, "but maybe it's because of all that went before. I'm not saying I'd change my mind, but it's still my history."

"All of our history," El murmured. "Plus, seeing as my parents don't wish to acknowledge anything, it's made me realise we have to treasure what knowledge we can get. Document it. All we have are the messages we discovered with these old grimoires."

"And your letter," Avery said to Helena, "in the back of mine."

El nodded. "With the great spell."

"Then perhaps," Helena suggested tentatively, "I should talk to all of you, either individually or together, and maybe I should start to write it down. My own diary of that time, free of censor and fear. Once this is over."

"Thank you." El turned her attention to the spell Avery had thought most useful. "This looks fascinating. Any reason why you think this one?"

"Well, you have several on this topic, spread throughout this section and time period. They are far more detailed than the ones in mine. Ours." She corrected herself. "All vary slightly. Some are verbose, whereas this one seems to have the most practical applications."

El read the title, *"For Understanding ye Tongue of Fire-Wyrmes.* Direct and to the point. There's a huge list of ingredients."

"For a potion," Diana said. "Although, watching you with the salamander a few moments ago makes me think you won't need that."

El looked at her, surprised. "Why do say that?"

"It responded to you, and you said yourself that you felt it. Maybe that spell is for someone who has no natural affinity. There are degrees of knowledge associated with salamanders."

"That's an interesting observation from someone who professes to have abandoned their magic," Avery said, looking at her mother with suspicion.

"You don't know what kind of library I work at, do you?" Diana said, eyes on the books, lips tightening with apprehension, or maybe disapproval. El couldn't quite work it out. It was as if the air had thickened around them. "Or where you might have got your love of research from?"

"Well," Avery said, bristling already, "it's hard to know when you're not around, and it's not as if you have been exactly forthcoming since your arrival, either."

Diana smiled tightly. "Touché. I haven't been entirely honest with you. I have been used to keeping things locked away, and it's become a habit. However, considering everything that's going on, and the scale of the problem, I think it's time I do. I work with a private collection of Medieval and Elizabethan manuscripts, some of which are herbal treatises, and there are some bestiaries, too. Stunningly decorated manuscripts."

Avery took a sharp intake of breath. "I wondered why you made so many salient comments the other night, and yet you didn't say a word!" She drew breath again, eyes wide, and El braced herself. "You still work in magic."

"No!"

"Yes! You abandoned your magic, supposedly—and me—and yet, you work with old manuscripts. No wonder you look so at home with them. You've been holding back!"

"I don't work with grimoires, Avery. They are not magical texts, either. There are all sorts of books…"

"Oh, as good as, Mother," Bryony chastised, rolling her eyes. "Old documents about herbs and bestiaries are one step away from magic."

El exchanged a look with Helena, both knowing they needed to avert this now.

"Perhaps," El said swiftly, seeing that Avery was about to strike again, "I should be out of the way when you have this particular family discussion. For now, let's get this done. I have to get back to Dante, anyway."

"Mother," Avery said, a spike to her tone, "considering your observation, of all the spells we've identified, I think this one then is best." She paged through El's grimoire, opening it to a much simpler spell titled *For ye Understanding of Tongues Spoken in Flame.* "But what do you think?"

"Not that one," she said, shaking her head almost sheepishly as she flicked through a few other pages. "This one. *A Charme for Parley with ye Spirit of Living Flame.* It sits side by side with *The Summoning and Parley with ye Fire-Spirite.* It has been summoned already, so we clearly don't need that, and it's a simple incantation."

El was already scanning and interpreting the language, and she read it aloud. "A charm to unlock the ancient tongue of fire locked within the creature of living ember." Even just saying the description aloud made her heart race faster. "Yes, this one. I feel it. It asks for dragon's blood resin mixed with honey. Avery?"

She was already searching her bottles. "Yes, I have them both, and dragon's blood incense."

"On it!" Helena said. "Let's set the mood." In moments, Helena had lit the incense and several red candles with magic, and moved around the room, quickly placing them out. "I feel we should build fire energy."

"If I'm honest, I think you four are doing that without any help," El said, amused. She took a deep breath to steady herself, knowing she was on the verge of something that would change her magic forever. "There's something else listed that I have never heard of. *Oculus Christi*."

"Clary sage," Diana said immediately. "It's the Medieval name."

Helena nodded. "Agreed."

"I have that, too," Avery said, grabbing another bottle.

"What," Bryony asked, watching their preparations, "do you do with the mixture?"

"Place it on my tongue," El said, reading the spell. "This seems to suggest that elemental fire witches already possess the knowledge. It just needs unlocking, which is exactly how it feels to me." She looked across the room towards the salamander, and with a shock saw it had uncurled and was now perched on the largest log, wreathed in flames, watching them all with rapt attention. "Holy shit. It knows."

"And it's bigger," Helena noted.

"They have poisonous skin, according to lore," Diana said, "so most are warned against touching them."

"If they're burning hot, that's not really an issue, is it, for most people?" Bryony said.

"Or for elemental witches," El said. "Hopefully. Look, there's this line here. *Witches not of ye fire element must take great care, for ye touch of ye Salamandre is death to those lacking flame within. The venomous skin of ye Fire-Beast holdeth no peril for witches of the flame element.* By the Goddess, this is feeling very real."

"A salamander is in our fire," Helena pointed out, amused. "It's already very real."

El settled her hand on her clavicles as if to subdue her panic and growing excitement. "If this works, I can speak to it."

"It will work," Avery said, grinding the resin and clary sage with her pestle with such intent that El thought she might crack the mortar. "I feel it."

"I know it," El said, annoyed with herself for her previous oversight. "I can't believe I haven't paid more attention to these spells before."

"There are hundreds of spells," Helena said, moving to her side. "It's impossible to know them all. I certainly never used the oldest ones in our grimoire. They were interesting but old-fashioned, even then. Plus, you never had a salamander before either, and I bet you didn't plan on summoning one."

"No, but I feel as if I'm unlocking a piece of my past. This is almost overwhelming, and yet so exciting, too."

"Sometimes things have to happen at the right time. This is one of those times. Just as Bryony and Diana were fated to be here, too. For Diana to point to the spell that made the most sense to you, out of all of them."

"Well, I'll be studying them all now, that's for sure."

"Any other ingredients?" Avery asked, as she finished her task.

"No. Just an incantation that I need to say when the herbs are added to the honey."

Avery handed her the mortar containing the ground herbs, and the jar of honey. "Time to mix it then."

Checking the words of the first part of the spell, El measured a large spoonful of honey and added it to the herbs. As she mixed them together, she said, "May honeyed words of wisdom flow forth, may fire feed our discourse."

El was waiting to feel a tingle of magic rise up the spoon, but so far all was normal, so she picked up the bowl and grimoire, and walked back to the fire. The salamander was fully awake now, its dark eyes fixed on hers, and she could swear she felt the tickle of its thoughts, like an insistent tapping on the edge of her awareness. The four witches gathered behind her, but she knew she didn't need their help anymore. This was on her. She read through the spell again, assured herself she'd missed nothing, and then smeared the paste across her tongue, saying the incantation afterwards.

"Creature of fire, close to my heart, let the flame within answer the flame without, that tongues may be understood." El's tongue tingled as the faintest whooshing sound started in her ears. Every fibre of her being trembled, as taut as a wire. "By the spark divine within me, I open to thy fiery words, o creature of living ember. Grant us discourse so that we should make great magic together and honour the element that binds us."

The salamander leaned forward and extended a long, slender tongue of pure flame towards her, and although the spell didn't ask her to do it, El knew exactly what the salamander wanted. She scraped out the last of the mixture with the spoon and held it close to the salamander, and in seconds it lapped up the final mouthful and wrapped its tongue around her wrist.

Instinctively El tried to pull away, but then realised she felt no pain, just a gentle heat that raced from her hand, up her arm, and across her body. But it was her head and tongue where she felt it the most. Her tongue felt as if it were on fire too, and a roaring sound filled her ears. For one horrifying moment, the heat intensified, and she thought she was going to burn from within and be left in a pile of ash on the grate, but it ebbed away, leaving crystalline clarity in its wake.

The salamander gave an impish smile. "Welcome, sister of fire, to the realm where flame lives and breathes. All you have learned before this moment was but the first spark. Now your true apprenticeship begins."

Twenty-Six

T he atmosphere in Ravens' Wood had changed again, and Briar shivered, wondering if she'd done the right thing by bringing Tamsyn with them.

Not that Tamsyn seemed the least bit worried, nor Moore or Cassie, for that matter. All three looked around with keen-eyed curiosity. Only Eli seemed to share her misgivings, and his lips twisted in a half-smile as he said, "This place feels even more watchful than yesterday."

"That's a nice way of putting it. I thought more threatening."

Water dripped from the branches, the mist hanging thick and heavy so that they could see only a small circle of trees around them, trunks looming as they progressed. Grasping branches reached overhead, catching in Briar's hair, despite the fact that she ducked to avoid them. The others were having similar issues. It was as if the wood was checking who they were, like a blind person used fingers to discern a person's features.

"And ghostly," Briar added. "It's Beltane, Eli. I feel anything could appear around us."

Everyone froze as a branch cracked nearby, a collective inhalation as they searched the mists, but then silence fell again.

Moore turned to Tamsyn. "Does this feel like your vision?"

"Yes, but wetter." Her hand, small and wrinkled, fingers slightly bent with rheumatism, touched the damp bark. "I smelled smoke, but I don't here. Yet. However, seen like this, I think it's the place." She shrugged and laughed. "Where else could it be?"

"It certainly feels older to me," Eli said, resuming walking again, sword in hand. "As if the place has withdrawn in time. Regressed."

"I hope not as far back as when Ben visited," Cassie added with a shudder.

"It does to me, too," Tamsyn confessed, "although I was last here in the summer, and it was bright and cheerful then."

"It's preparing for battle, perhaps," Moore suggested. "Alderic threatened that the wood would advance to the coast and sweep through White Haven, if necessary. As unbelievable as that seems, they would need to draw on ancient magic and power to do that. We all know its roots can tap into that. Maybe it's doing that as we speak."

A flicker of movement in her peripheral vision made Briar stop. She turned, magic tingling at her fingertips, and then smiled as she recognised the gentle presence of Deer. "My familiar is here." She held her fingers out, and Deer stepped delicately out of the mist to nuzzle her hand. Peace flooded through Briar as she greeted Deer silently. "*Dear heart. I've missed you. Thank you for coming.*"

Cassie gasped. "She's beautiful!"

"I can see it! Am I supposed to?" Moore asked, shocked.

"See *her*," Briar corrected. "She's like Raven, Avery's familiar. She can be as visible as she chooses, but she speaks to me alone. She's a very reassuring presence. Just bear with me a moment."

The others withdrew to give them privacy, falling into a hushed conversation. It had been weeks since she had last seen her familiar. Deer sometimes joined Briar on her foraging trips to the wood, but that hadn't happened for a while.

Talking silently, mind to mind, Briar asked, *"How are you, my sweet?"*

"As always. I keep busy. However, I felt your fear—for her." She nodded towards Tamsyn. *"Problems?"*

"Several." Briar quickly updated her on their troubles with the djinn. *"But I'm more worried about Tamsyn, even though that's incredibly selfish of me. She has seen the white stag again. I'm scared what it means."* She tried to marshall her scattered thoughts. *"I don't want to lose her. Do you know why he's here?"*

"He steps out of my time. Out of all." Deer stared through the trees as if trying to see him. *"He comes only in times of great need. Or,"* she lifted her head to stare at Briar with liquid brown eyes, *"to those he deems most worthy. Your grandmother is interesting, Briar."*

"She's that and more. She's brave, and bore more grief than most could." Briar glanced at Tamsyn again, seeming tiny and insubstantial next to the other three. Almost a wraith in the wood. *No.* It struck Briar suddenly, as the suggestion of death rose again. *"The Cailleach. The old woman of winter."*

Deer nudged her. *"It's not winter, and she's not the Cailleach. Crone, yes. Seer, yes. You see your own fears."*

"I know." Briar fought her rising panic down and changed the subject for a while. *"Any insights with the fire elemental?"*

"It will consume everything if left unchecked."

"So the dryads fear. How do we stop it?"

"*With guile. He's strong and wily, but that's as much as I know. I feel his magic here, though. It's tainted everything, even though the wood tries to wash it away.*"

The comment made complete sense to Briar. "*I never thought of it like that. So although they mourn, the mist stops the risk of fire and tries to wash his magic away.*"

"*This mist has many uses. It hides their actions, too. Already they plan to march.*" Deer stamped on the mossy earth. "*The roots are shifting beneath us.*"

Briar stared at the ground as if the roots would suddenly grab her ankles and pull her down into the earth, but of course Deer meant it was all happening far beneath the surface. "*We have to stop all of it.*" Briar's fears started to spiral again. "*Ravens' Wood and its dryads waging war on a djinn is not good!*"

"*But you're right to rely on the dryads, although it might feel counter-intuitive,*" Deer said. "*Use their strategies to help yours.*"

"*How?*"

"*By trapping the djinn here. Closing paths, moving paths, herding him.*"

"*It's certainly an interesting idea, but he's quick. His magic is far stronger than ours. He killed a dryad!*"

"*Because they were taken by surprise. That won't happen again.*"

"*Even with a new weapon he's crafted? Forged in fire with potentially the aid of his own salamander? His own Otherworldly magic? Ghost OPS has recorded it all. The metal made music.*"

"*This place is Otherworldly magic. So is he, behind you.*" She nodded at Eli.

"*He is not of the Otherworld, and the djinn easily swept him aside yesterday.*"

"He is most certainly not entirely of this world. He is part angel. He uses brute strength first, when he has other skills to offer."

Briar huffed. *"He uses plenty of other skills, and I don't mean just his apothecarial talents."*

"Oh. Those skills." Deer's lips lifted in a snicker. *"Do they appeal to you?"*

Heat rose in her cheeks, and she glanced back to Eli, but he was still talking to Moore and Tamsyn. Her own desires rose again, and thoughts of his strange behaviour with Newton earlier.

"No. I'm just confused, that's all."

"And yet you would be a good match, in many ways."

"Don't. Just don't. I'm confused enough. In fact, I'm just sex-starved. Can we change the subject, please?"

"Certainly. Perhaps," Deer suggested, a smile on her expressive face, *"your salamander could enhance their weapons. The Nephilims'."*

"Actually, that's a great idea, if El has time." Plans began to take shape. *"If he wants the dragon eggs, we need to offer them as bait, but we need to be certain first that we can catch him. I just wish I knew what the white stag's presence meant."*

Deer lifted her nose, and her ears twitched. *"He's coming."*

Briar whirled around. *"What? Where? How?"*

"He approaches on pathways only he can create."

"Briar, are you okay?" Moore asked, obviously seeing her agitation.

"No. Deer said the stag is coming."

She looked to Deer for confirmation, but her familiar was silently staring into the mist, her flanks trembling gently, and when she turned to her grandmother, she saw she was staring intently between the tree trunks.

Eli grabbed Briar's arm and pulled her close to his side, drawing his sword with his other hand. "Moore, Cassie, Tamsyn—closer to me," he instructed.

Tamsyn, however, took a tentative step forward, hand outstretched, and although Briar was tempted to follow her, she knew she shouldn't. She was comforted by the fact that Deer was still there, looking as intrigued as the rest of them.

Suddenly, the mist cleared, and Briar gasped as a magnificent stag stepped into view. It was enormous. Taller than Eli, its many tined antlers spread as far as the canopy of a small tree, and they were covered with deep green moss that trailed from the highest tines. Its chest was broad and thick, curled hair ran down its front, so plush that Briar wanted to plunge her fingers into it, but it was too terrifying to approach. Its flanks were broad, its legs powerful, and its hooves were enormous, although they left no mark upon the ground. It was so white that it gave off its own light.

Briar corrected herself. *Not it. He.*

The magnificent stag looked as if he stepped through worlds unconcerned by time, place, and matter. Even the trees moved aside for him, the close-knit branches forming a spacious aisle for him to walk through. A pagan temple for the king of all beings. Deer dropped to her knees, front legs bent, and Briar felt as if she too should prostrate herself on the ground. He approached Tamsyn who was barely the height of his chest, and lowered his head, and she raised her hands and placed them on his forehead. Tamsyn spent a few moments silently with him. Briar knew they were talking, and her heart ached with the uncertainty of it.

Finally, Tamsyn turned to them. "I need to go with him, but you mustn't worry."

"Go where?" Briar asked, mouth suddenly dry.

"On paths that only he knows." She smiled, looking so peaceful that it should have comforted her, but it didn't. "Don't worry," she repeated.

"But how will I find you?"

"I will find you, but be careful. This djinn is tricky."

Tamsyn turned back to the stag who knelt upon the ground, seeming to shrink as he did so. With a swiftness that belied her age, Tamsyn clambered on to his back, and once again of enormous proportions, the stag stood, turned, and vanished beneath the trees, taking her grandmother with him.

Briar turned to seek reassurance from Deer, but found she had gone too.

"Well, this is a bust," Reuben said to Zee and Ben as they reached the centre of the dunes. "What a waste of bloody time."

"Hardly a waste," Zee said, slicking back his wet hair. "We needed to do it, and now we know. We just need to search elsewhere."

"Are you sure that thing is working?" Reuben asked Ben as he adjusted his modified EMF meter.

"Yes, and seeing as the others are coming and looking equally as pissed off and wet, I'd say that confirms the djinn isn't here."

The weather had relaxed into a steady drizzle, and the mist had thickened so that even the town beyond the harbour was barely visible anymore. The mist had settled into every crevice, including in Reuben's body, and although he hated to admit it, he was seriously sick of being wet.

"He's underground," he said to the rest of the team as they gathered together on the crest of a dune. "He has to be. We should check the base of the cliffs while the tide is out."

Nahum nodded as he looked across the beach, beyond the harbour to where there was another much smaller beach, and the cliffs beneath the castle. "I suppose we should, but I'm beginning to think he's watching us and laughing his ass off. By the way, the Wayfinder did pick up shifter energy. Therians. They're around, but not close."

"Could it just mean they were here earlier?" Ben asked.

"Possibly. Or," Nahum swung around, aiming the Wayfinder at the gulls scattered across the beach, "they're watching us from a distance."

All six of them studied the birds, Reuben wondering how much more paranoid he could become. "I hate this. There has to be a way of spotting them before they're under our noses."

"I'd say they were regular gulls," Nahum declared confidently. "The dial isn't moving. But those gulls," he pointed to the cliffs they were going to investigate, "are suspicious. The pointer is flickering over their image when I face that direction. I suggest we keep an eye on them."

Half a dozen gulls clustered on the craggy rock face, indistinct in the mist, but all focussed on their group, until a couple suddenly wheeled away.

"Let's concentrate on finding the djinn for now," Dylan said. "Reu is right. He's not out in this. I mean, I know he's magical and everything, but he's a djinn. A fire elemental."

Sceptical, Alex scowled. "So you're a djinn expert now?"

"I'm being logical. He likes deserts and the heat, and we're soaked through."

"But he travels at ridiculous speeds," Zee pointed out. "He could be anywhere."

"Not true." Alex was over it all, that was obvious, but they all were. "He sped off in a whirl of wind and sand before, but he might not be able to sustain that for long. Plus, if he's planning on taking the dragon eggs, he'll be close by, biding his time. We wondered if he could be under our feet, in the sand somewhere, but how hot does it need to be to create a cave?"

Nahum laughed. "Biblically hot. Volcanic melting of landscapes over eons hot."

"Or djinn hot with crazy fire magic?" Reuben asked, liking where Alex was heading.

"That, my friend," Nahum said, shaking water off the Wayfinder, "is an interesting suggestion."

"In fact," Reuben added, warming to the idea, "he could create tunnels, even in the sand. He could create sand caves with superheat, deep underground."

"It would need an entrance though, right?" Zee said, frowning.

"Maybe." Reuben shrugged. "Probably."

"I'm just happy to be in any cave right now," Ben said. "Let's head to the cliffs like you said, all of us."

Within fifteen minutes they had trekked across the sodden sand, around the harbour, and were approaching the cliffs under the castle. The sea was already curling back in, and if they weren't careful, they could be cut off from the shore. At high tide and during storms, the waves pounded this stretch of cliffs. In fact, months before when the Winter Witch had invaded White

Haven, towering waves of ice had clung to this part of the beach, clutching at the rock face with frozen fingers.

A series of narrow caves, some so narrow that they could only enter by turning sideways, stretched under the cliff face. They entered in twos, looking for signs of habitation or disturbance, and Reuben investigated with Ben, seaweed tangling around his feet as water dripped from above. The strong smell of brine and urine bloomed around them, and a few empty cans of beers were wedged in the corner of a cave that was wider at the back than the entrance suggested.

"This is fucking grim," Reuben said, kicking a can aggressively. "Fancy hanging out here for your jollies."

"No, thanks. Sharing a flat with Dylan is bad enough," Ben quipped.

Hearing a distant shout, they sprinted from the cave to find Nahum gesturing in the corner where the cliff turned at a right angle and jutted out to sea.

"Success!" he said, gesturing to the Wayfinder when they reached him. "It's spinning to the djinn. Not excessively, but enough. In there." He gestured to a narrow crevice that looked suitably ominous, with green algae and clumps of seaweed clinging to the rock face. "It's narrow here, but opens up at the back."

"Could it be a trap?" Alex asked, throwing his shoulders back as if preparing for a fight.

"To be honest, there's no sign of another cave beyond, and no disturbance on the ground, but this Wayfinder detects djinn. We made it back out again, so that's something."

Dylan nodded in agreement. "Nothing obvious, but I saw the Wayfinder's pointer move."

Reuben fished his phone out of his pocket and started messaging the others. "Just in case," he said to their quizzical looks. "If we're trapped, I'd like the option of rescue."

Zee laughed as he followed Nahum into the narrow entrance. "Positive thoughts! Nice."

Reuben was at the back of the line, and he looked up at the jagged rocks. The gulls were perched far overhead, and every single one was watching him. He gave them the finger, just in case they were therians, and debated whether they could spell the entrance to stop them from following, but he wasn't sure which spell would be effective, and he certainly didn't want to conceal the way in from everyone else. Turning back to the dark opening, menacing in the gloom, all he could think was that it was a good place to get lost, or crushed by rockfall into a pulp.

Alex had already conjured several witch-lights by the time he entered the cave, and the team was examining the back wall.

"See?" Nahum said, fist hammering the surface. "Solid rock. Looks undisturbed too, and yet the Wayfinder likes this place."

"Could he have melted the rock and then resealed it?" Reuben asked, before immediately adding, "Of course not. It would look totally different."

Alex pointed high up the wall. "If we consider that he can turn into sand, then he could, in theory, seep through tiny seams in the rock. He could follow them to larger caves we can't find. There's a narrow opening up there, just by one of my witch-lights."

"Which leaves us with fuck all," Zee said, exasperated. "He's beyond our reach."

An idea struck Reuben. An unpleasant one. "He wants the dragon eggs that he knows are somewhere in Ravens' Wood. The dryads think he will attack from the boundary. Hell, we all do!

What if he's planning to emerge in their midst? Right in the middle—or as close as he can get."

"Tunnel up and across, you mean?" Alex asked.

"Sort of. It would mean avoiding their roots, which surely would be tricky. Unless," another theory struck him, "he destroys their roots with his new, fire-edged blade. Shit. That's a hideous idea."

"Bloody hell, Reu," Ben said, aghast. "That's horrible!"

"But is it possible?"

"I think we're giving the djinn way too much creative credit," Dylan said, "and yet we can't discount it, either."

"Zee," Nahum said, wedging the Wayfinder in his jacket pocket, "give me a leg up. I want to get closer to the gap." Zee boosted Nahum high up the wall, where he gripped the uneven surface, one foot on Zee's shoulder, another wedged in the rock face. Gingerly, he pulled the Wayfinder free and held it close to the narrow cleft in the rock. "The pointer is fixed on the djinn. It went this way, no doubt about it. Herne's flaming fucking bollocks."

Reuben considered their options and realised they were few. "Therians could get through that. Maybe we should ask for their help."

"The enemy?" Alex asked, incredulous. "Why would they help us?"

"They want to find him, too."

"To enhance their own power! We don't want them anywhere near him."

"And yet," a voice said from behind them, "we're here anyway." A naked woman emerged from the narrow entrance, eyes glowing yellow in the dark as if she were part animal. From behind her came the sound of rustling wings. "You've found him. Thank you. A djinn, no less. How very interesting."

"For fuck's sake, Jak," Alex muttered. "You're persistent."

"I told you, Alex, we want its power. I didn't know we were talking about a djinn, though!" Her grin was as feral as a fox's. "Maybe we follow the djinn to the dragon eggs and get both."

"And I told you," Alex said, conjuring a ball of magical energy into his palms, "to keep out of this."

He hurled the power ball at Jak so quickly that not even Reuben anticipated it. For some reason, he had assumed they would try and talk her out of it, but clearly not. Jak changed into a bat with blistering speed and darted forward, the energy ball hit the side of the cave, and shards of rock tumbled down.

In seconds, half a dozen bats were whirling around the cave, rock dust and sand filled the air, and everyone was shouting. Reuben was hit by a floundering Zee, and Nahum fell off the wall and crunched to the ground, almost flattening Dylan. Bats flitted around, limiting their vision, and Reuben tried to protect his eyes from their claws and wings.

"Bloody hell, Alex!" Reuben yelled, as another ball of energy smacked the wall and rocks cascaded around them. "Are you trying to kill us?"

"I'm trying to stop the bloody bats!"

Ben yelled, "Not like this! We need to get the fuck out of here!"

But it was too late. Another tumble of rock thundered down, blocking the narrow entrance, and the bats vanished like smoke into the crevice to follow the djinn.

In seconds, they were trapped.

Twenty-Seven

Helena wasn't sure what to think as she watched El reach into the fire and pick the salamander up as if it was the most natural thing in the world.

She was used to magic. It was part of the fibre of her being, but seeing the salamander whispering in sibilant tongues to El was distinctly magical and Otherworldly.

"This is a whole new aspect of magic," Avery said, echoing Helena's own sentiments. "It's amazing. I wish Raven were here. He would love this."

Bryony stepped backwards, fumbling for a chair. "It's unnerving. Uncanny. But I must admit, it's awakening feelings in me I thought were long buried."

"You can't get rid of your magic, my dear," Helena said, leaving El to have a private moment with the salamander, "it's impossible. However, when you leave here, I'm sure you'll be able to bury it again and pretend it doesn't exist."

"I'll have to," Bryony said, almost regretfully. "It has no place in my life."

Avery tutted. "But it could, if you let it."

Lips tight with spite, Diana's fury erupted. "You're such a romantic about it all! As if it's all candyfloss and starlight. But it's not. It's darkness, too. Elements that can't be controlled. Forces too strong to wield. Malevolent entities. Djinn and dragons and dryads and spellcraft. And spirits that should be at rest, but aren't." She levelled this at Helena. "I should never have come."

The air of wonder and magic that permeated every part of the attic, that seemed to dance in the shadows and light every corner, suddenly dimmed with Diana's words, and Helena, never one to mince words herself, snapped. "Diana, you are such a disappointment. So tight. So constrained. So predictably dull. I also wish you hadn't come. If you can't find a spark of wonder in what we're witnessing, you're dead inside."

"That's a bit rich, coming from a ghost."

"A ghost with a damn sight more life in her than you." Diana opened her mouth as if to respond, but Helena ploughed on regardless, aware that Avery and Bryony were watching, wide-eyed. "Hiding away in a private library, studying ancient manuscripts and pretending it's got nothing to do with magic. What utter bullshit. You're *scared* of magic. Scared of your own power. You're locking it in a box and peeking at it occasionally. Avery puts you to shame. She embraces all of it! And look what El just did. She has just opened up a whole new avenue of magic for herself. That salamander is hers now, I have no doubt. No matter where it came from, they are connected now, body and soul."

"Exactly!" Diana jabbed a finger at her aggressively. "Nothing like that should be connected to a human body and soul. It's wrong!"

"How dare you!" El said, finally speaking. She had been so caught up with her salamander that Helena thought she had forgotten they were there. "This is *not* wrong. In fact, nothing has felt more right in my entire life. Other than Reuben, of course." She held her arm out to them, the salamander perched on her flat palm, tail curled around her forearm. A ripple of flame passing over its body and licked up El's arm. The fire in the grate danced behind them both, and El was aglow with magic and happiness.

Avery bobbed on her toes. "El, I'm so excited for you. It looks so natural. I wish I could stroke it."

"Him, not it. Unfortunately, he would burn you. Not deliberately, of course, it's just his nature. This feels far more natural to me than my familiar, Bear, which is a terrible admission." El looked ethereal, her pale blonde hair also seeming to have its own platinum fire. "We have to go, right now. I need to finish the vessel for the djinn, and I know exactly what to do."

Helena turned her back on Diana and lifted the brass box. "Do you still want this?"

"Yes. He's quite happy to rest in it, aren't you my sweet?" She tickled him under the chin, and the salamander actually purred.

"Has he got a name?" Avery asked.

"Branthelios, or Bran for short. Bran, meet Avery, Helena, Bryony, and Diana. You might not see these two ever again. I can guarantee you will see Helena and Avery."

Bran turned his inky-black eyes on them that spoke of ancient knowledge and power, and he blinked in acknowledgement as a slither of noises slid from his mouth, sounding like shifting embers in the fire. Then he darted into the metal box and curled up tight. El sealed it shut and placed it on her bag. "He doesn't need air, and he generates his own heat." She gripped Helena and Avery's hands. "Thank you. And thank you, too," she said, turning to Bryony and Diana. "You helped—whether you wanted to or not. Now, I'll do my part and help send you home."

"If you need us, call us," Avery reminded her.

"I'll keep you updated, don't worry." El waved and ran downstairs, bag on shoulder and brass box in hand.

"What now?" Bryony asked.

"Now, we finalise the spell that will help trap the djinn in the vessel," Avery explained. "There are two parts to this. The spell that El wants to cast on the vessel itself to imprison him, and this one that captures him and drives him into his prison."

Helena addressed the disapproving Diana. "And you're going to help, Di, because if you want out of White Haven, this is how you do it. You, too, Bryony."

"I don't know if I can," Bryony said, heading to the table with Helena. "I mean, I'll try, but I'm serious when I say I don't use magic. And if I'm honest, I'm also scared. I don't want to die."

"None of us have any intention of dying," Helena said, "especially me. Been there, done that, and I'm not ready yet. Clea certainly isn't. That means we must focus and practise."

Avery nodded. "Agreed. Plus, you won't need to cast spells, hopefully. Instead, you will lend your magic to ours." She looked to Helena for confirmation. "That's the easiest thing. Like we do when we form a circle or cast other spells."

"Yes," Helena agreed. "Let's practice that once we've nailed this spell."

They were running out of time. She could feel it. The djinn was out there causing mayhem, and Ravens' Wood was plotting. And who knew what the therians were doing.

Cassie was still trembling ten minutes after Tamsyn had vanished on the white stag, caused by a mix of adrenalin, awe, and fear. *Where had he come from? Where had they gone?*

She checked her watch. It was early afternoon now, and yet it felt as if they were sliding towards nighttime. It was dark beneath the trees as their team sought out the dryads, and it felt like she had slipped in time. Ben's experience kept returning to her. *Was the same thing happening? Would they be pulled in the stag's wake, like into a whirlpool?*

She simply had too many questions.

Every creaking branch and cracking twig, every solitary bird call had her on edge. *Get a grip. You're a paranormal investigator.* She reached for her phone, needing to be reassured that she was still connected to the outside world, and called Dylan. When he didn't answer, she called Ben. When he didn't answer either, she panicked.

"Guys!" She caught up with Moore, Briar, and Eli. "My team isn't answering my calls. Are your phones working? It rings but is going to voicemail, and it's unlike them not to answer."

"They're hunting djinn," Eli said with a shrug of his enormously sexy shoulders. "They're busy."

"They always answer me." A nagging fear gripped her. "I hate this. And I hate that I hate this, because I love this place."

Moore gave her a reassuring smile. "It's not itself right now, and we've just had a distinctly surreal experience. Give yourself a break. I'm not half as composed as I look. At least, I hope I look composed."

"You do. Just hearing a human voice is reassuring."

Briar looked distracted, not surprisingly, but she stopped, her hand up. "Something is wrong."

"Something else?" Moore asked.

"Speak to me, Briar," Eli said, turning slowly, sword clasped firmly in his hand. "What do you sense?"

"The land is disturbed." She hurriedly pulled her boots off, thrusting her feet into the earth. "The roots."

"You did say that Deer said they were preparing to move," Cassie reminded her, thinking how freaky that sounded.

"It's not that. They're upset."

"The whole bloody place is upset, including you," Eli pointed out impatiently. "Be specific."

"I can't!" Briar whirled around, as if trying to place the problem.

"Honestly," Cassie said, gripping the EMF meter, "I am so disorientated right now. Do we know where we are?"

"Well enough," Moore said, but she knew he was just trying to reassure her. "Shouldn't we be hearing the dryads' singing now? It would carry in the silence."

Cassie wasn't so sure it would. The air felt thick, like treacle, as if it were absorbing all sound and light.

Briar huffed impatiently. "Wait. I'm so confused. That way, I think." She pointed into the tangled wood.

"That way what?" Eli asked. "The dryads, or something else?"

"Both."

"Behind me," Eli instructed, and Briar grabbed her boots and followed him barefoot, the others tagging behind.

The EMF meter whined as they progressed, and they left the path and plunged into the undergrowth. Cassie's training kicked in, as well as a healthy dose of self-preservation, and she swung the EMF in a wide arc. She had a couple of the witches' spells in her pack, and her knife, just in case. Then they heard shouts and thundering crunches that shook the ground so fiercely that she stumbled, and the EMF wailed like a siren. Goosebumps erupted on her skin as another unearthly sound scythed through the wood.

For a moment, she couldn't quite make out what she was hearing. It was like a choir—a choir of monstrous voices, ripe with power. Compelling. Demanding. Exhausting. She spun around, confused, the EMF meter's wail mixing with the wall of sound. Earth and thrashing roots thrust up beneath her feet, and a tree tilted ominously towards her. But that was the least of her worries, because the djinn was suddenly in front of her, shedding earth and sand as he whirled around, a wickedly sharp scimitar with a flaming blade slicing around him.

With horror she realised that was where the cacophony of voices was coming from.

Cassie screamed and fell backwards. The sword sliced mere inches above her head and embedded deep into the broad trunk of a tree that shuddered as if it was screaming, too. She could barely take it in.

Roots and branches whipped around, dryads emerged from the green depths, and the whole forest seemed to rise up and attack. Desperate to get clear of Eli and the djinn who were fighting within the confined space directly in front of her, she tried to scramble away, clawing at the tree root that pinned her to the ground. Moore shouted from a short distance away, but couldn't get close as the trees had erected a thorny perimeter. She had no idea where Briar was.

The root tightened, and Cassie squirmed beneath it, in danger of being crushed or trampled underfoot by Eli and Qabas. The ringing of their clashing steel and the blade's song drowned out the EMF meter, which she had dropped in her panic, until a branch landed on it, crushing it into pieces.

Cassie was pretty sure that Eli had forgotten all about her, he was so absorbed in his battle. He had to be. Qabas was fast and deadly, and Eli was already wounded. He needed all of his concentration and skills to fight it. The dryads darted in and out, but couldn't get close.

But if Qabas was here, where were their other teams? Lost? Still searching? Dead?

One thing was certain, and Cassie knew it in her bones. *They weren't ready.*

Cassie managed to twist enough to free her backpack wedged beneath her, and she dragged it out and fumbled inside for her weapons, desperate to free herself and help Eli.

The djinn whirled, sword slicing at Eli's feet. He leapt clear, but fell awkwardly, his huge wings now more an impediment than helpful in the tight space. The djinn raised his sword to strike Eli down, just as Cassie grabbed a spell bottle and threw it at him. It was short range, but her throw was off due to her awkward position. Fortunately, it struck the djinn on the shoulder and exploded, and ice spread across his back.

"Now!" she yelled at Eli. "Hit him now!"

Eli sprang to his feet, but it was too late.

The djinn turned his terrible fiery eyes on her as his body erupted in flames that melted the ice. He crashed his sword down inches from her body, shattering the root that trapped her, and grabbed her with one taloned hand as he pulled his sword free like a knife from butter. She grabbed a rock and flung it in his face, but the djinn pulled her to him, trapping her against his bulk, and blinding her with a blizzard of sand.

The forest vanished, leaving only the keening of the blade and a sudden fall into darkness.

Twenty-Eight

"How's the shop this morning?" Avery asked Sally, who was tidying books and adding new stock to the history shelves.

"It's dandy. How is it going up there?" Sally cocked her head. "And don't lie."

Avery groaned dramatically. "Mother is nightmarish, Bryony is trying to be helpful, and Helena is stoic and bossy."

"Sounds like a hoot."

"I actually think I'd get on really well with Bryony if we had time together properly, you know, without all this."

"Hopefully she'll stay, even if you find the djinn. Is that a big if?"

"We have plans. The guys are searching the beach, Briar is in the wood, we've refined our spells, and El... Well, El has a salamander now."

"The lizard in your fire?"

"Salamander, not lizard. Very different. And yes. They've bonded."

"Just when I thought things couldn't get any weirder. Where will it live?"

"In her forge, I suppose."

"Of course. So natural."

"You're taking this very well."

"My capacity for accepting new things is large, and growing larger by the day."

Avery laughed, despite the circumstances. The shop, Sally, and Dan were so grounding for her. A touchstone to normality in the face of extreme weirdness. *Home, in fact.* She wished she could stay all afternoon, but she couldn't. There was too much to do.

Her phone rang, and hoping it was Alex with news of their hunt, she pulled it from her pocket. However, it was Kendall, and growing worried, she asked, "Everything okay with James?"

"James is tickety-boo, all things considered. It's the others I'm worried about. Look, Avery, there's no easy way to say this. You have to come to the beach. Now."

"Why?" Her heart thudded in her chest. "Is Alex okay?"

"I don't know. There's been a rockfall, and I think they're trapped."

"Where?"

"Base of the cliffs. And hurry—the tide is coming in."

Avery was about to use witch-flight right in the middle of the shop, until Sally shook her arm. "What's happened? What can I do?"

"Tell Helena and Caspian I need them. I'll be at the base of the cliffs on the beach. Please tell them to hurry."

She raced to the backroom, and before the door was barely shut, and without even grabbing a coat, she used witch-flight to travel to the beach that she knew so well. She arrived facing the sea, and the encroaching waves filled her with dread as the dark grey, rain-soaked cliffs loomed over her. She whirled around, shouting, "Kendall!"

"Here, Avery!" Kendall was at the base of the cliffs, hefting rocks away with Stan.

"What the hell has happened? Why are you here?"

Kendall stood, slicking her hair back. "Didn't you see Reu's message? They headed in here fifteen minutes ago. We came to see what was going on when we finished with James, and found this. It's a fresh rockfall."

"Are you sure they're not elsewhere?"

"Look around! The place is deserted, and their footprints are here. Going in, but not out."

"Fuck!" Visions of Alex lying dead were almost overwhelming, but despair wouldn't help her now. "Are all six of them in there?"

"I presume so. The Wayfinder led them there. Short message, I'm afraid."

"Reu's not known for lengthy explanations."

Stan straightened up. "I'll call the Fire Brigade."

"No. Magic is quicker, I hope. If I can focus, I can sometimes speak to Alex with my mind." She pressed her hands to the rock face, willing herself to relax and focus.

"Alex, are you in there? Can you hear me?"

But panic clouded her concentration.

"Let's think logically," she said aloud to the others. "If we start to pull the fallen rock aside, we can use magic to hold the roof up." She didn't want to think about the fact that there might be no roof left.

Kendall nodded, still pulling debris from the entrance. "We're not making much headway at the moment, and what if they're trying to clear it from in there? Could they accidentally blast us with magic?"

"I'm hoping not. They could bring more down on them, and they're not that stupid."

"But it's how it happened in the first place that worries me."

A whirl of displaced air announced Caspian and Helena's arrival, and Helena fell to her knees next to him. He hauled her upright and raced to Avery's side. "I came as quick as I could, and picked Helena up on the way."

"Don't you dare race off and leave me behind again," Helena complained savagely.

"I was in a rush!" Avery pointed out.

"Later," Kendall instructed. She summarised the issue, and Caspian kept a far calmer head than Avery as he surveyed the scene.

"Avery, it's very clear where the roof was. We can even get slightly inside the entrance. I'm pretty sure this was just a small fall, but we need to work quickly. Helena, can you use a protection spell to keep the roof up? We'll use air magic to scoop the rocks out. Kendall, Stan—stand back in case we cause the rest to collapse."

"I can put protection over all of us," Helena said. "But I cannot hold back the tide."

Caspian nodded and grabbed Avery's shoulders, staring into her eyes. "Steady, slow, and sure. Okay?"

She took a breath. "I'm fine. Yes, slow and steady."

"Good. Let's begin."

El had never felt more alive. Magic tingled in her veins and at her fingertips, the flames in the forge responded to her every movement, and she heard the unmistakably faint song of the metals she was working to seal the jar that would contain the djinn.

Bran was weaving his own magic into the metals. He sang in his breathy, slithering-ember voice, and hardly realising she was doing it, she sang with him as she worked. She needed to engrave rune spells into the lid next, and she knew which she needed to use. Dante, however, was working on the vessel itself. Or she thought he was, until she straightened and found him looking at her with hooded eyes.

Scared of what he might answer, she nevertheless asked, "What's wrong?"

"There's a salamander in my fire, you're singing something weird, and you appear fevered. I can see pale fire licking your skin. It's extremely disconcerting—and that's an understatement."

"I'm sorry." She studied his face, hoping he wasn't annoyed—or worse, terrified and about to run screaming from his own forge. "I'm just so excited."

"I can tell."

"It's like the fire is alive. It's responding to me."

"I know."

"And the salamander is singing. It's teaching me songs to work into the metal. We've dived in together. I mean, it would have been good to start slower, but it's an emergency. I'm planning to go back to the basics after this."

He nodded, still staring at her as if she were a specimen under a microscope. "Good to hear."

She swallowed, fearing her friendship with Dante had changed substantially. "Do you want me to leave? Do you want to leave? You looked freaked out."

"I'm just coming to terms with it all. I thought I knew you, but now I'm not so sure."

"Of course you know me!" A weight settled in her gut. "I'm still me. Still El. I just have a few extra skills now."

"Normally that encompasses things like taking up painting or learning to use a drill. Singing along with a magical salamander is something entirely different."

"But you were okay with the djinn…" She trailed off as his expression darkened. "Weren't you?"

"I accepted it—in a sort of caught-in-the-headlights sort of way. But he was different. An interloper. Not you."

"Dante, please. I'm just the same, I swear, but I get it. It's big. It's like Medieval shit big."

Bran huffed. "*That is a derogatory term I do not like.*"

She glared at the salamander. "*Dante is my friend, and he's freaking out! I'm trying to reassure him. Until yesterday, I didn't even know you were a thing, and I'm a witch! You're like something out of a storybook!*"

"*Except I'm not, sister of fire. I am a fire elemental.*"

Dante broke into their conversation. "El, speaking in tongues is not helping."

She turned back to him, alarmed. "I'm not!"

"You totally were."

"Fuck! I'm so sorry. Please don't freak," she said again, almost like an incantation.

"I'm not freaking, I'm accommodating this new information."

"Can I stay?" She stepped forward, pleading. "Please don't let this drive a wedge between us. I'm still just me."

"So you say." He took a breath. "Of course you can stay, and of course I'll help finish this trap, but then I think I need some time to process it all."

She nodded, chest tight. "Of course. Whatever you need. He likes you, if that helps."

There was the faintest spark of amusement in his expression as his gaze slid to the salamander. "It's a relief, that's for sure."

She had of course introduced them earlier, but clearly Dante had hidden his shock well. *Time to keep them all busy.* "Well, I've nearly finished the lid, and then I need to engrave the vessel with Bran's help. The magic we weave will be stronger together. Is it finished?"

Dante made a visible effort to throw off his concerns. "Yes, I've just finished attaching the handles."

They turned to study the container they'd crafted together. It stood half a metre high, similar to an amphora in shape, with a wide neck and a narrow base. Two handles had been rivetted in place, and the jar's neck fluted outwards and up, like a cup. They had debated whether it would need the handles, but the jar was heavy and would be difficult to move without them. They had also decided against using a mould in the end, as Dante believed that pattern welding would create a stronger vessel. The previous night they had mixed the metals, deciding on the best quantity of each metal to create the most potent magical combination, and then layered and shaped the hot metal with the hammer. El had weaved many spells into it, and overnight she had protected the forge with more spells. That morning while she had been at Avery's, Dante had hammered it further into shape, and she noted it had a pleasing texture.

"You've made a fantastic job of it. I honestly couldn't have done this alone."

"I wouldn't leave you struggling. Just explain to me once more where the salamander came from. He just appeared in the fire?"

"Yes, in an orb. He floated down Avery's chimney."

"You said. But where did it come from before that? Are you sure it's not associated with the djinn?" He stepped forward, lips to her ear. "Can you trust him?"

El had been so excited to meet the salamander and gain new magic, and the events that morning had been so unexpected, that she had barely considered that. Now, she turned to look at Bran perched on the edge of the fire, watching them with his inky, unfathomable eyes. "I'm sure I can. I feel it."

"But you don't know. Have you asked him about the djinn? He's a fire elemental, too, isn't he? What if they have an allegiance?"

"We've considered that. In fact, we wondered if the salamander belonged to him, but now we think they're unconnected." She explained what Ghost OPS had discovered about the three different sounds associated with the djinn.

"So why is it here if they didn't arrive together?" The muscles in Dante's jaw flexed, and his shoulders stiffened. "It's quite a coincidence that both are here and supposedly aren't connected—two strange fire elementals. And don't say it's Beltane." Dante lowered his voice again. "I'm worried that he's pretending to be your friend, but is actually working for the djinn."

She was about to insist on how sure she was of Bran's good intentions again, and then realised that would be a lie. El certainly hadn't questioned him extensively. She had been in such a rush to start work, and it had felt so natural to speak to him, that she raced on, regardless. The others had been similarly accepting.

"That's a fair point," she acknowledged. "I'm just going to ask him a few more questions." She cleared her throat, feeling awkward, and then realised how stupid she was being. Just because it was an elemental did not mean she shouldn't question it. *"Bran, Dante has sensibly raised some questions that I need you to answer before we continue. Where did you come from?"*

"I am a fire elemental. I come from fire itself. I am fire."

"That's not an answer, and you know it. Where did you come from that you should be here in White Haven? Why did you end up in Avery's fire, of all places?"

"I thought you knew. I arrived because of a wish and an incantation cast upon the Beltane fire." Bran's tail swished in the forge's fire, stoking the flames. *"A fire potent with the sacred woods, the energy of the crowd, and the magic of the ancient wood on the hill."*

"You arrived in the huge fire on the beach? Not from the Great Wedding?"

"I have no place in weddings. I have no time for them. Besides, woodlands would not welcome me, would they?"

"That makes sense, but what incantation? Stan's?"

Bran smiled, revealing sharp teeth that his whiplike tongue darted between. *"The man who presided over the fire. He called me forth with such power imbued upon him by the gathered people and their energy that I manifested here with unexpected force. I admit the crowds were unnerving, sister of fire. I am used to working alone or with one skilled in magic, such as yourself. I seized my moment and drifted out of the flames and over this place. Then I felt the dragon magic and the summoning, and ever curious, followed it to the source. I am quite perceptive, you know.*"

"*So it seems.*" El was still dazed at Bran's admission that Stan had inadvertently summoned it.

"*But it was clear to me that the red-haired witch was not a fire witch, although skilled, certainly. I have not experienced dragon-based spells like that in quite some time.*" He dipped his head. "*Congratulations to the witch. However, I sensed it was safe enough so I settled in, knowing that normally where one witch is, another will follow. And thus they came, and eventually, so did you.*"

El was trying to process all this, and felt as if she was being extremely slow. Why on Earth had she not thought to ask all of this earlier? "*But what if there was no fire witch?*"

"*Then I would have left, eventually. Back to flame and source. But I knew there must be because I had manifested so strongly.*"

"*So, you really have nothing to do with the djinn?*"

"*Certainly not.*" Bran's chest puffed out. "*Arrogant creatures, normally. They do not need our help. If they did, they would treat us as servants, and in case you hadn't realised, I am no one's servant.*"

"*But Stan—your summoner—isn't a witch.*"

"*I know. Now that I know you, I sense your magic all over that spell.*"

Herne's hairy bollocks. She and Reuben had juiced up the incantation, but she hadn't realised how much a part that Beltane energy would play. "Oh, blimey." She turned to Dante, now very sure of one thing. "Guess what? Seems that I'm the one who probably summoned him all along."

Dante snorted as he sought to subdue a laugh. "Then we'd better get on with our amphora. We have a djinn to catch."

Twenty-Nine

For a few seconds, Alex could see nothing because of the rock dust that filled the narrow cave, nor hear anything due to the rumbling of stone cascading around them.

As soon as he'd realised the consequences of his actions, he had cast a spell to protect them from the rockfall, but he could feel Reuben's magic too, and knew he'd done much the same.

"Is everyone okay?" he asked, in between coughing fits.

"Barely," Reu grumbled.

"No, I'm bloody not," Dylan complained from somewhere to his right, amongst general groans and complaints. "A huge bloody rock hit my shoulder. Were you trying to kill us?"

"Sorry, I was cross," Alex explained sheepishly, casting another witch-light and trying to see how bad things were.

"I'm alive, but only just," Ben said.

"You fucking muppet," Nahum said, emerging in front of him as the dust settled, aided by a cool breeze that it seemed Reuben was casting. "She was provoking you."

"I know. I snapped. Zee? Are you okay?"

"I ended up with Nahum's foot in my ear, but I'm otherwise fine."

He heaved a sigh of relief. "Good, so we're all okay."

"No thanks to you," Reuben said, cutting him a side-eye before studying their surroundings. "Rule 101, do not throw energy balls in a small cave. Holy shit, if you're of a nervous disposition, do not look up."

Of course, everyone looked up, and the light revealed the fractured roof and several large rocks suspended by the witches' protective shield that could easily have killed them. The creaking of settling rock and another shower of debris confirmed it wasn't over, either.

"Please tell me your shields will last a long time," Dylan said.

"Long enough to ensure we might die of oxygen deprivation instead," Reuben quipped.

Nahum and Zee headed to the narrow entrance that was full of rocks and examined the roof. Neither needed to use a torch, as their eyesight was good enough without their aid.

"The roof will come down if we start moving rocks," Zee said, "unless you can hold this one up, as well as the one above us."

Reuben exchanged a quizzical glance with Alex. "If you can manage this one, I'll focus on that one."

"Done." He felt the faint change in magic as Reuben's focus shifted, and adjusted his own spell to cope. Another trickle of rock slithered down the walls, and Alex realised they had been seconds away from dying, and it was all his fault. "Did you catch one of the therians?" Alex asked the Nephilim.

"Dude!" Dylan said, rolling his eyes, "Wouldn't one be here if they had?"

"Of course not," Nahum said, as he started to dig them out, rock by rock, working from the top down. "Bloody bats tried to take my eye out! I almost caught one, but then I nearly died by rockfall."

Alex was positioned in the middle of the room, his magic spreading in all directions, and he focussed on the crevice the therians had aimed for. "That cleft has opened up more in the rockfall."

"Not enough for us to follow," Ben pointed out. "You'd have thought they might have checked on us."

"And risk dying?" Reuben asked. "Of course they wouldn't have."

For the next few minutes they worked in silence, grunts and tuts the only noise, but it became clear that it was extremely slow going.

"Should we try a focussed blast?" Alex asked Reuben. "We have therians to chase and a djinn to catch."

"Oh yes, more blasting is exactly what we need."

"Wait!" Zee held his hand up. "I feel fresh air seeping through the gaps."

"And I sense magic," Reuben confirmed. "Avery's, Caspian's, and Helena's."

The sound of grinding rock filled the small space, and the mass of rubble that choked the entrance started to wobble and collapse.

"Back, now!" Nahum instructed. "Hold up that damn roof, Reuben!"

The swell of magic in the tiny space increased, and Alex redoubled his efforts on keeping the cave roof at bay. More rocks slithered down the walls, and then the entrance popped like a champagne cork, allowing the sound of a pounding surf to rush in, and faint afternoon light to enter.

"Stay back," Nahum yelled through the choking dust that reared up again. "We're coming out. Ben, Dylan, go first!"

They raced through the narrow entrance, stumbling over the rock-strewn ground, as Alex kept the roof at bay. As the last one out, he only just made it. He threw himself out of the entrance and into the rain as the cave collapsed behind him.

One minute Eli had been fighting for his life against Prince Qabas, deafened and confused by the hideous sound that the djinn's sword was making, and the next he was whirling around in frustration, trying to find him.

"Where has that bastard gone?" he yelled to no one and everyone. "That coward has vanished."

"We were too much for him," Alderic the dryad said with visible relief. "But it's where he came from that's worrying me."

Eli caught his breath and lowered his sword. "What do you mean?"

"He didn't come through us. No one detected him. Not one single tree. Not by normal means, at least. He entered from below."

"How is that even possible?"

Alderic shrugged. "I don't know, but he must have found a way. The trees' roots identified his approach, and that's what finally alerted us."

Briar stepped out of the tangled undergrowth, still barefoot and with twigs in her hair, like a woodland nymph. Moore was at her side, distinctly nowhere close to being nymphish.

"I felt it, Alderic," she said, concerned. "Were the roots hurt?"

"Hurt?" Eli asked, thinking he was hearing things.

"His sword was made for destruction on a lethal scale," Briar pointed out. "Look around at what's he done. This is terrible! Branches have been hacked off, and trunks have been damaged. If he came from below and slashed at them..."

Eli finally took in the devastation and realised how right Briar was. It was as if a tornado had ripped through this part of the wood. The earth was rumpled, roots snaked across the ground that should have been underground, shrubs were completely uprooted, and numerous branches of various sizes were hacked into pieces around them, the pale fragments of fresh wood bleeding with sap. It was sickening.

"How long did it take him to do this?" he asked Alderic.

"Seconds only. You arrived almost as soon as he did." Alderic shook his head. "He must have tunnelled up somehow, so no, only minor roots are affected, but they felt him. As for these trees, they will recover, as long as he doesn't damage them further. It was lucky we found him so quickly." He turned to his companions. "Spread out, send the alert. He's still here somewhere, and he won't be far."

The dryads vanished into the gloom and the canopy of leaves shivered, a ripple effect that travelled what Eli imagined was the length and breadth of the wood.

"Hard to mask djinn energy, I presume," Moore said thoughtfully. "And he's a fire elemental, so he'll stand out here." He started pulling branches aside and peering into the undergrowth with increasing agitation. "Where's Cassie?"

"She was right there," Eli said, sure he'd seen her close by while he was fighting. "I heard her EMF meter until that damned sword drowned it out."

"The music of metals, I guess," Moore said, not looking at him. Suddenly, he pounced on an object on the floor and lifted it up for them all to see. "Her gizmo is smashed."

"Any blood?" Eli asked, kicking aside the undergrowth and hoping not to see a severed body part.

"He took her," Alderic said with conviction. "I heard her screams."

Eli rounded on him. "And you didn't think to say so straight away?"

"Like you, I was busy." He glared at Eli, the normally diffident dryad now confrontational. "Plus, the wood is my concern, not humans."

"She's helping you, so she should be your concern, you ungrateful—"

"Enough!" Moore shouted. "Let's focus on finding her. Alderic, where did Qabas emerge from?"

The dryad turned and pointed behind them. "That way, I think, but not far."

They followed the dryad through the trees, and Briar hurried to Eli's side. "Cassie was helping you. I saw her throwing one of the spells we made, just a glimpse through the trees, but I was stuck back there." Her expression twisted with annoyance, and because she wasn't concentrating, almost tripped over. "The wood was fighting everything and everyone—even me. And my gran is out there in the middle of all this. What was I thinking?"

"You did the right thing. The stag came for her, which means they have a purpose in all this, even if we can't see it yet. She went willingly."

"Like a sacrificial lamb." Briar was hurting and angry, but he knew better than to doubt her now. If anything, it would spur her on even more. "I will not let Cassie die at his hands."

"None of us will," Moore said, stopping as they entered an area where the ground looked more disturbed.

Alderic placed his hand upon the closest trunk and lifted his face to the canopy. The shift of shadows across his dappled skin made Eli blink as the creature dipped in and out of vision. While he conducted what Eli presumed was a conversation, the others examined the ground for signs of entry, but although roots and rocks were upturned, there was no visible entrance.

"How," Briar asked, "could he take Cassie? She's flesh and blood."

"He's a powerful fire elemental who has the ability to bend matter to his will. Or some of it, at least," Eli said. "Surely it's just like Cas and Avery when they use witch-flight and take others with them."

"I guess so."

The trouble was that this djinn was unpredictable, and like nothing they had faced before. Even the djinn in the desert millennia ago had not behaved like this one.

Alderic broke into their conversation. "They are somewhere below us. That is as much as we can tell. Not too deep."

"Buried alive?" Moore asked, horrified.

"In a cave. The roots detect a structure of some kind, but that's not unusual. There are many such places in the cliffs below us."

"So how the hell do we get to her?" Moore asked. "Can we dig a tunnel? The roots could, surely. Let's face it, they don't behave as normal roots do."

"They do not dig like bears," Alderic said.

Eli considered their options. "So, we think they're in a cave, which technically means she's safe. Hopefully. There has to be a way to reach her. Your magic perhaps, Briar?"

"If I can get a fix on them, possibly, but it would create devastation, and there are far too many roots. Big, thick, deep roots. I don't think I can. They're like a huge cage beneath our feet. What does he want with her?" Briar asked.

"Knowledge? To use as leverage, perhaps?" He turned back to Alderic. "Are the eggs safe?"

"How many times do I have to say yes, Nephilim?" His voice was steely. Impatient.

"I'm thinking of strategies." He was already missing Nelaira, whose teasing, seductive ways were preferable to this young dryad's blunt manner. "I'm thinking that perhaps we need to use them as a bargaining tool."

"I had the same idea," Briar said eagerly.

Moore's eyes widened with horror. "No! I don't even want to think what Newton would say to that. We wait for the djinn's next move and work out a way to find him."

Before Eli could argue his point, another round of shouts broke out in the distance, and he ducked as he was suddenly bombarded by bats.

Thirty

T he first thing Reuben had wanted to do upon escaping the cave was plunge into the sea, wash the dust off, and celebrate being alive. Then he wanted to race up to Ravens' Wood and hunt djinn and therians and inflict as much damage on them as possible.

Unfortunately, he could do neither of those things. Now, almost an hour later, he was in Dante's workshop with a bunch of agitated witches and one watchful blacksmith. What was worrying was that the team in the wood weren't answering messages or calls, so the Nephilim had flown there with Ghost OPS and Kendall, safe in the knowledge that the thick mist would hide them from view. Briar was still in Ravens' Wood, somewhere, so the coven would have to manage without her when they cast the spell on the djinn trap. Bryony and Diana looked disconcerted to join them, but had no choice.

At least there was the interesting new addition of Bran the salamander, who would be an integral part of the proceedings.

His wife was in raptures. "Can you believe it, Reu? A salamander!"

He watched the creature basking in the flames. "Just another member of our varied family. Fun times."

El kissed his cheek. "You'll love him, I know it."

"He's staying, then?"

"I hope so." El was aglow with heat from the fire, the hum of magic, and the lick of flames that seemed to shimmer just under her skin.

"Just when I didn't think you could become any more amazing, you go and prove me wrong. However, now is not the time for this. We have a spell to cast."

"You are very sweet, and I am very lucky. As for the spell, it's going to be brilliant. I can feel it." She turned back to the gathered witches. "Right, time to begin."

The metal vessel had been placed in the middle of a circle marked on the floor at the far end of the workshop, and both El's and Avery's grimoires were on a work surface next to it. The container was impressive, larger than Reuben had expected, and the magic already imbued in it gave off a steady hum that made his skin tingle.

"What now?" Bryony asked, looking nervous. "Bearing in mind I haven't done this for years."

"It's simple," El said. "We are casting a spell to strengthen the metals, activate the runes and enchantments, and make this jar a prison. It will contain the djinn for as long as we need it to. The metals we have used all have magical qualities. Iron, silver, brass, and a little copper. Spells were used while mixing them, to strengthen, add protection, and prevent combustion. With Bran's help this afternoon, we have cast a song into the jar, too."

"A song?" Helena asked. "How?"

"Bran suggested something tantalising," she threw him a smile. "Djinn are drawn to the beauty of well-worked metal, too, much like dragons are drawn to metals and jewels. It's why they hoard treasure. Apparently, some fey are sensitive to it, too. It's like a drug for them. This jar will not only act as a prison, but as a lure."

"Sneaky as fuck," Reuben said in admiration. "I love it."

"Agreed," Alex said, nodding. He was still caked in rock dust just like Reuben, but didn't seem to care. "Is the song active? Is that even the right word?"

"Yes, but you probably can't hear it. Although, I can now—thanks to Bran. It's quiet, but it's there. The spell," she said, all business, "will add power to the enchantments engraved into the metal. See," she pointed to the lid, the shoulders, and the base of the jar. "Once the djinn is inside, a simple incantation will activate them, sealing him in. Well, once the lid is fitted, too."

"Ah, yes," Caspian nodded, leaning against the counter nonchalantly. "I love the way you make it sound so easy, El, when the reality will be mayhem, spells flying everywhere, and an outraged djinn seeking to cause as much damage as possible."

Reuben cast a wicked grin at Diana and Bryony. "It's more fun than it sounds."

El drew herself up to her full height, sending both of them an imperious glare. "I'm simplifying the process, and you two aren't helping."

Diana shook her head, not amused at all. "I don't understand. Why were we working on another spell, as well?"

"To control the djinn enough to actually get it in the jar," Avery explained. "It's not going to just walk in. Caspian has a point."

"Just when I thought you knew what you're doing, you prove you don't," Diana said, tone icy.

"I can assure you, Mother, we all know exactly what we're doing. We work as a team. Now do your part and help us."

The uncomfortable atmosphere intensified, and Reuben hoped that once this was done, he'd never have to see Diana again.

"And that," Dante said, heading for the door, "is my cue to wait outside. I've seen enough for today."

"Trouble?" Reuben asked El after he'd left. It was obvious that the blacksmith, normally so relaxed and upbeat about everything, was decidedly tense.

"It's been a lot today. He's coped well, all things considered."

"One of those days for all of us, then."

"Right," El said, addressing everyone, "this is a straightforward ritual in which we link our magic, call upon the elements for support, and cast the spell. I will lead us, but we need to be inside the sealed circle."

"And Bran?" Caspian asked, catching Reuben's eye.

"Will aid me."

That in itself was interesting. El had never wanted to lead a spell before.

While the others assembled, Diana and Bryony placed between more skilled witches, El strolled to the forge, picked up the salamander, and carried him to the circle. It perched upon her arm like a falconer with its bird of prey, tail curled around her forearm, upright on hunched back limbs, the stars down his back ablaze. El spoke to it with words that slithered in Reuben's mind as he tried and failed to make sense of them. *This was going to take a lot of getting used to.* Alex caught his eye, his expression hard to read. This was turning out to be an interesting Beltane, and their coven was once again evolving.

Reuben pushed his concerns away and focussed on the job at hand. Helena sealed the circle once they were inside, and they joined hands as El began by calling upon the elements. The familiar rise of power made Reu's skin tingle, and their combined magic swelled, pulled together by El's mastery and confidence. He felt the flicker of Bryony and Diana's magic, but El coaxed both forth even more. Reuben noted Avery was by her sister, but not her mother. Instead, Helena and Caspian were on either side of her.

The cone of their power was high now, and a gentle wind swirled as the heat intensified. El held out her forearm that supported Bran, and unexpectedly broke into a distinctly odd song that had no words, only sounds, and unearthly chords that caused a vision to manifest in the centre of the circle—just like the djinn's music had done. Another forge with another fire that was distinctly Otherworldly.

What the fuck was happening?

He doubled his concentration as their magic formed what he could only describe as a golden, fiery arrow that El directed into the vessel. Instantly the metal was bathed in light and the enchantments and runes blazed. A visible sweep of magic started at the base of the jar and spiralled upwards, and the music rose to a crescendo with it. When it reached the lid, El shouted something utterly incomprehensible that Bran echoed, and the slither of his words grated along Reuben's nerves.

A white snap of flame enveloped the metal jar and just as swiftly vanished, leaving the engravings glowing and emitting a resonant hum of power. The strange vision faded away, and the coven took a collective breath of relief.

But it was El he became suddenly worried about. She too was bathed in a nimbus of light, and when she turned to face him, thrilled with the spell, he was alarmed to see a white fire within her eyes.

Cassie was trying to work out if she was terrified, excited, or just plain fascinated by the situation she found herself in.

Prince Qabas deposited her unceremoniously on the floor of a large cave that had highly polished, reflective walls of black and grey that she could almost see her reflection in. She wouldn't go as far as to say that it was luxurious, but the ground was comfortably flat and dry, and the small, smokeless fire burning merrily in the centre of the room gave warmth and light.

For a few moments after catching her breath, all she did was watch the djinn pace and mutter, the firelight dancing on his burnished skin as his huge, taloned feet slapped on the hard ground. Yes, feet. Human feet, with the talonlike nails of a great bird. He had cast aside his great cloak so that she could see his muscular figure clad in clothes of rich gold and red—a voluminous shirt and loose trousers that made her think of storybook djinn—and she wondered where his cloak had gone, until she realised she was sitting on it. It gave off a faint sandy smell of beaches or hot deserts baking beneath a cloudless sky, with a whiff of smoke mixed in.

It seemed he had forgotten about her after he dropped her on the ground, and although she had endless questions, decided to take advantage of being ignored and find a way out. Except it took only seconds to realise that there was no way out. The place was sealed as smoothly as an egg. It was then that fear—a cold, hard punch to the gut—hit her. She rose to her feet, heedless of the djinn, and prodded the walls.

"What are you doing?" Prince Qabas asked, voice silky smooth but hard as the rock they were encased in. When she turned, she found his dazzlingly blue eyes fixed on her.

Her mouth was suddenly dry, and she backed up. "Trying to find a way out, because there must be one. Has to be. You have kidnapped me!"

"I wouldn't call it that."

"Well, I would! I'm here against my will."

"You will be useful to me." He narrowed his eyes as he examined her. "I encountered more resistance above than I expected."

"Ravens' Wood will defend itself, and my friends will help. They will also rescue me!" *I hope.* Her anger rose, and it gave her strength. "You killed a dryad. How could you? She was our friend."

"She refused me," he growled, jabbing a large, pointed talon at her.

"How very petty! Is that what you'll do to me if I refuse? Because honestly, there is no way I can help you anyway. You may as well let me go."

He grinned unpleasantly. "I don't think so. I have options to explore."

"I don't even understand how I can be here. There is no way in!" Her voice was rising, and she could feel hysteria bubbling. *Calm the fuck down. I am a scientist*, she reminded herself. *Study him.*

"A way out? Of course there is. For me. Not you."

"Where?"

He pointed to a tiny seam in the roof above them, almost imperceptible in the dark. "There. Easy for me."

"It's tiny!"

"As I can be, when I choose."

"And me?" She patted herself down as if pieces of herself were missing. "How did you get me here?"

"When you are with me, you are of me. Now," he folded his arms across his chest, tapping his long fingernails against his burnished skin, "tell me how to reach the dragon eggs."

"How should I know?"

"I smell dragon on you."

"You can't possibly! That was weeks ago."

"So I was right." His gaze sharpened.

She stepped back as he stepped closer. "It was a baby and didn't live long, unfortunately."

His eyes flashed. "It's dead?"

"Yes." And she damn well wasn't going to tell him how that happened. "I don't think this world agreed with it."

"But there are others here. Eggs."

"You're imagining it. There was only one."

"Lies!" he roared, and it was like being caught in the blast of a furnace. "I know dragons, and there are eggs here. Tell me how it happened."

"I don't know."

"Lie again," he pressed his talon against her chest and ran it down her skin to her stomach, "and I will cut you open like a peach."

"What will you do with them?"

"Nurture them, hatch them, and make them mine."

"In your own world?" she managed to ask as he pushed his face even closer to hers. It was hard to concentrate as his eyes were dazzling and fathomless, as if staring into starscapes. There was no humanity there, just cold, hard analysis, and she felt as insignificant as an insect.

He grunted and moved away, allowing her breathing to settle again. "That way is closed to me for now, but I see potential here."

"For a djinn? A prince, such as yourself? There is nothing here for you." She thought back to what he'd said outside Dante's smithy. "This world is a pale imitation of your own. What's the point? Focus your energy on returning."

"In the spring the Great Goddess will wed again, and I will return then—perhaps."

"That's a whole year away. Let me get this straight. You willingly explored Ravens' Wood, knowing you would miss your opportunity to return, for dragon eggs?"

"Yes."

"How on Earth will you keep dragons in this world? Where? You have nothing, certainly no home."

"I can conjure anything I choose. I'm sure I will find deserts in this world as I know we once did, millennia ago. They are still here, yes?" She nodded. "Good. There I will create a great palace of sand and rock, and I will raise my dragons. You know so little of our world and of my power. This place..." He trailed off, tone filled with disgust. "I will turn it into something new."

While he was willing to talk, she thought she may as well try to get as many answers as she could. "You killed two humans, as well as Nelaira. Why? Why did you need to if you're so powerful?"

"Because they insulted me," he snarled. "Laughed as if I was an imitation in a costume."

Understanding suddenly dawned. "It was Beltane. Lots of people had dressed up for the parade. You saw them?"

"The great fire on the beach? Yes, I saw it. The people. The frivolity. But I felt the magic there. Here in the wood, too. It is unusually strong for this world."

He must have been there while the town celebrated, after fleeing the wood, but surely he was too memorable to miss? But then again, everyone had been drinking, spirits were high, and there were lots of spectacular costumes that night. She ran through her memories of the events. *Had she seen him and not realised?*

One thing was very clear. "You killed them for nothing. You're a monster. A fragile monster with an ego to match. They were having fun and made a mistake, and you killed them for it." Cassie was suddenly exhausted by it all, and the deaths, especially Nelaira's, hit her anew, particularly as there was a distinct possibility that she too might die in this cave beneath the wood. But it still didn't make sense that this all-powerful Prince Qabas should choose to remain in their world, when he would have family and status in his own. A world where dragons lived. Lots of them.

She was missing something, she knew it. And then it struck her. "You're in trouble!"

"I beg your pardon!"

Cassie laughed, despite the risk of instant incineration. "You're in trouble in your own world. Why else would you be here? Stuck in what you call a second-class place. You've pissed someone off. Family, perhaps? An enemy?"

"Enough questions," Qabas roared, and strode back to the fire that blazed at his approach. "I need to enhance my blade so that if they refuse to let us pass—because you, my dear, will be my bargaining tool—I will kill you and hack every single tree to pieces to find the eggs."

"I can assure you that I do not wish to die, so I'll plead on your behalf."

He had to take her with him, because to be left in the cave would mean death. Better to risk death at his side than down here.

Thirty-One

Newton extracted the Tasers from the boot of the car, ensured they were loaded, and placed extra cartridges in his pocket. He added torches, including head torches, into his pack, and strode to the start of a path at the edge of Ravens' Wood.

He had experienced a frustrating few hours at the post-mortem, during which he learned nothing new, but at least had confirmed the victims' names. They were out of towners, and now another poor sod had the job of telling their nearest and dearest of their demise. Then Jasper phoned, telling him that several people had left St Michael's Mount, one of them being Lord Wentworth, and had piled into cars, headed east. He couldn't say where, but having heard Kendall's news, Newton knew exactly where they were going. Right here. Hence, the Tasers. He would not be vulnerable again, and neither would his officers.

Kendall met him partway down the path, and he handed her a torch and a Taser. "Wentworth is on his way. Don't hesitate to use this if you or anyone else is threatened. Have you found Moore and Briar?"

"Yes, and Eli, too. We followed the shouting."

"Are they all right?"

"Shook up, but fine. There's no sign of the djinn, and the bats have disappeared, too."

"Bloody Therians," he muttered savagely. "We cannot let them get those eggs, Kendall."

"Alderic swears they are safe, and Eli trusts him, but things here are uncertain, and the djinn has already wrought havoc. We've split the team up, as you suggested. Eli, Zee, Alex, Ben, Stan, and Moore have gone with Alderic to the ancient grove—or as close as he'll let them get. The rest are trying to find Cassie and the djinn, although I suspect he'll find us first."

"Stan? You let him come?"

"I couldn't stop him. Well," she shrugged, "I could have, but he wanted to help, and we need it."

"Fine. He's proved his worth before, I guess. And the other witches?"

"With Dylan and Nahum, deciding where to set up the djinn trap."

Newton was in no mood to take in his surroundings, other than noting they were gloomy and menacing in the thick mist. He handed Kendall a head torch, then wrestled his own into place and flicked it on.

"I'm impressed you know where you're going," he told her. "It's not easy today."

"I come here fairly regularly, so I'm familiar with the outer part at least, plus the dryads have provided help." She pointed to a raven perched on the branch ahead. "He's leading us back."

"They're helping?" He watched the raven loop from branch to branch, leading them from one trail to another. "Wonders will never cease."

"They need us, and you should stop being so cynical."

"I'm just worried, for everyone."

"Whereas I am worried about you."

"Me?" he asked in surprise, stopping abruptly. "Why?"

She paused too, tight-lipped, as if wondering how much to say.

"Kendall, spit it out! You've started now, so you have to finish."

"Are we friends? I mean, you're my boss, obviously, but are we friends as well?"

"Yes, of course. You and Moore."

"Good. Then don't take this the wrong way, but you're getting grumpy again."

"What do you mean, again?"

"You find it hard to see the light in anything, but you did at the wedding, and it changed you. You looked all bright and breezy. And now you're not."

"It was a wedding. It was nice," he said awkwardly. "Is this really the right time for this conversation?"

"There is never a right time for this, so yes, it is, but I'll make it quick. You were happy, you embraced the team, the paranormal, everything. But you're slipping again. It's all doom and gloom."

"Have you looked around? It's very grim right now," he said, deliberately misunderstanding her. She frowned and he sighed. "It just gets to me, sometimes. You chose this job. It chose me. My association with the witches—and my family's association—goes back centuries. I don't think I told you that."

"No, you didn't, actually."

"Moore never said?"

"No. He's very loyal to you."

Newton smiled. "He's a good man. In that case, I will tell you all, just not now, obviously. Later. But suffice it to say I was thrust into this role, and it's taken me a while to come to terms with it. Moore dived in like he was born to it, which should have been my attitude. And then things became messy."

"With Briar."

"He told you that?"

"No. I'm a woman. I can tell. A baby could tell."

"Oh. Well, I fucked up. And now Eli..."

"Forget Eli and his potential moves, and try again. She's not with anyone, is she? If it doesn't pan out, accept it with grace, and be happy in this job! It's a great job. It's interesting! Fascinating, in fact. Better than dealing with regular murder and drugs and crap. Open your eyes, look around, and appreciate what you have. Weird friends are the best, and you have loads of them. I love living above The Wayward Son and having Zee as a roomie. It's brilliant!" The raven squawked so loudly they both jumped. "Talk over. We better move on."

"Sorry," he said, striding alongside her. "I didn't realise I was getting everyone down."

"You're not, at least no one has complained to me. I'm just worried, and I had to say something. It was killing me not to."

Reassured that he wasn't the subject of everyone's conversations, and determined to push the issue to the back of his mind for later consideration, he wondered how far in they were going, but just as he was about to ask, the raven abruptly plunged left through a tangled path, and he ducked under a low branch to follow.

As he straightened, he saw the scene of destruction. "Oh, shit! The djinn did this?"

"And the trees when they fought back. But hurry, we need to get through here."

He heard the sound of raised voices, and as they emerged into another clearing, found the witches, Dylan, and Nahum, gathered around a metal vessel shaped like an amphora, in fierce debate. Or rather, some were arguing, while Bryony and Diana stood apart.

"Newton!" Reuben said, turning to him. "We're just deciding on the best place to put the jar. The cave where he took Cassie is below us."

"You know this how?"

"The Wayfinder," Nahum said, wiggling it. "It's fixed on him."

"Plus, I can feel them," Briar added. "So can the trees."

"Bloody hell," Newton said, unable to stop himself as he saw her dishevelled appearance and multiple injuries. "You're bleeding. What happened to you?"

"The djinn. The trees. The fight in general." She looked down and grimaced at the scratches. "I can't feel them, I'm fine."

"If you're sure. What's the plan?" he asked, addressing everyone.

"Well," Avery shrugged, "that's what we're debating. This place is huge, and he could go anywhere. He's below us now, so this seemed like the right spot, but he moves so quickly, and we can't risk trapping Cassie, too. That would be a disaster!"

"How did he even take her?"

"He grabbed her, as best we can guess," Briar said, "and vanished, just like witch-flight. The trees are trying to break into the cave with their roots, but he's strengthened it, with magic, probably. He could emerge anywhere, let's face it."

"So why are we here?"

"Because this is where he emerged last time. He burst out of here like a damn jack-in-a-box," Caspian said, "according to Alderic."

"Well, he's not stupid, so he won't do that again," Newton pointed out. "Especially if he knows you're here. I don't understand why the therians aren't trying to get to him."

"Maybe they think the eggs are the easy target," El said, "and they'll come back for him later. With reinforcements."

Briar nodded, eyes hooded with worry. "Especially if they witnessed him fighting us."

"Yes, Wentworth and his clan will swell the ranks." Newton nodded. "That makes sense. Jasper reported they were on the move." He did a double-take as he looked at El. "You look different. Sort of glowy."

"It's the salamander. He leaves aftereffects. I'm sure it will pass."

He wasn't sure quite what to say to that, so instead said, "Well, the one thing we know the djinn wants is the eggs, so if he's going anywhere, it will be there. We need to move."

"But we can't get to where the eggs are, no one can," Avery reasoned.

"So Alderic says, but Qabas has got his great big bloody sword that has caused a lot of damage already, so he'll try again. Maybe the attack back there was a test run, or maybe he got caught out. We need to follow the others and get as close to that place as we can."

"But Cassie is down there," Briar said, pointing downwards. "We can't leave her."

"We can't get to her, and if he took her, it's with a purpose. He has a strategy, and we need to play the long game. We need to move. Avery, you have a plan to catch him?" He nodded at the jar, which was exerting an almost hypnotic attraction. The engravings flickered with white fire in the low light, and with difficulty, he dragged his gaze away again.

"Yes, but the more I think about it, the more I realise we'll have to adapt as we go."

"Don't we always?" Then he realised who else was missing, and that Kendall hadn't mentioned her. "Briar, where's Tamsyn?"

"She went with the white stag. I don't know where they are, but I believe he's here to help. Somehow."

Bollocks. This was getting more convoluted by the second, but he kept it positive for Briar. "Then we talk it through while we walk, because I think we'll have one chance, and then we're screwed. We need a perimeter, and we need to defend it. Someone grab the jar, and let's go."

Ben knew they were on the edge of somewhere special, because it reminded him of the feeling he'd had the year before and thought he'd never experience again. The feeling of crossing out of one place and into another across an unseen, liminal borderland. Despite the near darkness, mist, and constant drizzle, the way ahead was lit by a golden light without any discernible source.

"Feel familiar, Stan?" he asked, noting Stan was looking around with wide-eyed trepidation.

Stan nodded. "Yes, unnervingly so."

"This is as far as I can take you," Alderic said, drawing to a halt.

Zee rolled his eyes. "Not true. You've taken us further before."

"When you had a job to do. That's not the case now."

"We're trying to help," Eli said.

"You will help from here by defending our borders."

"But how big are your borders?" Alex asked, scanning the area. "That does not look like a small place."

"It isn't, but we have our own defences, too. Several of them."

"Care to share?" Moore asked.

Alderic grimaced. "No. You will see."

Alex rolled his eyes. "You expect us to fan out around the whole area? That will weaken us."

"No. I expect you to remain here." He gave them a warning look, as if to ask no more, and Ben suddenly had an inkling of what he meant.

He explored to the right, skirting the area ahead along the unseen but clearly felt boundary, but within a few feet, the light vanished, and the dense interior of Ravens' Wood looked as usual. Well, with an extra dollop of threatening thrown in. Passing the still arguing group, he moved in the other direction and discovered the same thing.

He returned to the group, and butted in. "This is a funnel."

Alderic nodded. "Of a sort."

Ben explained what he found to the others. "This is the only place you can see inside. A choke point."

"A lure," Eli said nodding appreciatively. "Now we're talking."

"This might seem a silly question," Ben asked, "but doesn't opening it up even slightly invite disaster?"

"The djinn will keep desecrating this forest unless we stop him," Alderic said. "I appreciate your question, but this is the safest option. We cannot risk another death."

A calculated risk. Ben couldn't argue with that.

"Any sign of therians?" Alex asked Ben.

He checked the EMF meter. Earlier, he'd had the uncanny feeling of being watched, but maybe that was just the wood. "This place gives off a low-level magical hum all the time, and it has spiked because of where we are," he said, nodding to the way ahead. "Consequently, it's effectively useless right now for detecting anything specific. But we're being watched," he said lowering his voice. "I'm sure of it."

"There are lots of things in here that are watching." Alex pointed to the ravens clustering in nearby branches. "Power is building. Can you feel it?"

Stan nodded. "Something is coming."

Ben cocked his head at Alderic. "What do you know of the white stag?"

Alderic just smiled, and Ben realised he knew plenty, and he wasn't sure if it made him feel better or not.

Briar had reluctantly followed the team, hating to leave Cassie behind, but knowing that Newton's suggestion was logical. The raven darted ahead, leading the way, but they hadn't gone far when they were suddenly attacked by bats.

"Hit the ground!" Nahum roared, as he swung his blade high around him, and extended his wings like a shield. "Therians!"

The bats darted through the branches, aiming at their faces with outstretched claws. The witches hit back, spells zig-zagging back and forth. Briar scooped up a handful of earth and flung it in the air, casting a spell. In seconds, the earth had transformed into a fine net that caught a couple of bats mid-flight. Unfortunately, by the time they hit the ground, they had changed into large cats that ripped the magical net into threads.

The cats pounced towards the jar in the middle of the group, and El threw herself across it to protect it, just as Newton fired his Taser. It hit the hind of one of the leaping cats and it howled, altering its trajectory midway through the jump. It landed short and twisted to attack Newton, but Reuben caught it with the well-timed blast of a power ball that sent it reeling backwards.

Ravens emerged from the trees to join the one who'd been their guide, and screeches and raking claws rent the air above them. The other therians changed shape, transforming into ravens too, so that it was impossible to know which ones to attack, and the light, already poor, vanished in a flurry of feathers, claws, and beaks.

Bryony and Diana were terrified, huddling in the centre of the witches, and Briar wished they hadn't brought them here. This experience would certainly not do Avery any favours with her estranged family. But they had no choice. They were all part of this now.

"Run!" Caspian yelled. "While they're busy."

Briar ran ahead, realising that she knew the wood better than most, and keeping to the direction that their guide had set. *Was this what Alderic had hinted at earlier? Their extra defences?* The birds of the wood would help defend it.

An outraged squawk drew her gaze upwards to an enormous owl, and as soon as their eyes met, he launched like a ghost, wings spreading wide, and led them further in. By the time they arrived at the gateway to the grove, they were exhausted, scratched, and bewildered. And there was still no sign of her gran and the white stag.

"Fuck me," Dylan said, as he skidded to a halt in front of the other team. "Where the fuck are we?"

"The borderlands," Moore said, without a hint of irony.

"About bloody time," Zee declared, "because we need to set up the trap."

Thirty-Two

"Thank the gods you're safe," Avery said to Alex as they stood at the threshold of the inner grove. "This place suddenly feels a whole lot more dangerous than usual. I swore I'd never come here at night again, and here we are. Idiots."

"Needs must," he said, "and actually, it's interesting to be so close to that place. It feels a little like when I venture into the spirit world. Another liminal zone, but earthier."

"I think that's where my gran is," Briar said, gazing almost vacantly down the golden path.

Avery stared at her. "What makes you say that?"

"I think the ravens and the owls are from there. They are not like normal creatures. They're bigger, for a start, more aware. I think the stag is from the same place." She sighed and shook her head. "Maybe I'm imagining it, but time will tell."

"I think you're right," Alex agreed, "but there's nothing we can do about it now."

Eli nodded. "The dryads have a plan. This gate is a lure. Combined with that metal amphora and your spell, it should be a winning combination. Alderic went to prepare, whatever the fuck that means."

"I've started some of the spell work for the trap," Alex said, "but there's a lot more to do. We need to hurry."

"I know. What role will you three Nephilim play in all this?" Avery asked as Nahum joined them.

"I've had a brilliant idea," Zee said, a questioning glance at his brothers. "I think you should cast a shadow spell on us. Then we can hide out there. Ninja-style."

Reuben high-fived him. "Yes. Love me some ninja-ing. Now?"

"May as well, before the therians catch up."

"Works for me," Nahum said, and Eli nodded in agreement.

"Leave it to me," Reuben said to Avery and Briar. "I'll offer the spell to Newton and the others, too. You guys carry on without me for now. This part is your baby, Ave."

El was already organising the area, and had placed the spelled vessel in a prominent spot close to the gate. Her mother and sister huddled under the branches of a gnarled old tree while Helena, Alex, and Caspian drew runes and sigils in the air with magic, each working on opposite sides of the small clearing. Caspian was in the trees, marking the outer perimeter, and the ghostly outlines of the sigils hovered for a moment before vanishing, but Avery could feel their effects. Kendall and Newton were out of sight, already on patrol with Ben and Dylan. They were all working quickly, knowing that the djinn or therians could arrive imminently.

Before she joined her coven, Avery spoke to her mother and sister. "Are you two all right?"

"Do we look all right?" Diana asked, a fierce edge to her voice, eyes hard. "This is everything I left White Haven for, and now I'm in the thick of it. I can't believe you have dragged us into it!"

"In my defence," Avery said, trying very hard not to lose her temper, "I had no idea this would happen when I summoned you, and just to point out *again*, if you had kept in touch with me properly, I wouldn't have felt compelled to do it."

Unexpectedly, Bryony looked sympathetic. "I didn't want any of this, and admit I am *way* out of my depth, but I'm enjoying seeing you again, and what you do now. It's eye-opening. But you're too busy for this now. Go help your friends. We're okay."

Diana just snorted, but Bryony gave Avery a knowing smile.

Feeling at least one of them was on her side, but also very guilty about dragging them into the whole situation, Avery said, "Thank you."

"How will this work?" Moore asked Avery as she helped Briar complete the enchanted perimeter. "The spell?"

"It's essentially a trap around a trap. When the djinn enters our perimeter, we seal it and hope his magic can't remove him. Then we draw it tighter, sort of like a noose, that will drive him into the amphora and seal him inside it." She frowned as she considered it, hoping she hadn't missed anything important. "Plus, we have the added advantage of the salamander's fire magic."

"That will help?"

"Most definitely. Haven't you noticed El?"

"The glow? Of course."

"Salamander aftereffects. He's not here, but she's learned a trick or two from him already. Or perhaps *trick* is the wrong word..."

"I think she's learned plenty from him already," he said, watching El's progress, before nodding, seemingly reassured. "I'll join my team, but be careful, Avery. I don't like this place. It feels like anything might happen in the borderland."

"But you love it here!"

"I'm not blind to the dangers, though." He urged her to stay safe, and then vanished into the mizzle.

They worked quickly to add rune traps, aware all the while that they were taking too long. The intensity of the unseen watchers grew, as if they were urging them onwards, and then they heard thunderous crunches and crashes as the trees started thrashing around them.

A mound of earth erupted a short distance away, and the djinn spun into view, showering everyone with earth and sand and smouldering embers that buried into the undergrowth. Despite the pervading damp, fires erupted as if accelerant had been thrown on them, and within seconds, flames were building, and smoke was billowing.

With a sickening clarity, Avery realised it wasn't the djinn that was trapped. They were.

Caspian acted on instinct as the djinn whirled through the incomplete trap, slashing wildly with his flaming sword, embers showering off him like a Catherine wheel.

There was no sign of Cassie at all, and he wasn't sure whether she was still bound up in his being somehow or in the cave, but as Qabas barrelled straight towards an unmoving and clearly shocked Bryony, he used witch-flight to tackle the djinn, manifesting right on top of him.

The djinn crashed into him with surprising solidity that sent a thunderous shock right through Caspian, but the creature was equally as shocked, and they went down in a tangle of limbs, rolling over and over, across the ground. Unfortunately, Caspian was no match for the djinn's strength or his dazzling eyes of blue flames that almost blinded him. As the djinn gained control, Caspian vanished using witch-flight and reappeared right behind him. But Avery had beaten him to it. She materialised onto the djinn's back and smacked a huge, concussive spell against his head. He bellowed and roared, shaking Avery off like fallen leaves, and it was as if a thousand voices roared along with him.

The witches fell back, almost bowled over by a fiercely hot wind that spoke of baking deserts under a midday sun. The mizzle that had hung thickly over everything steamed in the fearsome heat, and the various fires that had erupted around them blazed even brighter.

The prince leapt to his feet, and it was as if he saw the gate to the golden grove beyond for the first time. He moved towards it, a low growl in his throat, sword sweeping a broad circle in front of him, until something struck him from behind, and he hit the ground with a thump.

The Nephilim had attacked.

Dylan had climbed a tree and perched in a lower branch, using the leaves as camouflage, and aided by the shadow spell, he couldn't see himself or the others who had fanned out around him.

They were the outer perimeter, watching for the therians and the djinn they knew would be with them soon. They had turned off the EMF meters so that no sound would give them away, and he settled in silence, feeling an ache in his hip from the knobbly trunk, his spell bottle readied in his hand. This one was a lightning flash in a bottle, designed to alert the others whilst blinding their enemy, giving them precious seconds of an advantage.

Just as he was beginning to think he was in completely the wrong place—they had spread themselves in a broad area, anticipating that their enemies could approach from any direction—he heard shouts and the sound of fighting back near the grove's entrance. Alarmed, he twisted, trying to see the details, and with horror noticed the fire through the trees.

The djinn. It had to be. He was desperate to race back and help his friends, but knew he had to keep watch, so he tried to block out the sounds of battle behind him, and the stink of smoke. With every passing second, he felt their control of the situation was slipping away, and then he saw movement.

The rustle of the undergrowth gave them away, and a huge wolf padded silently under him, leading a few other wolves, panthers, bears, and a score of varied birds. Before the last few could pass beneath him, he uncorked his bottle, threw it into their midst, and released the spell.

Light exploded outwards, jagged, hot, and bright, and he turned away for a few seconds, dazzled. *Holy shit.* That was way brighter than he had anticipated. But from the howls and roars below it had worked, and the forest erupted into chaos around him.

He readied another spell, positioned himself, and threw the next one, watching the mayhem below as his team ran in to assist.

Now this was fun.

Until he looked up just in time to see an enormous owl barrel into him and drag him off the branch into the melee below.

Reuben realised that unless he did something quickly, they would all burn alive.

The coven and the Nephilim were tackling the djinn, and a large raven and owl had joined the fight, which meant he needed to tackle the fires alone. A few dryads emerged from the shadows, trying to stamp out flames, but dryads were not equipped to fight fire. Racing to the nearest blaze, he collected Bryony and Diana on the way. Both looked as if they were hanging on to their reason by a thread.

"I need your help," he said to them, flexing his magic. "I need water, lots of it, and I need your magic to get it."

"How?" Bryony asked, squinting at him through the smoke and steaming mist.

"Your hand, and yours, Di. Just like earlier, I'll draw on your power. Don't resist, just let me do it."

This wasn't something Reuben normally did. Other witches led this type of spell, not him, but he didn't have the time to second-guess himself now. He pulled the mist to him and turned the moisture into storm clouds that settled above the canopy, constantly feeding them as he pulled water from further afield by using Bryony and Diana's magic to supplement his own. He could barely see what he'd created but he could feel them, and had helped Eve enough when she did weather magic to know how she did it. He certainly didn't have the range that she did, but he didn't need to for this situation.

Blocking out the shouts behind him, he focussed only on his spell. "Stay with me," he instructed Bryony and Diana as he pulled their magic to him.

"It's too much," Diana said, voice cracking with the effort. "We're not used to this, Reuben."

"Just a little longer!"

He tried to ignore the flare of white light that suddenly exploded a short distance away, and knew the therians had arrived. He couldn't delay any longer, and besides, he could feel Diana and Bryony's strength ebbing. They still needed them for the bigger spell, too. Hoping the clouds were water-filled enough, he released a deluge of rain upon the wood, and at that point, realised he might have overdone it.

Briar, like the rest of her coven, was floundering in mud, which made it harder to fight the djinn, and very difficult to stand upright.

The soupy, steaming fog surrounding them was mixed with thick, choking smoke. Dozens of witch-lights barely penetrated the gloom, but the djinn's flashing blue eyes at least meant they could keep track of him, just about.

However, the rain made it hard for the djinn, too. He had visibly slowed, and trying to fight three Nephilim and witches all at the same time was taxing even for him, especially when the trees became involved. Branches and roots thrashed, trying to pull the djinn to shreds, even when his fiery blade sliced them. But his sword's song was strong. A chorus of voices that carried screaming winds and scorching heat. Briar was simultaneously soaking wet and searingly hot, both horribly uncomfortable, and her feet were stuck in mud.

"Reuben!" she yelled, turning to find him. "Stop the rain!"

But he was nowhere in sight, and that's when she realised that Bryony and Diana stood alone, and that she could hear shouts from the other direction, where the police and Ghost OPS were hiding. *Shit. Had the therians arrived, too?*

"El!" She blasted the earth at her feet, sending the mud oozing away from her in a wave, and hurried to El's side. "He's weakening, we must do this now!"

"But where's Reuben?"

"I don't know, but we have to manage without him, because we haven't the strength to keep this up. He's incredibly powerful, and I think the therians are also here."

El took a breath and nodded. "Then you gather the others and finish the spell while I stall him, because we have to prevent him from leaving—and we have to find Cassie."

"Good luck!"

Briar signalled to Helena, Caspian, Alex, and Avery, and within seconds they withdrew from the fight to continue rune-spelling, then she beckoned to a visibly shaken Bryony and Diana. "Stay close. Not long now."

She took a brief moment to look between the trees, and then at the beckoning glow of the grove through the gate. Still no white stag.

And still no Tamsyn.

Newton fired his Taser, watching with grim satisfaction as a tiger twitched and howled on the forest floor. "Serving you bloody-well right!" he yelled. "Bastards."

Other howls and shouts confirmed Kendall and Moore's success too, and Ghost OPS continued to bamboozle and slow the therians' attack with spells. But it was too soon to be celebrating. The therians changed form to best suit their fight—and their defence. Ravens and owls descended from the forest canopy to attack the therians, and he couldn't risk hurting the wood's own creatures. The therians knew it, too, and the ones that weren't Tasered were already changing into birds and continuing to charge ahead.

Reloading his Taser, Newton charged after them. One therian in particular was not changing. The huge, black wolf at the front of the pack snarled and snapped as he raced ahead, swerving to avoid dryads, or launching straight at them to make them scatter.

Wentworth?

Newton ran after him, leaping over the thrashing branch of a tree enroute. "Watch out!" he yelled. "I'm helping you!"

Was he actually shouting at a tree?

The bright fire ahead showed the outline of the approaching wolf. He wouldn't get there in time. He'd be on the witches in no time, and they were too busy fighting the djinn to notice.

And then a branch snapped out, catching the wolf full in the chest and virtually throwing him at Newton's feet. Newton fired the Taser, striking its flank, and the wolf howled with ear-splitting rage and pain that sent Newton stumbling backwards. The creature rolled to its feet and leapt at him, eyes burning with the desire to rip Newton's throat out.

Newton fired again. "It's a double-cartridge, you bastard, and I've got plenty more."

The second Taser struck and the wolf dropped, limbs contorted in painful spasms, just as a deluge of monsoon-like rain caused his surroundings to blur. A full-throated growl had him spinning to his left, and he fumbled to reload, hands slick with water.

Too late, the wolf was on him, and he thudded to the ground, the wolf's teeth inches from his throat.

El stepped in front of the djinn who, despite his injuries, had managed to throw all three Nephilim off and was marching towards the gate, the sloshing water and mud undisturbed beneath his taloned feet.

Heedless of the rain, and too focussed on the djinn to even think about protecting her companions from the water, El cast her spell to set the jar ablaze, activating the muted enchantments. Song burst from the blazing script and metal, and the djinn suddenly stopped as the battle-scarred Nephilim circled.

"What is that?" Prince Qabas asked El, his expression a mix of rage and confusion.

"A gift. Would you like to see it?"

"I can see it, and it is not possible in this world." For the first time since he had roared into their presence, he looked uncertain. "It reeks of elemental fire—and dragon magic."

She lifted her head, proud of her work. "And yet it is in this world, because I have made it." With a word of power, she changed the song of the metals to enhance their allure, and a dazzling landscape of sculpted dunes with an enormous castle glimmering within their midst manifested between them. The sunlight was so dazzling in the rain-filled gloom that a rainbow appeared. "I gift you a glimpse of the Realm of Fire."

As intimidating as he was, the prince looked wary, eyes darting around before settling on her with his dazzling blue fire. "How have you done this?"

"I am a fire witch, and I wield elemental fire using the power of my ancestors who have gifted me their knowledge."

The djinn inhaled, eyes narrowing with suspicion. "And yet there is some other magic here."

"Perhaps you should step closer so that you can see better."

She manipulated the metal's song again to magnify the image as Bran had taught her. It was odd how quickly it felt natural to her. He had suggested new ways to add power and depth, and as he was of fire, had cast some of his own elemental magic into it. It was the purest fire spell she had ever cast, and even now couldn't believe that she had done it. And it was most definitely Otherworldly. The pull from it was almost as strong as the pull from the gate behind her.

The djinn shook his head. "I am no fool, witch. You seek to trap me in a gilded cage."

"Not a cage. A gift to keep you comfortable while you await your home."

"I don't want to go home. I wish to stay here with my dragons and create this world anew."

"That's not possible," El said, aware that the witches were hurriedly finalising the rune trap. "In this world there are weapons that will destroy both dragons *and* you. This is no life for royalty. Best to return to your own world." She stoked the song of the metals, making it melodic and hypnotic as she drew on knowledge she didn't even know she possessed until the salamander awoke it. Fire raced under her skin, and she knew she was burnished with a silvery light, just as the djinn had skin of lustrous copper. She was transforming into flame.

Interesting.

The prince clearly found it so, too, and stepped closer to her, alight with curiosity. "You are worth saving. You may come with me when I create the world anew. Help me find the dragon eggs, and together we will rule. My queen." His voice sang with temptation, and visions that rivalled her own sprang between them. She tried not to show her surprise as she saw herself clad in silks, fingers and wrists adorned with jewels, a heavy pendant around her throat, reclining on a divan in a leafy oasis. The djinn, half-naked, his muscular chest oiled and gleaming like the setting sun, lounged beside her.

"See," he whispered, drawing closer, "we would rule in luxury, and as my queen, you would want for nothing."

With a great effort, she resisted his words. "I think not. Now, where is Cassie, our friend? You took her."

"She is of no consequence," he continued in silky tones, weaving music that spoke of star-filled nights. "If you want her back, I will make it so, but I must have you in return."

Her heart thumped at the thought of it, and Reuben's face rose in her mind, anchoring her in the present. "Bring her here, and I will consider it."

Qabas tutted. "I think not."

"But our haven awaits," she said, glancing at the jar with meaning. She wafted the heady scents of sandalwood and oud towards him and stoked the flames in her own skin so that she was luminous. "A place where we can be alone. We do not need others. We do not need to conquer worlds. We don't even need dragons."

"Oh, my dear," he said, a dangerous edge to his voice, "we most definitely need dragons."

She inwardly cursed herself for even mentioning them. She was trying to sweeten the deal, not piss him off. "Perhaps you are right, dragons are a great prize. I will negotiate with the dryads for the eggs, and then we will find a place that serves us both, but we do not need Cassie. I will not entertain the presence of another woman in our sanctuary. Bring her here so that I can see she is alive. *Now.*" She magnified her voice with the song of fire, surprising herself by how loud she became. Her voice rattled the leaves in the trees, and she felt her coven's shared surprise.

The djinn's eyes widened with pleasure. "A true mistress of elemental fire." He snapped his fingers and Cassie appeared at his feet in a heap, sprawling in the mud.

El almost stumbled back in surprise at the speed of his action, but held her nerve. *That was some magic.* "Thank you. Cassie, you may leave," she commanded, lacing glamour into her voice to make the clearly bewildered Cassie move quickly.

The djinn placed his taloned foot on Cassie's back. "Perhaps," he said, "I will have both of you."

And with unexpected speed, he lunged forward and grabbed her hand.

Reuben ran towards the howls and snarls just as the wolf attacked Newton, teeth inches away from his throat. He swiped it away with a scooping motion that picked the wolf up and slammed it against a tree.

The strike wasn't enough to stop it, though. The therian bounced off the tree trunk, landed on its feet, and made for the gate again, more therians in tow, just as Moore arrived. This time, the shifters didn't engage the humans. They avoided them, zigzagging through the trees, some turning into ravens again, racing to the now smouldering clearing where the distant glow of the grove could just be seen at the end of the path.

They all gave chase—humans, dryads, ravens and owls, angling in from all directions as the therians cleared the trees and burst into the clearing where the other team fought the djinn.

As Reuben reached the perimeter, he saw Prince Qabas grab El, just as the therian at the front shifted to a huge wolf and sprang on the djinn's back. They both tumbled to the muddy ground, and El was knocked clear, rolling in the mud. Zee lunged for Cassie, who was partially trapped under the djinn and the wolf, and dragged her clear.

Avery yelled at him. "Reuben, now!"

He grabbed her hand, and with a snap, felt his magic connect with his coven's.

The scene was chaotic, everyone fighting the therians as the witches sought to contain them within the spell intended for the djinn. The sparkling visions vanished, but the bewitched vessel continued to exert its pull. El struggled to her feet and started to sing, her clear and commanding voice weaving with the hypnotic song of metals, and the spell affected the therians, too. Their fighting grew half-hearted, their movements slow and laborious.

But now the gateway was clear, and the grove beckoned at the end of the long path between ancient trees. The djinn lunged for it, and just before Avery closed the circle, igniting the runes into a magical trap, the djinn escaped and slipped through the gate.

Alex watched in horror as the djinn raced down the path, his mighty sword swinging and crunching into trees and hacking off branches, and fire erupted again in his blazing wake as cinders landed in the undergrowth. The wood screamed, and Alex couldn't work out if the sound was real, or only in his mind.

They were too late. After all their plans, they had failed. The grove would burn, trees would fall, and the dragon eggs would be stolen. Alex could barely hear the tumult of the fight around him. The hum of the circle, the song of the enchanted jar, the slither of metal and crunch of bone on bone as the therians tried to escape and the team pursued them.

And then something shimmered on the path, a vision through the flames and smoke, and the white stag with a small woman on his back stepped into view. The djinn halted, almost comically stumbling over his feet as the stag leapt over him, leaving him wheeling in his wake, and thundered up the path towards them.

Unexpectedly, Qabas turned and followed, and for a second, Alex couldn't work out why.

Until he felt wild magic. *Dragon magic.*

Tamsyn, mounted almost regally and with astonishing poise, was carrying the dragon eggs, keeping her seat as if she was born to it. The stag cantered through the gate and the rune circle as if the spell they had cast wasn't even there, the djinn following in his wake. The therians—the howling, squawking, roaring clan of them—fell silent and dropped onto their haunches or perched on branches to watch the stag, transfixed.

The stag halted in the centre of the circle, broad-chested, magical, radiating the wisdom of ages, and instantly the rain that had been falling since Reuben cast his spell stopped, and the blazing fires were extinguished. A peculiar, hushed silence fell, but unlike the therians, the djinn did not fall into meek obeisance.

The prince swelled in size so that he was of the same height and stature as the stag. "I do not bow to the Lord of Beasts. Give me the dragon eggs, and I shall take my prizes," he glanced at El, making his meaning clear, "and leave. Do with the other beasts as you will. I have no interest in them."

Alex felt Avery pull their magic closer, and with unspoken agreement, they all stepped forward, tightening the circle, tension on a knife's edge. He studied the dragon eggs that Tamsyn held in a large basket, wondering if they were the real ones. *They certainly felt and looked like it, but would Alderic really risk them? Could they make fake ones seem so real?*

Either way, they certainly held the therians' attention. Or perhaps that was the Lord of the Beasts. In fact, the entire group of people—Nephilim, witches, humans, and therians—were spellbound. Dryads materialised out of the shadows, and from the grunts, snuffles, and squawks, it was clear the forest animals had gathered, too. The ancient magic of Ravens' Wood, never far from the surface, suddenly became more palpable.

Tamsyn, silent up until now, suddenly spoke, but it clearly wasn't her voice. The stag spoke through her, and Tamsyn's Cornish accent and gentle tones were swallowed by a deep, resonant voice that was far too big for her small frame to encompass. It boomed across the wood and vibrated through Alex like a bell. "*This is not your place, Prince Qabas, and as you have demonstrated that you cannot be trusted, and that you disrespect my realms, you shall inhabit the prison that has been made for you.*"

Alex almost staggered with the dissonance of it, attention split between Tamsyn and the stag.

The weight of the stag's magnificent stare fell on El, as Tamsyn instructed her, "*Once more, Mistress of Flame and Shadow.*"

Once again, El called forth the song bound into the metals, and the enchantments that had faded blazed into life again, exerting hypnotic power.

This time, the deep-rooted, earthy magic of the white stag was in there, and Tamsyn tipped her head back to stare skywards as she projected her voice—the stag's voice—into Ravens' Wood in an unbridled song that spoke of roots, earth, caves, the rich sap of trees, spring growth, dappled summer sun through verdant leaves, autumn colours, and winter ice that snaps branches.

Fire and Earth, working together as one.

Compelled to help, Alex and his coven repeated El's words, and even Diana and Bryony joined in.

The djinn bolted for freedom, struck the rune circle that he had entered so easily, and fell back, frustrated. He tried to resist the vessel's pull, sticking his taloned feet into the ground, even digging his sword in to try to slow himself down. He clutched at roots that shrivelled beneath his touch, dropped his sword and dug his hands in the earth, but the vision of the palace and the desert once more bloomed, growing larger and larger, until a sandstorm manifested and swept the djinn up.

Hot air and scouring sand raked Alex's face, half blinding him to the vision that was suddenly and frighteningly very real, and the creatures cowered and staggered back under the force of it.

El stood with Reuben, hair streaming, a subtle shimmer of silver rippling through her, and the enchanted scripts blazed. She swept her hand towards the djinn, and the script leapt off the metal and wrapped around the prince like silver shackles, as Avery commanded the rune spell to join in. The circle of swirling runes homed in like bees to honey, wrapping around the djinn.

Although he twisted and roared, cinders flying from him once again, it was all in vain. The djinn's size diminished, and slowly and weirdly silently, he was sucked into the vessel. The top flew on and El changed her tone. Within moments, the jar was closed tight, the spell complete, and the djinn was trapped.

"*And now,*" Tamsyn said, her own eyes sightless as the liquid brown eyes of the stag turned on the therians, "*I must deal with you. These dragon eggs held by the Seer are not for you, and never will be. You are beasts of this Earth, not of other realms. Is it not enough for you?*" The therians didn't answer, but they shuffled, some looking at the ground, others into the trees, and many stared at the black wolf at the front who led them. "*Answer me,*" Tamsyn roared, "*or I will strip you of your gifted power right now. Do you understand?*"

A cacophony of yips, howls, and screeches answered him, but none louder than the howl of the wolf at the front. Alex had no idea if the stag, the Lord of the Beasts as Alderic had called him, could do such a thing as take their power, but after what he'd seen so far, he thought it was highly possible.

The stag lowered to the ground so that Tamsyn could slip from his back. Alderic stepped forward to help her, relieving her of the basket of the eggs, but she waited close to the stag, hand resting on his flank as he stood again.

"*Take one final look at these eggs,*" she said to the therians, "*because this is the last you shall ever see of them, and if any one of you so much as steps foot in this wood again, I will hunt you in dreams from which you will never awaken. Do you understand?*" she asked again. A stunned silence of mute nods and creatures pawing the ground followed. "*I am the Lord of Wilderness and Crag, Beast and Forest, Transformation and Boundaries, and I will seek retribution, should you transgress. This has been witnessed by all. Now leave whilst I allow it.*"

The stag roared, jaw wide, huge antlers shaking, and with startling speed and without a backward glance, the therians raced away, streaking through the forest on wing and paw.

The stag, clearly a powerful figure of great reverence, bowed his head to Tamsyn, and if he spoke again, it was only to her. Her eyes returned to their normal beetle-black, and she pressed her forehead to his for a moment before lifting it again, eyes filled with tears as she stepped back.

The stag stared around the glade at all of them. His glance fell on Alex as light as a kiss, but with the sound of a tolling bell. Then, throwing off his grandeur, he raced out of the clearing, tossing his magnificent antlers and throwing off golden lights like fireflies as he raced through the trees.

In seconds, he had gone.

Thirty-Three

Helena felt the mood lighten as soon as the stag and the therians left, and a distinctly celebratory atmosphere entered the clearing as their friends mingled and the dryads cavorted. Yes, *cavorted*. There was no other word for it.

She felt giddy with it all, and could see that everyone else felt the same. *This place*, she thought, watching the golden light spreading under the broad canopy as far as the eye could see, *never failed to surprise her*. She felt as light as a feather. The dragon eggs had already been moved by a dryad back to their most secret and hidden place, and the gateway had closed.

"Are you two all right?" she asked Bryony and Diana, both of whom looked starstruck.

"Of course I'm not!" Bryony said, pink-cheeked and slightly breathless. "I'm utterly shocked. What on Earth have we just experienced?"

"Magic," she said, not wishing to reveal quite how mad it all felt, "in its purest form. And the King of the Beasts, of course, something I didn't anticipate." She glanced over at Tamsyn who was being hugged tightly by Briar.

"Did you anticipate any of it?" Bryony asked.

"Some of it, but no, not all. We expected the stag to make an appearance at some point, because Tamsyn had seen it, but not in such a dramatic fashion. However, I have learned to be flexible when it comes to White Haven. It's all quite splendid, in fact. Is it making you reconsider using your own magic?"

"Yes and no," Bryony admitted. "Something to think on."

"Absolutely not," Diana said. "This skirmish might have ended well, but we could have all died. Look at the Nephilim. They're covered in blood! They are wielding actual swords! We're drenched in mud, half-drowned, and I feel as if I have been hit by a lorry after being dragged into several spells. It's like my core has been ripped out."

Helena's joy at Bryony's admission evaporated. "Don't be ridiculous. Of course it hasn't. Just stop overanalysing," she said, trying not to be cross, because Diana was as white as a sheet, "and try to step beyond reason and enjoy it. The important question is, do you feel released now?"

Mother and daughter studied each other, and then nodded.

"Yes," Bryony said. "The feeling of being tethered has gone, but I'm not going to rush off. It's the weekend—if we haven't lost time, because I feel we might have—so I'll stay. Is it likely anything else will happen?"

"No, of course not," Helena reassured her quickly. *Not yet, at least.* "Thank you. I would love to get to know my great-grandchildren, and Avery will certainly want to spend more time with you. That is why she cast the spell, after all. She has a temper, but I can assure you that she has a big heart and genuinely summoned you here for the best." The thought of Bryony staying thrilled her, and if she could wrangle staying at El's place for longer, that would be even better. "Diana, I also think you should stay, now that you're here. Please," she added, seeing her waiver. "All three of us would like it, and I'm including Clea in that. A proper family reunion." She glanced over to where Avery stood with Alex and her coven. "As I said, Avery would not have summoned you otherwise. It's been too long. Certainly too long to harbour resentments." And then, because she really couldn't resist prodding Diana, said, "You must miss *something*?"

Diana stared at Avery, and then at Bryony. She finally said, as if it really cost her ego to admit it, "I have missed seeing both of you grow into adulthood, and as for Avery," she stared at her again, brow furrowed, almost perplexed, "I am astonished at her power."

"You are looking at," Helena said proudly, without the tiniest bit of doubt, "the future High Priestess of the Cornwall Coven."

Avery vowed that now this whole mess was over, she and Alex would go away together. They needed a holiday, time to be alone without all *this*. They had both been so busy lately that she felt she'd barely seen him. Stupid, of course; they shared a house and slept in the same bed, but she craved some alone time with him.

"Somewhere peaceful," she said to him, dragging him aside.

"You love all this," he said, smiling lazily as he pulled her towards him, enfolding her within his strong, safe arms. "But what the lady wants, she shall have."

"You have to admit, it's all a bit mad sometimes."

He laughed. "Sometimes?"

"Often, lately. Just a little break. We need a hotel, a flash one, with a spa and fabulous food, and long, lazy days. And plenty of shops. Maybe nice walks."

He smirked. "Am I picking the hotel, or you?"

"As if you would be the slightest bit interested in choosing."

"I suggest that before we dive into that, we finish this, which means spending time with your family."

"I will." She glanced over at them, suddenly nervous of what might ensue, but grateful she'd have the chance to explore it. "I just figure I'll need some respite afterwards."

"Shocking, Miss Hamilton."

"Oh, piss off."

"Oi, you two," Reuben shouted over. "It's time to go."

"Go where?" Avery was not ready to leave yet. The forest was aglow with the stag's enchantment, and she needed to decompress and talk things through. She still couldn't believe that the therians had fled with literally their tails between their legs, or that the djinn was now safely contained in his bewitched amphora. "Aren't we going to celebrate?"

"Of a sort," Reuben said, crossing to her side as the group made moves to leave. "We are mired in mud here—sorry for that," he added apologetically. "Eve makes it look easy, but it's really not. Anyway, Alderic has invited us to Nelaira's wake." He shrugged. "He didn't really call it that, but that's essentially what it is. Partying and dryad finger food, although I would kill for a burger right now."

"Maybe not the 'K'-word," Alex remonstrated.

"You know what I mean. And I think," he added, gaze sweeping the damaged trees, burnt undergrowth, and fallen branches, "that the dryads want to nurture the damage. We may have trapped the djinn, but he destroyed a lot before we did."

Their surroundings were a sobering reminder of the cost of the fight. A few dryads had been injured, but at least none had been killed, and Avery hoped they would heal without lasting issues. She sensed a sort of collective healing power in the wood, but perhaps Briar might understand that more than she did. Or Tamsyn, maybe, who had bonded with the stag in unexpected ways. As for El, her friend looked like her normal self again, composed as she talked to Moore, but what was she really feeling after that display of power?

And how did Reuben feel about it?

Avery and Alex fell into step beside Reuben as they followed the others down winding paths and onto solid ground.

"I have to admit," Avery said, boots still squelching, "that was an impressive spell you cast, and it put the fires out, so essentially it was a success."

"If a little overcooked," he admitted with a sheepish grin. "Your sis and mum helped."

"Did they?" she asked, surprised but pleased. "I was so busy, I didn't notice."

"Your mum wasn't thrilled, but Bryony was solid. You going to play nice this weekend?"

"I'll try." Then she corrected herself. They were here at her bidding, and their arrival had filled her with excitement at the possibilities of a future relationship, of any sort. "No, I absolutely will. In fact, I'll do everything I can to make this work. Are they okay to stay at yours still?"

"Sure. Maybe I'll cook Sunday lunch."

"Or perhaps," Alex said, alarmed because they all knew what Reuben's cooking was like if it wasn't curry, "we can eat in the pub. I'll reserve the back room. Jago would love to put on a show."

"How many we talking?" Reuben asked, nodding ahead to the whole team—witches, Nephilim, and humans. "All of them?"

"What do you reckon, Ave?" Alex asked her.

She smiled. "Why not? My family needs to see that White Haven is not all madness and spellcasting. I'd like to invite Sally and Dan, too, actually," she added, thinking how much poorer her life would be without them around. "They're my family as well as all of you. And how are you feeling," she asked Reuben tentatively, "about El's new skills?"

"Ah, that," he said, focussing on his wife who strode ahead talking to Moore and Stan. "Yes, they are quite something. I think Bran is here to stay."

"Are you okay with that?" Alex asked.

"Sure. I've always known El had skills she hadn't tapped yet, and now I'm pleased she has."

Reuben was always generous with everything, Avery thought affectionately, *especially those he loved*.

"Plus," he added, "she's always been the better witch between us, and I'm cool with that. I'm going to build a forge in my garden for her—or convert an existing outbuilding, perhaps."

"Are you?" Avery asked, surprised. "How come?"

He beamed. "She's going to move in permanently, and will be working magic and practising her new skills all the time, so rather than lose her to the shop, we'll build a brilliant forge and workshop at home. Plus, best keep Prince Qabas nearby. And it will be Bran's new home, too."

Alex laughed. "Mate, you are going to get so many brownie points."

"I know." Reuben grinned, and then nodded towards Helena. "And guess who gets first dibs on her flat?"

Alex punched the air. "Even better."

Briar was trying to get back to Tamsyn's side, but she was surrounded by dryads who were escorting her as if she were royalty.

Eli fell into easy step alongside her. "You'll talk to her soon enough. Let her enjoy her moment."

"I just want to make sure that she's all right."

"Of course she is. Look at her. Must be something to get picked by the King of the Beasts to help him."

"I know, and I'm excited for her, but also scared at what it means," Briar said, still watching her grandmother. "Did he just need her because she's a Seer?"

"Maybe? I'm sure she'll tell you. If she knows."

"Or perhaps Deer will know," she suggested. Her familiar had arrived when the stag did, loitering on the edge of the gathering, as transfixed by him as the other animals, but she vanished before they had a chance to speak. Briar was determined to find her over the next few days, thinking all insights would be useful.

"Seems we all had weird experiences today," Eli said. "Just think, Tamsyn saw the golden glade, a little of whose magic is around us right now." He gestured to the thousands of twinkling lights that illuminated the wood. "A gift, for a brief time."

"You've seen it, so if you think that is what this is, then I believe you."

"An unforgettable experience. I've had a few of them here."

She knew what he was referring to. "I'm really sorry about Nelaira. Of all the dryads he could have killed... I mean, any would have been awful," she clarified hurriedly, "but you know what I mean."

"I do, and I know I still haven't processed it properly. It feels better to know we caught the bastard, though." The bewitched amphora was being transported by Nahum and Zee, who carried it between them. For ease, Briar suspected, more than weight. "I thought the dryads would hide him in their grove, though."

She shook her head. "No, El wants him, so she can make sure the enchantments won't ever weaken. I doubt they will, though. Not after that display of magic." Her clever, amazing friend who had taken her own special magic to another level.

He looked down at her, speculative. "Newton is happy, too. Well, as happy as he gets. Therians now banished from Ravens' Wood. That's going to kill their aspirations, and has given Newton a bit of a swagger."

"Why is he still scowling at you, then?" she asked, catching Newton's darting glance.

"Who knows?" He shrugged, and then turned his dazzling smile on her, eyes alight with mischief. "I have something to show you." He pulled her off the path and pointed into the distance. "You know, I think we should come up here next week and collect some herbs and roots. I spotted wild garlic and lots of mushrooms—morels and puffballs. I have some great ways to use them."

"Really?" Eli was very close now, his size blocking out the others.

"Yes, and I've noticed we're out of a few basics, too. Very unlike you, Briar."

"I know. I've been busy, and so distracted by, I don't know, life."

"Easily done." He threw his arm around her shoulders as he pulled her back on to the path, but for moments only, hand soon resting on his sword hilt. "A trip out is just what we need to put this behind us."

"Sure." Briar frowned, convinced she was missing something. "You don't often want to come to this place."

"Things change. My apothecary roots need recharging."

"Is this Nelaira again?"

"Sort of. Anyway, best catch up with the others. Newton is really scowling now."

"But I can't even see him."

"I can." He smiled down at her again, smug. "Get a wiggle on. Dryad beer is supposed to be excellent."

Cassie was still dazed, and the flickering lights that illuminated the woodland canopy didn't help.

"I feel like I'm dreaming," she said to Ben and Dylan as they approached Nelaira's fallen tree. "I think it must be djinn-travel."

"Is that what we're calling it?" Dylan asked.

"Have you a better idea?"

"Not really." Dylan exchanged a nervous glance with Ben, and then asked, "Did he hurt you in any way when he kidnapped you?"

"No. He shouted and snarled, and then cast spells on his blade again, and I just kept out of it, hoping not to die. I did offer to bargain on his behalf after he said I was his bargaining tool, but then," she said, the feeling of dread sweeping over her again, "he left me there without a backward glance, and I wasn't sure he'd come back." She had already described the cave to them. "There was a tiny seam in the rock high above my head, and that's how he left. He did the big flashy whirl of sand thing and vanished into it, like smoke up a chimney. I have no idea how he took me there or pulled me out. I heard the *tap-tap-tap* of something and shouted myself hoarse, but I think it was tree roots, although I was imagining giant spiders. And then I was in the mud at his feet, filthy and soaking wet. I thought for one horrible second that I was underwater."

Ben nodded. "Yes, Reuben put on a storm show that was almost Biblical. At least the witches have dried us out a bit."

Cassie rubbed her head, still finding it hard to focus. "I think we should run brain scans on each other, just to make sure it hasn't done something weird to us."

"I'm sure," Ben said, stepping in front of her so that she had to stop and look up at him properly, "that if I can survive time-travel, you can survive djinn-travel with no ill effects long-term."

"But I feel so weird."

"Displacement, that's all. You need food and drink, that helped me, but of course we'll run the scans tomorrow, just in case. A good night's sleep will help, too. In fact," he said, eyeing Dylan, "we should make the scans a regular thing."

"Sure," Dylan agreed, as they started walking again. "Do we get hazard pay, as well?"

"No."

Dylan winked at her. "Thought it was worth trying."

Newton was finding it hard to settle as the group gathered around Nelaira's fallen tree that was now fully submerged into the earth, except for a tangle of roots.

He had expected a mournful atmosphere, but it seemed that had passed. Perhaps it was the double victories that had stoked the dryads' mood; they had certainly improved his. He had managed to give Wentworth a victorious smirk before he slunk into the wood. They would surely cross paths under other circumstances, but it felt good to know that this particular issue was well and truly over.

Plus, the djinn was contained, there were no more deaths, and beer, inexplicably, had appeared out of nowhere. The only thing that was bothering him was Briar's relationship with that smug wanker, Eli. He had seen him pull her off the path, swaggering in his over-sexed way. He wasn't with her now, though. She was talking to Kendall, and worryingly, Kendall was giving him what he could only call a Paddington Bear stare over Briar's head. *What the fuck did that mean? Was it already too late?*

A dryad thrust a carved wooden cup filled with frothing liquid at him, and after a tentative sip, he took a larger mouthful.

"Herne's bloody horns," he said appreciatively as his worries, aches and pains, and near-death experience seemed to fade into insignificance. "This is bloody brilliant."

Moore shuddered as he sipped his own. "Guv, this is one of the best beers I've ever had. I can feel it down to my toes."

"Do you think they're drugging us?" he asked, wondering what it had been brewed from. It was earthy, malty, and sweet, and he was pretty sure it was very strong.

"Only in a good way," Moore said. "Alcohol is a drug, after all."

"Course it is. Sorry. I'm distracted."

Moore followed Newton's eyeline. "Ah, of course. I suggest you take your Dutch courage and put it to good use."

"Don't you start."

"Kendall had a word, then?" Moore smiled, eyes slightly glazed already. "'Bout time."

Newton grimaced. "Have you two been talking about me?"

"No. We don't need to. Now, go on." He nodded towards Briar.

"I'm a grown man! I don't need egging on like a randy teenager."

"I beg to differ."

"You two are getting distinctly cheeky."

"I blame the beer."

Newton decided he should act before Moore chose to say anything else. As he arrived at Briar's side, Kendall made swift excuses and vanished, and Newton realised she had conveniently pulled Briar out of the general group. They stood under a large branch, cloaked in shadows.

"You must be happy," Briar said.

Her hair was tangled, and mud streaked her cheeks, but she looked radiant. *Eli's doing? Damn it, forget him.*

"Of course. Same for you though, right?" He couldn't bring himself to ask about Eli yet. "Is Tamsyn all right?"

Briar sighed as she sought her out in the crowd that milled about the clearing. "More than all right, which is a relief, but I'm worried at her connection to the King of Beasts. That he sought her out. If he's so powerful, why?"

"I don't pretend to know the workings of the Otherworld. I have enough trouble with this one."

She laughed. "Hardly. You head up your own team and deal with all this magic stuff remarkably well."

"I didn't. I struggled with witchcraft at the start, and fucked things up with us because of it."

Her eyes widened with surprise at his admission, lips parting in shock. "That was a while ago, and completely understandable, all things considered."

"Not that long ago. Coming up on two years. And that wasn't what you said at the time."

"I was angry. Disappointed. But a demon attacked you and gave you serious burns. That's enough to freak anyone out."

"That you healed."

"Then the Nephilim arrived, courtesy of our spell, and they were huge unknowns at the time. And bloody mermaids! Your life had switched from normal to magic-filled craziness. Anyone would have acted the same. I wasn't very understanding back then," she said, surprising him. "Too caught up in myself and my own needs."

He shook his head, refusing to let her take the blame. "No, you weren't. You are never caught up in yourself. I'm sorry for my behaviour. I don't think I ever said so."

"I'm sure you have."

"Not so directly, perhaps. I moan a lot, too. Kendall pointed that out to me. Sorry." He sighed and stared out in the wood, finding now that he had started this conversation, it wasn't as hard as he had anticipated. Just sad.

"Blimey, Newton. You're down on yourself after we've had an amazing victory and are standing here alive! I don't see it as moaning. We're all allowed to vent on occasions. I should probably do it more often."

He glanced at her again, almost scared to look directly into her eyes. "You're perfect. You don't need to change a thing."

She flushed. "I'm not."

If he didn't ask now, he never would. "Are you with Eli?"

"What? As a couple? Eli, harem Eli?" She glanced at his mug. "Are you drunk?"

"No! Fuck. Sorry. I didn't mean to blurt it out. It's just that he seems to be paying you a lot of attention."

"Just the usual Eli stuff. Unusually flirty with me perhaps, but I don't read anything into it. Is that why he said you were glaring earlier? We were talking about collecting herbs." She frowned. "What does it matter, anyway?"

"Herbs?"

"We work together, you twit." She shrugged and sniggered. "He's unnervingly good-looking, of course, but no, we are not a couple." And then she looked at him, really looked at him, and her expression softened. "What's going on, Newton? I'm not blind to you, or your attention of late, but I'm confused."

Newton glanced behind him to look for Eli, also confused, and saw him standing head and shoulders above the rest. He lifted his eyes to Newton and smiled. A nice smile. An encouraging, I got you sort of smile. *Bastard.*

Newton looked back down at Briar. "I'm not perfect, Briar, but I mean well. I moan, complain, stamp about and shout sometimes. Well, many times. But you *are* perfect, witchcraft and everything, so I really want us to try again to be a couple, not just friends, because honestly no other woman even comes close to you. None. I fucked up before, and I want to make it right."

"We both fucked up." She smiled. "A date?"

"Many dates, providing I don't bollocks up the first one, which I assure you I have no intention of doing."

"Permission to tell you if you are?"

"Of course."

Briar laughed, but then sobered quickly. "But I need to be honest, Mathias." His heart pounded. She hadn't called him by his first name for ages, and he liked it. "I've been thinking a lot about what I want lately. About what would make me happy. Or happier. I love my coven, magic, and my shop. I love my friends and my life, but I am a little lonely. I want someone to share thoughts with, ideas, dreams. Plans. A life. Love. Passion. I'm not made for flighty relationships." She stared at him, honest and direct, a quality he appreciated. "If that scares you, or if it's not what you want, then this," she gestured between them, "won't work. That's why I will never be with Eli. It's also why it didn't work with Hunter. I want it all, and that includes children someday. If that doesn't work for you, then say so now, and let's stay friends."

His throat was so full that he could barely choke out his next words. "I want that. I want it all with you. And I can be that, I promise. When I think of you, I see colour and light, and without you, the world is just grey."

Her eyes filled with tears, and for a horrible moment, he thought he'd said something wrong, but then she smiled. "No one has ever said anything like that to me before. Thank you. But we are not going to The Wayward Son for our first date."

"Absolutely not." He felt dizzy with the possibilities, and as he looked over his shoulder at his gathered friends, he realised he did not want to join them just yet. He reached for her hand. "Shall we walk for a while?"

"Yes, please."

El watched Briar and Newton walk into the wood together, and nudged Stan. "I think we have more romance in our group, Stan."

Stan's eyes widened with intrigue. "No! Who?"

"Briar and Newton. At least I hope so."

He bobbed around, trying to see them through the gathering before giving up. "Good for them. I always thought they'd make a good couple. Anyway, how are you feeling? You put on quite the show."

"I must admit that it felt good, if unexpected. It's like I tapped a well that I didn't even know I had."

"Which could be much deeper than you realise?"

"I suppose so, although," she said, feeling fire ripple through her, even now, "I need to learn how to control it first before it consumes me."

"Good grief!" Stan looked horrified. "What a statement. It seems to me that you're doing just fine. You trapped a djinn!"

"With help from the Lord of Beasts—and our friends, of course."

"Nevertheless, you worked together, you and your coven. You created visions." His voice dropped as if it shouldn't be talked about. "Visions, El! Incredible."

She should be excited, and she was, in a way, but she was also trepidatious. "It's just new."

Before Stan could respond, Tamsyn pulled him into a dance with a wink. "I'm stealing him, El."

The dryads' mournful singing when they first arrived had been replaced with cheerful jigs, and a few of them had produced strange string instruments that looked a little like violins, but weren't. She shook off her sudden unease, deciding she was worrying excessively.

The salamander was now a permanent resident in her hearth, and she needed to adjust her magic to accommodate him. Plus, she was moving in with Reuben full-time. Helena would move into her flat, and from the animated discussion she saw her having with Avery earlier, she looked as if she was pushing for more time in Clea.

It would be okay. It was just change. Instead of worrying, she chose to enjoy the moment.

In the midst of dancing dryads, Zee danced with Kendall, Nahum with Cassie, and Eli was talking to Diana, exerting his usual charm so that she finally looked relaxed. Her silly husband was dancing with Bryony, who looked like she might actually be coming around to magic, and Moore, the wonderfully adaptable Moore, was dancing with a dryad. Ben and Dylan looked tipsy on dryad beers, and Alex and Avery were giggling as he dipped and twirled her as if they were in a ballroom.

Caspian loomed before her, muddy, dishevelled, and looking lighter, as if he'd shed a load—or perhaps many of them. He gave a small, polite bow, and then extended his hand. "Mistress of Flames and Shadow, may I have this dance?" He grinned and pulled her to her feet before she could even think of refusing.

Another surprise. Caspian danced.

Thank you for reading *Cinderveiled Magic.* I would love you to review it please, on any retailer of your choice, but particularly in my shop, Happenstance Books.

Newsletter

If you enjoyed this book and would like to read more of my stories, please subscribe to my newsletter at https://tjgreenaut hor.com/landing/. You will get two free short stories, *Excalibur Rises* and *Jack's Encounter*, and will also receive free character sheets for all of the main White Haven witches and Hunters.

By staying on my mailing list you'll receive free excerpts of my new books, as well as short stories, news of giveaways, and a chance to join my launch team. I'll also be sharing information about other books in this genre you might enjoy.

Ream

I have started my own subscription service called Happen-stance Book Club. I know what you're thinking! What is Ream? It's a bit like Patreon, which you may be more familiar with, and it allows you to support me and read my books before anyone else.

There is a monthly fee for this, and a few different tiers, so you can choose what tier suits you. All tiers come with plenty of other bonuses, including merchandise, but the one thing common to all is that you can read my latest books while I'm writing them – so they're a rough draft. I will post a few chapters each week, and you can read them at your leisure, as well as comment in them. You can also choose to be a follower for free.

You can comment on my books, chat about spoilers, and be part of a community. I will also post polls, character art, share rituals and spells, share the background to the myths and legends in my books, and some of my earlier books are available to read for free.

Interested? Head to Happenstance Book Club. https://ream stories.com/happenstancebookclub

Happenstance Book Shop

I also now have a fabulous online shop called Happenstance Books where you can buy eBooks, audiobooks, and paperbacks, many bundled up at great prices, as well as fabulous merchandise. I know that you'll love it! Check it out here: https://happensta ncebookshop.com/

Substack

I now write over on Substack, and my page is called Where the Witches Gather. I'd love to see you there. Substack has a wonderful community of witchy writing and seasonal celebrations. You can find me here: https://substack.com/@wherethewitchesgat her

YouTube

If you love audiobooks, you can listen for free on YouTube, as I have uploaded all of my audiobooks there. Please subscribe if you do. Thank you. https://www.youtube.com/@tjgreenauthor

Please read on for a list of my other books.

Author's Note

Thank you for reading *Cinderveiled Magic*. After writing fourteen books and one novella, this series still feels fresh to me. I hope it does for you, too.

I always have so many threads to pull on in White Haven. First, the five wonderful witches who continue to grow and change and surprise me. No, I don't always see it coming. Reuben is forever evolving, and I love his relationship with El. It seemed the right time to expand El's magic, but again, I hadn't mapped it out when I started writing this book. It just unfolded. El's relationship with the fire elemental could prove fascinating!

I love Helena, and am really keen that she should take part in more stories. She gives me a little wicked glee with her honesty. I thought it was about time that we explore Avery's family, so I had fun looking into their past and exploring what they might have been doing in those years. I think there will be more to come from them, and I hope you've enjoyed meeting them.

Let's address the potentially contentious issue of Briar and Newton! It felt the right direction to have them try to make their relationship work, but I know that this will divide readers. Some of you love Newton, some of you are exasperated by him. Is he perfect? No. But none of us are. We all battle with our insecurities and doubts, and have parts of our job/life/work that we are frustrated with. Some of you love the idea of Briar being with Eli, but honestly, I couldn't see that working. Besides, who knows what might be in store for Eli! Both Eli and Zee are now part of the White Haven landscape, so their narratives will continue to grow, too.

Of course, I must mention Caspian. When I first introduced him in the first book, I had no idea how his character would change and become so important to the stories. I always love writing him, and from the many comments that I receive from you, I know you love him as well. I always aim to keep him integrated in the plot, but am wondering whether the occasional short story about him might be interesting, too. However, that comes down to time, so it might not ever happen. I always have so many plans!

And talking of short stories, this might well be the year that I look at telling Helena's story of the events in her original time. Investigating the ancestors of our current White Haven witches will be interesting, and I enjoy writing about the Moonfell Witches' ancestors, so this is a continuation really. I am not making any promises, but I'll see how my time allows, and my creative juices flow.

Ghost OPS continue to entertain, and I'm excited to explore more of Moore—who I adore—and Kendall in future stories.

I have no intention of stopping this series yet, so I will write another book next year. I feel drawn to standing stones, so the story might include those, but I have plenty to write between now and then, so that might change. Next up is the fourth Storm Moon Shifters book, and then the third Moonfell Witches book. There will probably be another book next year, but I am still ruminating on what.

Thank you to my ARC team and beta reader, Terri, for their early comments, and my wonderful subscribers to Happenstance Book Club on Ream and Where the Witches Gather on Substack. You always leave such encouraging comments. Thank you! Very importantly, thank you to Miriam who suggested the name of the beach front coffee shop, Tide and Thyme. It's perfect! Also, thanks to Fiona Jayde Media, my wonderful cover designer, and Missed Period Editing for sorting out my manuscripts.

Writing stories and creating worlds is one of the great joys in my life. From developing characters, to crafting plots and places, and then developing the merch, images, and extras that accompany my books, is so much fun for me, and extremely satisfying. It would not be possible without you. In this ever complicated world of ours, we must take solace in beauty, truth, and compassion. I try to bring those qualities to everything I write. Take care, my lovely readers, and thank you always.

About the Author

Author of paranormal and witchcraft fiction, TJ Green crafts vibrant stories filled with memorable characters, atmospheric settings, and a signature blend of action and humour. Originally from England's Black Country, she embraced international living, making New Zealand her home for sixteen years before settling in Portugal's sun-drenched Algarve in 2022.

Drawing from her experiences as a practicing pagan and witch, she weaves authentic magical elements throughout her work. Her diverse creative background includes performing as a band vocalist and acting with a theatre company, experiences that inform the dynamic performance aspects of her storytelling.

When not writing, she can be found tending her garden, practicing yoga, or indulging in her lifelong passion for science fiction – particularly Star Trek, with "The Wrath of Khan" holding a special place in her heart. Her eclectic influences range from classic detective series to urban fantasy, all of which shape her unique narrative voice.

TJ Green's work explores the intersection of modern life and ancient practices, reflecting her personal journey and open embrace of her identity as both author and witch. She shares insights about her craft and spiritual path through her blog, where readers can discover more about her grunge music roots and her evolution as a writer.

Please follow TJ on social media to keep up to date with news, or join the mailing list here: tjgreenauthor.com/landing

facebook.com/tjgreenauthor/

pinterest.pt/tjgreenauthor/

tiktok.com/@tjgreenauthor

youtube.com/@tjgreenauthor

goodreads.com/author/show/15099365.T_J_Green

instagram.com/tjgreenauthor/

bookbub.com/authors/tj-green

https://reamstories.com/happenstancebookclub

Other Books by T J Green

Chaos Magic #9

Stormcrossed Magic #10

Wyrd Magic #11

Midwinter Magic #12

Sacred Magic #13

Cinderveiled Magic #14

White Haven Hunters

The action-packed spin-off featuring Shadow and the Nephilim.

Spirit of the Fallen #1

Shadow's Edge #2

Dark Star #3

Hunter's Dawn #4

Midnight Fire #5

Immortal Dusk #6

Brotherhood of the Fallen #7

Storm Moon Shifters

Paranormal Mysteries set around the wolf shifter pack, Storm

Moon.

Storm Moon Rising #1

Dark Heart #2

Wolfshot #3

Moonfell Witches

This series features the mysterious and magical witches who live in Moonfell, the sprawling Gothic mansion in London. They first appeared in Storm Moon Rising, Storm Moon Shifters Book 1, and then in Immortal Dusk, White Haven Hunters Book 6, and features characters from both series. However, this series can be read as a standalone.

If you love witches and magic, you will love the Moonfell Witches.

The First Yule: Novella

Triple Moon: Honey Gold and Wild #1

Amber Moon: Secrets, Ink, and Firelight #2